The Ondines of French Camp

ISBN 978-1-62806-438-4 (print | paperback)
ISBN 978-1-62806-439-1 (print | hardback)
ISBN 978-1-62806-440-7 (ebook)

Library of Congress Control Number 2024925958

Published by Salt Water Media
29 Broad Street, Suite 104
Berlin, MD 21811
www.saltwatermedia.com

Cover art and author photo by Kelly Russo
Back cover image of the Oxford Cemetery used with permission from the photographer, Laura Otts Ramsey
Interior map by Derek Lingle
Interior illustration by Joseph Traylor
Cover and interior layout by Salt Water Media

The Ondines of French Camp

Andrew Heller

For Eva

Contents

Author's Note

As I sit to begin work on this note ... it feels less like a foreword or introduction and truly like it should be a note from me, the author. Much like a Director's Note for a play, the purpose seems to be to give one a little extra to ponder as they delve into these pages. I like the thought of it being a Director's Note as it allows me to direct—to direct your attention, your thoughts, your emotions. That is what a director does for their actors and audience.

Adding to that theatric sense, stylistically I wanted something cinematic. This story feels like a movie to me; it did to other early readers as well—or like one long monologue interrupted occasionally by Randy's thoughts and memories and relations. That is how my son, Sam, described it. He also described Randy as an unreliable narrator. And not because of any malicious intent or fallibility; but for the very human reason of memory being what memory is—fluid.

Memory does have a fluid, water-like quality, doesn't it? Or perhaps life itself does. We begin at the headwaters, a spring, the melt from millennia of compacted ice in a glacier—or just a season of hard-packed snow. We trickle down a path created by the generations of melt before us. We are joined down this path by other sources, other tributaries—and we grow. A rill, a creek, a river ... we grow. There will be bends and breaks; we may even get dammed up or fall, but the river has a goal it must reach. And water will always find a way.

If memory is like water, music is too. And music, like water, will evoke so much from deep within. There is a fluidity to music, a meandering or rather a purposeful flow ... I use music as part of this journey. I believe every generation has a connection to a sound or style that defines it or touches it. Husayn told me he could hear REM and *Nightswimming* specifically. And of course their song *Find the River* ... and that carries me to so many other sounds and notes and callings of deep dark moody undergrad nights—clove cigarettes and red wine and Enya or a smoky haze in a club with Depeche Mode, Bau Haus, or The Church.

And of course within all of that music and water are the people. The human connections that make life so real, both bearable and unbearable, and beautiful too. Mine started at the source: my mother. How funny to call my mother "The Source." Anyway, I owe my family connection to her, her stories, and the fluidity of their nature. I genuinely believe the closeness of my familial relations, the level of connection and relatability—I owe all of that to her. Mom's stories of her childhood can take on an idyllic nature or one of hardship, and both were true. And she had a connection to her aunts and uncles, her in-laws, her cousins ... and she has a story or memory for all of them. And she passed that connection and the appreciation on to me.

I was so lucky to grow up surrounded by family. Our home was so often inundated with relations as I was growing up, whether we went to them or they came to us. Multi-generations of relations. And all of them like those rills and creeks and streams pouring into the river that would become my life.

These particular stories were inspired by those stories my mother told—by those connections I felt and by the complications of love and relationships and the defining moments when childhood memories meet adult sensibilities. Or vice-versa. And that is a universal story, isn't it? Reconciling one's adult sensibilities with the childhood distortions we place upon memories, perspectives, and defining moments. We reflect, and they are distorted like our reflection on the surface of the water. If we look deeper, we may find we are actually beneath the surface looking up or out or beyond ... but never back.

And like the complications of love and relationships and all of those defining moments, *The Ondines of French Camp* went through so many iterations. The book was almost a play. That is how it started. On the front porch. Rudie, Vilma, and India arguing as children. Only they were not named Rudie, Vilma, and India. (Not true—India was always India.) Then it was going to be a story about just Rudie and Vilma. And then several years ago I received a package from my cousin Eva ...

Eva's Grandpa and my Nana were brother and sister, and as close as any brother or sister that ever brothered or sistered. They were quite the pair. (My mother could tell you.) Eva and I would occasionally message on Messenger or maybe send a random text. But our relationship began to grow more and more as we discussed old photos and memorabilia she would find in her grandfather's attic. And then she sent me this package: a vase that is not to my taste, two brass deer, a measuring cup, and a lamp—and a note that tied a reason or a memory to each of these random and forgotten items. The vase broke on the way. My mother sort of fixed it.

The conversations grew from there, both in frequency and depth. And *The Ondines of French Camp* also began to find its depth—along with its shallows and bends and tributaries and headwaters. My conversations with Eva allowed this book to find its way. Like water.

And then my dog died. Mrs. Molly Bell "Moo-Moo" Magoo. She was actually my son's dog. And when Sam was not around, she was my husband's. But damn if I wasn't the caretaker. I fed her, I cleaned her, I nursed her, and I slept downstairs with her

for the last several months of her life when she couldn't nego-
tiate stairs anymore. And after the heart-wrenching moment of
saying goodbye to her ... I received another package.

Eva used to talk about Mrs. Magoo to her family, as I would
evidently write some silly, anthropomorphic version of her life
in the end stages and post it on social media. I likened Mrs.
Magoo to a Gloria Swanson-like character, a silent movie actress
with a glass of gin and a long skinny cigarette. Eva found it both
hilarious and very sweet. Her brother, Joseph Traylor, is an artist, and he made a little sketch of this rather anthropomorphic
Mrs. Maggo. It was so sweet, hilarious, and timely ...

Eva has been an intrinsic part of this project ever since. She
was an early reader. She was a later reader. She sent me photos
and we talked and talked and talked. I shared with her the many
iterations of cover art. (That Kelly Russo is amazing.) And she
made one comment that really brought it all home to me. We
were discussing titles—oh, the journey to find a title for this
book was long—and I had sent her a list. Her reply: "I don't
know how you are going to decide, but we'll get there."

"We'll" get there. We. How beautiful is that?

And we did. *The Ondines of French Camp* is named for that
beautiful play by Jean Giradoux, *Ondine*. And also for those
amazing, beautiful, and perfectly imperfect people who inspired
this story, this journey, this long meandering tube ride down a
river filled with so many twists and turns and bends. Undines
and Ondines—every one of them guiding us, cautioning us, loving us ... as only they can.

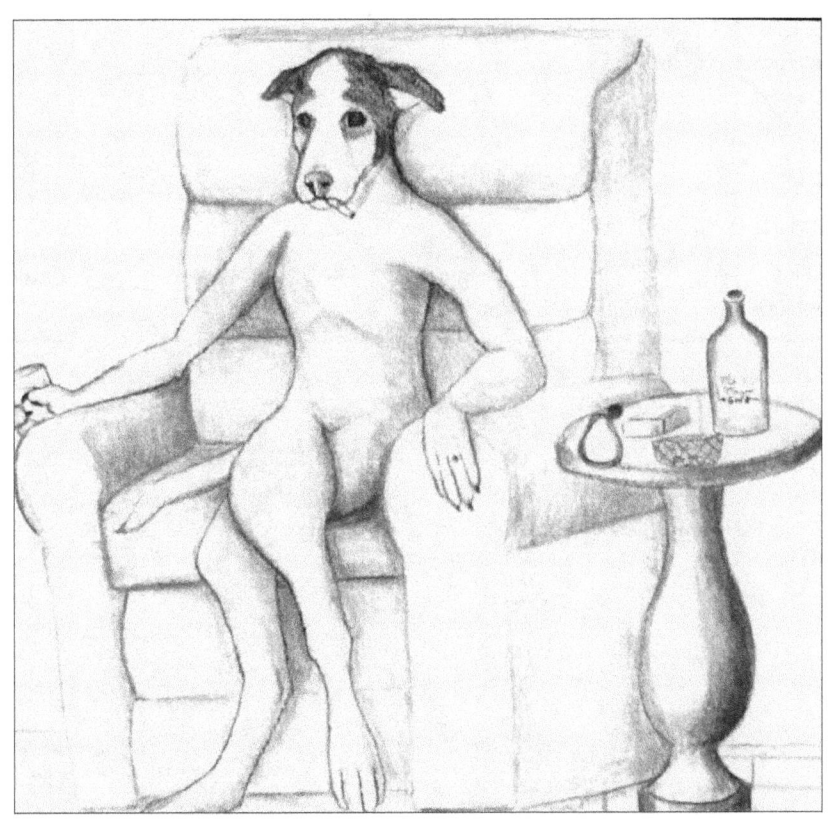

Artwork by Joseph Traylor

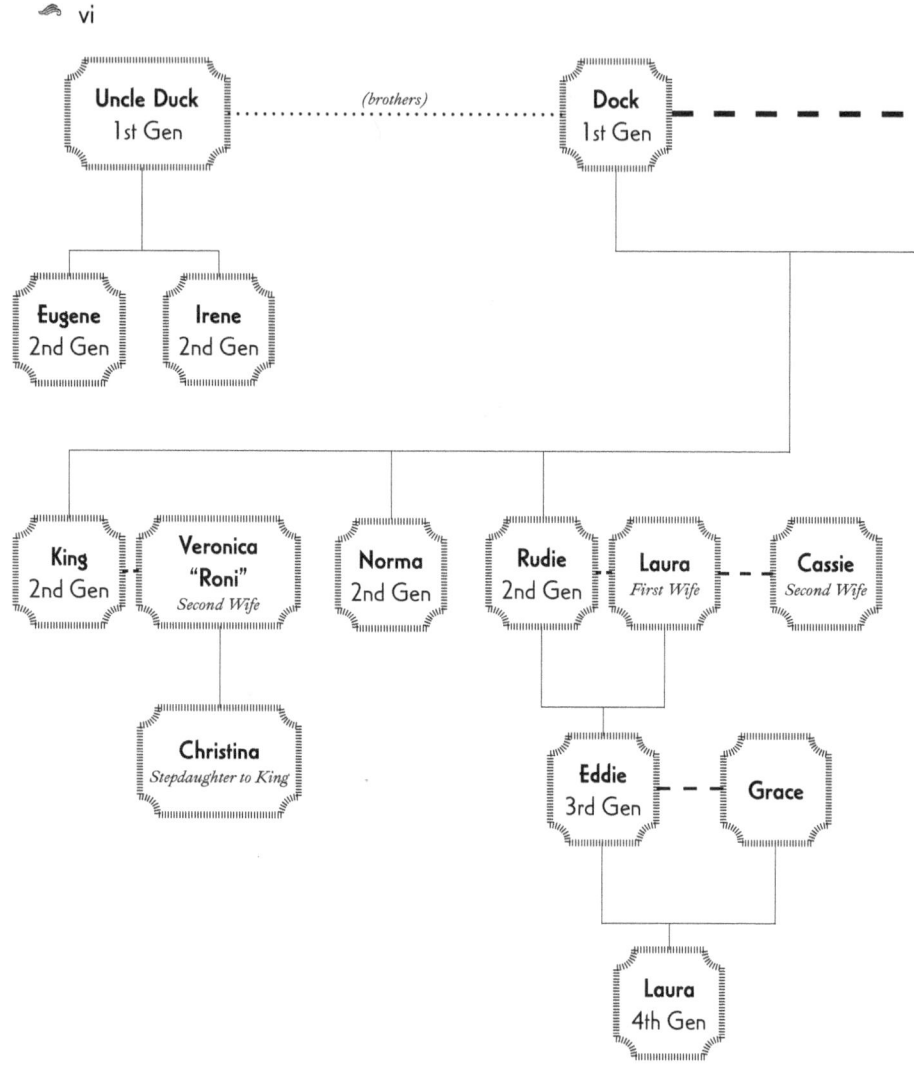

LEGEND

Denotes a marriage — — —

Denotes a sibling relationship in older generation • • • • • • • •

Italics indicate a relationship qualifier

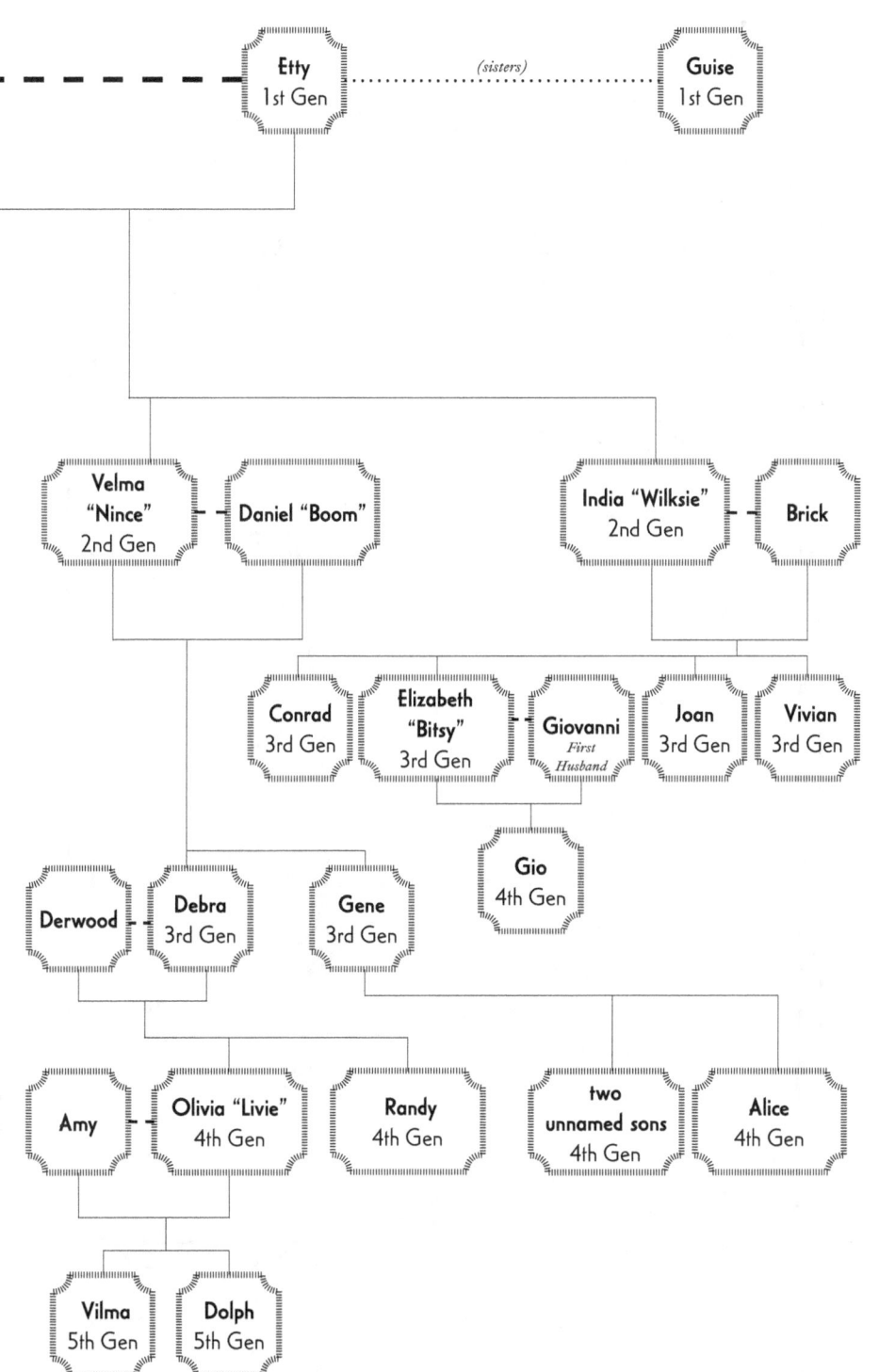

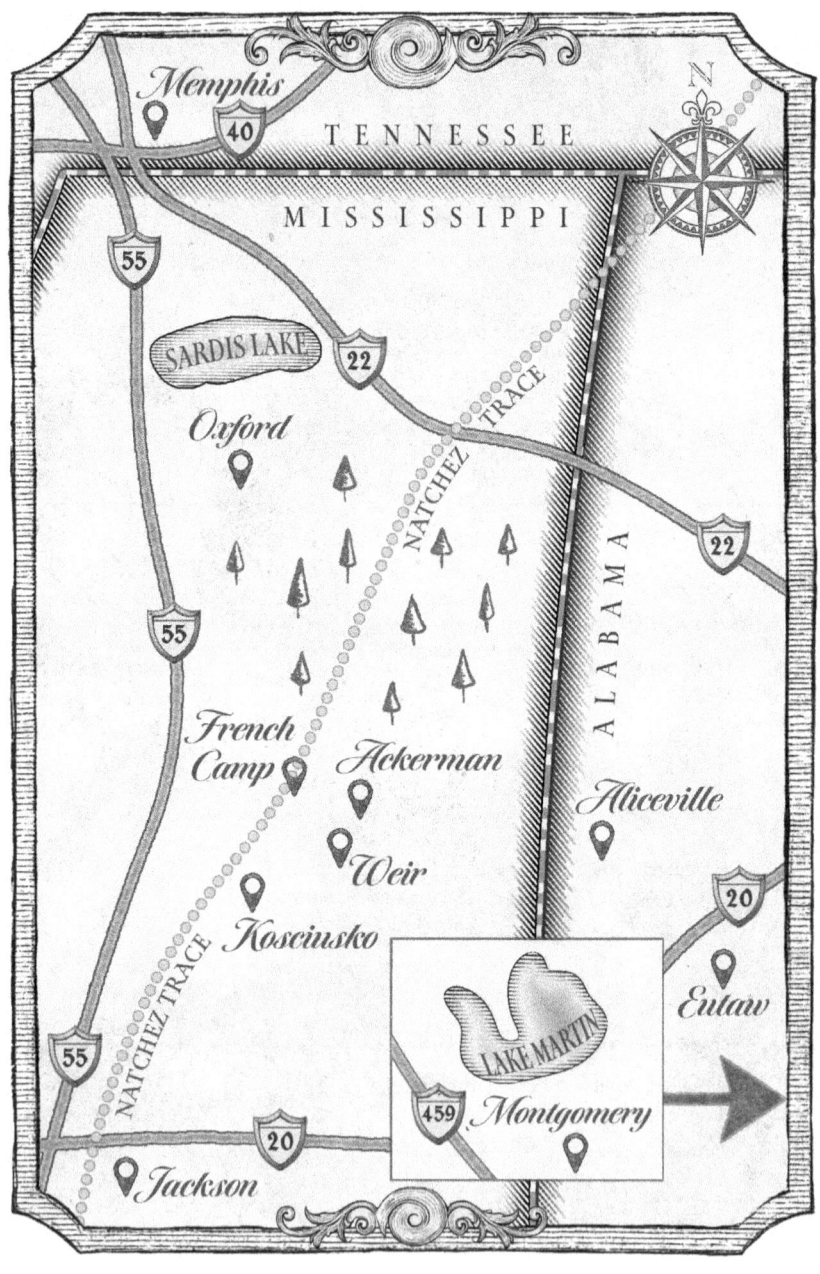

"It's between
Ackerman and Weir ... "

Chapter 1
Headwaters and Tributaries

One Should Never Start in the Middle,
Yet Here We Are

"It's between Ackerman and Weir," my mother told me. It was a Wednesday when she called. I remember the oddest things. That is what my mother says, anyway. She was explaining who would be staying where for my grandmother's various funeral services. "It's where your grandfather was born, Weir."

"I thought it was Ackerman."

"He was born in Weir but lived in Ackerman." She was agitated.

"Ahh."

"Olivia will be staying at the house with us, and my brother and the boys are all at Rudie's. I know it's two hours from here, but everything after the church service is in French Camp—not here at your grandmother's. And with everything going on, I just didn't think that the couch or the floor ..."

"I'm good with the hotel, Mother. Besides, I'll have a rental. I've made that drive countless times. It will be fine. I'll be there tomorrow."

"It's the same one we always use."

"Yes, our own Bates Motel for funerals. I remember it well."

"Don't be ... funny. Not this weekend. Not at the funeral."

I started to form a clever comeback and had landed on one that was quite witty, but alas, "Yes, ma'am" was my reply.

"Your father will pick you up in Jackson. What time do you arrive?"

"I'm actually flying into Memphis."

"Memphis? He is not driving to Memphis to get you."

"I told you. I'm going to rent a car. I want to spend a little time in Oxford after the funeral."

"Hmm. Are you bringing someone?" I wasn't sure of the tone. Hopeful? Disdainful? Plotting? I would not put it past my mother to try to set me up with someone while at my grandmother's funeral.

"No, ma'am," I replied, hoping my own tone might indicate no further discussion was needed over this topic. "I am not bringing a date to Nince's funeral." (We always called my grandmother that—Nince.)

"And you have pants and shoes."

"But the invitation clearly stated clothing optional ..."

"You're being funny," Mother said with zero humor. "I asked you not to."

"Yes, Mother." I am pretty sure she could see my eye roll across the miles. "I have appropriate shoes and pants. Nince would be proud."

"That's all I ask," Mother replied, and the call was over.

That's all I ask. That's all she ever asked, when I look back on it.

I took a shower. A hot one. I wanted a bath, but there was no time. I had to pack for French Camp—French Camp, Mississippi. I made sure to bring my favorite pair of Johnson and Murphy oxfords. They were still a little dusty orange from the last time I was there ...

So Let's Start with Shoes and Introductions, and When I Was Just a Kid

" **R**andolph Scott, take off your sister's shoes!" Mother was in the midst of a wrestling engagement, dragging her ten-year-old daughter, Olivia Joan, from under the bed in order to get her to wear the white tights that complemented the new dress that was to be inflicted upon her in round three of this epic ten-round battle.

Her seven-year-old, Randy—me ... I was in front of the mirror sing-shouting "Lucy in the skyyy with diamonds" while dancing in my sister's brand new, kitten-heeled, white pumps.

Randolph Scott is my name—Randolph Scott Fennig. And yes, I was named after *that* Randolph Scott. It is a family tradition, started by my great-grandmother—naming the children after movie stars. And perhaps there was a little providence in my mother naming me after a man who was just as infatuated with Cary Grant as I would become. We were at *this* time getting ready to visit that place I have only visited a handful of times; it's one that very much shaped my life—French Camp, Mississippi. And my poor mother was a pre-judged frazzled ball of nerves. I say "pre-judged" as her own mother, Velma (Nince to Livie and me), was to be a part of this journey. And, honey, let me tell you, Nince could judge.

We were traveling from our home on the west coast of Florida to Montgomery, Alabama to meet my grandparents. They had recently retired to the woods of west central Alabama. We would all make the few-hours drive to French Camp the next morning.

To add to the excitement, we were *flying* from Tampa to Montgomery. And Livie and I were oh so excited. We got to fly in not one, but two different planes. There was a brief layover and change of gates in Atlanta. Livie and I didn't know what that meant; we just knew there would be two airplanes.

It was 1974, and travel by air was quite the thing. One did not fly whilst dressed in sweatpants or shorts or what are essentially pajamas that people (like me) have been guilty of wearing today. No, one "dressed" for the airline in those days. Especially when one was to be picked up by her mother. Hence the pink and blue checked dress of my sister, with white tights, and the aforementioned kitten heels my scrawny ass was still wearing.

Mother also wore low heels and white stockings beneath a light blue skirt suit. She even wore a matching little hat that Dad insisted made her look like a movie star.

"You look beautiful, honey; you have nothing to worry about. The kids look great, you look great, and your mother will be very proud."

"Thank you," Mother replied before launching into her next tirade. "Randolph Scott, I am not gonna say it again—SHOES!" My mother screamed as she tore from my crying sister's room and headed toward mine.

I met her in the hallway. I was also crying and for no other reason than my sister was—and if she was crying, I should be crying because then maybe no one could be blamed. Well, that was the theory. But the hysterical young woman we called "Mother" found a way to blame us both. She was armed with her favorite weapon—a wooden spoon. I, on the other hand, was armed with my inherent cuteness, quick wit, and natural born survival skills. Olivia sat on the floor in her room, still crying—pulling on those dreaded white tights.

"I was just breaking them in for Livie 'cause they hurt her feet," I said with my baby blue eyes as wide as they could be.

I held my sister's shoes out before me as though I was offering Mother a bouquet of freshly picked weeds and dandelions.

She rolled her own blue eyes as she turned and marched back down the hall toward my sister's room. There was a brief argument over the shoes, but Olivia acquiesced, and Mother focused her ire now on our father. He was neither loading the car nor helping with the children "in any way, shape, or form" apparently.

In this story, my father doesn't get to use his actual name. Were this a story about his side of the family, he certainly would have a name—perhaps with the added signature of Lord or Prince. He was the golden child of that side of the family after all, a pronouncement that was passed on to me as well. His mother and grandmother thought I walked on water. But no, alas, this is about Mother's side, and Nince and my grandfather did not like him from the start. Boom-Pa warmed up to him, but not Nince. The warmest she got was tepid.

Nince, to Olivia and me, was just a human dynamo of energy and fun: the lady who descended upon us with a trunk load of Christmas presents; the lady with the amazing laugh; the lady who, from the perspective of TV-raised children, was a brilliant blend of Endora, Jane Hathaway, and Aunt Esther. She was just Endora to our father. Therefore, our father shall be referred to as "Derwood."

Derwood would not be going on this trip. He would just be taking us to the airport—it was across the bay in Tampa. And he would surely pick us up when we flew home; this was his purpose. So we were off to the airport. My father drove, my mother painted her nails, and Olivia Joan and I sat in the back of our 1970 Ford Country Squire. It was a "wood-grained" panel-sided car. The rest of the body, however, was an off-yellow gold. It was not the cool looking 1958 Ford Country Squire. You know the one that looked like surfboards or luggage would be right at home on top. No, the best we got was groceries in the back and a third-row seat that faced the wrong way. No cool fins or lines or curves ... this was just a long gold and brown rectangle. And that super cool third-row seat was folded down for all the luggage—so we could not even ride backward.

By the time we reached the Courtney Campbell Causeway, Olivia Joan and I were doing our thing—the thing we were best at: making our mother's life a living hell.

"Stop it, Livie. You're on my side."

"The line is right here, Randy. I am not."

"It's hot and Livie is taking up space where the fan is blowing."

"Liar, I'm on my side, and the air goes right in the middle. Right, Daddy?"

"Move your arm, Livie; stop!"

Then Derwood would interject, "Stop whining, Randy!"

"Take your feet off me, Livie! Mom, Livie is touching me with her feet!"

"My feet hurt. And you don't have to wear these stupid stockings."

"Well, Mom says you have to."

"Daaaad!!"

"Randy, stop whining!"

"But Livie ..."

"Nu-uh!"

"Stop it!" Our mother's sudden eruption set the rest of the car to dead silence. "Stop it now!" She continued to scream as she pawed through her purse for that dreaded pink plastic hairbrush with the very stiff white bristles. It was like her concealed carry ... She left the wooden spoon at home. "You two will not speak again until we are at the airport. Is that understood?!"

Livie knew better than to actually answer. I was the one who tested everything.

🐚   🐚   🐚

IT WASN'T TOO MUCH LONGER before we were entering the Tampa International Airport. It was a newer and more modern airport with what was, at the time, the tallest air traffic control tower in the world. It stirred excitement and interest in Olivia Joan and me, while inducing great anxiety and nervousness in our mother. Derwood dutifully checked us in, checked our luggage, and escorted us to the gate. You could do that then—it is amazing to look back sometimes and consider those little things we have lost; or maybe we hid them ...

I squealed with audible delight as we boarded the monorail to ride to the gate. Livie stood, holding the metal pole rather than sitting, and shifted her weight from one foot to the other.

"Do you have to go to the bathroom?" Mother asked Livie with a tone that suggested she had better not be complaining.

"I do!" I sang as I leaned back and forth, catching the pole with one hand before falling backward and then clanging my enormous cowboy-riding-a-bucking-bronco belt buckle against the metal pole. I loved horses. And I also loved cowboys. And I loved the shirtless or scantily clad "Indians" who often rode horses in cowboy movies. And I clearly loved clanging my belt buckle while repeatedly thrusting into the metal pole.

"Stop doing that, Randy," Mother said as she glared at Derwood. "You take him. Olivia Joan and I will go freshen up."

"I wanna go with Livie!"

"You are still not allowed to talk," Mother snapped at me.

"Besides that—it's the girls' bathroom. Are you a girl?"

I stuck my tongue out at Livie and resumed clanging my buckle against the metal pole. The monorail came to a stop, and our happy little family walked to the gate. Livie and Mother disappeared into the ladies' room. Dad sent me to the men's room and waited outside.

While I lost all track of time in the bathroom (I could sit

and sing all the songs I knew for hours), Mother and Livie had another wrestling match in the ladies' room. It was more of a mental and emotional battle of wills than an actual physical altercation. But it is not unimaginable that the pink brush with stiff white bristles might have made an appearance. The result was Livie coming back out of the bathroom, her face puffy from tears. Mother was right behind her with a face more like stone. She shot my father a "Where is Randy?" look; he failed to answer satisfactorily. She stared hard at Derwood as she made her way into the men's room and shrieked my name.

"RANDY!!!"

THE FLIGHT FROM TAMPA TO Atlanta was rather brief and uneventful. It was the first time on a plane for either Livie or me, and of course we both wanted the window seat. Mother's compromise: Livie would sit there from Tampa to Atlanta; I would get the window from Atlanta to Montgomery. The quick duration of the flight combined with the novelty of flying allowed for Livie and me to thoroughly enjoy this first leg of our trip. Our mother sat proudly as her two well-dressed and well-mannered children looked out of the window and "oohed" and "ahhed" as they pointed. And then we landed. And then we had to change gates. And then Mother became a little less proud.

DRAGGING HER TWO CHILDREN BY their respective left arms (I'm sure you can already guess who was walking backwards.), a harried mother was seen running through the Atlanta International Airport. Flight information and gate changes were announced over the intercom system, and rows of television screens displayed the comings and goings of passengers in this major travel hub.

"I gotta pee!" I whined.

"Well, you'll have to hold it; we're trying to find our gate," Mother barked.

"I don't like these; they hurt, and it's hot ..."

"Livie, stop complaining about those damn stockings."

We knew Mother was *really angry* when she cussed. Derwood cussed all the time; Mother never did. So Livie just pouted while I continued to push.

"I need to go ... bad."

"They hurt!"

"Stop it! Both of you! We are not having this. Randy, you go right over there. It's just across that hall. And use the men's room. I can see you from here. Do not wander off, and do not play with the water in the sink, and do not sit there and sing all day. We have a plane to catch." She said all of this while squeezing my arm tight and pointing in the direction of the men's room on the other side of two intersecting concourses.

I took my time walking toward the bathroom while I was passed by travelers moving in all directions—carrying luggage and running to make connections or getting their bags or saying hello or goodbye to relatives and loved ones. I passed by a line of folks on one side who were checking through security. On the other side, folks passed quickly by me on their way to luggage pickup. I meandered my way to the restroom. I found an empty stall. And I promptly sat down and started to sing.

The chuckles of the other occupants of the long row of stalls—well it was all the encouragement I needed to continue my impromptu toilet concert, with my rendition of "Aaaa-aaa-aaa-aaa-afternoon delight!" being my final encore. We were all suddenly interrupted by a loud scream.

"RANDY!"

Quickly I slid from my perch on the porcelain throne and left. I did not wash my hands, but then I did not actually go to the bathroom. Even as a child I got some weird thrill hanging out in the men's room. Coming out would certainly be easier if parents would just connect the dots.

"RANDYYY!!!"

I emerged from the bathroom, looked about the crowded concourse, and spied my mother just across the way. She was in some line—waiting, panicked—and the signs of the glue coming undone were clearly surfacing. Joining her in the queue, I took her hand. She looked down at me and her tight, yet frazzled frown softened into something almost resembling a smile. At that point, it was Mother's turn to walk through the scanners. She did. And then she walked promptly toward my sister who was standing in the exact spot where Mother had clearly threatened her life if she were to move. Livie, of course, was crying.

"What is your problem!?!" she whisper-screamed at Livie.

I stepped through the scanner.

BEEP

"Randy?" My mother turned only to watch as I was whisked to the side by two security officers. "RANDY!"

"They hurt ..." Lizzie sobbed.

Mother shouted, "Then take the damn things off and throw them away! I don't care anymore!" And then she ran toward the two gentlemen who had escorted me to the side.

The men got a good chuckle out of discovering it was my belt buckle that had set off the alarm. As they gleefully waved the wand over my buckle to demonstrate to Mother what had happened, their smiles faded. Mother unloaded the frustrations of her day upon them, only to be interrupted by a boarding call on the flight to Montgomery. I had never heard an actual human make the noises Mother made at that point, except for when Livie and I would watch Dr. Paul Bearer's Creature Feature on Saturday afternoons.

Racing down the concourse to our gate, Mother had me by the arm as she screamed at Livie to keep up. The "now boarding" call came across the airwaves again, and Mother let out a sigh of relief as she spied the gate. She turned to look for Livie, who was several yards back and getting up off the floor.

"Livie! What are you doing? Get off the floor!"

"I keep slipping and sliding ..." To be fair to Mother, Livie did always whine.

"I wanna take my shoes off too!" So I did. I was also a whiner. Our mother had two whiny children.

"Where are your shoes?" Mother asked, already knowing the answer.

Bursting into tears Livie screamed, "You told me to throw them away!!!"

The final boarding call for our flight came while Mother was digging through her third garbage can. We boarded the plane in silence. We sat in silence. And I knew better than to complain when I realized that the flight to Montgomery was shorter than the one from Tampa to Atlanta, and I got robbed because Livie had more time by the window. Sort of. I might have mentioned it once or twice.

Nince and Boom-Pa were there waiting for us when we got off the plane. We had to walk down steps to the tarmac; it was all very exciting. Boom-Pa hugged us both, picked Livie up, and carried her the whole way to the car. Nince kissed our cheeks and gave Mother a rather pity-filled hug. Our drive to their place was not as silent as the plane ride. Livie and I took turns telling them all about the flight, the monorail, and the security guards. I sang that old classic from the men's room. Mother sat in the backseat with her eyes closed; she complained of a headache.

Later that evening, as I lay on the couch not sleeping like I was supposed to be, I heard Nince on the phone with her sister, Wilksie (or India, which was her actual name).

"You tell me what you think when we get there tomorrow. I don't know what to think. I mean she shows up looking an absolute mess, Randy is a handful of energy ... I know, India, I know ... but listen to this: Livie wasn't even wearing shoes. I am beginning to wonder if Derwood has a job."

I Guess It Really All Starts at the Movies, Way Before I Was Born

Nince was the middle of three sisters. There were also two older brothers in the mix. And all were named for movie stars (well, with the exception of India). See, Nince's mother, my great-grandmother, loved the movies. She was the youngest of twins—Ettienne and her twelve-minute older sister Guise—and also the youngest of several brothers and sisters before her. Her mother died in childbirth; her father died in a horrible accident in Memphis. She was raised by the eldest of the clan. He was a prominent attorney and owner of the family lands.

Mornay was the family surname, and, according to India, "It was actually derived or evolved from Monet, but was bastardized when the Huguenots came to South Carolina."

My great-grandfather, who grew up in the "county," referred to them as the Moneys, and always referred to his wife's brother as Uncle Money ... a thing Nince and her younger sister disdained. Ettienne thought it was harmless and hilarious.

Despite the monied privileges that accompanied wealth, being the oldest of a brood of children, Uncle Money still had the challenge of getting his younger sisters married off to the right families. And, well, he admitted that he did not rise to the challenge for his youngest of sisters. But Ettienne, or Etty, disagreed and always said she married for love—not for her family's comfort or amusement.

My great-grandfather was a farmer and a mason with a penchant for baseball. He came from a poorer family of sharecroppers who eventually garnered their own small plot of land just before my great-grandfather was born. He was named for the new dock his father had built on the pond. In his teen years, Dock was scouted by the newly named Yankees, and went to New York in 1914. There he practiced with the team and was considered quite the new pitching find. But an accident in 1916 led to his leaving baseball and never picking up a glove, ball, or bat again.

It was batting practice early in the season. Dock was warming up his arm. The Yankees were about to enter a three-game series with the White Sox. He threw a pitch that was perhaps his fastest ever, but as the batter leaned in to swing, the ball curved in an unexpected fashion and struck the batter square in the temple. He immediately fell to the ground, the batter did, face up toward the sky. Dock was the first to get there—even before the catcher who had run for the errant ball.

"He smiled at me while he was tryin' to git up," he told my great-grandmother many nights, over many years, after waking from the same horrible dream. "Etty, he was smilin' when he tried to git up. There was blood in his ears. Then he stopped smilin' and he looked confused, and he said to ... he said to nobody, 'I'll tell him ... I'll tell Dock right now.' Then he looked me dead square in the eye, Etty, and he said, 'It is not your fault Dock. They say to tell ya' it is not your fault.' And then he collapsed. Dead."

He took his Yankee money, and (with the help of Uncle

Money) he purchased about thirty acres of land which surrounded the twenty-two acres he had acquired through his sharecropping family. It wasn't the largest of the family farms that surrounded the small crossroads town of French Camp, Mississippi, but it was just off of the main highway, and it was the closest to town. Dock also studied masonry from one of the men in Uncle Money's employ—a young Black man named Thurgoode.

Thurgoode's father worked for Uncle Money's father, though for little to no pay. Well, let's say *no pay* as this was Mississippi and humans owned other humans in those days. In Dock and Thurgoode's case, ownership of humans was now outlawed, so it was described as an internship where Dock was considered the master and the "boy" who taught him, the apprentice. But Dock would learn from this man. And Dock did honor him in his own way years later.

The masonry work took Dock away from the family farm, leaving Etty to maintain the home, raise the children, and manage the work on the farm. A tiny woman in stature, Etty was a force to be reckoned with. She managed several sharecropping families who did the actual work on the farm. She minded the children and oversaw their work on the family portion of the farm. And without fail, every Saturday afternoon she would walk into town—into French Camp—and go to the movies. It was her time. It was her escape.

French Camp was a place she visited from the time her brother had helped finance the construction of the Picture Palace and Vaudeville House by lending his "boy" and my great-grandfather's services to the project. By all accounts, Ettienne was a practical woman, a frugal woman, and a woman who knew how to live without luxuries ... save for the movies. And through the magical lens of Hollywood and all its glamor, she was inspired to name her children.

ᴈ   ᴈ   ᴈ

KING WAS THE OLDEST OF her children, a true first-born son. Dock was so proud and looking forward to raising his namesake. But it was not to be, as this bundle of joy was not named for my great-grandfather, but for a man named King. He was named for King Vidor, the famed director of the 1920s and beyond. Etty convinced Dock that King was the perfect name as he would grow up to be a strong and powerful man, King Edward Taylor. Dock liked the sound of that.

This also opened the floodgates for naming the rest of her children after Hollywood notables. Norma was next. Etty had just seen *A Slave of Fashion* with Norma Shearer. Dock was taken with both the beauty of the actress and his first daughter, so he agreed to Norma Katherine Taylor.

Ettienne wanted a boy and a girl next to name Rudolph and Vilma. She loved *The Son of the Sheik* and even saw it twice. Oh, how she fell in love with that movie and with Rudolph Valentino in particular. She hoped for twins; she and her husband were both twins, after all. But that was not meant to be. Etty did carry twins, for about four months—but she lost them during one harsh winter. However, Rudie, or Rudolph Mornay Taylor, was born just three years after Norma—a year after the twins were buried.

But it would take three more miscarriages and a stillbirth before my grandmother was born and Etty got her Vilma. Well, Dock fell in love immediately with this child who just fit into the palms of his enormous hands. He held her and looked at his wife with tears in his eyes and declared he was not going to call his favorite daughter "some dirty Hungarian name like she was some ..." I'm sure you can think of the word he was going to use in 1929 Mississippi, so Vilma turned into Velma—Velma Irene

Taylor. And Velma turned into Nince. We don't really know where Nince came from, and Dock was the only one who ever called her Nince ... until Olivia and I came along.

And finally, there was India. Etty was reading *Gone with the Wind* when she was pregnant with her last surviving child and declared India Wilkes to be "the only sensible character in the whole dern book, so that is what I am going to name my child."

Meanwhile, India would swiftly self-identify as Scarlett and she detested her name. She lived as a devastated martyr until That Sable Boy started calling her Wilksie.

"And he said to me," she would share every time she felt the need to explain her peculiar name, "Why Miss India Wilkes Taylor, if you dislike your name so, may I have the honor of calling you Wilksie?"

It really isn't a good story, but she told it all the same. She reiterated it to both Livie and me when we met her that next day after Airport '74.

🌀   🌀   🌀

Chapter 2
Branches and Confluents

Lessons on Little Ladies and Boys:
A Childhood Tutorial

I awoke to the sounds of dishes being removed from the dish-washer and placed in their proper homes. The soft clinks and clanks of Nince's everyday china, a high-pitched ding from a glass, and the flat metallic taps of the silverware as Nince quietly put the dishes away, as though her actions themselves were a whisper. They are sounds I can close my eyes and hear even now. Though distant or maybe hollow is the better word, I can hear the clinks and dings and taps as though underwater, warped and bent. And it is a far better sound than the recording of dishes NPR always uses when the radio journalist says, "We are at a dockside cafe in Copenhagen ..." It was early, 4:30 or not quite 5:00, but Nince was always up early. So was I. I am even now.

"Good morning, Randy," Nince whispered softly. But it was more like 'Rain-Dee' or 'RAIN-de' with the emphasis on rain.

"Ga' Mornin."

She sipped her coffee as she continued her early morning chores. The dishes were all put away. It was time to start breakfast. She patiently washed the shells of the eggs she planned to use, then allowed me to crack them into the bowl.

"Don't get any shells in, right Nince?"

"I washed them just in case, but no—no shells."

She watched but did not wince as I did my best to crack the nine or so eggs she had given me. Instead Nince pulled out jars of a variety of shapes and sizes containing jams and spreads she had purchased at some church bazaar or another. She used her everyday china, the incomplete set Boom, or Boom-Pa, brought back from England. She placed them all on the oversized kitchen table, leaving room for the breakfast dishes yet to come. She then turned to the other items she needed to cook. While reminding me to be careful with the eggs, she started the grits and pulled a chair over to the stove. I whisked the eggs as she instructed, using a fork to do the whisking ... always use a fork. Then we moved to the stove where she already had a stick of butter melting in the pan for the eggs.

"I could have cut it with a little hot bacon grease," Nince offered, then advised: "If ever you cook bacon, save the grease."

She poured the whipped-up eggs into the hot sizzling pan and handed me a large metal tablespoon. Standing on that kitchen table chair before the stove, I cooked the eggs while Nince continued to scurry about the kitchen. Every jar had a spoon. There was a special little knife for the softened butter; a cloche to keep the toast warm. Nince filled that oversized kitchen table.

"Your Boom-Pa never thinks I need the leaf in this table," she muttered as she shuffled things around to make room for the plate of ham and the grits.

Mother came out of her room and went straight for the coffee. And then to the ceramic pig Nince kept as a cookie jar— or in this case a "lemon square" jar. Lemon squares are really just a goo cake, a sticky sweet and cake-like brownie often made from a boxed cake mix, butter, eggs, and cream cheese. Did you notice I did not mention the use of lemon? Yeah, me too. It is because there is none. Nince was not a fan of lemon, so she left it out of the recipe and just never worried about it until I questioned her one morning while we made them together.

"Why are they called lemon squares if you don't use lemon?"

"Because they are yellah." Nince offered this explanation simply, matter-of-factly, and it somehow made sense.

On this particular morning, just as Mother reached into the ceramic pig, Nince asked, "Debbie? Is that something you should be eating this morning? I'm not sure that lovely blue traveling suit of yours is gonna fit you any better today than it did when you got off the plane. Have some dry toast."

"Can I have one?"

"Of course, Randy." Nince smiled. "Let me get those eggs in a bowl. Go wash your hands and tell Livie to come to the table."

"Yes, ma'am!" I cheered as I hopped from the chair and ran to get Livie.

"You know we don't make the children use ma'am or sir at home," Mother whispered to Nince.

"Yes. Derwood doesn't like it," Nince offered and smiled. "Or some such ..."

"Well, it is not the way they were raised ..." Mother tried to defend her stance.

"But it is the way you were raised."

"Leave it alone, Velma." It was Boom-Pa. "Where are my grandbabies at?!?!"

Livie and I came running, "Here we are!" And we were ushered to chairs around the kitchen table as Nince set a plate of eggs, grits, and sliced ham ... and lemon squares before each of us.

Nince was buttering my toast as my mother sat down. "Fix your father a plate, dear, while I help the children."

Mother set her plate down and got back up to get Boom-Pa's. I wondered why he couldn't get his own breakfast; it was all right there on the table in front of us. Boom-Pa was pouring coffee and beaming at his daughter as she spooned eggs and grits onto his plate.

"Now see Velma, she's gotta lean all the way across to reach them grits. We don't need this damn leaf in this damn table."

Nince shot me a look before rolling her eyes and smiling. I let out a little giggle. Then Nince gave me a wink and removed the lemon square from Mother's plate and rested it on her own.

I whispered to Livie as quietly as I could that the reason Mother couldn't eat lemon squares was because she was too fat to fit in her clothes. Mother set Boom-Pa's plate in front of him before picking up her coffee and heading to her room to get dressed.

"She should eat somethin' before she wastes away, don't ya think, Velma?" Boom-Pa said while dumping Tabasco hot sauce on his eggs.

"I don't think she is well." Nince agreed with Boom-Pa before getting up and walking toward the closed hall bathroom door. "Debbie, don't you worry dear; I'll get the children ready while you do something with that hair."

Livie and Boom-Pa sat and talked at the kitchen table while Nince made sure I was dressed and ready to go. I got to watch Boom-Pa shave while Nince and Livie had a very hushed conversation about little ladies and expectations. And then Mother came out of the room.

"I've got the children's things packed up." She was wearing her blue traveling suit. Debra had freshly pressed the suit that morning. Her gloves were perfectly white. Oh, and the little pillbox hat sat perfectly on her blonde hair that was stylishly somewhere between a wedge and a pageboy—but with a cute little flip in the back.

"Well, it looks like Randy and I got the prettiest little traveling companions any man could ask for." Then Boom-Pa whistled and said, "Right Randy?"

"Yes sir!"

"Oh Debbie," Nince beamed in my mother's direction. "That hat is perfect. It covers that thing with your hair."

◈   ◈   ◈

IT WAS NOT SO MUCH the sound of the tires that woke me up, but the change in sound as we left the highway and pulled to a stop beside a pair of gas pumps. There is something about the sound of tires, that low hum, on a long asphalt road that lulls one to sleep. Like a white noise machine or the sound of the ocean waves crashing on the shore. But the sound changed to one of crushing gravel or rather the crunching bits of orange and crusty earth that had baked in the Mississippi sun.

Boom-Pa stepped out of the car and chatted with the man who pumped the gas. We were at a little roadside station. A small restaurant and shop were a part of this mom-and-pop establishment somewhere just on the Mississippi side of the Alabama/Mississippi state line. We would be in Columbus soon, and then Starkville, home to that dreaded Mississippi State University.

"You will go to Ole Miss, Randy. And that is all there is to that," Nince would pronounce at every passing through Starkville I ever made with her. Ole Miss, the University of Mississippi, is located in Oxford. And I did go. I studied theatre; I studied a lot of things ...

"Come on out here, kids!" Boom-Pa shouted from outside the car. "Go on inside with this boy here; I gave him enough money for y'all to pick out a candy and get each of us a coke."

"Yay! Come on, Livie!" I shouted, crawling through the window while Mother was opening the door.

Livie slid along the back seat; the side of her face imprinted with a red splotchy line matching the design of the seam along the leather seat. She yawned as she took my hand, my other in the hand of the tall Black man who pumped our gas. He was probably my grandfather's age. And he was sure patient as Livie and I oohed and ahhed over our candy choices and all the different kinds of cokes.

The sunlight dappled its way through glass jars filled with nothing but flavored sticks of sugar in a rainbow of colors and flavors. I stood mesmerized before the jars and barely took notice of Nince and Mother conversing thirty feet beyond that corn syrup and dust filled storefront window. Apparently Nince was taking the opportunity to stretch her legs and offer Mother a little parenting advice. At least that is what I put together from a story Mother told me years later—sometime after that middle part where I began this whole story.

"The children were awfully well behaved on this car ride, don't you think?"

"The children were asleep," Mother replied.

"Yes," Nince smiled, "because I gave them one of these."

Mother looked at the yellow cardboard box which contained several chalky white pills Nince had handed her. "You drugged my children?"

"Oh, it is just Dramamine. And yes." Nince smiled as she put the box back into her purse. "And so will you."

Livie and I ran back to the car with our cokes held high, "I have a purple one and Livie's is orange!" I shouted the obvious as we climbed into the backseat.

The crushing orange clay from the tires turned to the smooth low hum as Boom-Pa turned back onto Highway 12, leaving the roadside station and the man my grandfather called boy behind in a sepia cloud of Mississippi dust. That is not all we left behind, just as the cokes and candy were not all Livie and I picked up. I stared out the back window for a long time, even after the image of the nice man who held my hand in the store had vanished. When I turned back around, I saw my mother looking out of the passenger side window up front. Nince had taken her place between Livie and me in the back.

"We're passing State, Velma," Boom-Pa announced.

"That's right, and you will go to Ole Miss, Randy. And that is all there is to that."

"Where will Livie go?" I asked.

"Wherever Livie wants," Mother replied.

"We have an hour and a half left if we take 12. Two hours if we take the Trace." Boom-Pa looked up into the rearview mirror toward Nince.

"Take the Trace," Nince answered as she opened her purse and removed the yellow cardboard box.

"Oh, Mother, they will be groggy and cranky when we get there; let's not give them any more."

Nince offered a condoling look toward her daughter. "Dear, I have something to perk them up before we get there."

And with that, Boom-Pa's Cadillac rolled on down the Natchez Trace—that beautiful park-like drive that follows an old Native American route from just southwest of Nashville all the way to Natchez, Mississippi. We would pass through French Camp on our way to India's ... or Wilksie's, as she preferred. She lived in Kosciusko, just beyond their childhood home. Livie and I were both asleep as we drove through French Camp. And like the Luft children before Mama gave a concert, we were offered some candy and a beverage just as we left the Trace and entered a whole new world.

⁂

LIVIE AND I BOLTED FROM the car as soon as we pulled into

the driveway. We were eager to stretch our legs—to move, to run, and to get out all the stiffness of being on your best behavior in the car because Nince was in the backseat with you. And Boom-Pa encouraged us to run a little energy out. And run we did, around what we learned was called a magnolia tree. Wilksie had it planted recently. It was part of a fundraising and beautification project that Wilksie was spearheading for the DAR. The DAR, if you are unaware, is the Daughters of the American Revolution. And Wilksie was serving as Immediate Past President of the DAR, President of the Botanical Society, and a member of the Artists Guild—so hers was the first tree planted.

"Oh Livie, no!" Mother tried to shout, but it was too late.

Livie had taken a tumble in the freshly watered orange clay that surrounded the newly planted magnolia. Her traveling clothes, with those dreaded white tights that only Nince could convince her to wear without the requisite wrestling match, were now stained with muddy orange streaks. Livie immediately started to cry. And I quickly began to offer my defenses of both Livie and me, throwing our grandfather under the bus; he was the one who told us to run. Boom-Pa just laughed and laughed and lit a cigarette and began to unload the car. Mother tried to whisper-scream at us, as our relations were now coming out of the house to greet us, and she did not want to be embarrassed. And Nince? She offered only a withering stare at our mother.

"Oh, poor Debbie!" Bitsy, Wilksie's eldest daughter, wailed before pulling Mother into an uncomfortable hug. "Don't you worry, hon; I'm going to take your precious children inside and help get them settled. You go on back to my old room and freshen up. I'm sure you'll find what you need. Oh, bless your heart."

There were a lot of hearts blessed that weekend—and also the weekend of my grandmother's funeral, which happened roughly 30 years later ...

Three Sisters: There Are Two Sets, and I'm One Confused Adult

I saw them as soon as I walked in. They could not be missed. They all wore black, because that is what you do on days like these—black or some other dark hue. High and buoyant was their hair. And blonde. Not in the sense that it was natural, because it wasn't. But blonde and peroxide have had such a long relationship with these three sisters that anything other than boxed hair color would somehow seem, well, unnatural.

They were hovering about the free coffee and "breakfast" of plastic wrapped pastries and assorted flavored creamers offered by the roadside motel located somewhere between two small towns in rural Mississippi.

"It's between Ackerman and Weir ..." Mother had reminded me.

I stepped in line behind these three sisters to get my own cup of coffee and vaguely plastic pastry. While not black, I too wore the traditional dark colored mourning attire. Be it tradition or respect or simply because we were told to by our mothers—it is like a costume one must don in this oft-performed pageant play we call a Southern Funeral. And if you are a lady, you had best not wear the same dress to the viewing, the second viewing, the family viewing, the memorial services, the funeral service, the graveside ... and don't forget your pearls. If you do, there are at least two sets of three sisters who may whisper about it. Well, there used to be.

"Well good morning," the eldest sister said to me and smiled. Her left hand held her paper cup of coffee while she delicately traced the requisite string of pearls she wore with her French manicured right. "Aren't you a broad-shouldered and handsome man," she stated, not questioned.

I smiled with a mixture of discomfort, nausea, and hilarity while the middle of the three just laughed.

"Bitsy, that's our cousin, Randy!" Vivian, the youngest, gasped.

The way she said it, the way they all do, I will always hear it in my mind. Randy with a long A, Rain, and a quick D. But the emphasis is always on rain, RAIN-de. Just like Nince used to say it. Only not at all.

"My, my, Randy, you're all grown up," Elizabeth Wilkes Taylor Sable Gregorio Wiltson Hamilton Gray said, with the emphasis on Rain and all.

She was my grandmother's youngest sister's eldest daughter, so my first cousin once removed. Did you follow that? Because I believe I got that right. That whole first cousin, second cousin, and somebody being removed always confuses me. Bitsy would eventually garner two more husbands than her actual namesake. And Bitsy didn't cheat ... and by that, I mean she never married any of them twice like Liz did. I can't vouch for her fidelity.

🦿   🦿   🦿

UNTIL THAT MOMENT IN TIME, I mostly remembered her as I had when I was young. Bitsy and Mother were roughly the same age, and they sometimes grew up together. See, my grandfather—Boom-Pa, we called him—was in the military. The Air Force stationed him all over the country and sometimes even the world. He was originally in the Army. Then toward the end of his career, he made the move from the Army Air Corps to the Air Force when it was officially established. Sometimes his family would join him, and sometimes they would not. There were

several summers and a few school years during the more difficult transitions when Mother lived on the farm owned by her
grandparents, Dock and Etty.

Bitsy and her twin brother, Conrad, were essentially raised
on the farm as well. Their grandmother and grandfather, again
Dock and Etty, did the raising though, because their mother,
Wilksie, was often away. Sometimes she was visiting their father in Alaska, and sometimes she was just busy living her life.

My mother, Debbie, was the first grandchild for Dock
and Etty. Nince followed tradition and named her for Debbie
Reynolds. Bitsy and Conrad were just a few months later and
were named for Elizabeth Taylor and Conrad Hilton. Wilksie
swore they should never have divorced, and Liz should have just
dealt with it.

"Women were born to bear the burden of men." Wilksie
would often share her little wisdoms of life to anyone or no
one—it did not matter. "Their accomplishments and their short-
comings." These were alway punctuated with a smile. One that
both invited you to share in her opinion and cautioned you not
to do otherwise.

As is often the case with siblings or cousins or friends, there
was sometimes a bit of unspoken competition between Bitsy and
Mother. To be fair, sometimes it was spoken. They were both
pregnant at the same time with their respective firsts. Both, as
hindsight and proper math would indicate, were pregnant a bit
prior to their nuptials. And both were eager to provide Dock
and Etty with a very first great-grandchild. Mother won out
with the birth of my sister, Olivia Joan Fennig. It was a weekend of tears, laughter, and joy when Livie was introduced to her
great-grandparents and to Mother's sometimes childhood home
of French Camp. She introduced me as well, three years later.
But Bitsy beat her to the punch with a first BOY great-grandchild. Gio came shortly after my sister. Births and introductions

were our first reasons for travel. And funerals ... but they came later.

᷎   ᷎   ᷎

THE BOXED BLONDE BEVY (BITSY, Joan, and Vivian) and I laughed through that ticklish breakfast exchange of Bitsy and her overly eager need to shower a man with attention. My heart was blessed multiple times by each sister as we laughed at the awkwardness of the scenario. Then we discussed my mother, a topic I skillfully sidestepped by bringing her grief over the loss of her mother into the conversation. And of course, they, the Garnier Girls, had much to say in the way of condolences over Nince. My heart was blessed a few more times before I managed to take my coffee and my vaguely plastic pastries back to my room—and I quickly called Liv.

"Yeah?" Liv answered. Thank God it wasn't Mother.

"Um, I may need therapy?" The trauma hung in my voice.

"What?!?"

"Our cousin, Bitsy ...?"

"Which one is she?" Liv asked. She was never one for whom the ability to keep track of the ins and outs of family dynamics, history, and politics came naturally. She preferred to simply put her head down, do her thing, and avoid the drama. She took after Derwood in that department.

I, however, majored in Theatre. And now I made my living as a stage manager and a director and lecturer on said things. I knew all the players. I studied them. I knew where they were and how they stood—what their proxemic choices and all those other nonverbal bits of communication and gestures conveyed. I studied their interactions and dissected their relationships: I had an eye for the drama. "Wilksie's oldest girl, Elizabeth Taylor? Gah, how do you not know these people ... I ran into her and her sisters, Joan and Vivian, you know ... *The Three Sisters?* Not the originals—the *next* generation." We always referred to Nince and her sisters (Wilksie and Norma) as The Three Sisters. Livie and I did. So, the progression or next iteration only made sense. But I always made up a nickname just to differentiate between the generations.

"Yeah, yeah, yeah ... the Lemon Fragrance Added Girls." Livie had just as many names for people as I did.

"Yeah, she just hit on me!"

"What?!"

So I relayed the entire traumatic story, embellishing where appropriate, and Livie and I shared a much-needed laugh. Our Lady of Perpetual Martyrdom, whom we sometimes referred to as Mother, could be heard in the background, "Olivia Joan, I don't know what nonsense your brother is sharing, but the laughter is not appropriate. Not today."

"Yes Mother." I joined her in saying it, despite the fact that Mother could not hear me.

"And tell him I told him already not to be funny."

"Mother says don't be funny."

"It's a funeral for crying out loud! His grandmother's!" Her voice carried across the room and through the phone my sister was holding.

And Now for a Brief Aside on Funerals

We have all done it, been there. You have; I have. It's all been done countless times before. Attending the funeral of a loved one. Or the funeral of a loved one of a loved one. The funeral of a venerable stranger with whom you are only remotely connected via circumstance or happenstance—or perhaps some obscure relational contact. And that really just amounts to those same two things, doesn't it? We have all sat on the hard cold wood, shifting cheek to cheek; leg crossed this way, now that. Listening to most of what is said, because you can't seem to do anything else. The ceremony or service or whatever secular solicitation being offered is only marginally reminiscent of the person you may or may not have known—the individual who once occupied the painted and costumed shell that lies in a decorated and flower-filled box before you now.

And I have made that long drive before. My tires, sometimes rented, sometimes my own, (and sometimes the vehicle of my relations) have traveled those gentle ascents and downgrades and turns through fields of scraggly brown sticks capped by fluffy white cotton, forests of tufted green pine needles, blacktop that gives way to the orange ruts and lanes of a tired old lady named Mississippi. My Johnson and Murphy wingtips swing around and step from my pickup ... my parents' car ... my rented SUV ...

It was raining that day, and we remarked how it was like Jesus was weeping over this good man. Or it was unusually cold, and we remarked that God was helping us find comfort and warmth in each other's arms as we gathered to celebrate the life of this matriarch of matriarchs. It was sunny because we were being smiled upon. Every graveside service I have attended is met with a discussion of the weather, and the resulting divine commentary as suggested by said weather—a consistency that has often provided comfort. At least to me.

And I always found comfort, at a Mississippi funeral anyway, in the inevitable deep orange ruts in the ground. They may be baked brick-hard by the hot Delta sun, they may be frozen solid in the perpetual frosty damp gray that is a Mississippi winter. Or they may be what I seem to remember most days ... a combination of wet concrete and clay, like burnt orange

quicksand or an over-baked sweet potato pie—perfect for en-
casing your wingtip or less than practical spiked heel in a suc-
tion-like grip that cannot be released without the aid of the
shoulder of whomever is standing with you. They are always
there; those rolls and ripples of burnt tangerine. They were that
day at my grandmother's funeral.

I was a pallbearer for this one. Nince had asked that a few
friends from her church and her three grandsons carry that position. She had been sick, quite a while, Nince, and she had organized her funeral plans to the last detail. She let it be known
what it was she wanted for this event. Two separate viewings:
one for family and one for everyone else. A memorial service
was held at the last place she was employed—and where she
volunteered her time for years after. It was a "special camp for
children and adults." That was the '70s and '80s; its moniker is
something a little more politically correct now.

There was also the service at her church, where we were
now—and then a smaller one at the family church back in
French Camp. And of course, the graveside service and burial. Nince had it all planned to the last dotted "i" and the last
crossed "t".

She had discussed everything she wanted with her children,
Debbie and Gene. Gene was almost three years behind Mother.
Nince and Grandmother Etty both enjoyed *Singing in the Rain*
immensely.

Betty-Girl, however, did not enjoy *Singing In the Rain*. I
don't actually know that as a fact; I am merely speculating.
Betty-Girl Monroe was the rabid funeral director Nince chose
to run this Southern Baptist rite of passage. She had little time
for the wants and needs of family. She also had little time for
the wants and desires of my grandmother—well, the ones she
felt were just not appropriate. She had a job to do. And she was
the wife of the preacher, after all. The preacher who asked to

be affectionately called Brother-Man Bill, or just Brother-Man. I never understood the aggressive familiarity of some southern nicknames. Also, Betty-Girl had it out for me, for my sister, our mother, and oddly enough Bitsy—although that tale was told at another funeral, years before this one.

↝   ↝   ↝

Chapter 3
Ole Miss and Auld Lang Syne

I'm at Ole Miss,
and That's All There Is to That

"Now *who* died?" she asked in a drawl that had come home to roost, much like Lorraine herself—an actress who had returned from a stint in the Big Apple. She took her bite; it bit back—and now she and I sat bathing together in our respective tubs.

I could vaguely hear the words, as vaguely is the only description that comes to mind when hearing while submerged. I suppose there are others. Actually, I know there are others. But I was underwater—and I couldn't think of them at the time. I could only concentrate on losing myself in the distortions of the world above. I stared up at the ceiling, my eyes open as my head rested against the hard porcelain beneath the surface of the warm but-not-too-warm water. The beige square tiles, yellowed walls that refused to give up whether they were paper, plaster, or just a poor and aged choice of decor. The ceiling was high, and of a similar cigarette-haze hue as the walls. But the tub! Oh, that tub was incredibly long and deep, and it allowed for my large, six-foot-plus frame to fully sink down. I watched the bubbles trickle from my nose and rise to the surface as the vagueness of the words became clearer.

"Hello!" Lorraine banged on the thin yellowed wall that separated our two tubs.

Although our bathrooms shared a wall, we did not share an apartment. This was years earlier when I was a grad student at Ole Miss. Lorraine lived with a design major. I also lived with a design major. And our apartments shared the first floor of a building that also housed two very quiet undergraduate gentlemen in an apartment upstairs.

The bubbles escaped faster now as I exhaled and sat up, the warm water cascading down as I wiped my face, shook my hair out, and took a deep breath. "No, I'm here!"

"I should be at class with Ho-Ho, but I chose to take a bath with you. Now, who died? Do I need to come with you anywhere?"

"No, no, nothing like that. I think I'm good," I said. "He and I were not really close. Not at all; I can probably count the times I've met him on the fingers of one of my hands."

"He's your uncle?" she asked—not judging.

"My great-uncle. He is, was ... is? He is the husband of my grandmother's sister," I answered. "So there are going to be cousins, extended relatives ... The Three Sisters, ha! There will be a lot of folks there."

"And we can't have them talking. Not now. Not at a time like this."

"I guess?" I took a sip from the beer bottle resting on the side of the tub and puzzled for just a moment about what she had said. I imagined Lorraine drinking a Mimosa from a champagne flute—I never knew her not to have a pitcher of Mimosas available. "I think I'll just be preoccupied with Nince and her sisters. They are something else, these ladies, that ..."

"A single man, bringing a girl home for a funeral. Oh no,

that's bigger than a wedding. I'll have to go with you some other time."

"Yeah, I'd like that. But I still don't think it would be a fuss if you came today ..."

"Really? Don't you? You don't think those three sisters are gonna have something to say about each and every person at that funeral?"

"Well yeah, that's probably just about accurate." I laughed. "It gets a little confusing because there are actually two sets of what we call 'The Three Sisters.'"

"Like Chekhov!" Lorraine also laughed.

"More like if Tennessee Williams was carrying Albee's baggage in addition to his own ... and then wrote a play in the style of Chekhov."

"Oh, my ..." Lorraine clearly took another sip of Mimosa. "Now I think I do wanna go."

"It is always an adventure," I assured her.

"So tell me about your uncle. But hurry, the bath is getting cold."

"You better add water then; I'll talk a little louder while you do ... It's hard to condense these stories."

Tides and Tales and That Sable Boy

India's husband was always "That Sable Boy"—or "Wilksie's husband." I mean that is all I ever remember him being called. He would probably say the same. He had a name; of course he did. It was Brick. Brick Sable. He sounded like a movie star, so naturally her mother, Etty, approved. He was handsome and he was rugged, and he worked the pipeline in Alaska. And you'll remember, he is the one who christened my Great-Aunt India Wilkes Taylor as Wilksie—a name she carried from that day forth. And from that day forth everyone called her Wilksie ... even her children. She was never Mother, Mama, or Mom. She was Wilksie.

It was during that visit when Livie wore those orange-stained tights that I learned this fact about Wilksie. We were a little more settled. It was after dinner, and I probably needed to go to the bathroom or get a glass of water or find an excuse to walk down the hall where that nude painting was.

"Um, Aunt India Wilksie, um ..." I sputtered.

"Oh, just Wilksie, Sweetie. Everyone calls me Wilksie. Why I can't believe no one ever told you—it's just the sweetest little ol' story ..."

"Here we go ..." Norma, Nince's older sister, said and rolled her eyes.

We never addressed our aunts and uncles as Aunt Whomever or Uncle So and So; we always used their first names. Certain members of Derwood's side of the family found it disrespectful, I believe. Nince's side would have somehow been offended had we used such formality. It could be a little confusing when we were young, so Livie chose to just never speak. I chose to listen.

"She's gonna tell him, and he is only seven years old." Nince called me over to her. "RAIN-de, you don't want to hear this nonsense."

"Oh, y'all hush up now." Wilksie was clearly relishing the attention. She smiled and twirled and winked at everyone in the room.

King and Rudie (Nince's brothers) and Boom-Pa raised their glasses as King offered a toast. "To That Sable Boy, who married my sister after the first visit home from the pipeline ..."

"... but didn't tie the knot 'til after the fourth!" My grandfather finished to the roaring laughter of his brothers-in-law and much to the chagrin and scolding of his wife.

Norma howled and said she was gonna pee herself.

"Now y'all wouldn't say that if Mama and Daddy were sitting here." Wilksie laughed, as Nince was clearly the only one not enjoying the joke. "Besides, it was twins with the first visit, and a vasectomy after the third, not the fourth. I didn't have another baby after Vivian."

Norma leaned back, looked at Rudie, and said, "And Mama raised every one."

"Y'all there is a child in this room," Nince reminded everyone as though announcing it for the first time.

"Yes, and I was just about to tell him ... Come here Randy and sit with your Wilksie," Wilksie said as she flopped down on a large poof and patted the cushion beside her. "I was named for a character in *Gone with the Wind*, a novel of antebellum antiquity and grace, as penned by Ms. Margaret Mitchell."

"Wilksie is cut off; she doesn't need any more," Rudie said, and for some reason Rudie raised his own glass and giggled while clinking glasses with King and Boom-Pa.

"She didn't need the first three," Nince said quietly under her breath and loud enough for everyone to hear.

"And though I respect and never want to insult Ms. Mitchell or the character she created, and I love Mama dearly ... I just never felt comfortable being called India."

"Not since she studied it in geography, third grade. Remember, Velma?!"

Nince finally laughed. Nobody could get her laughing like her brother Rudie.

Wilksie shushed the room and continued her story. "Be that as it may, I am never gonna get through this story if y'all keep interrupting me. Now Randy, you'll get to see the old family homestead tomorrow—and you'll see. I was in the front parlor ... a young and handsome boy by the name of Mr. Brick Sable had come courtin'. Daddy was off to Baton Rouge building on the school there and of course King had gone on to Philadelphia.

I am not sure who served as chaperone, unless it was Rudie or you, Velma."

"The way I remember it is Mama was in town, shopping or at the movies, and you begged Rudie and Velma not to tell that you had a boy coming." Norma offered her own take on history.

"Oh, you were in Memphis doing hair," Wilksie shot back.

"Correction. I was in DC doing hair."

"Still, you weren't here."

"And with distance comes clarity," Nince interjected. "Norma has that part of the story right. Partially. Rudie was gone by then too; I was the one she begged."

"Anyway, RAIN-de," Wilksie emphasized my name as she was done talking to anyone else. "We were sitting in the front parlor, and he took my hand and knelt down, and he said to me, 'Why Miss India Wilkes Taylor, if you dislike your name so, may I have the honor of calling you Wilksie?' And because of that dear, sweet Sable Boy, I am who I am."

～　　　～　　　～

HE WASN'T THERE ON THAT particular trip, That Sable Boy. He was off working. He made a good living in Alaska and was able to send more than a respectable income home. And Wilksie managed what she was given, always making it appear to be more than what it was. She did not live beyond her means, oh no. But like most Depression-era children, she knew how to stretch a resource. And she also knew she would never go back to living so thin on resources so greatly stretched. It was a lesson all five of Dock and Ettienne's children learned and learned well as each made good for themselves or married and supported a spouse who provided well. And all, save Wilksie, tried to leave French Camp behind.

Brick Sable supported Wilksie's desire to cling to a French

Camp and an upbringing that existed only in her mind. He did not see the harm in elevating the old six-room farmhouse into "the old homestead" or "my family's country home" if that is how she dealt with the hardship. Wilksie did not have the years and experience that King and Norma possessed. And she did not have the tenacity and grit of Rudie and Velma. She had her mind, and she had her artistic sensibilities, and she had these and only these to manage the difficulty of being but a woman in Mississippi in the 1930s and '40s and '50s and '60s and now the '70s (where we were that day).

It was all very surreal, being a seven-year-old in that moment, in that time, in that very adult space of my grandparents' generation. Siblings of a generation removed from mine, yet so like Livie and me—reminiscing over concepts and experiences, the context of which I could never begin to understand. They laughed and argued and loved each other the way they always had—the way only siblings can. And they shared that with me, whether intentional or because they just forgot that I was there ... I don't know. And though I didn't understand it, I was cognizant enough to be aware of that moment and understand how very lucky I was.

⌒   ⌒   ⌒

THE LAST TIME I SAW Brick, he was quite ill. Amyotrophic Lateral Sclerosis (ALS), a stupid, horrible disease that often leaves one well aware of what is happening to them. It did in the case of That Sable Boy. Lou Gehrig's Disease, some call it ... named for a baseball player who also played for the Yankees, just a few years beyond my great-grandfather's time.

Brick Sable could not eat; he had to be fed. He could barely speak, like, not anything intelligible at all. Yet you knew behind his eyes there was a world of memories and understanding and presence. And a deep, desperate pain because none of that could be articulated beyond a nod, a groan ... and his wife constantly dabbing at the moisture that collected from his open mouth.

Oh, and Wilksie could translate. She understood his every "word" and his every look and gesture and tremor. She knew it all. She did it all. He had made sure, after all, that for the better part of her life, as well as for the years that would come after he was gone ... that she was and would be more than well provided for. She loved her husband. And she would provide for him now.

We talked about Ole Miss, Brick and me. And Wilksie added Bitsy's experiences at Mississippi State into her translation. Mother laughed and nodded at all the right places during that portion of the conversation, and she took the lead when appropriate as well. Mother was charming and animated and free without her own mother watching over. And Mother demonstrated why she was clearly the favorite grandchild and the most doted upon of all the nieces and nephews of her generation. It was always refreshing to see her in those moments. Those moments, she naturally shone.

🐌 🐌 🐌

WE WERE ON THE TRACE, somewhere between Kosciusko and French Camp, on our way to take some atrocious plastic poinsettias to place on my great-grandparents' graves—Wilksie insisted.

"These will be lovely for the holidays. I have enough for your grandfather too. They're silk." Her smile had a way of convincing one to do as she bid.

The cemetery was roughly a third of a mile from "the old homestead." We were hoping to visit both places before dark, as we still had to drive back to Oxford that night. Wilksie thought the power company had taken it down, but she wasn't sure. I was pretty sure it was still there.

Mother was looking out at the swiftly graying sky; the late autumn evening was going to fall fast. It would be dark soon. I turned the volume knob on the radio. A mixed tape of some of my favorites was in the cassette deck. A pair of lesbians started singing about the South in the spring and how lovely it all was and how God was teasing them when he made them born Yankees. I was singing along, adding a deep dissonance to their woven harmonies.

"It was quite the deal when Bitsy went to State," Mother said out of the blue.

I turned the volume back down. "Is that why you were so quiet?"

"I was quiet?"

"I mean, for you," I said. "But just when Wilksie mentioned that Bitsy went to State."

"She couldn't get in." Ahh, my cryptic, dramatic Mother.

"What?"

"To Ole Miss. She couldn't get in." And then she said quietly so whomever was driving by on the Natchez Trace at a swiftly darkening 5:30 p.m. with their windows open could not hear, "And not just because of her grades."

There was no other explanation, and I never got one later. Not from Mother. But we arrived at the cemetery and walked toward what was an obviously chained and locked gate. It is not a large cemetery, maybe an acre of land. The road to town from my great-grandparents' home used to run right behind it; then they put in the highway, and it cut through on the other side. Both Mother and Nince were filled with tales of walking past, no, running past the cemetery after walking home from the movies or a dance at the Academy. French Camp Academy, the local school.

"Well, open it," Mother said impatiently, as she was trying to straighten out the stems from the plastic poinsettias.

"Oh, yes, let me just pull this key out of my pocket."

"Oh, don't be smart. I was thinking it had a combination!" Mother snapped.

"Ahh, and what is the combination to this lock?" I asked.

"Well, I don't know."

"Correct, because it doesn't have one. Not that we would know it if it did, but it has a key … which we also don't have."

"Climb it," Mother said.

I turned to look at her; Mother had already thrown the flowers over the fence and was putting her foot through the chain link. I rolled my eyes and followed her lead, surpassed her lead, and was over the fence and picking up the flowers when I heard the thud of my mother hitting the ground.

"It is over there, to the right," she said, dusting her knees off and straightening her blouse. Her sweater was still hanging on the top of the fence.

I walked in the dim light toward the gravestone of my grandfather. I stared at the words and numbers carved into the stone: Daniel "Boom" Boone Holloway, 1920 - 1982. My eyes shifted to the left; carved there, Velma Irene Taylor Holloway. The dates were open ended, to be filled in a little more than a decade later.

I said a few words in my head to Boom-Pa and placed some of the ugly plastic flowers in the little cup beside his headstone. I moved to the left, and there was the stone my great-grandparents shared: Dock Randy Taylor and Ettienne Mornay Taylor. I kneeled down as I arranged the remaining flowers. I was saying a few more words in my mind and pondering over the family names on this side of the cemetery when I heard my mother scream.

"Oh my God, Randy, run!" she shrieked.

I whipped my head around only to see my mother straining to get back up and over the fence. She used her tangled sweater like a tie line.

"RUN!" she screamed again.

And I ran. As fast as my skinny theatre major ass could carry me, I ran. I reached the fence only to find my mother still struggling to get her leg over. She did not have a skinny theatre major ass. I crouched down to put my shoulder beneath her heavy, rounded bottom and shoved like I was breaking down a door.

As she went up and over, she let out a surprised yell followed by another thud—my mother hitting the earth once more. I jumped up and over in a feat of athleticism that I have never displayed since. I helped my mother to her feet, and we ran as best we could back to my truck. I gripped the steering wheel with both hands as I caught my breath, then started the truck. My mother sat panting, tears streaming down her face as she caught her own breath. I looked over to my terrified mother, wanting to offer some comfort and also find out what the ever-living fuck was that? My mother sat crying ... crying tears of uncontrollable laughter as that is what she had been reduced to at this point.

I joined in the laughter, as laughter is even more contagious than a yawn. As we settled down, she finally offered her explanation: "I was thinking about that time I walked back with Gene and Bitsy after we saw some movie ... oh, what was it?"

I covered my face with my hands as I continued to laugh.

"*Dr. Jekyll's Son* or *Son of Dr. Jekyll* ... I got a little spooked." She had regained her composure and was now just relishing in the hilarity of it all.

We drove by the house, but it was too dark to explore the empty and abandoned structure—not to mention the scare we had just received from Dr. Jekyll's imaginary child. We drove on back to Oxford, back to my apartment. The plastic poinsettias stood sentinel, in all their red and white and pink and green holiday glory. They were gone by the time I returned in the spring.

"SHE'S NOT GOING TO LIKE these," I said to myself as I turned onto I-55 South.

I was on my way to the funeral of my great-uncle, That Sable Boy, and opted to take the interstate rather than the Trace. It would save me some time getting there, and Mother (who could not be there) desperately wanted me to go. I was there to both assuage her guilt of not being there and to gather any talk or gossip or news.

Oh, and I was talking about my pants. Before. Nince. She wasn't going to like my pants. I wore a dark brown jacket and dark green pants. I liked the pants because there was a soft crushed feel to the fabric. They were comfortable looking, yet still nice. But they were too long. Not that I am short; I am not. They were too long for my already long legs. I rolled up the cuffs the very best my impatient fingers would allow. It was fine, but not great.

It is embarrassingly stupid that I can blame my inability to do something as simple as cuffing my pants on a lack of patience—and also the ensuing anxiety that arises at my inability to take my time and allow my admittedly poor hand-eye coordination to work. So, yeah, I looked a little sloppy from the shins down. But my shoes were nice, ox-blood oxfords ... I always loved oxfords.

I pulled into the hotel drive we always use for funerals, somewhere between Ackerman and Weir. Boom-Pa is from one of those towns; I never remember which. I parked my little Nissan pickup next to Norma's colossus of a vehicle. It was a 1980 Cadillac Fleetwood Brougham, a pearlescent white four-door with a luxurious white leather interior that somewhat exemplified this Auntie Mame-like great aunt of mine. My truck was also white.

The Unsinkable Norma Katherine Taylor

She was named for Norma Shearer, though Ettienne Mornay Taylor had no idea her own daughter would grow up with the same determination. She left when King left for the war, although the war would not happen for a few more years—not for the United States anyway.

"We ain't goin' to war. There's no way!" their father exclaimed as he read about the German invasion of Poland.

"And I promise ya we are," King stated simply.

"Dock, King ..." Ettienne was less simple with her statement. "Perhaps you could sound a little less like the people who tend our fields" ... or something to that effect.

When France fell to the Nazis that early summer day in June 1940, Dock began to believe his son's statement. The truth of it all would hit very close to home, and very soon. King left to join the Army.

Norma was charged with driving him to Memphis. She was also charged with bringing Rudie and Velma, or Nince, but only their father called her Nince. Ettienne had had a troubled pregnancy with her youngest child, India Wilkes Taylor, but that was nothing compared to this daughter's colicky, needy, demanding infancy. And even though India was now almost six years of age, she still required an inordinate amount of attention. It would be a nice respite to have only one child to tend to for a few days, even if it was her neediest. Besides, Etty had made herself a plan. She was going to take time every day to reread *Gone with the Wind*. She loved the book so much and was terribly disappointed when she was not able to see its premier release.

Velma had sweetly suggested it might remind her of why she named her sister "that name you did."

The air hung damp and chilly in the early pre-dawn Mississippi morning. The sun had not yet risen, but you could see the pink and orange glow in the mist and dew that would give way to something moister and more humid by mid-morning. King and Norma broke the stillness as they argued about who would drive.

Norma finally won that battle as she reasoned, "I was tasked with driving you to Memphis, not with driving the damn truck home!"

Nince and Rudie loaded the luggage and climbed into the back of the truck. It was an old one, a Chevy. They each had a pillowcase tied in a knot as they were only staying one night. It was a simple pack for King as well, just an old cardboard-sided suitcase from a five piece set. Norma had just a few bags, four of them to be precise—the remaining four of the five-piece set King was using. It was why Rudie and Velma were using pillowcases. She also had a trunk—an old chest really.

"I can't very well stay at the Peabody Hotel without a change of clothes ..." Norma said to her mother.

"No. I guess you very well can't," was her mother's simple reply. And then she offered to no one in particular, "I like that trunk."

Ettienne knew what was happening. Dock did not.

And they did stay at the Peabody Hotel. That part, at least, was not a lie. Nor was the part about King joining the Army. Only he didn't join the Army; he joined the Navy. It was for no particular reason other than that happened to be the line he stepped in when at the recruiting center. Norma, however, had accommodations at the hotel as an employee. She was to share a room with three other girls, all of whom were employed at the newly renovated hair salon on the first floor of the Peabody Hotel. Rudie and Velma slept on the floor in their sister's shared room. It was only for one night. King slept in a single bed in a triple room in a pre-barracks setup at a less swanky hotel down the street.

Norma fretted over her decision to leave French Camp and stay in Memphis, having answered an advertisement in the paper her father was reading over coffee one morning. The *Daily News* out of Memphis; it was his preferred publication. He didn't like the news out of Jackson, and that "damn *Clarion-Ledger*."

"Ever since they dropped the *Daily*, I just don't trust 'em," he told Norma as she read over the Want Ad section of the paper.

And here she was now. In Memphis. And she didn't even say goodbye to Daddy.

"Mama's gonna be mad," Velma insisted.

"She is gonna whip us good," Rudie complained.

"Mama already knows," Norma answered.

And she was right. Ettienne knew her daughter was not coming home. What she did not know was how her other two children were going to get home.

"So here, Rudie, you drive." She handed the keys to her twelve-year-old brother. "And Nince, you be sure to follow the map and keep track of where y'all are."

Rudie snatched the keys like they were a bag full of candy and climbed in the truck with no further argument.

Velma was less convinced. "You're only calling me Nince so I'll do what you say. You're not Daddy."

"I'm not going home, Velma. I'm not. Not ever." Norma's tears betrayed only her determination, nothing else at all. "And I'm never driving a stupid old truck like this again."

Velma stared at her older sister for a moment, working out in her head just how she felt about what her sister was really saying. Without a word, she gave her sister a hug and then turned and walked toward the passenger side of the old Chevy. "It's Daddy who's gonna whip our asses," Velma said to Rudie as she climbed in.

"I love the both of you! So much more than you can know ..." Norma said out loud, but to no one, as Rudie and Nince were driving away in that stupid old truck. The empty trunk sat safely secured in the back.

⌒   ⌒   ⌒

NORMA STAYED IN MEMPHIS THROUGH the war. She gathered quite the clientele and developed a particularly friendly relationship with one who just so happened to be the wife of a Tennessee state representative. Their friendly relationship developed into a friendship, and soon enough Norma was introduced to the lady's son.

Wilksie explains it best, and she delighted everyone with the scandalous affair after sharing her own courtship story with a seven-year-old me. And I eagerly ate up every word.

"Well, it is just as true now as it was then. We all know it doesn't take long for her natural charm and caustic wit to move one to overlook Norma's Rubenesque stature ..."

"Says the Quentin Matsys over here ..." Norma laughed a somewhat unamused laugh.

"Oh no. I've changed my mind. Get her another drink." Nince was also clearly enjoying herself.

I sat cross-legged in front of an enormous white fireplace and watched the adults in the room. The children—Joan, Vivian, Conrad—and Mother were out in the courtyard of Wilksie's spacious home. King's stepdaughter, Tina, sat with King's wife, Roni, in the kitchen. They were drinking coffee.

"I'm sorry, but I just can't think of anybody who likes Veronica or Christina." That was Bitsy. Everyone in the house overheard this and more as Bitsy explained to Livie who everyone was while cleaning her up after the magnolia tree incident.

But the rest of us—King, Rudie, Boom-Pa, Norma, Nince, Wilksie, and me—we were there together in that family room, swapping stories and sharing memories.

Wilksie went on with her story: "As I was saying ... it wasn't long before Norma and the wife of this certain prominent state representative became fast friends. And it wasn't long after that before Norma was introduced to a certain prominent Tennessee state representative's son. And it wasn't long after that, a certain state representative was running to be the representative, not in Nashville, but in Washington, DC."

"Imagine that!" Boom-Pa said in a silly voice which had everyone laughing. I laughed too.

"Let her finish or it will never end," Norma groaned.

"There was a wedding to quell a few rumors ..." Wilksie alluded to something more, as she comically held her hand to her lips like a fan before letting it fall limp as if she were showing us all her rings. I didn't know what she meant, but I knew she meant something.

Nince coughed and Boom-Pa said, "Mind the boy, Wilksie."

"Anyway, they were married, and Norma moved to Washington, DC. Only she and her mother-in-law came home one day to find the son of a certain prominent member of the House of Representatives from Tennessee in flagrante delicto with the boy who drove the member to and from the Capitol Building."

King made another joke about a member that I didn't understand at the time. And now that I'm old enough to understand it, I can't remember the joke.

"There was a divorce, of course, and Norma made out quite well as nothing was ever made of it in the papers ..."

"Not true, Wilksie; Daddy read about the divorce in the *Clarion-Ledger*," Norma interrupted. "Remember? He used it as another reason to hate the paper whenever Mama came home with it."

Wilksie laughed. "And then you married that ... artiste."

Norma stopped laughing. And she stopped smiling. "You mean my husband."

"Yes. The artiste," Wilksie added.

"You mean my husband. The artist who actually has work displayed in museums and not ... well ..." Norma looked about the room.

"I think we should go. Mama and Daddy are waiting for us back at the house," Nince said, then stood and called me to her. "Randy, go tell your mother we need to head out. It is getting late."

I reluctantly obeyed and ran to get the others, but I also knew I was about to miss something good. Norma and Wilksie continued their heated yet comical confabulation. I can distinctly remember Norma screaming the words, "And it's a shed!" through the sliding glass wall as Wilksie stormed off toward her art studio.

As Boom-Pa drove along the Trace toward French Camp, leaving Wilksie and Bitsy and the magnolia behind, my mind raced. Livie was asleep, her head in Nince's lap. I sat between Mother and Boom-Pa up front. And my mind wandered over the many possibilities of what an in flagrante delicto boy was— and how could I be one?

Introducing the Dowager Countess of Kosciusko – India Wilkes Taylor Sable

He was the last of The Three Sisters' husbands to go. Brick Sable, That Sable Boy. Nince and Norma shared their praises and whispered their criticisms over Wilksie's introduction to society as a widow—as though this were some sort of Gothic-themed debutante ball rather than their brother-in-law's funeral. And they were not short on criticisms of me and my long pants. I knew she wouldn't like them.

Nince's words were the harshest as they included the word "disappointment" in multiple ways and shapes and forms. Norma stood up for me by letting Nince know that I was representing my side of the family, after all, and how proud we should all be that I drove all the way from Ole Miss to represent them. This was followed by Nince giving me a heartfelt hug, tears and all, and telling me she was indeed proud. I looked at Norma, who mouthed "You're welcome."

It was as Norma was selecting her jewelry from an assortment of Ziploc bags that she said to me, "You would think someone like you, you know, someone in the theatre, would know someone who could sew."

She didn't say it unkindly. But her point was clear. And soon she was regaling me with a tale about why she carries her jewels in Ziplocs and about that time she tackled a would-be purse snatcher.

"She chased that boy half way down Connecticut Avenue—in heels, mind you—and tackled that little ..." Nince said as she stepped out of the bathroom of their shared motel room with two queen beds. Her colorful description of the culprit as she fixed her hair and reapplied her lipstick was out of a time capsule, like a snapshot of quintessential Southern beauty and ugly rolled into one. I have so many, so many snapshots emblazoned in my memory.

⌒   ⌒   ⌒

"HE IS SO UGLY," NINCE whispered, pointing out an arguably half-plucked chicken-looking man in a dark gray suit jacket and dark gray suit pants—not the same dark gray, not the same suit.

"Who, Vernon? Ohhh, yes," Norma interjected with her version of a whisper. "He was an ugly child too. Oof, and he just got uglier as he got older."

"Mmm. Bless him," Nince muttered, although it did not sound like a blessing at all.

"Remember when Debbie brought Olivia Joan to meet Gussie?" Norma's stifled laughter at the memory was clear in her voice.

"Oh Lord, yes!" Nince smirked. "Randy, you weren't born, but your mother and Derwood came out to Mama and Daddy's. I think Livie was just two."

"And Gussie was visiting from Mobile. She and Mama were twins, Guise and Ettienne. We always called her Gussie," Norma explained.

"Daddy did, anyway." Nince added, "I'm not sure Mama ever did."

I stood between the two sisters. Norma and I were arm in arm, our eyes scanned the room for more opportunities of pettiness. Nince held the funeral program for Brick Alfred Sable, fanning herself in the warm and crowded room.

"Daddy was also a twin. We always called his brother Uncle Duck. Even Daddy called him Uncle Duck." Norma continued, enjoying the family history lesson she was giving as much as I was in learning more of it. "He was an hour and 25 minutes older than Daddy, as the story goes, so Daddy called him uncle."

"And Duck? Where did Duck come from?" I asked.

Nince answered this one: "Well, they named Daddy Dock, after a new dock his daddy had built. And Daddy always made up names like Gussie for Mama's sister ..."

"And Nince," added Norma.

"And Nince." Nince smiled. "So if his name was Duck because they had a favorite duck or if it was just what Daddy called him—we never knew. And Mama and Daddy never said."

Norma continued her lesson: "And Uncle Duck had two children—Irene, who was just as lovely a child as one could ever imagine. A pretty little thing ..."

"Yes," Nince agreed. "And she is still just as lovely. A Christian woman."

"And Vernon," Norma said flatly. "When Mama first saw him, she said she didn't know if she should give him a bottle or stuff him with cornbread and roast him."

"Y'all talkin' about Vernon?" It was Joan. The middle child of Wilksie and That Sable Boy—Joan Collins was who Wilksie decided to name this one after. (Etty had never seen one of her movies and had no idea who this Joan Collins was.) "He was always so ugly. Remember the time he met Livie?"

"We were just telling Randy about it." Norma smiled.

"Well, hey Randy!" Joan said, pulling me into an unsolicited and demonstrative hug of familiarity that I did not know we shared ...

I hugged her back and struggled to breathe a little. "I'm so sorry about your father," I managed.

"Oh, and what a fine representation of your family. Your Mama must be so proud," Joan said, still holding my arms, yet leaning back as though she were sizing me up.

"She is," Nince and Norma said.

"Well, RAIN-de," Joan did that thing where it was a long "A" sound too. "We were all at Grandmother and Grandfather's home in the front parlor. Gussie had come to visit. And, well, ol' Vernon came a-knockin' on the door with Irene. Irene was always so lovely, and she wanted to meet your sister too. So they come in the door; your Mama hugs Irene, and your father hands Livie to Vernon. Well, that child took one look at Vernon, his arms outstretched to take her, lookin' like the Grim Reaper himself. Lord, your sister cried and carried on so."

"Thank you for telling the story for us," Nince said.

"And you told it so ... well." Norma smiled.

"Oh, of course." Joan's smile was rather aggressive, and then she became serious. Her eyebrows lowered almost as much as her voice. "Wilksie sent me over to warn y'all. SHE is here with Rudie."

Yes, the brothers were there too—Rudie and King. They had all come to be with their sister as she suffered this rite of passage into Southern Widowhood. She was the last of her sisters to lose a husband, which is only fitting in her role as the youngest sister.

King was there with Roni and Tina. Roni would be playing the organ at the service. Roni always played the organ (or piano) whenever the occasion warranted. And there was Rudie, standing with King. Rudie's new wife—she was and would always be the "new wife" until the day they divorced—was "laughing like she was at a cocktail party" between the two brothers.

"Diamond Lil" they called her. The Three Sisters did—the original three—or they chose from a host of other names. Never using her actual name, Cassie, they had come up with quite a list. Cassie was an attractive woman with what some would describe as "too long of hair and too short of skirt for a woman of her years." That some, of course, would be my grandmother, Nince. Norma's descriptions had a little more bite.

"Look at her, standing there like she's got a sourdough starter in her underwear," Norma whisper-shouted—think Ethel Merman quietly singing "Anything Goes"—through her toothsome grin.

"What makes you think she is wearing any?" Nince replied, with no sense of humor to her tone, pointing to her own teeth, indicating to Norma she had a lipstick smear.

Norma ran her tongue across her teeth and snorted, "Remember the reunion?"

Nince rolled her eyes at the memory while I also snorted a stifled laugh. Picture, if you will, an attractive, well-made up, and tastefully nipped and tucked woman of a certain age. Imagine her wearing a lovely white linen tank dress, cute strappy sandals, appropriate jewelry. And she is standing before a beautiful plate glass picture window overlooking the lake, the sunlight showering its beams of light and warmth through the clear glass. Her legs splayed just enough to allow the light, the shadows, the silhouette ... making it all perfectly clear that not only was this attractive woman of a certain age not wearing any undergarments—she was also well groomed all over. And now imagine this plate glass window as the perfect picture spot for many, many family photos. And finally—imagine, if you will, all the looks on all the faces of all the relatives, old and young, as, one by one, they took notice of the silhouetted, clean-shaven nether regions in a variety of those photos.

"I shared those photos at church!" Nince said, horrified.

✑   ✑   ✑

MY COUSIN, GIO, GAVE THE sermon or eulogy or pretty much led the entire service for his grandfather's funeral. It was the hallmark of pride for many in the family, as Giovanni Leonardo Gregorio IV was the first great-grandson. Because of the Roman numeral following his name, his family's tradition of naming children after members of their own family outweighed our family's tradition of naming children for famous members of other people's families. He was Bitsy's boy.

"His father was the reason his mother couldn't get into Ole Miss," Nince added in a whisper decidedly quieter than Norma's guffaw at the comment.

I admired his calm and collected nature, Gio's, and the ease with which he was able to speak so eloquently, so passionately, and yet in a manner that brought one a sense of peace and comfort. He was in seminary studying to be a Southern Baptist preacher.

His father, "G the 3" they called him, was a used car salesman who made more money than a used car salesman should.

But he kept Bitsy in cars and furs—for a time. That time came to a close when she learned that he was keeping others in cars and furs as well. But then she learned that others would also buy her cars and furs and so many other things—so she got over "G the 3" rather quickly.

And by the time her son gave the eulogy at her father's service, she had moved on to Gordon. He was an undertaker. Gordon's family owned the funeral home in Ackerman. Not that it matters—Gordon was also on his way out (and was not at the funeral). He was talked about as though he were there.

We sat in Wilksie's front parlor. The white fireplace had since been through several transitions and was now a sleek red marble. Wilksie sat in an oversized armchair with lion claw feet. Lion heads were carved into the wood of the hand rests. The seat and back were upholstered in a chic, sleek, perfectly gold and black leopard print. She wore all black, of course, that is what one did—save her pearls, which were brilliantly white. And her final reveal of the day's services was a stunning A-line, tea-length dress, with crinolines and a veil.

Her girls, Bitsy, Joan, and Vivian, were dressed in similar Gothic prom attire and sat with that same charm school poise in armchairs of their own. They were like a convention of Mourning Barbies, these three Sable sisters. The Goldilocks Girls were each named for three lovely actresses—Elizabeth Taylor, Joan Collins, and Vivian Leigh, as was the tradition. These namesake actresses were widely known for their striking dark features, style, and grace. These three sisters—Bitsy, Joan, and Vivian—also had parents who, genetically speaking, were unlikely to have light-haired children. Yet there they sat: Ultimate Lightest Platinum, Warm Ashe Medium, and Ultra Cool Light Bleach.

Oh there were a lot of stories, a lot of laughter, and a lot of booze. And it felt like we had left the Gothic prom and settled into the Edward Gorey after-party. All of us dressed in black and each of us holding a drink. Some of us held more than one as a wide variety of beverages were passed around.

Wilksie had the caterers turn her ornate dining table into a buffet of elevated funeral fare. Funeral potatoes in a silver chafing dish, chicken skillfully pan fried in batches, and enough nibbles and small bites and pastries to feed the entire county. There was even an ice sculpture for some weird reason.

I sat on the fireplace hearth. The marble felt nice and cool for a moment, as it was getting rather warm. There was a small gas fire—enough to strike a mood, but not enough to make the room feel any warmer than it already was. The body heat from the mass of people in attendance put the room just over the edge of comfortable. The view of the room was impeccable from this fireside location, and my less-than-padded ass was now making the cool hard marble a little less cold.

"Slide over," Norma said, as she scooched me over with her hip. "This is the best seat in the house." She was holding two glasses of champagne. "One of these is for your grandmother."

Rudie and Nince soon walked over, each carrying two glasses of their own. Nince handed me one of the glasses and told me to sip slowly. Norma laughed as she downed one of the glasses like a shot and set it to the side. Nince sat in a dining room chair that was brought into the room, while Rudie, who was especially jovial, stood beside us. He had dropped Cassie off at the hotel before coming over. Apparently Casiphia had a headache.

⁂

"AND JUST WHAT KIND OF a name is Casiphia anyway? What will she even look like?" Nince whispered this last as she and Norma were discussing Rudie's new girlfriend one day several years earlier.

"It is Hebrew, from what Cassie says; it means money or the place where money is kept or something like that."

"They should have called her Piggy Bank," Nince muttered.

"And she is a rather attractive woman, though I'm sure she has had work done."

"Penny Dreadful," Nince continued to mutter.

"But she always carries herself well ... lovely and stylish, and she is quite attractive, you know. She did catch our brother's eye." Norma had not yet experienced Cassie's penchant for transparency in her clothing choice.

"Or Diamond Lil."

Norma laughed. "She is not chasing our brother's money; she's got plenty of her own. She is just new money."

"And not Baptist," Nince added, her muttering a bit clearer.

🐌   🐌   🐌

RUDIE CAUGHT A LOT OF flak over his new girlfriend and the inappropriateness of a grown, unmarried man, a widower, shacking up with some "Jewish Floozy" from New York. Nince and Wilksie were the harshest of critics as Norma was less concerned about the Jewish part. But Rudie took their criticisms to heart and knew what he was doing was inappropriate in the eyes of his sisters.

Besides, "what would Mama say?"

So, he married her. It was a small courthouse wedding, attended by Cassie's sister, niece, and nephew—and Norma. Rudie's son, Eddie, and his granddaughter, Laura, were at the wedding ceremony too.

🐌   🐌   🐌

"IT'S BITSY'S FIFTH ONE, GORDON; who's throwing this

thing?" Rudie queried with an impish smile; he liked to stir the pot. "I wonder where he's at?"

"Bitsy said he was at a convention for undertakers—or whatever title he goes by," Nince whispered this second part. "But we all know it's something else."

"Well, he left his new assistant, Betty-Girl, in charge. They are pretty tight, they say. Maybe that's why Bitsy's got her girdle in a bunch." Rudie did not whisper any of the parts.

"Who are 'they'"? Norma asked with a knowing look.

It was Joan who spoke next. She was the least favorite of the three girls. She was the plainest—the one who was Warm Ashe Medium. Joan had swooped in from no one quite knows where, and quietly too, despite the yards of black tulle and taffeta she wore.

"Bitsy is divorcing Gordon because he spends too much time antiquing with our brother ... or another of Conrad's associates."

"I told her not to marry an undertaker," Norma said to me with a wink.

"No, Bitsy's issues with Betty-Girl go way back—further than her working for Gordon," Joan Collins Sable exclaimed as she flounced herself down with the style and fluidity of Grace Kelly, but with the appearance of Mary Wickes in the same dress. "Bitsy and Betty-Girl did pageants together. I believe this one was the Miss Magnolia - Starkville. She was at State then, Bitsy was, bless her heart."

"Why didn't you ever enter the pageants?" Rudie asked.

"Oh, I entered a few. There were just parts I didn't like." Joan smiled neither kindly nor unkindly.

"Winning." Nince coughed.

I stifled a laugh; Norma did not. And Joan settled in on the large ottoman or poof or whatever Conrad called this thing he had purchased for Wilksie. Rich in color and price tag, jewel-tone green, soft and plush. It looked striking amongst the mismatched occasional chairs and red marble fireplace of this oft-redecorated room. She was holding court, as it were, chatting and gossiping away.

I looked about the room and saw Bitsy, similarly dressed and with her own audience, or court, about her. She held Gio's arm as they listened briefly to a friend from seminary Gio had brought home. He didn't actually go to seminary, the friend. He was at Belmont—a small music college in Nashville. And there was Vivian, chatting politely with Roni and Tina. King was sitting with his sister, Wilksie, and a cabal of relations I could not begin to accurately sort or identify.

Joan's hushed voice brought me from my distraction. "It was the eve of the final night of the pageant. Bitsy and Betty-Girl were favorites for the Top Ten—the Top Five even. And a few of the girls were discussing their make-up and face-care routines as they were getting their things ready for the next day's event. Well, Bitsy has always had naturally flawless skin; all of us Sable women do."

"It's all that Alaskan oil," Norma said, rolling her eyes.

Joan had a remarkable ability to tell a story without missing a beat, despite the quips and sarcasm, and under-the-breath comments that might be made. "Well, Bitsy was not gonna let them in on her little secrets, so she told her one she learned from your first husband, I believe, Norma. The congressman's son."

"He knew all about facials." Rudie laughed out loud. "What? His parents owned hair salons," he added defensively as Nince shot him a look.

"It was the hemorrhoid cream," Norma said, shaking her head.

"It was the hemorrhoid cream." Joan nodded. "Bitsy told the girls all about her uncle who was 'in the know' and had shared some secrets of the female illusionists he knew. For puffy eyes, or sunken eyes, or droopy eyes ... just a little dab of hemorrhoid cream, and it would all disappear. Then Bitsy let them know she was going to return to her room for her 'special night mask.' She swore she had to wear it for at least eight hours."

"Oh no." Norma already knew where this was going. Nince and I looked at each other, a little taken aback and embarrassed that we were now interested in this story. Rudie had wandered over to King.

"Well, the way I understand it, everyone on that same hotel floor could hear the scream coming from Betty-Girl's room. When the floor mother of the pageant girls went to investigate, along with all the other girls on the floor, she reported seeing Betty-Girl in a heap on the bathroom tiles clawing at her face; the mirror had been shattered to bits."

"What happened?" I asked.

"Betty-Girl decided she was going to one-up my sister, Bitsy, and put on her own special face cream blend. And she apparently smeared that hemorrhoid cream all over her entire face *and* neck *and* decolletage. When she woke up, however many hours later, well, bless her heart—she looked like raw meat. She didn't make the top ten. One little girl cried when Betty-Girl walked across the stage in her swimsuit. Bitsy, of course, won big that day. And the two never really spoke again. Well, not until Gordon hired her. But that was years later. I'm sure she has forgotten all about it."

My sides were splitting, as I tried not to be rude and contain the laughter. Norma had slid to the floor; she was sitting with her legs straight out in front of her, tears streaming down her face. Nince sat tall, as though everything was perfectly normal.

The rest of the evening pretty much followed that routine. We shuffled from court to court, sibling to sibling, and finally landed at the feet of Wilksie. She looked tired. She looked wonderful too. Her dark hair was still flawless and held in place by that large blue—not pink—can of Aqua Net hair spray. Her strands of pearls still shone white. But her smile was worn and less natural. And her eyes. Her eyes conveyed that she had long since retreated to her own thoughts.

We said our goodnights. Norma and Nince were nothing but praises and pride as they discussed their sister on the ride back to the hotel. Her debut as a widow was a success. The next morning was uneventful. I brought coffees and those plastic pastries back to Nince and Norma as they dressed for the graveside. We drove separately to the cemetery. I would be heading back to Ole Miss from my great-grandmother's and great-grandfather's. I wanted to stop and see Dock and Etty's place before I headed back.

🙟   🙟   🙟

I DON'T REMEMBER IF IT was cold or warm that day. I do believe it was gray and wet, however. The service at the graveside was simple, though not small. Everybody had a fondness for That Sable Boy. And for that odd man out who didn't—well, Wilksie held a spell over that town as though she were its sole benefactor and matriarch. She was now the Dowager Countess of Kosciusko.

I said a few words in my mind over my great-grandparents' graves, and then I sat for a bit with my grandfather. The plastic poinsettias had been replaced with real flowers from Brick's service. Wilksie had insisted it was the best use; there were so many flowers after all. I picked one up and held it to my nose. It smelled of refrigeration and perfume.

The Three Sisters stood under an umbrella held by Rudie— so I guess it was raining after all. Wilksie stood in the center, framed by her taller sisters, her older sisters, her sisters who had both buried their husbands and stood strong and proud with their siblings as she now did the same. King held the umbrella for Roni and Tina. The Blonde Contingency stood in solidarity with Conrad. Gio stood with his friend. I stood by my grandfather's tombstone. I was the lone representative of my family; Mother must have been so proud.

After dueling fried chickens, potato salads, baskets of cornbread, biscuits, and a vast array of other baked goods and funeral foods; after chatting with Irene and Vernon (who agreed none of these ladies' fried chicken was as good as Etty's); and after saying my goodbyes to two sets of three sisters, my heart had been blessed, I recognized how proud my mother was of me, and I packed a plate to take home for dinner. I was finally on my way to the old family farm ... or homestead, as Wilksie called it.

Chapter 4
The Source of Water

The Homestead:
We Are Backtracking Again

It was dark, of course, when we pulled into the drive. It was just off the new section of Highway 407. The State had built it, as the old orange clay road that meandered to the south side of the property and then way back behind the pond was not a direct route from Weir to Winona. It also passed by the group of homes, or shacks, or as Wilksie called them, "shanties"— where several families who were not well off lived. They were the sharecroppers of the land my great-grandfather owned, but, by the '70s, the practice of sharecropping had all but dwindled, for the Taylors anyway.

Grandfather Dock still farmed, as Grandmother Etty insisted on a full vegetable garden—tomatoes and corn, yellow and green squash, peppers of both the bell and hot variety. My Boom-Pa loved hot foods, and Grandmother Etty made sure her favorite son-in-law had plenty of hot peppers in her husband's garden. Tomatillos were added; a migrant family who had come to work a part of the land had introduced them to Dock. And of course he grew his favorite, some yellow-meated watermelon.

Not a cantaloupe, although he grew those as well, but a water-melon. Just as juicy and watermelony as you can imagine—but yellow inside, not pink.

Boom-Pa carried me into the house; I was asleep. And Livie walked, tucked into Mother's arm, I am sure—shy and tired from the long day's travels and adventures. The orange stains in her tights were barely visible any longer. I remember very little, as I was truly sleeping and not faking it, for that secret enjoyment and comforting feeling of security I always found when being carried into the house by my father or grandfather ... or a fireman or a soldier or some other strong man who might enter the imagination of a seven-year-old in flagrante delicto.

We were put to bed in a small back room just off another larger room. I learned later that the latter room used to be the living room, but it was turned into a bedroom when the front porch was converted into the "front parlor." The former of the two rooms, the one in which Livie and I slept, was the room both our mother and grandmother were born in.

"Same bed too," Etty said as she kissed our foreheads and bid us goodnight.

She probably didn't mean to scare the bejesus out of Livie and me that night. All I could hear was the limb scratching at the window, imagining my great-grandmother's bony arm reaching out to pull my hair from my forehead, while Livie was concerned that they never washed the bed. She eventually cried herself to sleep while comforting me over the scratching. I didn't sleep, not really; I just stared out the window at that tree.

⌒   ⌒   ⌒

DOCK MADE THE BISCUITS AND Etty fried the chicken. I picked that up real quick on day one. It was still dark except for a little light creeping through under the door and a slice of silver beginning to glimmer low on the horizon. Or perhaps I was just suddenly aware of that light as I had clearly finally fallen back to sleep. Livie was drooling on her pillow, her arm draped over the side of the bed and her torso twisted so her leg was draped over mine. I was pushed up against the wall and window. Carefully, I extricated myself from the pretzel that was my sister. My feet found the hardwood covered in thin blue carpet. The room was blue too, sort of a hospital blue. I made my way through the former living room; Nince and Boom-Pa were sleeping in the king-sized bed that just seemed so enormous and grand to my seven-year-old self. Quietly, I made my way into the hall that led to the kitchen, the new living room, Etty's room, and the bathroom.

The kitchen was an open room with a small metal dining table. There was a window over the sink and over the head of the table. Between the two windows was the old stove—a white, enameled marvel with several doors and drawers and odd shaped burners; it was nothing like the avocado green we had at home or the harvest gold of Nince's. A counter of sorts divided the kitchen from the dining area, where there was a door to the side porch. I made my way to the table.

My mid-century loving-today-self would have gone mad over it, but on this day in 1972, it was just a kitchen table with chairs. I quietly sat in one, my legs dangling in the early morning light, and watched as Dock did something with his enormous hands in a pink mixing bowl. He nodded when he saw me, and then just continued about his business of making the biscuits.

The smell of bacon was strong, and it made my stomach grumble a little. Dock pulled a large skillet from the oven; that's where the bacon smell was coming from. He poured a splash of grease into the large bowl then placed the iron skillet back on the stove. Another just like it was also resting there, shiny and dark black from the bacon grease that coated it. Dock washed

his hands then poured two cups of coffee from some weird looking glass-knobbed pitcher or pot that he took from the stove. He
caught my eye again and mumbled something under his breath.
He then poured a healthy amount of milk and sugar into one
of the cups. He set the cup with mostly milk and sugar in front
of me.

"Nince said you would be up early," Dock said to me.

"Ga mornin'," I said, taking a sip of the coffee he had set in
front of me. It was bitter and hot, despite the sugar and milk,
but I knew without knowing that this was a little test—and I
was going to pass it. "You call her Nince, too?"

"Of course I do," Dock answered with a smile. "I named her."

He went back to the biscuits, threw some flour on the counter, threw the large ball of dough on the counter, and he began
rolling them out with a long wooden handle; it looked like the
end of a baseball bat. He cut each biscuit with a teacup, then
placed them in the hot iron skillets on the stove.

"They have to touch. But they don't need to be too friendly." This was the only instruction he offered ...

I sipped more of my coffee and let my legs swing, my eyes
never leaving the large man's hands. Those hands worked the
homemade-looking rolling pin; they eclipsed, yet gently han-
dled, the delicate teacup he used to form each biscuit. He fit
each one into a skillet just so—touching, but not too friendly. I didn't notice Nince. She had come in from the door that
led to a small pantry, and that pantry had a door that led to
Etty's room, the bathroom, and the hall. She didn't say a word;
she just watched. It wasn't until I noticed Dock fixing another
cup of coffee, just like he fixed mine, that I knew someone had
joined us.

Nince sat down next to me, in front of the coffee Dock had
set down with no commentary. They nodded at one another,
and Nince sat and sipped her coffee while Dock cleaned up the

flour from the counter. There were a few moments of silence, and then we heard the creak of wood on the floor coming from Grandmother's room.

"You've got the eggs?" Dock asked as he walked back to the stove and poured a final cup of coffee.

"Yes sir," Nince answered. "And the grits. I've got help this morning." And she goosed me a little; I giggled, and she stood, pulling her chair to the stove. That was my cue to follow.

Dock began the process of cleaning out the stove top percolator for more coffee, while Nince and I cracked eggs into a bowl. A large crock of butter sat ready on the counter. Nince used a smaller version of the pink Pyrex mixing bowl Dock had used for the biscuits to measure out the grits from a bag in the pantry. Setting a pot on the stove behind my skillet, she used another, similar sized Pyrex bowl to measure out water and milk. I stirred the eggs in my bowl with a fork, and Dock stepped behind me and gave them an extra good whisk. He handed the fork he used to me, and then I practiced doing the same. Dock walked over to the refrigerator and pulled out a mound of white something, wrapped in cloth and tied tight. I couldn't tell what it was. He also took out a small white cube from the freezer.

Nince poured two bowls of milk and two bowls of water into the pot. She threw in a healthy spoonful of butter and a few pinches of salt and pepper, then turned up the heat. Dock handed her the cloth-wrapped wad of white from the refrigerator.

"Mama made cheese?" Nince asked Dock.

"Of course; her farmer's cheese is the best," he said, then he placed the frozen cube of milk into the last cup of coffee he poured. "Grits are always four to one with liquid. Half milk and half water is best. And if you ever git you a wife who makes cheese like Etty—well, it always adds a little something extra to the grits," he said to me, patting me on the back as I stood waiting for Nince's cue to start cooking the eggs.

"You better git those biscuits before they burn." It was Grandmother Etty. It is as amazing to me now as it was then: This tiny little woman, thin, petite, and not even five feet tall, yet her presence filled the doorway she stood in. Watching us.

"Woman, I do the biscuits," Dock said with a wink and a smile in my direction.

"Yes. And they are burning." Etty also smiled. "You also do the coffee, which is way over there."

Dock howled with laughter. "Nince, grab them biscuits out the oven."

"Yes sir," Nince answered immediately.

"Randy, you be careful; them skillets hot! And you, my lovely bride, set right down and enjoy your coffee."

He took my giggling great-grandmother by the arm and escorted her to the chair in front of the coffee that held the cube of frozen milk. Nince opened the oven and grabbed a dish towel from the counter. It was the one Dock had wiped his hands with after handling the flour. She folded the towel over several times and then carefully pulled the skillets of golden-brown topped biscuits from the oven.

Oh, they smelled delicious—*warm*. You know how *warm* adds that special comforting scent when biscuits are right from the oven? It may not make sense when you think about it. But when you feel it ... oh, you can smell the warmth. And the butter, and the hint of bacon grease ...

Livie was up next. She came out of the pantry because she was coming from the bathroom. She still had toothpaste in the corner of her mouth. Etty opened her arms wide, and Livie shyly walked over and accepted the hug. I didn't understand why she was so shy at the time. I mean she had known these people longer than I had. I was seven and she was ten; she had met them at least two more times than I had.

Dock walked over to the stove and looked over the grits

Nince was stirring. He smiled at me as I stood in the chair waiting for my next instruction. I knew the grits took longer than the eggs, so the eggs had to wait a minute. And I didn't know if that cheese they added would make the grits take longer. It didn't. (And I will still add a bit of cream cheese to my grits to this day. Not quite the same as farmer's cheese, I think it's pretty close but then I am not a farmer, or a farmer's wife.) Dock put a spoonful of bacon grease in the pan before me, and then a spoonful of butter. And then he fixed a small cup of coffee, with milk and sugar, just like he did for me, but this time it was for Livie. Livie stared at the coffee, but she didn't touch it.

Dock laughed and Etty gave her a hug. "Dock, put one of my milk cubes in it."

He did as his wife suggested. And Livie, with all eyes on her, took a hesitant sip. She didn't like it. Etty looked almost hurt, Dock looked confused, and Nince looked worried. Livie looked like she was about to cry.

She reached out to take another taste when I blurted out in her defense, "Livie only likes orange juice!"

"We don't got orange juice," Dock said.

"Dock," Etty seemed exasperated at her husband's inability to solve this simple problem. "Take Livie out to the porch and get her an orange coke."

We discovered at that moment, Livie and I did, that our great-grandparents had one of those old Pepsi coolers on their porch filled with every flavor of coke you could imagine. Now coke in the South is more than Coke. We call all of it coke. Even the ones not made by Coke proper ... we still call it coke. Or at least we did. And as far as the Pepsi cooler, it is an unclear misty memory. I could be getting it confused with an old country store in a podunk little town in Florida that Derwood moved us to, or it could be the machine that was at another warehouse where Derwood worked. But that one was clearly

Coke proper, and it was like an upright refrigerator. You put in your quarter and opened the door and selected your glass bottle. No, it was a Pepsi cooler, because it was blue. And it was filled with all the cokes.

"I brought you a purple one, Randy!" Livie said, coming back in from the kitchen door that led outside to the porch and the garden.

"Wilksie is pulling in with her gang," Dock said. "Git them grits in a bowl, Nince. And Randy, start them eggs."

"Yes sir," Nince replied, and I did too.

Reckless Water and the City Grocery

I pulled into the drive—though it was not much of a drive any longer. Wire grass and sandburs, fleabane and chicory, and an assortment of other yellows and blues and whites of the wildflowers covered the forgotten ruts and tracks of orange clay disturbed by tires in years past. And it was getting dark. (I had allowed myself too much fried chicken and that extra slice of cake back at the church. Irene could sure bake a cake.) But I told Mother I would stop at the house. I told her I would snap a few pictures since she and I were unable to stop before. I knew she regretted our not stopping—but after the self-induced scare at the cemetery, well, it didn't work out. And so here I was, in front of my great-grandparents' old home—sitting in my truck. My hands gripped the steering wheel. Michael Stipe was singing about photographs reflecting clarity in the windshield — and something about the recklessness of water. A tear rolled down my cheek, I don't know why—and then another.

I don't like to cry. I did enough of that when I was a whiny little kid with Livie. I thought I had taught myself to stop, to avoid that particular emotion. I was wrong. The tears welled up from some spring I had left untapped. And the stream turned to a river—and the river found its way home. I did not go inside. I did not take any pictures. I didn't even get out of the car. My thoughts were indeed "flower strewn" as the next song pulled me into an undertow of memories and vulnerabilities—a riptide of emotions from which I could not seem to escape.

And then I saw the headlights of a car or truck coming down the old orange clay road from around past the pond. The road that used to bring you to town by the cemetery ...

"Run!" I remembered my mother had screamed.

So I did. I put my truck in gear and ran. I drove back to Oxford. Back to where I could put everything where it belonged. Back to where this, whatever this was—it didn't exist. It was light years ago.

⌒　　⌒　　⌒

"ARE YOU GOIN' TO CITY Grocery tonight?" Lorraine asked, sipping her beverage of choice from her champagne flute.

"I'm not sure," I said, and I didn't know. I mean, yes, probably, the answer was probably yes. And, as it turns out, it was more than probably—but at the moment, I was letting the warm weightlessness of water envelop me in her comforting embrace.

"It's Bellini night. I'm going for a little bit." Lorraine had already gotten out of her bath, the water gurgling and glugging as it slowly made its way down the drain of her clawfoot tub. She sat on the toilet now, wrapped in a large and fluffy white terry-cloth robe. A similar towel held her pixie cut in a soft warmth, wrapped tight like a turban. She slowly, carefully painted her toenails a soft rosy pink—her foot outstretched on the edge of her tub. "So why were you crying?"

"I'm not sure."

"Well, you need to go back."

"What? To City Grocery? I'll probably go."

"No, dummy ... your family home. Your great-grandparents' place. Oh, you need to go back and go inside. At least for the closure."

"Closure?"

"Well of course, Randy." I could picture her sitting tall on her closed toilet, her white fluffy towel piled high on her head, hand waving the brush of her nail polish like a small sword or baton for emphasis.

"I don't think I feel the emotions you think I am feeling," I parried.

"And I think you don't let yourself get emotional," she countered, "like you are afraid."

I took a deep breath and let myself sink under the water. Lorraine launched into a good-hearted speech about crying and purging of feelings and letting one's emotions out, and something about Meisner and Stella Adler was eventually worked in. I stared at the ceiling, the distortions and movement of light from my watery vantage point complimented the hollow echo of Lorraine's voice from beyond the walls and water of this porcelain womb.

"I know you're underwater because you're not answering," Lorraine said sharply. "I also know you can hear me. We are going next week. We are both free on Wednesday; Ho-Ho had to go out of town, remember?"

I sat up, the water poured down, and I took a deep breath to fill my aching lungs. "Where are we going Wednesday?"

"French Camp," she said. "Now hurry up and get dressed. I don't wanna walk into City Grocery by myself. And don't spend the whole night on the balcony; it's easier to pretend you're my boyfriend when you are actually standing next to me."

"You know, neither of us is gonna find a husband if you keep pretending I'm your boyfriend whenever we go out." I laughed.

"Yeah," she said. And then with no malice, "Sometimes I think about how much easier things would be if you weren't gay."

"Me too," I said and slid back down into the water.

🐚   🐚   🐚

THE CITY GROCERY, ON THE Square of downtown Oxford, Mississippi is not an actual grocery. Nor is it a store. It is actually a fine dining establishment. Now, whether it is "fine dining" or simply "fine" dining, is up to the consumer, I suppose. But it is an acclaimed restaurant noted for elevated southern cuisine. And, back in the day, after the dinner hour had come to a close, the City Grocery became a happening cocktail bar with a convenient name for students to defend their purchases that showed up on their parent's credit card statements. And on Saturdays, until 11:59 p.m. when the bars had to close down completely for the Blue Laws—it was the closest thing Oxford, Mississippi had to a gay bar.

Like a nod to Gatsby, Lorraine was fabulous in her little drop waist number, tights she managed to put on without tears, and a not-quite-lavender, not-quite-lilac cloche. I wore a tight t-shirt with Natalie Merchant's face on it, an untucked and unbuttoned, torn pink oxford, a pair of loose-fit jeans that sort of disguised my commando status, and Birkenstocks. We met outside my apartment door, but I didn't use it. Rhiannon would never let me use the door.

My door, our door (I shared the apartment with Rhiannon, the design major.) was the original front door of this old brick home. I liked that apartment; the covered front porch extended from the front door to my window. I could open my window and didn't have to worry about the rain coming in. I had this habit, however, of coming home, unlocking the door, and leaving the keys in the door when I went inside. Rhiannon would come home, find the keys in the door, and bring them in and lecture me. Then she started hiding them. So I started using my window.

"Oh, well you look cute …" I said as I closed my window. "You gotta Woody Allen leading lady vibe about you."

"Oooh, thanks," she curtsied. "And you look like a hippie mechanic."

"And why did you take the time to paint your toes and then put on tights?"

She looked at me like I had said the most confusingly stupid thing ever to be uttered by a man and simply stated, "Because."

She took my arm, and we walked the few meandering blocks toward the Square. It was a bit dark at our end of the street, but the closer we got to town the more the walk came to life. It is a college town, Oxford, but with plenty of history outside of Ole Miss. Of course much of it is tied to Ole Miss. I mean, the Oxford Riots were over a Black man, James Meredith, being admitted to the school. There were not many in Oxford at that time, or in the South, including Nince, I would imagine, who would have said, "You will go to Ole Miss, James Meredith. And that is all there is to that." So they rioted instead.

But Oxford also had a vibrant literary scene—Faulkner, Brown, Grisham. The Kudzu Kings are an Oxford band. And there is poetry and theatre too, of course. Oh it was a progressive little oasis … a rare example of a town where the university was more conservative. Well, except for the whole dry on Sundays thing. But that was really Lafayette County. The entire University of Mississippi campus was dry. Unless, of course, you were tailgatin' in The Grove.

We walked in the door and immediately up the stairs. A few diners were still seated at the tables on the first floor, but our destination was the upstairs bar. Lorraine's Bellini was waiting for her, held high by the cute bartender who fancied Lorraine—though both Lorraine and his wife disapproved. He handed me my beer with less enthusiasm than he had offered Lorraine her Bellini. She and I clinked glasses and made our way to the group of undergrads from our department. They were bemoaning the fact that an excitable group of mostly young men had taken over the balcony.

"If you can really call them men..." a particularly obnoxious little twat who couldn't sleep her way to be cast as a chorus girl's alternate snipped.

That was Lorraine's description of the girl, not mine. I was too busy giving a knowing wink to the twink who was double majoring in Hotel and Hospitality because his father didn't think there was a future as a Theatre Major. He could also tap dance like there was no tomorrow and had a huge but muscular ass.

✍   ✍   ✍

ONE NIGHT AT A CAST party I remember making him awfully uncomfortable as we flirted in front of a rather large ferret cage. He proceeded to follow me around that night like a lost and hungry puppy. Eventually he left with that same untalented little twat Lorraine had commented on. They were running to the next county to get beer for an after-party. I skipped the after-party and went home. It was three a.m. when I heard knocking at my window; it was the twink. He was drunk. And the obnoxious no talent girl was nowhere to be seen. I opened the window.

"I need you to drive me home and fuck me!" he said as he grabbed my head with both hands and attempted to kiss me—or maul me, really—with his tongue.

"Why don't you just crawl through the window and we can do that here," I said logically.

"Shhhh. I don't want Rhiannon to tell. Nobody knows but you." He slurred; his tongue had almost made it back inside his mouth.

"Nobody knows what?" I smiled and kissed him again, but on my terms, with less mauling.

I told him I'd meet him outside. I threw on sweatpants and a t-shirt, brushed my teeth, and I told Rhiannon where I was going and that we would be doing very not gay things. She laughed and carried a large bowl of pasta back to her room. Her live-in boyfriend who did not pay rent was hungry. I left through the window.

We got in my truck and started to drive across town—he stared straight ahead and said nothing. Silence. We parked at his apartment and went upstairs, still no talking. He opened the door, we walked in, he closed the door. He went straight to the kitchen and grabbed a bottle of vodka from the freezer. He poured two shots, did one, and then ran across the room and jumped me. His legs wrapped around my waist, his arms around my neck, and we proceeded to do very gay things all over that living room.

It was just approaching dawn when I pulled back in front of my apartment. A car was parked in the street out front and that obnoxious twat was sitting in the backseat. She wasn't moving, she was just sitting there, my guess is she was still drunk. I climbed back through my window.

🌊　　　🌊　　　🌊

BACK AT THE GROCERY, THE twink caught my meaning and stopped laughing at the obnoxious twat's comment. Lorraine got bored and wandered over to her married admirer for another drink. She flirted. Then I saw her walking over to a group of grad students, no doubt they were going to abuse Ho-Ho—the acting teacher no one liked. I heard my name shouted from the balcony. I nodded at the twink, he blushed, and I turned toward the group outside.

It is not a large balcony; it held maybe two tables. But it was crammed full with folks sitting in an amoeba-like circle, drinks in hand, vapidly debating the Bible. Oh these folks were riled up, voices were raised higher than the shot glasses, and fingers were snapping in a Z formation. It was the Oxford Queers. Or, more fittingly, the gay boys and three lesbians who had found each other on campus, formed a low-key PFLAG group who met on campus in a different room each month out of fear, and for safety and attempted anonymity. They never actually called themselves "The Oxford Queers" either—that would have been pretty badass. No, this was a deeply closeted group. For, despite the alcohol-induced bravado and the perceived safety of numbers, generally speaking, it was an underground group terrified of being outed, beat up, or worse.

"They speak of Sodom and Gomorrah, they say that any man who lieth with another man is an abomination ... and I speak of David and Jonathon, Ruth and Naomi, and the time Jesus healed the young lover of a soldier!" It was a larger queen—a flamboyant young man holding court. And he knew his Bible! He could just about quote the entire thing, as he demonstrated with great aplomb. "Jesus never spoke an ill word about homosexuality. He actually never uttered one word about it." And he was correct; the word homosexual didn't appear in any Bible until 1946—a little tidbit I learned from this Queen of the Oxford Queers.

The others sat entranced by this young man's speech—one he would never launch into around his Grenada, Mississippi relations. Grenada is a small town (All of them are, really.) on

Highway 51, just off of Interstate 55. You can follow 51 from Granada, through Duck Hill, and to Winona, then turn right toward Ackerman, and it will take you right through French Camp as you intersect with the Natchez Trace. My great-grand-parents' farm will be on your left. So will the cemetery, just past the old homestead.

I spoke of it as a debate. But a debate would require two sides of an argument. There was clearly only one side being prof-fered here—and that was countering biblical verses that spoke of homosexuality as an abomination with those of Jesus talking about loving everybody. Some spoke with more knowledge and with more Southern Baptist preacher mannerisms. I immediate-ly thought of Gio, and wondered what he and his choir director friend might have to add.

A few of the others had things to add as well. Mostly echo-ing what Wesley, the boy from Granada, had to say. The Bible was thoroughly dissected. The sermons were quite brimstone-y. And then there were the cat calls and threats offered from the street below by the occasional hot frat boy in a well pressed blue, white, pink, or yellow oxford with khakis. An alternate uniform would be a crisp white t-shirt beneath a bright polo ... and khakis. If it were a casual day, a crisp white t-shirt with another t-shirt over it, a more colorful one, or one with a slo-gan or picture of Colonel Reb. Oh, and khakis. Depending on how far along The Oxford Queers were in their alcohol intake, those calls were met with uncomfortable silence, small mutter-ings, and discussions on what assholes they were or how hot that one was. *Fuck-yous* and *fuck-offs, you wish,* or finally, *come on up and I'll give you a blow job!* would round out a particularly shot-filled evening.

Frat boys and the Bible were not the only subjects of our discussions. Classes and professors were discussed, of course. Especially the hot ones. And stories about growing up—the high school bullying comparison dialogue. (Every queer has that discussion.) Since Oxford was Oxford, and we only really had the Grocery or random classrooms to meet in, Memphis was a big topic as well—and a must see destination. Memphis had all the dance clubs. And of course, back here in Oxford, there was Cedar Oaks.

"What is Cedar Oaks?" I asked with all of my Florida born naivete.

If he were wearing pearls, Wesley would have clutched them. And then he began to orate *The Tumultuous History of Cedar Oaks - Unabridged.* It was built in 1859 by a man named William Turner. His sister saved the house from fire during the Yankee occupation. Eventually the house fell into disrepair. It was saved by a group of ladies and their historical society. Funds were raised for the antebellum mansion. The home was moved roughly two miles and renamed for the stately oaks and cedars that lined the lane of its new address. Wesley's version was a little more frilly.

"And you live there?" I asked.

"Yes," Wesley said with pride."I am lucky enough to have been selected as a resident caretaker of the property. I live in one of the first floor rooms, off the kitchen. I mostly make sure the house is safe and in order. The historical society ladies come by if there is to be an event or a tour. And I don't pay rent."

"Damn," I said. "That's quite a gig. I bet it is beautiful."

"Beauty doesn't begin to describe it." Wesley launched into another monologue with words like *stately, majestic, dignified,* and *romance of a bygone era.*

"Tell him about your dream, Wesley!" one of the other queens insisted.

"Oh my, yes." And Wesley sat up straight and smoothed the folds of her nonexistent gown as it lay across the hoop and petticoats she imagined she wore underneath. And yes, I say "she."

Wesley's not so secret desire was to dress in one of the old historical gowns on display in the ballroom of the old mansion, step out onto the balcony, and wave at her throngs of adoring fans.

"And sing 'Don't Cry for me Argentina,' right?" I laughed.

"You're a church boy, aren't you Randy?" Wesley asked with no laughter in his voice.

My laughter left too.

See Ya in Choich!

I t is true; I did spend some time in the Southern Baptist Church. We also joined the Methodist Church, and we did a brief stint as Presbyterians. Derwood's best friend's wife was a Presbyterian. And despite the Fennigs of old being of Jewish descent, we always stuck to the Christian churches. Nince was not impressed.

Nince was also not impressed with our behavior—Livie's or mine—whenever we went to her church. And by *not impressed,* I don't mean in the sense that she felt we were misbehaving or our mother was lacking or we needed drugs, no. She saw how Livie and I both shrunk in church. We became not like ourselves and sat quietly, as though we were afraid to be noticed. And afraid, again, not of Mother, or of Nince, but of the words the sweaty man in an ill-fitting suit screamed at us. So Nince stopped making us go to church when we visited. Or maybe it was Mother. To this day, I am still not sure.

Oh, I went with her to a few special services or Christmas Cantatas. But they were not the regular services, and Rudie was usually there to offer a well-timed, not-quite-under-his-breath comment. So Nince generally had us skip church whenever I visited. I made frequent trips back to Nince's house during my

Ole Miss years. It was just a four-ish hour drive of rolling hills with little to no traffic and plenty of time to think. And Nince would call nearly every Thursday just to see ...

"RAIN-de," she would say when I answered the phone.

"Hi Nince!"

"Rudie wants to know if you are coming home this weekend or if you have practice."

"I am coming to see y'all, if that is still okay ..." I answered cheerfully. "I have rehearsals, not practice, and I don't have any this weekend.

"Oh, I know." Nince sounded a little distant—far away, not aloof. It was because she had her head in the chest freezer. Now that she knew I was coming home, she was deciding if she had enough frozen items to send back to Oxford with me. "Do you want half of a cake when you go home? And Rudie, bless his heart, he can't get it out of his head that you play football."

"Why does he think I play football?"

"Well, your mother said you were there on a scholarship."

"I have an assistantship."

"Lord, don't tell Rudie that. He'll think you're an assistant coach!"

⁂   ⁂   ⁂

I ARRIVED MID-AFTERNOON AND, THERE she was, waiting in the open garage, headfirst in the freezer. "Do you have your cooler?" she asked, shifting and reshifting various wrapped, freezer-burned, and ice-encased foodstuffs.

Not that they were bad; they were not bad at all—they were, in fact, delicious. Nince was a very good cook. She was just not so good at food storage. Or expiration dates. I remember finding a tin of sage dated 1972 in her cupboard. This happened when we were cleaning out her cabinets after she passed, and we were finally able to sell the place.

"I do have my cooler. But I'm not leaving 'til Sunday; we can worry over it then." I carried my things to the garage, setting them down when Nince finally closed the freezer and came to give me a hug. "How are you, Nince?"

"Rudie should be here soon." Nince grabbed my empty cooler and heaved it up on top of the chest freezer. I carried my clothes in a large backpack. "I called him when I saw you pull in."

"You were face-first in the freezer when I pulled in."

"The cord reaches to the garage, Randy," Nince said.

I laughed out loud because it did reach the garage—and all the way from the kitchen and through a laundry room. My mother loves to tell the story of the time we discovered Nince was dating and she had a boyfriend. This was several years after my grandfather had died. Nince's boyfriend was a widower as well.

🌊   🌊   🌊

"WE WERE ALL SITTING IN the living room just visiting," Mother would begin. "It was Rudie and Norma, Olivia, Joan, and Randy ... I don't remember if your father was there."

Mother always began a story by telling us who was in attendance—a trait I have picked up too, according to Livie. She told the story a thousand times and she never remembered if my father was there.

"Well, the phone rang, and Mother just about came up out of her chair to get to it before anyone else could," my own mother would continue her story. "Well, before we could say anything to her, she came slinking out of the kitchen with the phone to her ear, giggling and twirling the cord like a teenage girl. We all just watched her. All of us—and she didn't notice. She just kept on giggling and kept on twirling that cord and stepped right into the coat closet ... and then she closed the door. Rudie shouted, 'Hey Velma, is it your boyfriend?!' And then we heard Mother just laugh and laugh. Norma tried to tell us he was very sweet. Oh, and he was ... he was a very sweet man. And then Mother came out of the closet."

I always wanted to add a little joke after she said that line, you know:

And then Mother came out of the closet ... so to speak.

And then Mother came out of the closet ...
and our roof never leaked again.

And then Mother came out of the closet ...
and rented a U-haul and moved in with my P.E. teacher.

I used the last one at Nince's funeral. Mother shot me a corrective side-eye. Rudie and Norma burst out laughing. Betty-Girl stared at us like we were lunatics, or we smelled funny, or her face was scarred from hemorrhoid cream.

⌒   ⌒   ⌒

NINCE DESCRIBED HIM AS FAT. And we did not meet him that night as she hadn't prepared enough food. But we met him the next day. And the day after that. And several times more in the years they dated, or were companions, or were doing what is really no one's business. But small towns are a hub of getting into other people's business.

I went with her to his funeral. I was an undergrad when he died. But I remember Nince and me sitting together in his little church. My pants were not too long that day. And we were the only ones in our pew in that rather crowded church. The sermon was all fire and brimstone and condemnation—an odd juxtaposition to the lines of praise and respect for the dearly departed woven in. I thought it was just me, when we left the church and I felt as though I had been thoroughly dragged through the mud—being the lowly and vile abomination that I was.

"Hmph," Nince shook her head. "And that whole time I thought they were talking about me."

✥   ✥   ✥

RUDIE WAS QUICK TO ARRIVE, and as I was walking out of the guest room, I could see Rudie and Nince laughing and talking out on her back deck. I had put my things away, kicked off my shoes, and was looking forward to a great weekend. Nince was telling Rudie about the surprise she had for me. When she found out I was coming, she got us tickets to *Night of the Iguana* by Tennessee Williams. It was running at the Alabama Shakespeare Festival. We would attend the Sunday matinee.

"RAIN-de!" she yelled through the screen, "Make us a margarita!" Margarita possessed all the syllables and more. "Look under the cabinet, and see if I have the right stuff."

I looked under the cabinet of the island that separated the kitchen from the dining area of the small, three-bedroom home she built with my grandfather for their retirement. And sure enough, three bottles of tequila and two bottles of triple sec, Grand Marnier, and a host of other liquors that would make any Ole Miss tailgate gathering on The Grove envious. We were talking the good stuff too. There were no hats on the tequila. I debated whether there could be an expiration date on alcohol.

"I think we're good!" I yelled. And I went to work making us a round of drinks and filling the pitcher Nince had already conveniently put out. Lime wedges and salt too. She knew.

"So no football practice this weekend?" Rudie asked as I walked through the door with a pitcher of margaritas in one hand and a tray of glasses in the other.

"I'm in graduate school, so even if I wanted to play, I don't think I would be eligible," I reminded him and laughed.

"I bet your friend, ol' Tommy at Auburn ... Velma, call him." Rudie was determined. "I bet he could get you playin'."

"Are you sure you don't want to go to the play with us tomorrow?" Nince interrupted.

"Nah," Rudie grumbled. "I'm all cultured out with Cassie."

I'm not sure if they were married yet at this juncture, but it didn't really matter. Cassie annoyed Nince so much, she had to leave whenever the diaphanous nemesis from New York was mentioned. "We need to put the steaks on."

Nince went inside to get the steaks while Rudie poured us another round. Soon enough they were bickering over the steaks, and then bickering over the sides. Rudie set the table while Nince pulled baked potatoes from the oven. Nince reset the table while Rudie got the steaks. I helped by putting out the sour cream and butter, putting the green beans in a serving dish, and setting them on the table. We ate outside at a round metal table, spray painted black. The metal chairs were also painted black. The setup was in the corner where two wide decks met in an L and overlooked a creek below.

We chatted about everything and everyone. I certainly cherished this time, like a stolen moment with two siblings who also happened to be best friends. And I often found myself just sitting back and watching the show—the inside jokes, the jabs, and the love they so clearly shared. Or perhaps bond. Bond is the better word, as I believe one can have love without the bond. Because I do see that same love in Mother and Gene. I see it, feel it, between Livie and me. And even those three boxed blondes that Wilksie had her mama raise (according to Nince and Rudie anyway; one of their inside jokes). I can't say I see that same bond. Or quite feel that same tie. Certainly, I can't speak for the others. (There are days I doubt I'm even qualified to speak for myself.) But it is true. I don't feel that bond. I don't want to. I don't like being tied up.

I cleared the dishes from the table on the back deck, Rudie rinsed, and Nince put them in the dishwasher. I could not wipe the smile from my face as the laughter at the memories, the bickering of two siblings, and the love of family enveloped us. It was comfortable. It was safe. The two of them cut up as Nince loaded the dishwasher and criticized Rudie's rinsing technique. He sprayed her once, and she laughed herself into a coughing fit. She offered Rudie a dish of ice cream, but he opted to head home to Money-Penny, or Cassie if you asked him instead of Nince. And we turned in too. Nince had a big day ahead: lunch at the base in Montgomery, a quick trip to the commissary, and then that matinee performance of *Night of the Iguana*.

Rudolph and Vilma

Nince and Rudie were the middle two. Most of the responsibility for things was placed on the shoulders of King and Norma. It had been that way from the start. King helped their father manage the sharecroppers while Norma helped manage the home. Rudie came next. And while not as big a boy as King, he was just as strong and wily and ready to get into anything. There were several miscarriages after Rudie, and a stillbirth that was said to have broken Dock's heart—and then Nince was born.

Vilma Irene, or Velma, was born on Christmas Eve. It was a cold and rainy night; there was quite a blustery storm when Nince arrived. The doctor could not get through; there was a gut in the road from a washout that made it impossible to pass. Oh and the ice. The ice hung on the pine branches, the weight snapping them like gunshots in the night.

When Wilksie tells the story—and she does tell the story; Wilksie tells lots of stories—she blames the doctor's absence on "that white trash girl who had shacked up with the sharecroppers." But it turns out that "white trash Slattery girl" was a character from *Gone with the Wind* and not actually in the recesses of Wilksie's memory, though you could never convince her otherwise.

"Oh, she wasn't born for another four years; she doesn't know anything," Norma would say. "The doctor was stuck, Mama was in pain, and the baby was coming. That is all we knew."

King had gone out in the cold storm with Millie, the old mule, to try to pull the doctor free. Dock sat by his bride, Ettienne, his enormous hand holding her tiny one as he pressed compresses to her forehead and whispered how much he loved her.

Norma had Rudie boiling water and told him, "Git every towel, rag, and sheet you can find. And bring one of them boiling pots when you can—I need the clean water!" She may have been a child, Norma, but she had seen her mother give birth to Rudie, and she had seen her mother help the women from the shanties (though not with cholera and yellow fever as Wilksie might have one believe). And while she didn't understand all the whys of what they did to help a woman give birth to a child, she did know the whats.

It was Dock who did the delivery—well, Dock and Ettienne and Mother Nature. Rudie was only four years old, but he ran to get everything his older sister called for—except for the boiling pot of water; Dock had to carry that. And Dock was the first to hold this baby he would call Nince. He cut the cord where his eight year old daughter told him to. He bathed her the way she told him to—and he held his new daughter in his hands the whole night. Of course Ettienne had to feed her; only then could she hold her. She was Dock's little girl.

"And mine," Norma said. "It was Christmas Eve. I did all the work for her. I decided she was my Christmas present."

Everybody laid claim to baby Vilma. Dock and Norma would argue over who did more to birth her. Ettienne would argue that perhaps she had done the most. And King added that he was the one who finally got the doctor in ... after it was all over. But it was Rudie who grew closest to this new little wonder they now called Velma because the "dirty Hungarian" name had to be changed.

Rudie and Velma were inseparable. Rudie held her hand for her first steps. Rudie made faces to make her giggle when she was so fussy over cutting her teeth. Rudie taught her to swim in the pond—and they both got whipped good for it because of the snakes. Rudie taught her to ride a horse. Except it wasn't a horse; it was Millie, the mule. And they both got whipped good for that too, because Millie was for plowing—not for riding.

And then there was Jasper, the old horse that was "a mean sum bitch" that Uncle Duck had left at the farm one day. He knew his brother would take it. His brother always loved animals; he took every one Uncle Duck would dump on him. Jasper was no different. A little high-strung perhaps—and he'd bite you just as soon as look at you—but he was a pretty horse with an easy stride.

Rudie was riding Jasper and Velma was on Millie. They had done the loop around the pasture, and they did the road down to the shanties. And now they were riding between rows of cotton, watching the children of the sharecroppers while away their time stuffing cotton into long woven sacks.

"It's hot," Velma said, wiping her face with her shirt and staring past the crew of workers barely older than her eight years.

"Wanna go swimmin'?" Rudie asked.

"You know Mama don't like us swimmin' in that pond.

It's got them snakes." Velma wiped her brow and stared at her brother. She knew he would think of something.

"We'll take the horses," Rudie said matter of factly.

"Well, that don't make no kinda sense." Velma stared at her brother.

"'Course it does, Velma." Rudie schooled Velma on this subject he had put quite a lot of thought to over the past few moments. "The horses'll get washed off and cool, and then we won't have to do it back at the barn. We will get nice and cool without getting all the way in ..."

"And them snakes?"

"We'll be on the horses, higher up than them. They can't get us." Rudie *did* have it all figured out.

Velma was satisfied with that answer. Her brother had pretty much thought of everything. They rode along, patting themselves on the back for their good idea. The sun beat down through the canopy of trees along the orange, rutted road. It was a little cooler under the canopy—a little less hot, anyway. They discussed the children they had left behind in the fields, how hot it was, and how grateful they were that they weren't the children of sharecroppers. But they were; they were the children of a sharecropper. That part is often left out of the stories— especially if Wilksie is telling them. Only Rudie and Velma did not use the word "sharecropper." Theirs was a shorter and more distinct word. And that word cuts much deeper. So deep, in fact, that I believe it leaves scars upon both the subject and the user—and even on the young ones who listen.

They didn't reach the pond, although it did come into view. And it wasn't one of them pond moccasins that caused all the trouble; it was a rattler. Jasper saw it or sensed it (or whatever it is horses do), and he stopped short. Rudie hadn't seen the snake yet. He gave Jasper a swift kick to urge him on. Jasper reared back and turned, the snake coiled up and started rattling—and when Jasper came back down, his leg caught Velma's. Millie the mule bucked and ran as Velma cried out in surprise and pain. Jasper's blow to Velma's leg snatched her from Millie's back, and she tumbled to the ground. Jasper kicked and stomped at the snake; Velma's leg took two of the blows. Rudie was thrown from Jasper, but he got right back to his feet and ran to his sister. The snake disappeared into the crusts of orange clay and the spatter of leaves and shadows in the ditch between the road and blackberries growing wild. Jasper made his escape back the way they came.

The kids from the field came running when they saw a riderless Jasper. One of the young men was able to catch the reins and calm the horse. He rode to the house for help. Millie hadn't run far (She was for plowing, not running or riding.), and Rudie was struggling to help his screaming sister up and onto the mule. Velma had clearly broken her leg. They were soon met by the young field hands, and together they got Velma onto Millie's back. Ettienne came running when she saw the children all walking down the road. Surrounding Millie and her own children as they were, she almost reached for her shotgun.

"It was that Goodie boy who rode up on Jasper. He told Mama what was happening and she put the gun down," Nince said when she told her version of the story.

The doctor was called, Velma's leg was set, and Rudie received the whooping of his life.

"I deserved it—and more," Rudie would say. He never got over feeling like he almost got his sister killed.

When Dock came home and learned what had happened, he grabbed his shotgun and went immediately to the barn. It only took one shot. Jasper was dead. He sat in the barn for hours and hours, finally coming in after Ettie sent that Thurgoode boy in to talk with him. It was just Rudie and Ettienne at the dinner table that night, and baby India. Velma was in the back bedroom asleep. It was dawn before Dock came inside the kitchen door. He did not make the biscuits that morning. Instead, he kissed his daughter on the forehead, and then he made his way back to his room and slept.

"Your father is a kind and gentle man, Rudie. He loved that horse," Ettienne said quietly. "But he loves your sister more."

Rudie stared ahead; he was out of tears. It could have been the fear or it could have been the beating, but he had no more tears. "I do too," he said.

✍ ✍ ✍

THE FOLLOWING SUMMER WAS EVEN hotter. It seemed to start in March and last through November that year. King was in the Navy and Norma was just getting acquainted with her future ex-mother-in-law. Any young man of fighting age was being encouraged to either join the armed services or secure a position in a factory that made goods for the war, become a student at a university, or find some real work—a job of some importance—all to avoid a rumored draft. Many of the share-croppers who worked Dock and Ettienne's fields had made the choice to join the armed forces. The other options were not for folks who looked like they did. Well, they were allowed factory work. Their families followed or left or scattered to nearby relations. And the labor pool in French Camp had severely dwindled. Money was scarce. And Dock made it clear that Ettienne was not to go to Uncle Money for a handout. She was true to her word, and convinced her brother to finance a project at the school instead.

French Camp Academy, originally opened in 1885 as the Central Mississippi Institute for Girls, was started through the Presbyterian Church. They opened French Camp Academy for Boys later that year. A fire at the boys' school caused the two

schools to merge, though the boys' and girls' education and rec-
reation would remain separate for some time.

Mother was a student at the school a few times during a
few of those unsettled years when her father received a military
transfer. Nince and Boom-Pa would often leave first; Boom-Pa
would get established, and Nince would set up the home. The
children, Debbie and Gene, would be called later. So Mother
and Gene went to several schools across the country—and even
in England and Germany for a brief period of time. And those
schools included two stints at French Camp Academy. Her
greatest memory of the school, aside from the stories her parents and their siblings would tell, was that the playground was
segregated. And she did not understand why.

"And I don't mean by color," she added. It was not an in-
tegrated school; all the kids were White. "But I mean that the
girls could only play on one playground and the boys on another. We could not play together. I thought it was so odd to separate children like that."

The school had several fires, even beyond the 1915 fire that
resulted in the merging of the boys' and girls' schools. Not the
playgrounds, however; we have established they remained segregated. After one such fire, Ettienne had convinced Uncle Money
to invest in some new buildings—brick ones. And Dock, of
course, was a mason. Naturally, with so many in the labor force
having already joined the armed services or they found work at
a factory in the city, it was up to Dock and his apprentice (the
older Goodie) to do the work.

Dock wasn't a dumb man despite his lack of formal education. And though his family did not come from the same money
as his wife's, he was well respected in the community. He knew
where the work came from, but he also knew the work needed to be done. It was more important to the community than it
was to his pride. So he set aside his pride, along with his own

work (namely the crop on his land), and Dock took the job at the school. He and Thurgoode built the boys' dormitory and the foundation for the observatory.

And he still maintained the garden; Etty insisted on a full vegetable garden. The sharecrop work had just about dried up. All that was left in the shanties were some kids and their grandparents. They were trying to maintain their own sparse gardens, so they were of no help. With King and Norma gone too, it was up to Rudie and Velma to pick up the slack.

"We don't got no farmer's cheese?" Dock observed with great annoyance early one morning. It was before five. He was just putting the biscuits in the skillet.

"No sir," Nince answered her father. "Mama didn't make any. She didn't have the milk."

"You tell Rudie to get that cow milked for your Mama," he said firmly. Things were not getting done since he took this new job.

"Yes sir." Nince stirred the grits on the stove and decided she couldn't keep it to herself anymore. "Can I tell you something, Daddy? 'Bout Rudie an' me. We did somethin'. But we want you to be proud—not mad."

"Even when I am mad, I am proud of my girl and boy. I want you to know that," Dock said seriously to his daughter. "Now you tell me what you need to tell me, and we will see how I feel about it."

"Yes sir." Nince took a deep breath. This almost felt like talking back to Daddy, defending Rudie and herself. But she had to do it. "Rudie did milk the cow. And some days I did."

"I see" ... although he didn't see. He didn't know where his daughter was going with this.

"But Mama never made cheese with none cuz Rudie and I took it to the shanties and sold it." Nince did not look at her father as she told him this. She was too scared. She just stirred the grits and talked slowly. "I'm sorry Daddy, I know you don't like us going down there ..."

"What did you do with that money?" Dock asked. He didn't like them going down there. He didn't like them being around those ... those ... "What did you do with that money?" Of course he added another descriptive term, an ugly term, to help clarify whose hands that money came from. A term that sadly still hung around even as my generation arrived.

Nince was getting worried; she could tell her Daddy was about to be very upset. "We already spent it all, Daddy."

"Where is your brother?"

"Daddy."

"Where is your brother?!?" Dock almost never raised his voice.

"He, he is out hitching up Millie," Nince hesitated.

"And I told y'all never to ride that mule again." Dock was mad. As mad as Nince had ever seen him. Well, not as mad as when he shot Jasper, and not as mad as he would be in just a little over a year more, but he was mad. Oh, he was mad. "G'on and git your brother. And y'all best not come back without a good switch for each of ya."

Nince carefully moved the pot of grits from the fire and turned the burner off. She looked up at her father with silent tears rolling down her face. "Yes sir."

"I didn't think I married a fool," Etty said sharply to her husband. '

Dock turned, surprised by both her presence and her tone. He started for the icebox; Etty interrupted his movements.

"I heard Velma say distinctly there was no farmer's cheese," Etty said, the sharpness to her tone had not left. "Do you also think so little of your wife that you can even imagine she would make ice-milk cubes for herself—and no cheese for her family?"

"Now Etty," Dock started; he could never withstand Etty being sore with him.

Etty didn't look at her husband. She poured her own coffee; she took a small slice of butter and added it to the beverage. It wasn't the same as milk, but it was something. She stared at the small, yellow-white pat of butter as it slowly melted, tiny bubbles of oil and cream separating and then blending as she stirred occasionally with a small silver knife. She stared at the pat of butter as it continued to shrink and disappear while her husband ranted about his children taking money from a bunch of ...

"So what?!?" Etty finally said. "You take their money through the crops they grow. You take their money when you rent our land to 'em. So what?!?! So what?!? Did you ever stop long enough to get the answer on what they did with their money?"

"I asked 'em. They spent it."

"On what?"

Dock ripped open the door to the side porch and called out to his children. "Rudie! Nince! Y'all git in here now!"

Rudie and Velma appeared out of the dark morning mist; each carried a long thin, but not too thin, piece of branch or stick they had selected for their punishments. Choosing a switch was tricky business. If you tried to choose a small one, you would only be beaten all the harder with it. A really thin one was like a whip and stung even more. A big one felt like a bat and would leave a nasty bruise. Rudie's eyes were damp with frustration and fear. Nince had already cried her tears. She stared straight ahead, stone-faced; ready to be punished.

"Ask 'em," Ettienne whispered loudly at her husband.

"What did you do with that ..." He used that same ugly and angry adjective again, " ... money."

It was Rudie who tried to answer first, but the words caught in his throat.

Nince finally answered. "Cotton seeds, Daddy. We bought cotton seeds. An' Rudie an' me, we're gonna put in a crop. And we are gonna help Mama with the garden, and we gonna help make sure them ... sharecroppers that are left do their part too."

Dock didn't speak for a moment; he digested everything they said, his wife said, and the things he had said and thought and almost did ... He looked at his children, nine and not quite fourteen. "Rudie, you ain't strong enough, and Nince you ain't big enough for that plow."

"Millie is real patient," was all Rudie could manage.

Nince launched into more, and let their father know they already had three rows turned up and ready to plant. They weren't straight, not the first two, but they were gettin' better and Rudie was gettin' real good. And they hoped that, by to-day, they would at least have the field behind the barn planted.

They didn't. But when Dock arrived home that evening, he walked out to the field with his children and they discussed what needed to be done next. And he went out every morning before heading to the Academy, and gave them some instructions and told them what they should do that day. Of course there were a few older men, too old for service or a government job. They stayed and worked the fields alongside Velma and Rudie. So did the boy (Goodie) who rode ol' Jasper when Rudie got thrown and Nince broke her leg, although he was down at the school too, helping his grandfather and Dock with wheelbarrow loads of bricks. And several other children who had stayed with older family relations while their parents left for work in other parts came to the fields to help. The cotton was planted, the cotton was tended, and the cotton was harvested. It was not a large crop, and prices for cotton were not strong that year. But it was enough to keep several families through a rather harsh and cold winter.

THE FOLLOWING APRIL (APRIL 22, 1942 to be exact) Ettienne Mornay Taylor had both her best and her most horrible day. It was a Saturday and *Gone with the Wind* was finally playing again at the cinema in town. It was the day fifteen-year-old Rudie left. And Dock, he came the closest he ever had to striking his wife. And it was the last day Nince saw herself as a child.

King was rumored to be on the USS Roper, and he was also rumored to be in Bataan. King would later confirm that while both were true at one point, he missed out on any of their major significance. He saw his action, plenty of it, but he did not take part in the Battle of Bataan and does not remember if he was on board the Roper when she became the first United States Naval Ship to take out a U-boat.

"I think I'd remember that," he told me at some family gathering after my grandfather's funeral. It may have been Dock's funeral, I can't quite be sure. There was one summer the funerals sort of ran together.

Clearly, though, King could not have been in both the Atlantic and the Pacific at the same time. But that did not stop the family from worrying with every bit of news they read in either the *Clarion* or the *Daily News*. And it did not stop Rudie and Nince from worrying about their older brother fighting this war so far from home—or the other American heroes so bravely sacrificing for this war on other shores. It was the talk in the cotton fields; it was the talk at the Academy; it was the talk at church; and it was the talk on the way home from school. Everybody wanted to enlist or help or do something.

Rudolph Mornay Taylor walked with his mother to town that day. He held the paper from the recruiters who came to his school. They would be there today too. All she had to do was sign. He wouldn't drop out of school; they would educate him.

They would even make sure he went to college. He would have a career. He would have meaning. And he would defend this country and make sure King was safe. And at fifteen years old, he needed his mother to lie—and sign a form stating that he was seventeen.

Rudie had waited all week for an answer, for his mother to sign the form. Daddy was out of town on a job and wasn't due back 'til late Saturday or even Sunday. And then Rudie feared it would be too late. They were taking a group of fresh recruits to Mobile on Saturday, and Rudie was determined to go. He would run away if he had to.

"I think that would hurt Mama more. And if you hurt Mama, that would make Daddy all the angrier," Velma said wisely to her older brother. She didn't want Rudie to go, although she understood his determination. She wanted to leave herself, after all. But what was the ugly skinny sister with no real talent gonna do? Norma had a profession, skills, things to fall back on. India was a problem child with a wild imagination, sure, but it would carry her far. And of course the boys could join the military. But how was an almost eleven-year-old girl gonna escape this town? She wondered how she could join the military, or maybe work in a factory in Mobile or Birmingham. "No. You better get Mama on your side on this one, Rudie. It's the only way."

So Rudie tried. He got up extra early every morning to do the biscuits. Velma was glad, because that was her job and she didn't make the biscuits like Daddy—they were never as good, and it frustrated her. She was better with cornbread. And while India would eat a bowl of cornbread covered in buttermilk for breakfast, it was not as easy for others. And this was a practice as old as Millie: making biscuits with a piece of fatback (or bacon or ham if it was a hog killing month) and bringing them down to the shanties before work began.

"Them little workers will always git out there if ya tempt 'em with a little food," Dock's own Mama would say, using her own colorful and descriptive terms to paint a very ugly picture of what could have been a simple and potentially kind gesture.

Rudie made the biscuits better than Velma. And Rudie also milked the cow and made sure there was cream for butter, milk for farmer's cheese, and skimmed the milk for Mama's frozen milk cube too. He also took the biscuits down to the shanties and got the boys started out in the fields. Velma kept the kitchen going, and she tended the family garden, chickens, and minded the girl who came in from the shanties to look after India. And they both had schoolwork, though neither worried with it much.

On this particular Saturday, Rudie had gone out early to get the boys started. He wanted to be back and dressed before Mama went to town. Velma already knew his plan, and promised her brother she would do everything she could to help him. She had a small breakfast of eggs and ham for Mama waiting, along with her coffee. India was just getting through her buttermilk and cornbread mush when Etty walked into the kitchen.

"Good mornin', Mama."

"Rudie left early." Mama smiled—Velma had a way with India that none of the other kids or she possessed. "I'm not sure them folks are gonna like being woken up early on a Saturday. Your Daddy always gives 'em an extra hour Saturdays."

"Rudie talked with 'em all week and told 'em he would be there early today," Velma answered. "He wants to get back to walk with you to town."

"He wants me to sign that paper."

"He knows you are going to see *Gone with the Wind,* Mama, and that it is a special day for you."

"And he wants me to sign that paper."

"And he wants you to sign that paper," Velma finally agreed.

"I can't do it. Not without your father here. Dock would kill me if I let Rudie go without sayin' goodbye." Etty held her coffee but did not sip it. She just stared over the small teacup and puzzled over this problem in her mind.

"Well, Rudie's gonna leave anyway," Velma confessed. She was always honest, or tried to be. Velma only ever lied if it would spare someone's feelings—and sometimes not even then. She only ever got more honest as she got older.

"I know," Mama said.

"And he won't have said goodbye then either," Velma said.

"I know," Etty replied, still not drinking her coffee.

"I don't want him to go anymore than you, Mama." Velma sat down next to her mother. "But I want Rudie to do what he needs more than what I want him to do. I don't have to be happy. But I want him to be."

Ettienne looked up from her coffee and stared at her young daughter. "Don't you want to be happy?"

"Oh Mama," Velma said with a little eye roll, nothing too noticeable or disrespectful, and she turned her attention to India. "You all done, Sissy?"

A part of Rudie left that day he drove back from Memphis, after leaving his older sister and brother to start their lives. What remained had left the day he and Nince and those other children finished the last of the cotton crop that late summer or autumn before. Every news report, every bit of gossip about the war, and every time he saw a soldier on leave, he longed to leave this prison he called Mississippi. Or at least French Camp.

And though it pained Etty to see her children longing for a better life than the one she and her husband had provided, she also understood what it was like to be provided a life that you didn't want. She named her children for the stars so they could reach just as high. What if Rudolph Valentino's mother had kept him in Italy, making him garden and farm and tend the goats like he learned in Genoa? Well then, she would have had no Rudie of her own. And if Etty tried to hold on to him now, her own Rudie, she would still have no Rudie.

They walked in silence to town, Etty and her youngest boy. They walked past the cemetery and followed the orange, rutted road. The azaleas had reached past their peak, and the blooms lay yellowing, even browning on the edges—but the hum of bees still indicated they were filled with pollen. There is nothing quite like Mississippi in the springtime. The colors, the blooms, the cool mornings that give way to warm afternoons, and the budding trees. The magnolias become even greener, shinier— and the promise of their fragrant blossoms teases you for weeks and weeks as you wait for the heat of the late spring for them to offer their true bounty.

"Mama ..." Rudie began as they arrived beneath the marquees of the cinema.

"Don't you dare get yourself killed. Or your brother. Don't distract him with your nonsense if you two end up together."

"I'm sorry, Mama," Rudie tried to hug his mother, but she stopped him.

"No. Don't you dare say that," she said sternly, almost angrily. "Don't you ever say you are sorry for doing what you know is right."

The tiny woman seemed even tinier as she pulled her son into a deep embrace. They both cried; they shed tears of pain, sorrow, regret, promise, love, and gratitude. If anyone were to watch that scene, at that moment, on that day in April of 1942, they would see a truer picture of an old South on the cusp of change than the one that would unfold on the big screen for Ettienne. The overture was nearly over when Etty took her seat. It was the final boarding call when Rudie took his on the train. And Nince cleaned the house, and she minded India, and she brought lunch down to the fields, and she pulled weeds, she shot a snake, she milked the cow, and she started shelling some peas. She wondered if she would ever see her best friend again.

THE TABLE WAS SET. NINCE had even convinced Etty to let her use "the good dishes." They weren't certain Dock would be home for dinner, yet they knew Rudie would not be. Nince set the table for three anyway. India was with Dock's niece, Irene, for the weekend. The girl who usually minded India had given birth a few months prior. It was her third child, and her husband had left for the war. She needed money, but hand-me-down clothes and linens, and leftovers from any meals "the girl" helped prepare were all Etty would offer.

"And then she started bringin' them whelps and monkeys of hers and I had to draw a line," Etty had told Irene.

Nince was frying the chicken under Etty's watchful eye when Dock walked through the kitchen door. He had arrived home by bus. The Greyhound dropped Dock and a few of the older boys from down the road off at the Academy. Dock arrived just in time to wave at the last bus of new recruits who were leaving that day for Mobile. They would soon join the war effort—heroes, patriots, brave young men, every one. And Dock was grateful and proud of each and every one of those boys. It would be quite the surprise to learn that one of those boys was his own.

Dock was not excited by his surprise. "Weren't yall expecting me?" he asked his bride and his pride as Etty finished the chicken and Nince set the peas on the table.

"You better wash up," was all Etty said.

"Where's Rudie?" Dock asked, but he was starting to put it all together.

And Nince, well she was as scared as she had ever been at his anger. And now it was worse because Mama was not trying to calm him or console him. She fought back hard, her tiny body producing a voice and a will that was just as formidable as her husband's six-foot three-inch frame. The argument carried outside, then back inside. The ruckus carried down to the shanties where they all could hear the shouts and screams but not the actual words.

They were back in the kitchen when Dock started in on Uncle Money and the rest of Ettiene's "high falutin' and stuck up kin," while Etty countered with Uncle Duck and the rest of her husband's "white trash, no better than them dirty sharecroppers at the shanties" ... loosely quoted, but the words struck home. Dock lifted his enormous frying pan-sized hand in anger. Etty stared hard and dared her husband to make this very big mistake. Nince stepped in between the two.

"You gonna lose me too, Daddy!" she screamed at her father. "And you gonna have to beat me before you beat Mama because I convinced 'em both that Rudie should go. It was me, Daddy!"

The cry of pain and despair reverberated like that of an animal with its leg caught in a trap. Dock's fist landed hard in the plaster above his wife's head. The glass in the window over the dining table shattered as Dock slammed the door and stormed out into the dark Mississippi night. He didn't come home, not that night. And he spent a lot of time working in the barn, the fields, and tending his wife's garden—avoiding Ettienne and his Nince. He didn't speak; he just worked. It was a month of this—and then another few weeks. And then they received a letter from Rudie. He was gonna be on the same ship as his brother. They were headed to the Pacific Ocean. That was all Rudie could say. But it was enough.

"Etty, I never did ask you how you liked that movie."

Etty smiled at her husband, and looked up as he refilled her coffee. "I liked it just fine."

"Well that don't sound like you liked it at all." Dock put a fresh cube of milk in his wife's coffee.

"It's not that." Etty thought about how to explain it best.

"The scenes of them boys going off to war; well, of course that was hard. But it was that scene with that Melanie—oh, she was a mealy-mouthed ninny like they say—where she scolds the Meade boy who wants to go off and fight after he learns his brother has died. How dare she stand in the way of that boy growing to be a man? Doing right by his brother and hisself. Oh, I got so mad I almost walked out. And India, they hardly made anything of her character, and I thought she was the only sensible one of the bunch. And I still do."

Yes, Etty and Dock were talking again. Things were going to be okay, maybe even better than that. He was back to making biscuits, Dock was, and Etty? Well, she fried a whole chicken for dinner—they'd never got around to eating that last one. And that girl who minded India was back. She needed the material from the hand-me-downs to sew clothes for the new baby. Besides, India liked to carry that baby around like a little doll. And Nince put her dreams of leaving on hold. What good are dreams when one has work to do?

🖎   🖎   🖎

"IT WAS THAT BOY WHAT taught your Daddy to lay brick all them years ago that helped him," Etty explained to Nince as things went back to normal. "They sat in the barn all night, and that boy talked sense into your father. He was always good at that. Did it the night he shot Jasper too. Remember that, honey?"

"I do." How could she forget?

"And a little good hard work too. His own work. On his own place. That always does right by a man like your father. A man has got to feel like something belongs to him, and him alone." Etty continued: "We women aren't like that. We're built different. Our whole life we have to share; even our bodies aren't our own. Between birthing babies, and, well ... something doesn't have to be ours alone for us to know it belongs to us."

Dock had a different take: "It was Nince who saved me." That was all he said, and that was all he would ever say.

◢   ◢   ◢

Chapter 5
Here Comes the Rain

Night of the Iguana

After an early breakfast with Rudie—he made biscuits while Nince did grits and bacon—we started our drive to Montgomery, Alabama. An hour and change, it was a pleasant drive through the rolling mounds and hills of this part of the country. Springtime had really caught hold ... the pinks and crimsons and purples of the blooms. The varied greens and almost blues or yellows of new foliage, and of course this was all highlighted by the vibrant orange of the tilled earth making way for crops of peas and melons and tobacco and cotton. The fields gave way to neighborhoods and strip malls as we approached Montgomery and then found our way to Maxwell Air Force Base.

We ate at the Maxwell Club. Back in the day, it was a rather exclusive officers' club. And since her late husband, my grandfather, was an officer in the Air Force when he passed, Nince was a welcome member of the club. He had made the switch from Army-Air Forces to the Air Force after World War II. She could go at least, but the Maxwell Club was a bit less club-like than it was back in the day. Gone were the days of it being a true hot spot—with live entertainment, dancing, and handsome officers back from the war. It was now little more than a fancy buffet-style cafeteria, but Nince had fond memories.

"Rudie would bring me here to go dancing." Nince looked about the room as though envisioning something else. "We would leave Mama and Daddy's, and stay with the sister of a friend of his from the war. That's where I met Daniel."

"Who?" I asked, not really thinking.

"Your Boom-Pa."

"Yes, right."

"Oh, he was a mighty fine dancer. And handsome too." Nince was clearly lost in her remembrance. "We drank champagne cocktails and danced 'til dawn. Well, almost dawn. I remember sitting outside, his jacket draped over my shoulders. We shared a cigarette while the sun rose that morning; it was the first time I had ever smoked. Oh, I felt like such a bad girl. Like Veronica Lake."

I laughed lightly and imagined my grandmother with her hair covering one eye.

"You know who that is?" she asked, briefly pulled from the trance of her memory. "Of course you do; your mother raised you on old movies. She's just like Mama."

"Yes. yes I do." And it is true—Sundays were all about the old movies. Mother and I would sit on the couch under a blanket; Derwood always kept the thermostat set on cold or Arctic tundra. We would have our breakfast watching Basil Rathbone solve all the mysteries. Or sandwiches and sweet tea while singing along with the ingénue. And of course ... Cary Grant.

"And I felt pretty, Randy. For the first time in my life, I felt like I was the pretty one."

⌖   ⌖   ⌖

BEFORE SEEING THE PLAY, WE had one more stop to make on the base: the commissary. It was off limits to the general public. Nince, being a military widow, was able to shop there and attend all of the Maxwell Club's finest buffet offerings, a true military widow bonus. The commissary stocked every item imaginable, from personal hygiene products to liquor, groceries to electronics. You could even get tires for your car, bicycle, or boat trailer. It had everything. Even the item that Nince was very annoyed I was without.

☙   ☙   ☙

"WHAT DO YOU MEAN YOU don't have a television?" Nince asked sharply. She and Rudie were arguing over watching *Step By Step* or *Major Dad*.

"I don't really watch TV; I'm generally studying or rehearsing or ..."

"Out with a girl," Rudie chimed in. "Leave the boy alone and let's watch *Step By Step*."

☙   ☙   ☙

SO I WAITED IN THE car while Nince ran into the commissary; it didn't take too long. And soon she was walking back with some older man carrying a box with a portable television and VCR combo. It didn't quite fit in the trunk, so the man stuffed it in the backseat and wished Nince a blessed day.

"Yes sir, you do the same, you hear?" She smiled and waved and then got into the car. "Well he was a well-mannered little ..." And she used that word I detest. And I said something.

"You know I hate it when you use that word," I said, confused, maybe annoyed by her use of sir and that other word all while referring to the same man.

"I know that you don't, but they like it."

"No, I am pretty certain they don't."

"Randy." (Long "A"; quick "D".) "You did not grow up with those people like I did. I know what I'm talking about."

"I'm also pretty sure 'you people' and 'those people' aren't high on the list either."

"Randy." Nince looked me dead in the eye as she stopped the car and said, "If I had known Ole Miss was gonna turn you into a liberal, I would have insisted you go to State." She winked, smiled, put the car back in gear and we drove to the Carolyn Blount Theatre and the Alabama Shakespeare Festival.

The Alabama Shakespeare Festival is nestled in a gorgeous park-like setting. Well, not park-like; it is in a 200-acre park. It is a beautiful campus, especially in the mid-to-late spring. A botanical garden of colors and fragrances. Small ponds and fountains add to the reflective and peaceful setting of this performance venue that offers more than Shakespeare despite its name.

I had never seen *Night of the Iguana* live, only on film. I had enjoyed it though it was not a standout for me. I had read the play a few times, mostly skimming for scenes to direct for class or quotes for tests. There was one moment I was especially excited to see how well they would pull off—the hurricane! There is a climactic moment toward the end where the metaphorical storms of the characters are swept right into the actual storm of a hurricane. Mentally, I questioned just how effective they could be. I mean, movies are one thing—but live and right there on the stage? Oh, and my design major roommate, Rhiannon, was also interested. She was waiting for a full report when I got home.

We took our seats; we flipped through the program; I shared my excitement over the impending hurricane.

"I know!" Nince whispered, then shushed me as the lights began to dim. "You told me at lunch. And Rudie at breakfast."

The lights grew dim, then black—and then the lights came up on the stage. I was not prepared. It was beautiful. Gorgeous even, or any and every other adjective or synonym or what have you. I'm not talking about the play or the scenery or the lights. I mean, they were nice too, but there was this one young man; he played one of the cabana boys, and he was just HOT. He was always shirtless and sometimes wore even less. And he was five feet from me—and my grandmother; she was right next to me. This Mexican-Tarzan-Adonis was five feet from me and Nince. And I was an enthralled and uncomfortable mess.

So while Nince watched the action on the stage and flipped through the program in an effort to follow who was who, I imagined all sorts of other action playing out. I swear I was not just about to reach up and touch the bare chest of that poor actor who was standing right there—my eyes tracing the path that little bead of sweat from his Adam's apple was going to make when the lightning flashed across the deep purple and gray sky. And then I don't know if I heard it or smelled it or felt it—the dampness one can feel and that electric smell; the first irregular drops one hears while sitting beneath an old tin-roofed porch before a summer storm.

The rain came, and then the wind. Those purples and deep violets of the sky, the ominous greens and threatening magentas of a storm ready to unleash its fury shone brilliantly across the cyclorama—that vast spread of muslin reaching beyond the rows of lights and scenery that hung above. I was all at once enveloped by the falling rain. It surrounded me, it penetrated me—my mind, my thoughts ... my feelings. I was caught in a maelstrom of visions and memories escaping from depths I could not fathom. The echoing of water crashing onto a hard surface, the dancing light as the water spilled from the tin roof, and the vague calls from the actors, both on stage and lost in the recesses of the many acts and many scenes of my life I had relegated to an echo, an impression, a souvenir. Where the fuck was all of this coming from?

I fought to focus on the technical elements. It was only a play after all. The wind came from a fan and the rain was produced by ... well, water can have some source other than God. This wasn't real. But the emotions that sprung from me were. And I fought it. I fought them, the emotions, the feelings, those souvenirs and snapshots I tried to lose or bury or hide. And the storm raged across the stage and right through me. Water will find its way. And then it was over. And the lights brought us through to the dawn. And I sat, embarrassed, as my eyes were still wet from the storm.

When we left that afternoon, we agreed that their performance of *Night of the Iguana* far exceeded the expectations either of us had. I drove back that evening, the TV/VCR combo strapped into the seat next to me. And I had a cooler full of miscellaneous items from Nince's freezer. Rhiannon would be happy; she loved it when I went "grocery shopping" at my Nince's. Nince and Rudie tried to convince me to stay one more night, but I did have class in the morning so I really needed to head back. And Rhiannon was dying to hear about the hurricane while eating whatever pie I brought home.

"Be good, Randy." Nince hugged me again. "And call your Mother more. I love you."

"I love you too." I kissed her cheek.

"And tell her to call me more." She waved from the garage as I walked toward my truck.

Rudie was still convinced it was football that was bringing me back to Ole Miss so soon. He waved too as I loaded the last of Nince's "groceries" into my truck and said, "You've got them big broad shoulders. You can carry anything ..."

A Good Funeral Requires Preparation

"You still play every now and then don't ya?" Rudie more stated than asked as he sort of fumbled through conversation. We didn't make a lot of eye contact; he just stared forward, or maybe backward ...

"No sir," I answered with a smile and a wink to Liv. "I can't remember the last time I played football."

Norma chuckled and put her arm around her baby brother. She sat somewhat perched on the arm of the sofa Rudie sat on. Liv was next to him. I was sitting in a random armchair, probably from someone's grandmother's dining set. Betty-Girl had commented that all the furniture in the "designated family waiting area" had been hand selected from the finest antique places throughout central Mississippi and Alabama.

"Why, this piece here—Brother-Man Bill and I picked this one up from a home in Natchez," Betty-Girl announced with the intent to impress as she pointed to the single captain's chair.

This was when we were planning my grandmother's funeral. Nince was quite wisely and rather macabrely clear about what she wanted for her funeral services. And we were now getting a tour of the back parlor by our very own family Julie McCoy for funerals—Betty-Girl Monroe. And I could hardly contain myself as Nince needled her with questions about the ins and outs of this lone captain's chair from a reproduction Queen Anne dining set. Nince asked her to go into detail about the period. Was it truly from the period or was it a reproduction? Some of them are very good, those reproductions. What home did it come out of? What family did the furniture originate with? Had it always been a part of that home, the chair? What happened to the rest of the dining set? Was it destroyed in the war?

And poor Betty-Girl did her beauty pageant best to answer the questions. "Well I don't know about all of that. But when my cousin was moving across town because it was closer to her new job at the Piggly Wiggly they just built—Brother-Man and me, we were helping. And Brother-Man, he suddenly screams and stops that truck we were driving. And there it was. This beautiful chair. Someone had set it out to the curb. Well Brother-Man snatched it up and threw it in the back of the truck and it was ours. It was a nice brick rancher, probably built before I was born. And my cousin lives in Natchez ... so ..."

Nince reached up for my hand which was holding one of the handles of her wheelchair. We were both doing our level best not to laugh. And the death grip the dying woman had on my hand as she was hilariously second guessing her request of this boob to be the one who was going to be in charge of her funeral ... well, it did little to stifle our laughter.

"You will have to excuse them ..." Mother said, giving both Nince and me one of her sternest wooden spoon looks.

🌊   🌊   🌊

I LAUGHED AT THE MEMORY and shared the story with Norma and Liv. Rudie had been there that day, but he hadn't heard the whole story about the chair. He was with Derwood receiving the spiel from Brother-Man Bill about what they would do for his sister's funeral. They all laughed; I did too. And Mother shot us all a glare from across the eclectically furnished room.

Mother was with Wilksie and King. They were standing by a glossy, black upright piano and a plastic-covered sofa, the only plastic-covered piece in the room, with a pattern that is best described as herringbone plaid, in oranges and greens and browns. It looked as though Dick Van Dyke might trip over it in some opening sequence of this family show we call a funeral.

The three formerly non-blondes, Wilksie's girls, sat on the very same sofa. These southern belles were able to sit with such delicacy, grace, and lightness. It is almost as if they levitated just above the clear plastic protective covering, because God forbid it should come in contact with their taffeta. Gene and his wife were talking with Roni and Tina. Roni would be playing the organ for her sister-in-law's service.

Liv was in the middle of telling Norma and Rudie about my breakfast encounter with Bitsy, Joan, and Vivian—Bitsy was the only name Livie got right out of the three—when Betty-Girl came bursting through the doors in a huff. She looked about the room with her blotchy, pink, plastic smile and wide, flaky eyes, searching frantically until they zeroed in on me.

"You are not where you are supposed to be." She tapped her black clipboard with her autumn frost nails and lost her fake smile.

"I'm with the family," I said, a bit confused. And also unable to avoid staring at the flakes that seemed to strain beneath the piles of pancake and powder this woman was wearing. Like a nearly smooth stucco or a poor attempt at scraping a popcorn ceiling—

"You sir, are a pallbearer."

—or perhaps she really did use Bisquick as foundation like Norma suggested. "I'm a grandson."

"Not anymore. For these services you are a pallbearer," she sniped. "You need to come with me."

"I'd prefer to stay with my family." I tried to argue, but she spoke over me.

"It is what Velma prefers, not you." And she turned toward the door.

I tried to catch my mother's eye as I followed, but she was somewhat trapped by Wilksie and Bitsy and couldn't get away. I followed the woman in the too-tight-in-some-places-and-not-at-all-in-others dark gray sweater dress and black flats. Her tights were red because it was almost Christmas—and also because she was a "tacky whore." That was how Norma described her. Mother agreed. Who was I to argue?

Gene's boys were already in the sanctuary, seated in a pew behind three other gentlemen whom Nince had also asked to be pallbearers. One of them would be singing. He was a good man. I had met him on a few occasions although I could not remember his name. Betty-Girl pointed at the pew behind my cousins. I took a seat and my cousins and I chatted quietly, hesitantly, as Betty-Girl seemed annoyed by any family warmth we exuded. After maybe the forty-third time she walked past us and made a quiet cough, I asked if she needed a piece of hard candy. She glared, my cousins laughed, and we sat silently after that.

I reached in my jacket pocket and pulled out a folded piece of paper. I had crafted a few words to say, nothing too terribly long, not like an entire eulogy. But I had wanted to share some thoughts and ideas and memories of who Nince was to Livie and me. Livie and I worked together on the contents; I added a little dramatic flare while Livie tamed it with some fact-checking and reality. It was even Nince-approved. She and Livie and I cried together as we sat on Nince's bed and I read the note aloud. This was the Thanksgiving before she passed—Nince always hosted Thanksgiving. Even Mother approved of our letter and told both Liv and me how proud she was that we represented our family with such beautiful words.

My grandmother's coffin was already in the sanctuary. The casket was now closed and covered in a spray of soft white and pale pink poinsettias. The light silver gray of the casket was actually kind of pretty, with the muted frosts of the flowers allowing for an absolutely gorgeous Christmas Cantata and funeral combo. Betty-Girl had worked her magic.

"In fact, one of Velma's last wishes—I added it to the clipboard the last time we spoke, bless her heart: She wanted some of the flowers to be used for the cantata tonight."

The photo of my grandmother that Betty-Girl chose to display beside the casket was lovely. Well, it was fine. It was from just before she was ill the second time around. I would have preferred a different one. One where you could not see the pain of sickness lingering, waiting behind her bright and brilliant eyes. But still and all, you could almost hear her laughter in her smile. And I did. I listened to her laughter as I stared through the blue stained glass out into the cold and gray and damp December morning. It may have even rained.

A Recollection of Undines

I don't remember if it was Laura or Aunt Nee's husband who died first. I was young. Seven? Six? Maybe even younger. Time is not always the mitigating factor of events that seem to take residence in our memories. But I am pretty certain this all came before that time we terrorized my mother at the Atlanta airport.

Laura was Rudie's first wife. Rudie said she was the first girl he kissed when he got off the ship in Maryland after the war. He settled in DC and got work initially through his older sister's first husband's family connections. Norma had introduced him to several well-connected folks in the District, and eventually, Rudie being Rudie, he made his own connections. What started as a secretarial position with an ambassador to the Netherlands landed him in a consulting position with an international hotel firm specializing in attracting American tourists.

Laura, I both remember and don't. I mean, how can one forget perhaps the kindest, gentlest woman who possessed that effortless beauty of kind and gentle ladies. And she was a lady—there is no doubt about that. And she met the approval of not only Ettienne, but of The Three Sisters as well.

Four of the Taylor siblings settled in DC after the war at least briefly, as my grandfather's remaining an officer in the military required that he and Nince (and eventually my Mother and Gene) move frequently. Wilksie was the only one who remained close to French Camp. She got as far as Kosciusko. But those other four siblings and their respective spouses? They made quite the group—their own Rat Pack of the political world and art scene in the greater DC area. They went to all the clubs. They went to all the shows. And the "artiste" of whom Wilksie spoke, the man who would become Norma's second husband, well, he managed to score tickets to one of Harry S. Truman's inaugural balls. It was unseasonably warm in DC that late January of 1949. The Two Sisters and their Sister-In-Law stunned the crowds, or at least their respective dates, in their strapless gowns.

⌘   ⌘   ⌘

I REMEMBER LAURA IN A loose sweater and capris as she stood in the kitchen fixing dinner while I sat on a stool and read to her. I have no idea what it was I was reading to her at the age of six or seven. I cannot imagine it was a very stimulating read—perhaps a dumbed-down Disney classic, a Dr. Seuss, or a P.D. Eastman. But she listened to every word, and she did so kindly. I will always remember that. How kind she was ... and I think they had sheep. I have a vague recollection of sheep.

I also remember Livie and me sneaking down to the basement to watch the adults play cards. Rudie and Laura had an octagonal, green velvet-covered card table. And Livie and I sat at the top of those basement stairs and quietly watched through the bannister as our parents and grandparents and other grownups we were really just meeting smoked and drank and laughed and argued and talked about all the inappropriate things adults talk about that Livie and I did not understand. When Mother noticed us, she shot us a look. Livie and I were about to run for cover, but Nince gently placed her hand on top of Mother's hand and shook her head. Laura excused herself and brought us a dish of vanilla ice cream with a cookie. She put chocolate syrup on it. And Livie and I sat at the top of the stairs, eating ice cream, watching the grown-ups play cards.

Oddly enough, Derwood is who I remember the most when Laura died. I was at the low peninsula of the kitchen counter, sitting in my chair and not eating my dinner. Livie was much better at discretely making the parts of our dinner she didn't like really small—and then she somehow made them disappear into her napkin. I tended to narrate my actions with a song, "I'm chopping, chopping, chopping my yucky tuna noodles." Where Livie was able to quietly smear the paste she created across the bottom of her plate like a sandwich spread and place her napkin across it so that no one was really the wiser, I had a small mountain beneath my napkin—and probably sang about that too.

"Mmm hello, Fennig residence?" Mother answered the phone in the kitchen. It hung on the wall, just like the one at Nince's, only it was avocado green and not gold. The call was brief, and Mother didn't really say much after her initial hello. She was quiet. She went pale and turned her face away from me and Livie. Livie was taking the opportunity of the turned head to make her paste. I tried to know what was going on.

Mother hung up the phone, left the galley kitchen through the dining room, and went straight to her bedroom. Derwood told Livie to clean up the dishes. Livie shot a glance at me as she stopped making her paste. I quickly handed her my plate of tuna noodles. Derwood went after Mother. And I didn't get to sing.

It was ten days later when Mother returned. We had been remanded to Derwood's care for those ten days. It was a free-for-all of fish sticks and french fries. Pizza Friday occurred four times. We also ended up at one of the neighbors' homes a night or two for dinner. Aunt Nee, who lived just down the street, brought us pork chops and apples one night. On the tenth day, I went with Derwood to Tampa to get Mother. Livie stayed with a neighbor, I think. On this excursion to the airport, I don't really remember the monorail. We took it, there is no doubt, but I really remember it being a little past my bedtime and the airport was rather empty. We sat at the end of a long concourse; everything felt white and sterile. I was sitting, holding a small paper cup of dimes, watching a little television that required a new dime every several minutes. I watched *Hot L Baltimore* and *The Odd Couple,* two shows Mother would never have allowed, but Derwood, who sat at the corner of the bar where he could see me—he was fine. I ran out of dimes, which was okay because I didn't get the jokes anyway. So I made the row of chairs bolted to the hard linoleum my own personal playground.

I heard my name, "Randy!" It may have been because I was standing on the backs of the row of chairs bolted to the floor practicing my balance beam technique, or perhaps it was because she missed her most favorite of sons—but I was soon enveloped in a giant hug from the familiar and safe arms of my mother. Derwood came running from the bar, shoving his wallet back in his pocket, and he and my mother embraced as well.

We never really talked about Laura's passing, not then. We just knew she was gone. Slowly the pieces of life came together, and, without being told, the understanding of what being gone meant found its home. It was her physical presence that left us—the slim lady with sleek gray hair and the kind face that I often confuse with the face of the mother of a childhood friend, Ruth-Ann was her name. But Laura's memory carried through like a presence or entity of its own. I'm certain Rudie's second wife felt it. And some forty years or more later, when we buried Rudie, Laura's presence was still felt. Her gentle, kind love was what held Rudie together when he buried their only child, Edward Rudolph Taylor.

Laura and Rudie were not buried in French Camp. And neither was Eddie. Where one generation came home from war and their soldiers were branded as heroes, another generation came home and they were spat upon, both literally and figuratively. Eddie's demons and addictions finally took his life. And even though he was closer in age to Gene, it was Eddie and Debbie, my mother, who were best of friends—much like Rudie and Nince.

⁂   ⁂   ⁂

I WASN'T ABLE TO GO to the funeral when Aunt Nee's husband died, either. I say either, but I don't really remember which funeral came first, Uncle Bill's or Laura's. I called Aunt Nee and Uncle Bill "Aunt Nee and Uncle Bill" not because they were my aunt and uncle—we clearly demonstrated that is not a thing we do with our actual aunts and uncles—but because that is what Aunt Nee told us to call her. All the kids in the neighborhood did. She lived two houses down at the end of our dead end street. The kids would gather at that end because there were fewer cars. We would ride our bikes and scooters and green machines; we would play hide-and-seek and freeze tag and kick the can; we would sit in her driveway and drink Kool-Aid with no ice. She also threw dinner parties for us kids. And she dazzled us with stories about her friend who starred in *Bewitched!* Not Endora, or Agnes Moorehead as that would have been just too cool. No. But Aunt Nee did know Elizabeth Montgomery and said she was very, very nice.

All the adults went to the funeral when Uncle Bill died. He had a heart attack, which my young brain had a hard time

understanding. I mean, how does your own heart attack you?
Everyone was dressed in black, of course, and it really struck me
when I saw Aunt Nee in her black dress and not her sun dress. I
understood the concept of death; I knew what being dead was.
But the concept of grief was much more conflicted. And the
sadness. I think perhaps because I did not know her husband
other than by his name, really, the grief seemed like something
... odd, or out of the ordinary. I don't remember how old he was.
I don't remember if they had children, or grandchildren, or why
I even spent so much time with Aunt Nee. I just did.

MEMORIES ARE LIKE WATER. I believe I've heard that
before (maybe in a Barbra Streisand song—or maybe it was
REM), but the fluidity of memories and their shapelessness that
takes form only as they surround what was once tangible—it is
reminiscent of swimming with your eyes wide open. You are in
a pool. The clear crystal blue of chlorine-infused water bright-
ens the surrounding sunlight more than it would your whitest
of whites. Your hair floats about you, and you lay your back
against the roughly smooth marcite at the bottom of the shallow
end of the pool. The bubbles of precious air rise to the surface
as you exhale all that you have to rest your head on the bottom
step and look up. Up at the brilliance of another world, another existence above the water. You see those fluid shapes of children running about the surface, a bird swims overhead, someone dives in or wades or does a "cannonball" and the images
sort of ripple away into a blur of colors and silver and light.

THERE WAS A GAY COUPLE in our neighborhood. Everyone

knew though no one discussed it—like a pre-Clinton *Don't Ask, Don't Tell* but with less nefarious implications. Reuben and Barry lived in an unassuming dark brown and white ranch home with a well-manicured front lawn and garden. As you walked through their double wooden front doors, you walked into an enchanted world of tchotchkes and hardcover books, paintings on the walls, and an array of potted plants. And through the back wall of sliding glass doors, you would walk into this amazing garden of waterways filled with koi, pathways of rocks and shells, and a botanical wonderland that, to me, was like the homegrown version of the Kapok Tree—a local restaurant known for its fancy and elegant atrium.

Hindsight lets me see that Aunt Nee actually worked for Barry and Reuben and she often took me with her. We would clean their home, dusting each tchotchke shelf and book. I would rearrange them to where I believed they should go, making little scenes and tableaus with the various porcelain or clay figurines, carvings, and statuettes that were most likely pricey pieces of art. Barry and Reuben always smiled as I led them by the hand to each of the new scenes I had crafted with their fine antiques.

Somehow, in the deep and dark and meandering river of my mind (or maybe it's just a retention pond), I can recall two figurines that fascinated me the most. They were men, shirtless—nude really—except where the interesting parts should have been, the men's bodies morphed into something with beautiful scales and fins and a flowing tail. Undines Barry or Reuben called them. I called them mermaid boys. They were based upon an old fairy tale, they said, a German one. They told me the tale, and I read the novella years later for research on a play I was directing. And I have somehow wound up with a copy in German as part of my collection ...

Out back, Aunt Nee would weed and plant in their gardens. I

walked the pathways, fed the fish, and caught lizards. Sometimes I daydreamed of finding an undine hanging on a rock or under one of the bridges in the garden. And of course I sang songs, demonstrated a few dances, and I talked with Aunt Nee.

"I miss him," she told me, as she removed her garden gloves and wiped her brow.

"Me too," I said, careful to match her tone of sadness.

She smiled at me, and she wiped something from my own forehead. "That is very sweet, Randy. Bill loved all of you kids too. It's lonely without him."

"You can come play with me."

"I know Randy, and it makes me so happy when you come help me at Barry and Reuben's. You have been a very good friend to me. But he was my best friend."

"And you miss him?"

"And I miss him, yes." She hugged me tight. "But do you know what I do when I really miss him?"

"What?" I asked, my wide blue eyes looking into her soft, damp, hazel ones.

"I talk to him."

I giggled.

She did too. "No, Randy, I really do. I pull out my pictures of him; maybe I'll set one at the table when I am eating dinner. And I talk to him."

"What do you tell him?"

"I tell him about my day. I tell him about you and all of the fun things we get to do," she answered, giving me a squeeze and a tickle. "And I tell him how very much I love him."

"I love you, Aunt Nee."

"And I love you, Randy."

We hugged for a long time. And then we just sat there, her arm around me. We were on one of the little wooden bridges among the pathways winding through our private backyard

Kapok Tree. Our feet dipped in the cool water; occasionally a koi would kiss our toes. I felt safe there, in that backyard paradise built by two queer men who must have known that I too was a budding little queerlet. I sometimes wonder if that is why I fill my own home with photographs and tchotchkes.

You Can't Go Home Again, Not Really: Ole Miss

"RAIN-de!" It was Nince on the other end of the phone that I broke my neck to get to from the bath. "Rudie wants to know if you are coming home this weekend."

"Oh no, Nince, I can't; I'm sorry." I explained that I had rehearsal for my second year show. I was about to launch into an explanation of the show, my concept, the playwright, and all of the things I was excited about, writing about, and getting ready to do.

She just answered, "Oh good!"

"Good?" I laughed. "You seem awfully happy I'm not coming."

"Well, Rudie is worried I won't be able to cook you a decent meal, so he said you shouldn't come."

"Why is Rudie worried you won't be able to cook me a decent meal?"

"Oh, I broke my leg."

"What!?!?"

"Don't start on me Randy; you sound like your Mother."

"I didn't say anything."

"No. But you were about to," she said. "I can hear you thinking all of the things your mother would say to me if I told her."

"Nince, you haven't told your daughter that you broke your leg?"

"No, I have not. And I don't want you telling her either," she scolded.

"And why not?"

"Ugh." I could see her roll her eyes through the phone. "I can just hear Debbie now: 'Why were you and Rudie out riding anyway?'" Nince's impression of her daughter Debbie was hilarious. I cannot explain it, I think it was in the tone—just know that it was.

Nince and Rudie had decided to go horseback riding. Rudie owned three horses and loved to ride. His wife, Cassie, owned three pairs of jodhpurs and had riding boots in brown, black, and oxblood, but she would no sooner straddle a horse than she would ride a rocket to the moon.

"Or a man without a substantial income." I can always hear Norma adding to any conversation.

So Nince was always Rudie's riding companion and off they went. They had ridden all across Rudie's property, and his neighbor's as well. And they just about traversed the length of the orange clay road of Booger Holler Lane. (Rudie named the road.) They turned back toward Rudie's and the barn, choosing to follow a small stream, just a rill that wound its way through the field and back toward a patch of woods.

"Wanna race?" Rudie beamed an impish grin at Nince.

But it was too late. Nince had kicked her horse with both heels before Rudie could finish saying, "Wanna ..."

It was Rudie's horse stopping short that caused him to be thrown. He went forward, up and over, and landed firmly on the soft ground. Nince was taken out by a tree—two actually— as her horse either miscalculated or didn't care about the distance between them. There was enough room for the horse and saddle, but not enough for Nince's thighs. They hit the trees with the full force of the horse's gallop. She was thrown backward from the saddle. The tree strike broke her leg just below the knee. When she hit the ground, it snapped a little further down. Rudie half-carried and half-helped and half-dragged his

sister—that's a lot of halves—back to the barn where both horses and a mildly panicked Cassie stood waiting. She had seen the
horses return to the barn with no Rudie and no Nince.

Nince was now in Hell as she argued with Rudie that she
should go back to her house while he insisted she stay with him.
He had it all figured out: Cassie would nurse her back to health.
I stifled laughter as she complained; my head filled with vi-
sions of my Nince in a bed with her leg propped up and "Hello
Nurse" doing all she could to help.

"You don't need me to come help with anything? I can make
a few arrangements," I offered.

"Do you like gefilte fish?" Nince asked. "Then stay home."

"You can tell Rudie I have football practice," I let her know
as we were hanging up. "And you need to call your daughter."

"Fine," she answered and hung up. Not angrily; she just had
a habit of hanging up when she was done talking.

I stepped back into the not-quite-as-warm-as-it-was bath and
I picked up my not-quite-as-warm-as-it-was coffee and slid back
down into a comfortable soaking position. I took a deep breath
and closed my eyes.

"Well—who was it?" It was Lorraine; she had taken the
opportunity to refill her mimosa. That was just a guess, but I
heard her step back into her own bath.

"It was Nince. She wanted to make sure I wasn't coming
there this weekend," I said.

"Why ever not?" Lorraine asked. "That seems like such a
loaded reason to call."

"Oh, it was loaded alright." I laughed. "She apparently
broke her leg and sort of accidentally told me as she was fishing
for a reason for why I should not come for a visit this weekend
in case I told her I was."

Lorraine giggled too, "I'm not sure I followed that, but I
think it means we're both free the rest of the day."

"Not quite. We have rehearsal," I said.

"Not quite," Lorraine answered. " 'Cause your lead actress is taking a road trip to French Camp with her director!"

IT WAS JUST A FEW hours' drive from Ole Miss, the University of Mississippi, to this little crossroads town on the Natchez Trace, French Camp. In it, a school, some houses, and a visitor center, for some odd reason. I say odd because I cannot for the life of me think of a reason the average person should want to visit this town. The visitor center is cute, though, with all sorts of gifts and history on the area. It just seems an odd choice of location for a visitor center. Like I said, I cannot imagine who visits French Camp. But then again, I did. And I brought Lorraine.

Originally a camp for French trappers and traders, the area was settled as it was a natural crossroad for two well-traveled trails. Eventually the school, French Camp Academy, was founded. My ancestors and relations made up much of the student body in its early years. My great-grandfather helped build the school—literally, not figuratively. And you may remember that even my mother attended the school here and there during her well-traveled, multi-homed, military childhood.

"Oh, they tore it down, the power company did. It was years ago after we finally sold off the last of the old homestead," Wilksie said, not sadly, as she ladled soup from a terrine that would have looked at home in some cabinet in a butler's pantry in Balmoral.

When I called to ask her about the house, she insisted Lorrane and I come for just a light supper of soup and salad and sandwiches. She wanted to meet this pretty little girl I had kept hidden in Oxford. When we arrived, she showed us to a long room that had formerly been a hall or breezeway connecting two sections of the home. Lined with floor-to-ceiling windows on one side and gilded mirrors on the opposite wall, it now served as her mini-Hall of Mirrors, her Galerie de Glaces. It is also where she ate when she wanted to impress the girl her great-nephew was bringing home.

And by "homestead" she meant plantation, as her Scarlet daydreams and Antebellum dysmorphia never allowed her to recognize the small wooden single story farmhouse and accompanying acreage as anything less than a plantation. To be fair, in her mind it was rather grand, as Etty and Dock had worked hard to make a home out of that old house. Etty always kept flowers by the front windows and steps. And her roses! She had the most beautiful array of roses along the north side of the house. Every color imaginable. Dock kept a vegetable garden for the family between the side porch and the barn. And the barn housed the plow, Jasper, Millie, and the chickens. Well, it used to. Wilksie said it was gone now too.

"When did they tear it down?" I asked.

"Oh, they've been threatening to tear it down for years," she said dismissively. "I imagine they've done it by now. Why would you want to go back?"

"Curiosity."

"Oh, well, there's probably nothing to see."

"And because my mother told me to."

"Now see, that makes more sense." Wilksie laughed, "A boy must always strive to make his mother happy." And then she turned her eyes toward Lorraine.

Lorraine endured the interrogation with all the true southern-belle-debutante-pageant-girl decorum she could muster. She politely refused a glass of wine, opting for lemonade instead. She chose tea over coffee. And she made every appropriate and expected compliment on the china, silver, and furnishings.

Lorraine was also a ninja with her diversions and distractions as Wilksie tried to get personal, wondering aloud why my Nince had not spoken of this charming girl before.

It was time for us to get moving. We wanted the full tour of French Camp, after all. Wilksie urged us to stop at the visitor center. Mother wanted us to drive through the school campus. Nince wanted me to visit the cemetery. Wilksie also thrust more plastic flowers in my direction.

"They are silk," she insisted.

The flowers were placed on their respective graves. I said a few words to my grandfather and let him know where I was in school. I told him how often Nince reminds me that he would be proud of me.

"Are you going to be emotional?" Lorraine asked this question multiple times that day, or something very similar. It was very important to her that I understood she wouldn't judge me if I became emotional.

I placed some flowers on Brick's grave; I told him about lunch with Wilksie. And then I went over to talk to Dock and Ettienne. I introduced them to Lorraine, and I told Dock all about Rudie and Nince—her broken leg, and the fact that Rudie still thinks I play football. I told them we were going to their house, that Wilksie said it had been torn down, but I just wasn't sure. I told them all I loved them, and then I looked up and to my side and noticed Lorraine standing there, tears flowing down her face.

"Well if you're not gonna be emotional, I guess I'll have to." She laughed and blew her nose.

I wanted to scream, "Run!" But I wasn't sure, given her emotional state, if Lorraine would have gotten the joke.

_&_   _&_   _&_

Chapter 6
Divine Commentary of the Weather

The Stolen Summer of
Velma Irene Holloway – Boom

Wilksie called it The Stolen Summer of Velma Irene Holloway, or something like that. It was something she said years later, not during the actual summer. But she was correct. That summer was stolen from my grandmother, as was a bit of the glimmer in the light behind her eyes. That glimmer never quite returned, but was replaced by something else. Sadness for sure, but also something more akin to understanding, or percipience, or some other word that just doesn't or won't come to mind. She was both more cautious and more open. Adventurous but sad, as though she had found the freedom to do as she pleased but there was just nothing she wanted to do. Nince was always present when she spoke with someone, yet also very far away. Perhaps that is what it is to cross over to widowhood.

It was Boom-Pa, my grandfather, her husband, who stole first. He died from a heart attack brought on by the back-and-forth and back-and-forth and do-it-yet-again battle with cancer. Unless you are related and concerned about the genetics and passing on of said disease, it doesn't really matter what kind of cancer it was, does it? Because we all know it. We have all experienced it. Much like the funerals we have all been to. And they are often the source, the cancers, or the reason behind the funeral in the first place. That disease in all its guises has left its mark on all of us—with its scythe, its skeletal grasp, or shrouded smile. Boom-Pa had colon cancer. A life-long smoker, he had a few other issues as well. Somehow, lung cancer was not among them.

⌐   ⌐   ⌐

HE WAS BORN IN ACKERMAN or Weir. I always forget which one. And Mother always corrects me, impatiently, because she has told me she doesn't know how many times before.

"I don't know why you can't keep these things straight in your mind," she would say.

Regardless of my mother's ire, he was born in one and raised(ish) in the other. I say "ish" as it was only the first stop of the many homes of the many relations he was shuffled to during his youth. Daniel Boone Holloway was his name. He was always just called Boom. Maybe it's a southern thing, but it seems like half of my relations are named after animals, inanimate objects, movie stars, and now noises. But Boom served him well, especially in the Army where he ended up a tank commander during the Italian campaign. He mentioned to me once, when I was interviewing him for a report in middle school, that he was there when the people drug Mussolini's body through the streets. He was witness to so many things, he said—a thousand horrors lost or buried in his mind. He never liked to talk about it.

After Germany surrendered, he was in the Pacific. He was with the Air Force Division of the Army Communications and Command. Because of his red-green colorblindness, he was not permitted to fly. Boom was captured by the Japanese when their base was overrun on one of those many thousands of South Pacific islands that seemed to trade hands like hot potatoes among the Japanese and Allied Command. He was not a POW for long; his release was swiftly secured after two entire cities were leveled—the men, women, and children vaporized. The Japanese surrendered. I remember learning that the Japanese Emperor offered to convert his entire nation to Christianity. How sad that, in defeat, we feel we must relinquish our very souls. The war was over now on both fronts. And men who left as children were going home. Some of them.

Boom did. He had a wife at home waiting for him. Only she didn't. She gave birth to a kid who wasn't his. He left, and met my grandmother at an officers' club in Montgomery. The Maxwell Club, the same place where she and I ate before my life-changing attendance at the Alabama Shakespeare Festival's *Night of the Iguana*. It was Rudie who introduced them. King was there with his first wife, Kate. Everyone loved Kate. And Norma was there with her artist friend. They would eventually marry. But that night in the early summer of 1946, Boom danced and drank and laughed and fell in love with a skinny, awkward girl from French Camp, Mississippi. He thought she was just the cat's meow.

Boom went back to DC with Rudie. He was still in the military but was also attending school as an officer. King and Kate settled in the area as well. Norma stayed in DC after her divorce from the congressman's son; her artist friend was working for the government. Velma was not far behind. A few letters from Boom and a lot of encouragement from Rudie and Norma, and she was soon there.

It was a tearful day, a rainy day when she boarded that bus. Dock couldn't go, wouldn't go, to the bust stop. He just could not say goodbye to his Nince. Etty and India walked with her to town; Goodie carried her suitcase.

"I don't know how I'll manage without you, Velma," Etty cried into her daughter's shoulder as they embraced beside the old Greyhound bus.

"You'll manage just fine." Nince held back her tears. "Now kiss Daddy for me. And tell him I love him. And I'm sorry."

Etty stepped back and shook her head. "You and your brother. Like two dern peas in a pod. Always apologizing for being yourselves. That year y'all put up the cotton ... and the war. Rudie grew into his confidence. And he can charm the shine and the ding back into a rusty old bell. But I worry about you, Velma."

"Mama, I'll be just fine."

"I want more for you than that." Etty held her daughter's hand and squeezed. "I want you to want more."

"You be good for Mama, now. Don't let her write me that you've been acting too grown," Nince said to India.

Etty watched as her daughter boarded the bus and took her seat. Etty watched as the bus pulled away from the curb. And Etty watched as the bus disappeared in a low, lazy cloud of orange dust and memories. Velma did not look back.

Velma did not look back her entire trip to Washington, DC. She read her letters from Boom, and she watched the meandering orange clay roads of her childhood become hard, straight-lined streets and highways—planned, constant, predictable, and safe. Oh, she got off at a few stops—twice to stretch her legs and once to eat a cold supper. Etty had packed her a small basket with some chicken and pickled vegetables she could eat on the way. The small towns and cities and wide open spaces seemed to fly by as she worried over leaving Mama and Daddy behind. The rest she didn't care if she ever saw again. Norma and Boom were there to greet her. Rudie's girl Laura got Velma work at the Treasury. And let me tell you: The six of them were the toast of DC—in their minds anyway. And Velma thought she might be happy.

Fun times gave way to other times. Marriages, divorces, births, and a war in Korea. King and Kate were no longer together. They divorced after a series of rows that could never get settled. It was a "her money-his money-their money" thing. King wanted to get by on his talents and abilities while Kate occasionally accepted gifts from her relations that King did not appreciate. Kate wanted him to try to exact influence and assistance from the Mornay side of his family while King preferred the skills and ethics he learned from the Taylors. King did well for himself, though not well enough for Kate. They divorced. They tried to remain friends, but once Roni and Tina came into the picture ... well. King wanted that instant family and to settle down— and he got it.

Rudie and Laura soon married. Rudie traveled, but the couple was always ready to host a party or go out to the officers' club when he was in town. Norma and her "artiste" were also married. He settled into a cushy job with the government while Norma continued to do hair in the salon she now owned, thanks to her former in-laws. And Boom and Velma got hitched as well. He was at the University of Maryland in College Park—one of the District's many suburbs (though not as fine as Norma's Chevy Chase). Boom was working on a master's degree, courtesy of the United States Air Force.

And as marriages go, we cannot forget Wilksie's. She was still in French Camp. And if you were to ask Wilksie, hers was the only "proper" church wedding of the bunch. You may not even have to ask. My grandparents were married at the courthouse. While Rudie and Laura were married in a little chapel, it is true, only Nince and Boom were there, so Wilksie says it didn't count. Both of King's weddings were small, unassuming affairs. He was on leave in New York when he married Kate. And when he married Veronica, Norma went because she drew the short straw. Norma's second wedding was also a small affair, in the living room of the Chevy Chase house she and her artiste friend were already sharing—scandalous! But all the siblings except Wilksie were able to attend.

To be fair, Norma's first wedding was a family affair. And everyone from both the Taylor side and the Mornay side drove up to Memphis for the Society Event of the Year. Uncle Money's wife, Letitia, the woman who raised Etty and Gussie, took on the planning for Norma's wedding. Though Norma was her niece, Letitia always felt more grandmotherly to Etty's children. And while she organized all the lace and tulle particulars, Uncle Money negotiated that the bulk of the price tag would be carried by the groom's well-connected politician father. They wanted this match more than he did, after all, if you believe the rumors (which Wilksie did).

By all accounts, it was a spectacular affair. All of Memphis society came out for it—and all of French Camp society was there as well. Even Vernon, Uncle Duck's boy. That's right, Uncle Duck, Vernon, and Irene all came to the society wedding. Vernon made quite the splash when he asked one of the bridesmaids to dance. She screamed and fainted. Irene brought a cake.

Ettienne felt as though she were at a Hollywood movie premier. All of the ladies in their fine gowns and furs, the gentlemen in their tuxedos and top hats—it was easy for her to delude herself into thinking she was sharing the room with Cary Grant and Katherine Hepburn; Olivia DeHaviland and Joan Fontaine; Laurence and Vivian … it was the shriek and the thud of that poor girl hitting the ballroom floor that pulled her from her fantasy.

"Don't tell your father or my brother," Ettienne whispered to her daughter, Velma, as they sat on a well-cushioned bench watching some unlucky girl cry her way through a dance with Vernon. "But one day, I'm gonna have a nice, fine fur coat."

"Where're you gonna wear it in French Camp?" Velma asked.

"I don't know ... around the house." Etty giggled. Velma did too.

After the weddings, it was children—my mother being the first of the grandkids. Debbie. Debra Blythe Holloway. The Blythe was for her father's mother. Debbie was born in that back room Livie and I slept in. Boom was in Texas when his daughter was born. He did not get to see his little girl 'til she was almost four months old, and then again when she was two. Velma and Debbie followed Boom to Newfoundland and Oklahoma and back to Texas. Velma gave birth to Gene in Texas. My mother was shipped back to French Camp because of the difficult pregnancy. They were soon reunited and traveling the country once more—and even the world. With Boom still in the United States Air Force, they were a well-traveled family.

Mother recalls two things from her time living in England: the crowds and the parade for Queen Elizabeth II's coronation and the excitement her mother showed as she saw it all. The two of them drank tea from a fancy tea set Boom had purchased for Nince and watched it on television the entire day. It was one of Mother's favorite memories.

And she remembers the other American family across the street from where they lived. Boom never liked to live on the base; he preferred to "live where the people lived." There was a little girl Mother's age who was also American. They went to the same American school. Every day they walked together to the school, and then they would walk home. But they were not allowed to play together, Debbie and this other little girl. Boom would not hear of it. That girl's father was an enlisted man, not an officer. So there was that. But even if that were not the case, and this girl's father had been an officer, just like Boom ... Boom's choice of expression to label the man was more of a Mississippi term than it was a London term, so Mother and the little girl could never be friends.

They were back in French Camp for a spell, at least Debbie, Gene, and Nince were. Boom was in Alaska. He was not working on the pipeline like Wilksie's husband; Boom was monitoring the Russians. He did get to see Brick while on leave. Brick and Boom; Boom and Brick; the Pride of Mississippi in Alaska. And Debbie was able to learn that her London expressions and way of speaking went over about as well as Boom's Mississippi-speak did in London. Debbie was not the English princess she longed to be, and she was competing with Bitsy, who was a true princess from the South, crowned nine times in four different pageants.

But as it turns out, farm life was actually the perfect life for these two princesses; it prepared them for the world outside of fairy tales and romances. There were not a lot of princes or knights for them to encounter. And they had to battle their own dragons. Life was not going to be all tea parties and roses. One had to milk the cow if one wanted cream for the tea, and one had to shovel something else from the cow for the roses. And they did. They had to milk the cow, and they had to muck the stalls. They did this right alongside Rudie's son, Eddie, and Bitsy's twin brother, Conrad. And they did this right alongside the kids from the sharecroppers too. They were built-in friends for their built-in playground or kingdom.

And play together they did. The metal roof on the barn was their slide, the ladders and rafters and open windows were their jungle gym. They even had a pool. The pond. The one with all the snakes. It was also the watering hole for the cows on the other side of the pond. Between the orange clay bottom, the splashing children, and the cows dropping what cows do ... it was not a clear pond, not the kind of pond in which one might imagine finding a pair of swimming princesses or mermaids.

But swim, they did. And get in trouble for it? They did that too. Switches had to be picked, chores were given, and punishments remanded every time they got caught. And when you had a little brother like Gene, you were almost always caught. If someone was gonna get their leg scraped on the metal roof when sliding down, it was Gene. If someone was going to step on a sharp stick or bottle in the pond and cut their foot, it was going to be Gene. If someone was going to get wrapped in a hose and piece of fence, get two puncture wounds on their ankle, and then convince everyone they were going to die because they were bitten by a moccasin—it was going to be Gene. In later years, Debbie would wonder why her children took after her whiny, accident-prone brother. But now, she just took care of him. She just took care of everybody.

Debbie was the teacher when they played school. She was the mother when they played house. And she taught, minded, nursed, and schooled her brother, cousins, and the kids who lived another life down that orange clay road, just around the bend. I don't understand what the difference was between that enlisted man's daughter in London and the sharecroppers' kids in French Camp; it is an oddity of facts and circumstance I just can't wrap my mind around. Maybe Boom just never knew. I find that unlikely; parents always know. They just choose not to see.

Boom would eventually return, and Velma would be so excited. Always the same, Boom would arrive and it seemed like the whole of French Camp would descend upon the family farm. He would be home for just a few weeks, but oh how everyone celebrated! And then Boom and Velma would bundle up the family, pack them in his '52 Dodge Coronet, and head to their next destination. It was the Georgia coast, then the middle of Florida, and then west Central Alabama where Boom and his family finally settled. Despite being in the middle of "Bama" territory, both Boom and Nince preferred Auburn although Nince still held an affinity for Ole Miss. And of all the places they had lived, even London, their little country home overlooking a creek somewhere between Aliceville and Eutaw ... it was the place they both loved. It suited them. And it was, after all, The Big Compromise.

I didn't learn of The Big Compromise until sometime after my grandfather had passed. A good sometime because I was visiting with my grandmother after college, sitting in her kitchen while she made her famously buttered eggs and infamously weak coffee. I flipped through a black three-ring binder my grandfather had filled with papers and documents and a few pictures of Boom throughout his career in the military, both Army and Air Force. He was rather dashing with his Cary Grant hair on a more rugged face—like William Holden or Cornel Wilde.

"Boom-Pa got a divorce?" I read with astonishment, as this was information I had never been told.

Nince whipped around from melting an entire stick of butter for five eggs, her face red and flushed with embarrassment. She almost looked like a cartoon character as you saw the color change starting at her neck and moving right on up. You would have thought we caught her talking on the phone in the closet with her boyfriend.

"They did not have any children," she said adamantly.

I laughed and so did she, eventually. And then we chatted about my grandfather in a more honest way than I ever had before, with anyone. She told me that he divorced "that woman" and that, although she was pregnant, it was not his baby. He was devastated at first, but his friend Rudie soon introduced the two. Boom and Velma apparently hit it off right away.

"He liked that I was tall and that I wasn't fat, like his first wife," Nince said proudly. "Do you know she gained over thirty-five pounds with that poor little bastard child she was carrying? I only gained fourteen pounds with your mother and seventeen with Gene. A woman should never gain more than seventeen pounds."

I learned that, in addition to being color blind, he was designated as a DSM-I with a diagnosed "gross stress reaction." This would be a precursor to post-traumatic stress disorder. It was a further reason for his inability to fly. And oddly enough, despite being in the Air Force, Boom did not like to fly. He preferred his two feet on solid ground, and he preferred whatever vehicle he was in to be on solid ground too. He didn't even like boats, although he loved to fish. Oh, and when we were little, he would turn his little Datsun pick-up truck into a roller coaster.

ᔕ   ᔕ   ᔕ

"DO THE ROLLER COASTER, BOOM-Pa!" Livie would laugh.

"Make us fly!" I would giggle.

And Boom-Pa would speed up as fast as his little Datsun would go; fourth gear (there were only four) and the engine revved up high, screaming for all it was worth. Boom-Pa would take those curves and hills of those Alabama roads with such breathtaking speed. Then, for the briefest of moments ... weightlessness, like floating in air, as we crested some of the steeper hills. Maybe Boom liked to fly just a little bit.

Nince and Mother never approved. But for Livie and Boom-Pa and me, it was our time. It was our thing. It was our fun. Boom-Pa was never anything but fun for me and Liv—and he made everything fun—from weeding and picking vegetables in the garden to chasing armadilloes around the yard. Boom-Pa took us fishing off the dock using cane poles. We would hold those long pieces of cane, fishing line tied to one end, and watch the red and white bobbers dance so delicately on the surface of the water before being suddenly snatched from below.

And of course we rode the roller coaster on the way home from getting bait and cokes at the store. I can't really remember the store, I get it confused with that one back in that podunk

Florida town Derwood had us live in. But I remember the smell—rotting potatoes and crickets. It's funny how smells can thrust us back in time. Back to another place. A distinct yet gauzy picture. A snapshot of a nauseating and beautiful time.

Boom-Pa was the fun-loving, cuddly grandparent. And when you climbed up on his lap to watch TV or have him read you a book, you could smell his aftershave. His aftershave and cigarettes and pecans ... those scents always bring me back to Boom-Pa. He always ate pecans. He and Derwood would sit for hours drinking highballs and shelling pecans while Mother and Nince shopped.

There was this one particular nutcracker Livie and I liked, or I at least found it fascinating; it was a pair of women's legs. "You put your nut right between her legs and squeeze," Boom-Pa would instruct and laugh. Derwood would too. Mother and Nince would scold or roll their eyes or tell them to behave. I kept trying to figure out why the "in-between-the-legs" looked like they did.

Livie and I would play an invented game of "roll the ball" on the floor of the den. Born out of mind-numbing boredom as this was our grandparent's dream home, not ours (we preferred the one back in Florida with the pool), the game is as simple as its moniker. Livie and I would take turns choosing from my collection of Star Wars action figures or Little People (those legless and armless little characters made by Mattel or Playskool or maybe it's Fisher-Price.)

"You always pick Princess Leia," Livie would tease.

It was true. I always chose the Princess Leias. But I also liked to make Luke and Han hook up. I was a strange little child.

Sometimes the nutcracker was part of our game too. So after we chose our "people," we would choose sides of the room. Livie would set her people up on one side, and I would set mine up on the other. And then with a small rubber ball or golf ball or even a tennis ball, we would roll the ball (hence the name) to try to knock down our opponent's people. There really wasn't a whole lot going on between Aliceville and Eutaw.

✒   ✒   ✒

"LIFE IN ALABAMA IS WHAT saved him," Nince said seriously as we sipped her atrocious coffee and flipped through the large three-ring binder. "And you grandkids."

His PTSD was first manifested in dreams. Boom would become restless in the night and mutter all sorts of nonsense—at least Velma thought it was nonsense. Or gibberish. But that gibberish turned out to be Japanese. Boom would speak in Japanese in his dreams. It seemed comical at first, and Velma would laugh about it with her sisters or other officers' wives. But some nights he seemed so distressed. Even when he woke up, it took him a few moments to come out of it. Velma would do her best to calm and soothe him until he would settle, relax, and come around. Until he didn't.

A terrible storm in Oklahoma woke the family from a deep sleep. The wind howled and the rain battered the windows; the thunder was so explosive, it shook the house with every crash. And Boom woke up shrieking. His eyes were open and wide and filled with terror. It was the first time he became violent.

"An animal in a trap," Nince said. "He was like a terrified animal caught in some painful trap, so of course he lashed out at those trying to help."

Velma shielded her child and took the brunt of his terror nearly forty minutes before she was finally able to calm her husband and soothe him back to sleep. And once he was asleep, a battered Velma took the car. She and Debbie traveled the rest of the night back to French Camp.

These episodes came in waves. A stressful day or an argument or bad news and the dreams would start. The yelling in Japanese, the sleepwalking ... sometimes it would go away. Sometimes it would not. Something would trigger it—a backfiring lorry in London, a hunter's rifle in Georgia, a crash of thunder in Newfoundland, Texas, Oklahoma, or Florida ... and the violence would begin.

"It stopped when we left Florida. It was a few years after you were born. I told him it had to. Or I wasn't going with him, not this time," Nince said, unemotionally, matter-of-factly. "We moved here. We created a home for us—and we relied heavily on help from the church and from the base. Your grandfather received a lot of help there. I did too."

∽   ∽   ∽

I WAS JUST STARTING HIGH school when he died. Livie was just graduating. Mother had a large party planned for Livie's graduation. Nince and Boom-Pa were unable to attend because Boom-Pa was in the hospital. He was having a bad reaction to his latest round of chemo. It was his second time around with colon cancer, and the chemo was taking its toll on his body, though, surprisingly, he never lost his Cary Grant hair. It didn't even thin. But he did have a heart attack, then he was in a coma, and then his heart failed again in the hospital. It just quit, his body did. And he was gone.

"Yes Mother. Thank you. I will. I will. Yes. We will. I love you." I heard my mother on the phone with Nince that afternoon.

Mother's plan was to have the party for Livie and then head up to Nince and Boom-Pa's the next day. We knew Boom-Pa was in the hospital; that much they had told us. So of course they could not come for Livie's graduation. But the plan was to have a party for Livie—and we stuck to that plan. Somewhat. We attended Livie's graduation and then came home for the party. Derwood's mother and grandmother were there, and his stepfather. Mother's brother, Gene, had come as well. He looked terrible. And he brought the boys, a thing he was not supposed to do as both Mother and Nince thought they were far too young. And of course Livie's friends were there, and a few teachers too. It was quite the celebration of Livie's accomplishment of getting through a school neither of us remembers much about.

It was after midnight when Derwood asked us to come upstairs and check on the things we needed to pack for our trip to Alabama. He was pale and quiet and he looked as though he had the weight of the world on his shoulders. I guess he did. He certainly had the weight of his wife's emotions on his shoulders. It was his job to explain to us that our Boom-Pa had passed earlier that day. That they didn't want to tell us then because they didn't want to spoil Livie's day. That we were leaving for Alabama immediately; we hoped to be there before dawn.

NINCE WAS THE FIRST OF The Three Sisters to lose her husband. It was a rite of passage, a ritual of sorts that all southern women must endure if they are going to join the club. One simply cannot become the dowager of their community if one still has a husband. That is just not how it works. She accepted her role with great aplomb. She was appropriately graceful and lovely in her assorted black attire. She wore her reserved, yet strong demeanor as simply as she wore her pearls. She greeted mourners and well-wishers, she was appreciative of each casserole and plate of chicken delivered to the home. She arranged and rearranged the flowers. And she spoke to perhaps every member of that small unincorporated Alabama township. We must have looked like the ne'er-do-well relatives from Florida when we arrived in two cars filled with luggage, blankets, and pillows—three adults, two teens, and Gene's two young boys as well. And we did everything we could to test Nince's grace and reintroduction to society as a widow.

It began with angry whispering. Everyone had gone to sleep somewhere in Nince and Boom-Pa's small yet comfortable retirement home above the creek, on a partially wooded three acres. I was on the couch in the living room, and I could hear, almost plainly, the whispers coming from the hall closet. It was something about Gene and my mother. Somehow my mother had failed in getting Gene there appropriately. He was supposed to leave his two boys with his ex-wife. Nince felt they were too young to be there. And he was also supposed to have brought at least a suit jacket for the services and funeral. And since he had the boys with him, "Well, they could've had a decent set of clothes for their grandfather's funeral too, don't you think, India?"

And so Derwood and I were tasked with finding appropriate clothing for Gene and his two boys to wear to the funeral of our patriarch, Daniel Boone Holloway. We went to one of those local clothiers that small towns often have, not like a Macy's or even Sears, more like the name of some random family that has lived in the area since forever and this was their great-great-grandfather's old dry-goods store turned department store on the square. I worked with the plump and bespectacled overly friendly sales clerk on getting the appropriate attire for my uncle. Meanwhile, Derwood chased two rambunctious children as they climbed through racks of clothes, tossed all of the balls in the sporting goods section, and tried out every toy in the toy aisle. Gene broke down into tears about every five minutes. I did what I could to comfort him, but I was busy trying to get the clerk to leave me alone and fit my uncle. Despite the winks and nods and side glances from the man who looked like he and Judy Garland may have once saved a school by giving a show in the barn, my fourteen-year-old self was not interested in hooking up with a middle-aged closet case in the wilds of western Alabama. And certainly not during my grandfather's funeral.

We returned at just the right time for the boys, Gene, Derwood, and I to be late to the first viewing. The boys were deemed too young for this, and they sat in an anteroom of the funeral home with some books and toys and Roni. Apparently, in addition to her piano and organ playing skills, Veronica, King's wife, was also very good with children.

Livie was in a black dress, her eyes revealed the signs of an argument with Mother. And Mother's eyes revealed the signs of yet again letting down her mother. And Nince stood at the head of a greeting line as people flocked in to pay their respects.

Livie saw me walk in with Derwood; Gene sort of slunk off to the anteroom with Roni and the boys; she made a beeline for me. After thoroughly abusing our mother for a moment, we began to do what we do best—people watching along with the resulting colorful and petty commentary. Of course this garnered the attention of Rudie and Norma, and, soon enough, the four of us were laughing a little too loudly. Nince shot Mother a glance. Mother shot Livie and me a glance. And Norma snorted, ignoring the scolding looks she received from her sister and niece.

And then it all sort of fell apart for Liv and me. But very slowly. It was all rather surreal really. It was as though everything moved incredibly fast, but in slow motion—frame by frame—like the events of that moment were being dragged through the pull of an ocean tide. That resistance you feel when your open hand tries to push through water. The light in the room began to move, to breathe as things do when one is submerged. The light dances, the walls seem to inhale then exhale, bending with each breath, and the sound is a muffled deep tone beneath crashing waves, vaguely distant yet closing in on you all the same.

"I want to go with the children," the newly created Dowager of West Alabama said hauntingly. Her face should have been floating in a glass ball above a table on a ride at Disney.

The Dowager stepped between Livie and me, her arms slipped into ours as her black lace-gloved hands clasped our upper arms. I could almost feel the cold of her hands through the lace and my jacket. Livie's eyes met mine as we were guided toward the back of the room, toward a wide opening that led to yet another room. (Why are funeral homes just a maze of rooms and flowers and fragrance?) Our legs locked, Livie's and mine did, as we realized what was happening. She was taking us to see Boom-Pa.

Livie and I tried to resist; our legs pushed forward and we both leaned backward ... but like the moon and the tides, our grandmother's pull guided us into the room. Those in line to pay their respects parted like the Red Sea—or Dead Sea, I suppose—and Velma Holloway was cast as Moses in mourning, leading her people to the body. I understand the need to mourn; I don't completely see the need to look at the dead body. It is a weird custom, really, one that I have grown to accept and recognize as a part of the ritual we call a funeral. I don't really like it, but it is what it is. A viewing. Of a dead body. And for two somewhat sheltered kids bookending their high school years as well as their grandmother, it was a lasting impression of their Boom-Pa.

And there he was, Boom-Pa—our grandfather. The man who bought us cokes from that rotten-potatoes-and-cricket-smelling bait shop. The man who took us on the Datsun Roller Coaster Express. The man who happily drank high balls with my father and a sexy little nutcracker. And the man who lived terrible nightmares in a language that was not his own ... there he was. In a box. A nice silver one, but a box just the same. And he was dead.

"Look at him," Nince whispered deeply. I'm sure her mood was one of a grieving widow with her grandchildren, but I only heard Judith Anderson telling Joan Fontaine to look at the portrait of Mrs. DeWinter.

The graveside service was the next day. We all piled into various vehicles to make the trek to French Camp. It was an early afternoon service, to give us all time to make that trek across the state line into Mississippi and down the Trace just past Starkville, and on down to the old family haunts.

"You will go to Ole Miss, Randy," Nince said quietly as we rolled past the Mississippi State campus. "And that is all there is to that."

Norma winked at me from the front seat, and Rudie smiled as he drove. Livie was with us as well; we called it the fun car because we had Rudie and Norma. And the two of them did their best to keep their baby sister healthy, stable, and loved. And if that included a few wisecracks and inappropriate comments along the way, then Norma and Rudie were there for it.

It was warm, hot even, on the hard-baked earth of the cemetery. We all marched across the uneven ground, winding our way through family names etched in marble and granite—Taylors, Mornays, Edwards, and Stones. I stood amongst the names and the histories lying beneath the clay. I closed my eyes and breathed in the sweet, nearly overpowering fragrance of late spring and early summer blooms and fine fragrances worn by the delicate ladies gathered to mourn. And of course there was the Divine commentary on the weather ...

"God is sure smiling down on Boom today."

"What a beautiful smile from God to remind us all how loved we are."

"God is keeping us warm with his blessings for Daniel."

THE ORANGE CLAY RUTS WERE baked hard as pottery in the early June sun. Nince was surrounded by her siblings as we approached the coffin, suspended as it was over the gaping hole in the ground. Artificial turf or indoor/outdoor was used to offer less of a hole in the ground feel. They are an entire production, funerals are, complete with costumes and sets. There was a green tent for shade for the family; they always seem to be green or burgundy or black. And we were ushered to our assigned seats: immediate family up front; secondary family just behind; and the rest of the cloth-covered folding chairs were for the older and more feeble of the mourners.

I thought it sad that Nince had to essentially sit alone, up front, like she was on display. Her children were there, of course, but they were too busy mourning the loss of their father to offer comfort. Her siblings sat behind her. I mean, she knew they were there, but it seemed to me at the time a bit unfair to my grandmother to be left with her strongest support seated behind her. I listened to the twenty-one gun salute, the playing of Taps, and the presentation of the flag to my uncle by a rather handsome looking cadet. My eye caught my cousin Gio's at that moment, and we shared an uncomfortable nod.

Next up was the macabre garden party of standing about the cemetery in the blazing hot Mississippi sun, mixing and mingling with relations and family friends and those occasional folk who just like to go to funerals. Oh, they exist. I knew somebody once who did that. He raved about the food and he saved all the programs.

Livie and I stood with Gio and Roni. Gio was quiet that weekend, and less intimidating than he seemed the last time we had met. Perhaps it was the mood of the occasion or perhaps he had other reasons, but he was rather low-key and withdrawn as I recall. I almost felt sorry for him and I didn't quite know why. Livie said she still did not trust him.

Roni played the organ at that funeral too. It's funny how she willingly performed during all these rituals for a family that never really accepted her. She loved her husband, King, and she believed, deep down, that all of them were happy that their brother was happy. At least that's what she shared some years later at my grandmother's funeral. Mother and Gene stood with Bitsy and the rest of the Blondells. Conrad was there too, as were the other cousins.

There was no one from my grandfather's side of the family in attendance. If there was a cousin or distant relation, I am unaware. It struck me as sad. His parents were dead; I knew that much. And so were four of his siblings. Three others were scattered "too far" to make the trip for a brother they never really knew. I understood that his early years were difficult, but as I got older, and Mother became less guarded or less protective, I'm still not sure which, I learned more.

☙   ☙   ☙

AN ALCOHOLIC TRAVELING DOCTOR FOR a father and a brilliant, ahead-of-her-time mother who broke under the stress of being a brilliant, ahead-of-her-time woman in a world very much meant for men. Were she born a half-century later, she would have been a physician or physicist or the head of some medical science institute. Instead she was institutionalized, several times, and died a vacant woman after shock therapy and drugs could not control her moods—and a lobotomy was the final answer. Boom was just starting high school. He and his siblings had been traded from relative to relative between Ackerman and Weir, then God knows where ... until finally Boom just left. And when he left, he never went back. Only sometimes he would, in his deepest dreams. And these nightmares were not in Japanese.

🍥   🍥   🍥

NINCE WAS WITH HER SIBLINGS. She looked exhausted. And she wanted to go home. All she wanted to do at that moment was to go home—her childhood home—and hug her Mama and Daddy. They were not doing well that summer. Age and heat do not always mix. So they were to stay home during the funeral; it was just too hot. Dock was impatiently waiting to hold his little Nince and protect her from all of the sadness he knew she felt.

"We're expected at the church for a supper." Wilksie smiled behind the veil of her large black hat. She looked like a beekeeper. Livie laughed when I made the comment, Norma snorted, and Mother gave me one of her withering looks.

"I don't want to go," Nince exhaled.

"Oh I know. But you will." Wilksie continued to smile her trademark smile. "And you'll be glad you did."

And with those words, we were loaded back into the cars, and off to the little Baptist church we went. A white clapboard church with an impressive steeple and red door. We pulled into the partially shaded, partially paved parking area and made our morbid, black clad procession into the fellowship hall. It was a large paneled room with metal folding chairs and tables, a large counter with several pass-throughs to a more impressive and operational kitchen. And if you looked through one of those pass-throughs into the kitchen, you would see an impatient Dock Taylor. His tall, broad-shouldered, and painfully thin frame was giving instructions to some quietly smiling yet clearly irritated lady. He was telling her how to make the biscuits. He was not about to stay home while some ninny messed up the biscuits.

"Make 'em touch there, you gotta make 'em touch," he was saying, "but not too friendly, now."

Ettienne could barely be seen; she was in a wheelchair. She was also giving instructions—these were about the chicken that was being fried. "No skin, we don't want any of the skin." Etty insisted on her chicken being skinned because, "feathers are where chickens hold all their nasty, and you can't get all the feathers 'less you skin 'em."

If grief could make a sound of relief and longing and joy, it would have been the sound Nince made upon seeing her parents, not at home, but at the church making the fried chicken supper for Boom's after-service meal. Southerners so often pride themselves with the decorum and decency they display—rely upon, even—in the face of catastrophe. There was no care for appearance when Nince shouted for her parents.

"Mama? Oh Daddy ..."

They met by the door to the kitchen, and my grandmother vanished in the arms of her father. Dock and Nince held on to each other, while they each held one of Ettiene's hands. There was not a dry eye to be seen. Even Wilksie was seen to dab a kerchief beneath her veil.

We ate supper in the fellowship hall: chicken and biscuits and salads of both the congealed and not congealed kind, several versions of funeral potatoes, stuffed eggs, and casseroles. And cakes. And pies. Livie and I sat with Gio, who pointed out and identified the folks Livie and I didn't know.

"Which one is Vernon?" Livie asked, scanning the room.

"He's over by the buffet," Gio answered and pointed.

"Yes, look at how ugly he is," Norma said, walking up to the three of us. "We are headed back to Mamma and Daddy's to get them settled. It was a long day for them."

"Are y'all talking about Vernon?" It was Nince; her face was puffy and her eyes were running with mascara from her earlier tearful reunion. But now she seemed somewhat lighter. "Look at him. He's always been so ugly."

Livie, Gio, and I stifled our laughter; Nince gave us a wink, and Norma hurried us along. We walked back out into the late Mississippi sun. The sky would turn as fierce and orange as the clay earth it hung over, marking a brilliant Mississippi sunset to further mourn the loss of one of Mississippi's sons. God sure painted the sky bright for Boom.

We piled into various vehicles. Livie and I got stuck with Bitsy by virtue of the fact that we were hanging out with Gio. It was fine. She blessed our hearts several times on the short drive—our mother's too. Not soon enough we were pulling off the two lane highway and onto the crushed clay drive of my great-grandparents' home.

Missing Panes and Yellow-Meated Watermelon

The house was empty; it had been for years the day Lorraine and I made that trip home. It was never actually my home. I had visited several times as a child, and perhaps even more as an adult. But I was always a visitor; it was never home—not for me. The house stood, as it always had, small but proud, on the highest part of this plot of land tucked between an old road that was relocated long ago and the newly erected powerlines.

"The power company took it down years ago, I think." Or something like that; Wilksie's words stuck in my head. How many times had she said it? How many variations on the same theme had I heard? I heard it at Brick's funeral. I'm almost certain she said something to us at lunch. I would hear it again at the funerals yet to come.

Clearly they had not torn it down—the house. They had not kept it up, either. The shrubs and old flower beds were overgrown. Scrub pines and volunteer pecan saplings had invaded where Etty had kept her roses. She had quite the array of rose bushes lining one whole side of the house; they grew so well there. Reds and oranges, yellows and whites, soft pinks and a pale, pale lavender. Nince had recovered one of them after Etty passed. It died one winter when Derwood never got around to planting it. Nince had passed the winter before, and I believe Mother may have been in the hospital—and it just never made it into the ground. Mother was rather displeased when she learned Derwood had killed her grandmother's rose bush.

Wilksie managed to save her fair share of Etty's beloved roses before the power company swooped in. She had several of them moved to her home in Kosciusko. They transplanted well, and she spent many a summer cultivating new and interesting blooms of her own.

Rudie took one as well for his home on Booger Holler Lane. There were just a scraggly and leggy few along the side now. Clearly they were not the grand display they had once been—a veritable rainbow of color along the north side of the old home. If I had owned my own place instead of renting an apartment in Oxford, Mississippi, or maybe if I had lived in the home my friend Wesley did, Cedar Oaks ... but I always regretted not trying to take one of the rose bushes with me. Also, I didn't have a shovel.

The path to the front steps was covered with a suspicious looking ivy ... that whole three leaves and berries thing. The brick steps—made from the finest Mississippi clay and laid by one of the finest Mississippi masons around, Dock Taylor— were in need of his services once more. Crumbling on one side with another of those volunteer pecans trying to take root in the mortar, they were also covered with that same suspicious three-leaved vine.

The front porch was small, really just that crumbling set of steps and a covered landing at the front door. And the front porch was actually not originally the front porch. That distinction fell to the family room that had been closed in and converted so many years before I was born. It was closed in to make room for a growing family. Although I never knew it any other way ... and now I'm babbling. It's funny how memories can do that—like a meandering brook that seems to start from nowhere and then wander off to some other place.

Skirting the ivy and making our way to the side of the house, we stood in the late spring sun. The warm and golden light spattered through the branches of the old pecan tree that stood just as tall and proud as I remember. Even the old picnic table was there. That soft buttery pine color had aged and weathered into the brown-gray of dried sage or rose hips from a potpourri satchel left in a drawer or trunk for far too many years. I could see ourselves sitting there, eating at a watermelon my great-grandfather had just cut open.

🌊   🌊   🌊

"YELLOW-MEATED," DOCK DECLARED WHEN HE split the green melon in two. Instead of the expected bright pink flesh, a deep rich yellow was revealed. "... you ever seen one of 'em?"

I hadn't. But my cousins had. Vivian, the youngest of my mother's generation, was actually closer in age to Livie than she was Debra or Bitsy. And Gio, who was closer in age to Liv than me, I think he was there too. Even then, there was always something funny about him. Which is doubly funny because funny is the word Mother always used when she asked me to tone it down. "Don't be ... funny."

Gio was always nice enough, charismatic for sure. He went through a creepy phase, dealing with his own demons and questions and confusions I can well imagine. He eventually grew up to be a preacher, of course. I say of course because aside from the stereotype that one can form in their mind, this was a fitting career choice for Cousin Gio. From an early age, Gio knew exactly the direction he would go. And he was a Southern Baptist too—the correct kind of Baptist if you are from Mississippi. Yes, my sister and I long suspected him to be gay. A very incorrect thing if you are from Mississippi. But somehow the one (Southern Baptist Preacher) allows many to ignore the other (Southern Baptist Homo) as the two worlds are just not compatible. And none of it is really any of my business.

And none of it really matters either, not when you are sitting cross-legged on the picnic table, eating a half-moon of yellow-meated watermelon, and listening to the words of wisdom as issued by a gentleman named after a wooden structure erected over water.

ᔐ ᔐ ᔐ

I SQUINTED AWAY THE MEMORY as I stepped away from the old picnic table, overgrown as it was in some other ivy. It might have been poison. It might have housed snakes. Lorraine and I walked toward the side porch. A brief flash of Wilksie dressed as Maleficent flashed through my mind, surrounding her castle with not vines of thorns but poison ivy.

"Are you going to be emotional?" Lorraine asked. "Do you need a moment?"

I laughed; she did too, and we stepped up onto the side porch. The white of the windows and siding had long since lost its luster. The blue of the porch ceiling was peeling and faded to a light gray. The flowers that used to line the house in beds were gone, of course. And that old Pepsi refrigerated cooler filled with cokes—for some reason it popped into my mind—gone.

I told Lorraine how I remembered the old cooler, and that, to this day, I am mostly certain that this is a real memory and not one mixed up with one from my Dad's old office in Florida or perhaps that old store in some small town where we once lived. I laughed at my explanation. Lorraine gave me a hug.

"Bless your heart, you think of the strangest things."

A bird had made a nest above the window, and a few wasps had made some nests as well—those gray paper-like structures stuck in corners and nooks and crannies. Ettienne would have had Dock out there with a broom for sure. There were two windows onto the porch, and the door, of course, which was locked. I immediately thought of my mother and the cemetery.

"What are you giggling at?" Lorraine was not giggling.

"I'm being emotional," I said.

The window over the sink in the kitchen was covered in a film of dust and dirt ... and also a spider web. So that window was out. The other window, next to the door, led into the dining area. There was not the same film covering this window, though it was still not clean to Etty's standards. Nor was there a spider. And neither was there a pane of glass in that one corner of the window. I looked at Lorraine. She looked back at me. I reached in. I unlocked the window and it lifted.

"Are you goin' in there?" Lorraine asked.

"Should I? I mean..." I wasn't completely sure now. "Is it breaking and entering if the window is already broken?"

"I don't think it's breaking and entering when they are your people."

My people. They were my people. My family. Lorraine was right. I climbed through the open window from the side porch into the dining area off the kitchen. The smell is what hit me first. A damp and musty smell. The smell of old kitchen grease and steam and a million meals prepared and eaten and washed up. The smell of peeling wallpaper and old shelf liners. The smell of laughter and crying and loud discussions at the table. The smell of chicken frying or corn bread baking. The smell of sweet tea and black coffee. Of tobacco. Of catfish. Of freshly made biscuits that were not too friendly. Of time. I climbed through that window. I stood up—and it all came rushing back.

When I think about memories, what they actually are—I always liken them to a stone dropped in a still lake. The memories are not the stone, the cold hard rock that just sinks to the bottom, no—they are the ripples. They are the ripples and the waves and the currents and the tides—and they will carry you where they will.

And they did … to the night after we buried my grandfather.

✎   ✎   ✎

"RAIN-DE …" SHE WHISPERED. "RAIN-DE." IT was Nince. She was sitting on the edge of the sofa I was sleeping on in her parents' living room. "Are you awake?"

"Nince?" I let my eyes open and adjust to the darkness of whatever early morning hour it was.

"Are you awake? I was worried I would wake you," Nince said.

"Yes, and saying my name repeatedly while shaking me and asking if I'm awake is a great way to make sure you don't wake me."

"Maybe you should go back to sleep."

"Maybe you should tell me why you are up?" I asked more than stated.

"I'm going for a walk."

"Would you like me to join you?"

"I think I would, Randy, if you don't mind."

I didn't. "I just need to find …"

"Here." She handed me my shoes and socks. "And bring your blanket; it might get cold."

I got myself ready while Nince tied her own sneakers. I

quietly stood and made my way to the door while she lifted the window to the left. I looked at Nince; she looked at me. Both of our expressions seemed to ask, "What the hell are you doing?" Nince's look had more conviction, so I followed her through the window.

"The door ..." she said, still whispering, once we were down the front steps and heading toward the road. "Daddy always made sure it squeaked a bit when it opened, so we wouldn't sneak out."

"Did y'all sneak out a lot?" I asked.

"Mmm." she said, but didn't really answer.

It was noncommittal. I think it was more of an "it depends." I am sure Rudie and Norma snuck out every chance they could get, dragging Nince along with them. King was just too grown and Wilksie too spoiled; they probably didn't care about the squeak and just used the front door. But "Mmmm" was the only answer I got.

We walked in silence for a bit, down the side of the dark highway. The sliver of a moon did little to light the way. And at whatever o'clock in the morning it was, there were no head-lights. We walked maybe fifteen or twenty minutes—it's really hard to tell when walking in the dark—before we reached our destination, the cemetery. The tent was gone, and so were the chairs. And so was the hole in the ground, though the dis-turbed orange earth was still covered with a piece of that unnat-ural green carpet.

Nince took the blanket from my hands and threw it over the chain-link fence, then she started to climb over it herself. I looked around the darkness as though there was someone there to explain to me what the hell was going on. But alas, there was not. We were deep in the backcountry of Mississippi, climbing into a cemetery, in the dark wee hours of the morning. There was nobody there but me, Nince, and the current residents.

Nince began spreading the blanket out on the ground next to my grandfather. And then I finally got my answer.

"I just needed to lay down next to my husband one more time. Is that silly? Weird?"

"Yes and no. Mostly no," I answered honestly, and sat down next to her.

And we talked, my grandmother and I; perhaps it was the first "adult" conversation we had ever had to that point. I was a child before. I guess I was a young man now. She told me about Boom-Pa's last days in the hospital and how she would lay with him in the hospital bed, even though he was unconscious. (Boom-Pa had been in a coma since the heart attack.) But she would lay there and hold his hand and talk to him.

"I told him everything. Everything I never told him, Randy," she said. "I told him everything I was angry about. The things I was sad over. The things he did to hurt me. And I told him about the other things—the good things. The things I appreciated more than I ever was able to share. And I apologized; oh Randy, I apologized for so many things myself. He did not have an easy life. His childhood was a nightmare."

"And then he had them as an adult too, didn't he?"

"Yes. He sure did." It was almost a whisper.

We were silent for a moment, and then I felt the need to ask, "Do you want me to leave you alone for a bit?"

She shot me a quick look and said, almost laughing at the ridiculousness of it, "Are you crazy? We are in a cemetery in the middle of the night. I'm not sitting here all alone. Now keep watch, I'm going to lay my head down for just a moment."

"What am I keeping watch for?"

"Well, I'm sure I don't know. Just do it. And stop talking about it. You are making my beautiful moment with my husband all creepy."

We both burst out laughing. I wish I had a photograph of

that moment other than the one that resides in my head. We were silent after that. Nince even fell asleep, although she would deny it. And I sat, with my grandmother's head on my legs, and I played all my favorite memories of Boom-Pa on the projector of my mind. The deep purple darkness gave way to silvery light, and then that burst of fiery orange and yellow as Mississippi showed off her glorious sunrise.

"Where have y'all been?" Mother suppressed the screaming tone because she was speaking to her mother as well as her son, but she was flying hot with that kind of mad a parent gets when their worry over their missing child comes to an end because their child is now in front of them ....

"I thought it would be nice to take a walk to the cemetery. I asked Randy to join me," Nince replied with a tone so light you would think she was talking about a walk through the park after church.

"Told ya!" Dock said from his chair at the kitchen table.

"Daddy said he saw you crawling out the window." It was Norma. She was holding her coffee mug with two hands, enjoying the show.

"Why did you crawl through the window?" Livie asked me. She was sitting next to Dock at the table, biscuit in hand.

Norma answered: "The door squeaks, so we always used the window."

"Which was stupid, because so do the floorboards." It was Etty this time. Her housecoat looked as though it had devoured her as she made her way into the kitchen.

Dock stood laughing at his wife's comment while Norma got her mother her chair. He sat back down when his wife did. "Yep. That's how I knew you left, Nince. I got up and started the biscuits when I heard you in the hall."

"Did you know where we were going?" Nince asked her father.

"I figured you were going to see Boom. If it had been another boy you were sneakin' out to see, I would have said something. But you had Randy with you, so I reckoned yall'd be alright."

"A fine chaperone," Etty giggled.

"Well, you had us all worried," Mother interjected.

"Now Debbie, I told you where they were."

"Oh, Daddy had it all figured out." It was Norma again. She decided to bring the tension down, mostly because she wanted another biscuit. "He told all of us where y'all were. And he went to making breakfast like nothing was wrong. So I did the grits."

"Thank you, Norma." Dock nodded his agreement to all she had said.

"You're welcome, Daddy," Norma said, then she turned to look at me. "Your mother sent your father out to look for you."

"Oh great." Nince rolled her eyes. "And now who's gonna go look for Derwood?"

"Oh, let's just eat and we'll worry about that later." It was Mother. She had stopped being angry. There might have even been a glimmer of pride as I caught her gaze while spooning some grits onto Etty's plate.

Derwood showed up around lunch time. Nince had saved him a biscuit with a slice of ham.

☙   ☙   ☙

OH, BUT THAT WAS A long time ago. And the table we all sat around that morning was gone now. So were the chairs. I didn't go through the cabinets and cupboards, but I'm sure they were bare. It was dusty, yet oddly clean for a house that had stood empty all those years. I had been in abandoned dwellings; we took over an old funeral home once in a downtown area for a theatre company I worked for. It was our rehearsal space. It had also been a hideaway for the homeless, some animals, and probably ghosts. It smelled like death and shit. But where we stood, in the kitchen of my great-grandparents' home, all you could smell was stale damp air and a bit of whatever was blooming that wafted in through the now open window. And the memories ...

We walked toward the hall; the floorboards creaked beneath our weight. Lorraine asked if I thought it was safe. I told her they always creaked. I showed her the room my mother and Nince were born in, and we walked through the rest of the house—the small blue room that was Dock's and the small pink room that was Etty's.

"Didn't they share a room?" Lorraine asked.

"He is too big to be sleepin' next to; besides, he kicks and talks and gets up earlier than I do," is how Etty would have replied.

"Look at that old trunk." Lorraine pointed toward the corner of the room.

"Oh neat!" I exclaimed, and we walked over to investigate.

"What do you think is in it?" Lorraine asked wide-eyed. "Whose was it, do you suppose?"

"I'm guessing my great-grandmother's—this was her room."

"Oh, maybe it was her trousseau. How romantic would that be?" Lorraine mused. "Where did they go on their honeymoon?"

"What were they doing that she would need a whole trunk for her trousseau?" I laughed.

"A trousseau can be a hope chest too, silly."

We locked eyes and we both took a deep breath before opening the old trunk in Etty's room, and like Geraldo Rivera's finest moment ... it was empty.

We explored the rest of the house, the front room or parlor as Wilksie described it. I told her where everything was that I remembered, and where other things were based upon the countless stories I had heard. More and more came back to me with each story I told.

"Oh, we should check to see if the barn is still standing," I said as I headed back toward the kitchen.

"We should probably load that trunk into your truck," Lorraine suggested instead.

"We should steal my great-grandmother's trunk?"

"It's not stealing, Randy. She obviously left it for you." Her head tilted a little to the side as she stared at me. She was very serious. "I can feel it."

And so we did. We carried that trunk through to the kitchen where we still chose to go through the window rather than the door.

"Fingerprints." Lorraine suggested.

I gestured with a wide reach at everything else we had touched.

"Well, there won't be any on the doorknob." She was already backing out of the window.

We didn't go to the barn. And we didn't walk around to the pond. We loaded the trunk and drove away and took the interstate back. It was a narrow and winding road to Winona, but still quicker than the Trace once you got on I-55. We didn't speak much until we got to Granada. Then I just checked in to see if either of us were hungry. We weren't. When we got off the interstate in Batesville, Lorraine decided she needed a drink.

"Like a coke or a drink drink?" I asked, offering to stop at the pop-up Mexican chain or the convenience store.

"Mmm," Lorraine answered. "I need a mimosa and a bath before I decide on my drink. Probably a scotch or a gin. It's been an emotional day; I'm a wreck."

The Stolen Summer of Velma Irene Holloway – Etty and Dock

"Do you need something to drink?" Nince woke me from my "just resting my eyes." My head leaned against the damp glass of her silver Pontiac; I tried to right it.

We were driving back to Florida. Back to Derwood and Mother's. Mother and Gene had decided Nince wasn't ready to go back to the house so soon after Boom-Pa's funeral. Nince reluctantly agreed. Though she wasn't looking forward to an empty house, she was looking forward to the quiet which, now, she was not going to get. I volunteered to ride with Nince to keep her awake for the drive.

"Maybe a coke; maybe a cheeseburger," I managed through a yawn.

She yawned too. "I want some coffee."

We pulled into a truck stop somewhere in Georgia. Nince ordered coffee and a biscuit. I ordered an orange coke and a cheeseburger. I apologized for falling asleep; she said she enjoyed the company *and* the silence so it was okay.

"I'm only staying a few days," Nince blurted out in a moment of quiet. "I need to get back to Mama and Daddy. Wilksie says they aren't doing well. She said they had made a real effort to be healthy for the funeral ... I thought they looked so old."

"They are old," I said. "They earned it."

"Yes." She almost smiled. "And I need to do some things at the house, my own house, before I try to tackle anything in French Camp. And Wilksie is on me to help with Mama and Daddy."

"She takes care of them I guess?"

Nince harrumphed. She did, I swear to God; she

harrumphed. "Wilksie's checkbook takes care of Mama and Daddy. We all help too, of course, financially. India manages the folks hired to care for Mama and Daddy. The same bunch of ..." she whispered the next word and looked around to see if our dark-complected waitress was within earshot. "... that have always worked for them. Living just down the road in those old shacks. Only now they help cook and clean instead of working in the fields. India doesn't cook or clean."

Nince left money on the table and we both went to the restroom. I took an acceptable stall near the back of the long restroom. It was the cleanest of those available. There was a door by the last stall that led to a locker room and showers for the truckers. I prepared the seat with the appropriate amount of tissue for hygiene, pulled my pants and underwear down, and prepared to sit.

"Yeah boy. Take care of business here then let's step back into the showers and I'll clean you up." A low, deep, serious voice came from the stall beside me. "Now touch your cock."

"Uh," was about all I managed to cough as I turned to my left and saw a puffy semi-hard pink penis coming through a hole in the side panel of the stall.

"Or you can touch mine now, boy." He laughed.

I did not laugh. Nor did I touch any cocks. Not that day. I pulled up my pants, and I ran from the restroom without even washing my hands. I only managed to pee, so at least it wasn't gross or anything. I suppose that is debatable.

"Are you okay?" Nince asked. "You look flushed."

I still couldn't articulate much beyond "Uh."

It was another three hours and forty-nine minutes before we pulled into my parents' drive. I carried in the bags, hers and mine, and I put hers in the guestroom. When I came out of my own room, Nince was on the phone. It was Rudie. Ettienne had taken a fall in the night. She was in the hospital with a broken hip.

"I'll leave right now, Rudie. I can be there in sixteen hours." Nince was pacing as far as the cord would allow. "What? No. You didn't have to do that. Well you shouldn't have. I could have drove. Fine. I'll ask Debra." She hung up. "Rudie has purchased tickets for us to fly to Jackson tomorrow. We will leave out of Orlando."

"Yes. I know. He called an hour before you got here," Mother said. "I am already packed."

"Yes. I know," Nince answered, not warmly. "I would like it if Livie and Randy would drive my car back to my house. Rudie says he will run them over to French Camp."

"Livie is only 17 years old."

"I know how old my grandchildren are."

"And Randy is 14."

"I know how old my grandchildren are." The two women stared at each other for what seemed like an eternity. Nince finally added, "Randy always falls asleep in the car anyway. So Derwood will have to go too, I suppose."

Mother looked like she was going to say something, but she didn't.

"I'll ask him before I go to bed. But we have an early flight, and we're meeting your brother at the gate. So if you'll excuse me." Nince kissed her daughter on the cheek. She gave me a long, tight hug before thanking me, and she left for her room or to find Derwood, or maybe the bathroom. Mother looked terrible.

The drive to Nince's was quiet. I slept. Livie slept. Derwood drove. The plan was for us to stay the night at Nince's, and Rudie would come by the next morning and pick us up for the drive to Jackson. They had taken Etty all the way to Jackson for her hip. Livie and I were to be dropped off at Bitsy's on the way. We were too young to visit in the hospital apparently, or at least that's what we were told. Well, technically Livie wasn't; she was almost 18. (Nince knows that.) And I was certainly mature enough, at least I thought so. But Mother laid out the plan and it was not to be altered.

But sadly, even the best laid plans may come to ruin when life and death intervene. Ettienne passed before we made it to Nince's. Nince and Mother, thankfully, made it to Ettienne before she went. And Rudie was not coming to get us. We were taking Derwood to Montgomery, and he would fly back home. And Livie and I, at our respective ages, were to drive Nince's car to French Camp.

The main service for Ettienne had to be held in the auditorium of the school, French Camp Academy. Now, that sounds grander than it was. It was not like it was an opera house (or the old movie theatre that actually was torn down by the power company); it was a high school auditorium. But it was also the largest capacity room for a funeral attended by all the Taylors, all the Mornays, all the cousins and relations, and all of the folks who had ever worked their land or cared for them in the end. It was probably the most multicultural event French Camp had ever experienced since the French were there trading with the Native Americans. The procession by the casket seemed endless.

There was a private service for family at the church. And not a soul for thirty miles around failed to bring a dish for the supper. We ate good, though "nobody's chicken is as good as Etty's." We heard that remark often that day.

Dock wasn't at the supper. Nince and King took him home. He was out of sorts, having moments of confusion thinking that Nince was Etty and that it was Nince who had died. Telling him the truth only made him realize his wife of over 70 years had passed away—and he had to go through that shock all over again. It was Roni, King's wife, who thought to drive to the shanties and get Goodie. Goodie was what they called Thurgoode, the grandson of the man who taught Dock to lay brick. He had a way with Dock. He learned the mason trade from Dock as his grandfather was too old to pass it on to him. And he made good, making quite a business for himself, being the only trained Black mason for several counties wide. While the Whites wouldn't hire him, he did very well as an alternative for the minorities who lived in the area. In addition to a large Black population, Mississippi was home to a growing Mexican one as well. Goodie made enough money to buy some land from Dock and rebuild the old shack he called home. He did the same for his mother and sister, purchasing a small plot of land and rebuilding the old shanty that once stood. Dock helped, or supervised these projects, but Goodie did the work.

Etty would send for Goodie, just like she did his grandfather, whenever Dock had one of his spells. Goodie would find Dock in the barn or on the picnic table or down by the fields and they would talk.

"What do I do, Goodie?" Dock had asked Goodie countless times before. This time he was sitting on Etty's bed. Goodie was on a trunk beside a dresser. "I'm all mixed up. And Etty ain' here to set it right."

"Yes, Mr. Dock. I know. We just gotta talk it through 'til it's all straight in your mind. That's all. Like we always do."

And they did talk. For a long time. Livie and I were back from the church by the time Goodie was ready to go.

"Children, you'll walk back with him, won't you?" Nince asked us.

"Of course," I answered. "It's not past the cemetery," I whispered to Livie who was stepping hard on my foot.

The moon was maybe three-quarters full, certainly brighter than when Nince and I walked only twelve days before. But Livie and I weren't going to the cemetery. Tonight we were walking Goodie home. And on the way, he told us stories about Dock and our grandmother, some we had heard before, but these stories were from his perspective. Like the time he rode the horse that threw Rudie and broke Nince's leg; Goodie was the young man who caught the horse and rode for help. It was a different version of the story than I had heard; Livie acted as though she had never heard it. Maybe she hadn't or maybe she just forgot.

Perspective is everything, I realized, even more so for a man like Goodie. Given my own proclivities, I knew I always had to look at every scenario, every situation, with a more cautious or suspicious eye lest I be caught unaware or unsafe. I always know where the exits are, I don't sit with my back to doorways, and I listen carefully to the innuendo or dog whistle or left-handed compliment. I don't know why it didn't dawn on me until then that this was especially true, more so really, if you are a Black man in the South.

Livie asked a lot of questions. It was like this was her first time to French Camp and she was getting all the history. If the visitor center had been built then, I would have taken her. I had questions too, lots of them, and I was eager to ask them all. But I didn't—I dismissed them, each of them, as my mind kept going back to one question. It turned over in my mind and pushed all other thoughts and questions away. I did not know how to ask it.

"I'm good here, kids. Thank y'all so much. I can see the light from my porch from right here. I appreciate you."

"Yes sir," I replied.

Livie said, "Of course."

"Y'all are in for some changes," Goodie said. "And you gonna want to be there for Nince."

"You call her Nince, too?" Livie asked.

"That's all Mr. Dock ever called her. So that's all I've ever known."

"What did you say to Dock to finally settle him down?" This was my question. I had been pondering it the whole walk. I had finally worked out how to ask but I didn't know if I should. It just slipped out. Turns out all I had to do was ask.

"Well, Dock did say you were grown past your years." Goodie smiled at me before the deep brown of his eyes grew serious, yet softer somehow. "He told me he couldn't understand a world without his Etty and his Nince in it. I told him Nince would be just fine. She has her family to care for her. She got you two to look after things. But right now he needed to think about going home—going home to Miss Etty. His heart has done broken and died and has already made the trek. It's just waiting for his mind to catch up."

And so it did. Just six weeks later, Dock Taylor's mind and body joined his heart and Etty. Mother was preparing for surgery and unable to go to the funeral. Derwood wasn't leaving her side. And Livie had had enough of funerals. She did offer to drive me to the airport, Derwood bought me the tickets, and Rudie was able to pick me up this time. He and Norma met me in Jackson.

Dock's funeral would have been remarkable if it hadn't followed two others. The same throngs of people from Etty's funeral, the same casseroles and congealed salads. And the same comparisons to Etty's chicken, with the added remembrance of Dock's biscuits. We spent less time at the old home and more of it at Wilksie's. I think the siblings needed a break from French Camp. And maybe from the memories too. They each kept to themselves or their spouses. Or in Nince's case, me. She was an orphaned widow, and she had no one else. At least that is what she told me, a few times, right after she would tell me how proud she was that I represented my family.

I stayed an extra week with Nince; I helped her and the other siblings with the mundane chores around a house none of them had lived in for longer than two of my lifetimes. Of course they shared stories and memories with me, though the best ones were when they almost forgot I was in the room. Like lowering a veil, they revealed themselves just a little differently. They were siblings, after all, and they were siblings before they were ever anything else.

Nince Goes Home

The man who sang for Nince's service, whose name I cannot remember—he sang beautifully. "Ave Maria," one of my grandmother's favorites. Schubert wrote the music in 1825 when it was titled "Ellen's Third Song." It was written for Walter Scott's poem, "The Lady of the Lake"—a useless bit of trivia, yet one that struck me as fascinating as I stared out of the blue stained glass of Nince's church, trying to think of anything else. The gray outside had not cleared. My turn to speak had not yet come. But Nince had lived on a creek that emptied into a lake, and I casually pondered if that was why she chose this song.

Betty-Girl stepped up to the microphone and thanked Brother Richard (It was Brother Richard; that was his name.) for singing so beautifully. "And now we have a special treat as a member of the family has some words of comfort and love for us all."

I pulled the folded piece of paper from my coat pocket and I stood. Mother looked over at me proudly; she nudged Derwood, who looked up too. His eyes were bloodshot and he wiped something from them. Livie sat tall and gave me a little nod. And Gio walked up to the microphone and began to speak. Betty-Girl walked over to me and not so subtly indicated I should sit and be respectful.

"Family is speaking," she spat.

I slowly sat back down onto the hard wooden pew of my grandmother's church. Gio's words were ... lovely. And he painted a lovely picture of a strong Southern lady who embodied family and Jesus and generosity. A true steel magnolia with her fortitude and femininity. A God-fearing woman, a good Christian lady, a mother, a grandmother, a sister, and a wife. He said all these "somewhat true of any Southern matriarch" things—things any Southern family would want said about a beloved female member who had passed. They were not specifically about or for my grandmother. There was nothing Velma Taylor Holloway, nothing Nince about Gio's eulogy at all. It was sterile. It was hollow. It was not what I was going to say.

The time for my role in this pageant play was now. Betty-Girl indicated with a snap of her fingers that my cousins, Gene's boys, and I should rise. We followed Brother Richard and two other gentlemen I did not know to the casket. Betty-Girl hastily arranged us around the casket and told us to walk with dignity out the door. So the six of us wheeled my grandmother out of the church like she was contained in some fancy version of that audio-visual cart with the boxy television bungeed to the top of the cart, VCR underneath, one wheel always squeaking and wobbling—like back in high school. I had a moment of eye contact with each of Nince's siblings as we did our best dignified walk out of this overly large small town church on the Alabama side of the Mississippi border.

Livie wouldn't look at me. She was fuming and staring daggers at Betty-Girl. Derwood kept his head down. I never saw him so sad before, so moved. And Mother, she just watched the casket, her eyes never left the vessel that contained her own mother's body. And as the casket glided by, squeaka-squeaka-squeaka, because of the very dignified loose wheel (Brother-Man Bill probably found it on the side of the road in Vicksburg.) ... Mother's right hand reached out and let it glide along the casket as it passed. Her gloved hand hung in the air, as if in a frozen wave goodbye.

◢   ◢   ◢

"Pictures!" Betty-Girl screamed as she walked into the room—a bright white room with white linoleum and white folding tables with white folding chairs. When she initially led us to the room, she announced it was normally the 'Kindy Garden" room, as she gestured to the white board on the wall which had, no lie, "Kindy Garden Room" written in blue. "Now I know y'all do things a little different in French Camp, but we always use this room for the reception and Dead Spread after a funeral. It is far more bright and cheery than the fellowship hall, which is set up for the Christmas Bazaar anyway. Help yourself to refreshments." She pointed at the array of store bought cookies, a vegetable tray, and onion dip. There was a bag of chips too. The solo cups for the punch or Kool-Aid were black, a more respectful choice for the Dead Spread. Also the green and red ones were being used for the bazaar ...

Norma and Rudie shared a judgy glance about the room with me, and I pointed at Wilksie. Wilksie looked as though she was walking on a pathway lined with front-lawn reproduction furniture, cotton blends, feces, and yellow fever. One hand held a kerchief over her veil-covered nose while the other hung in the air, as if she could somehow not touch each particle and molecule that floated about. Norma snorted and Mother shot me a dirty look.

"Pictures!" Betty-Girl announced again. And she went about placing us in a variety of poses, groupings, and arrangements. She had the siblings up front, seated, Mother and Gene with their respective spouses on either side. This one had to be repeated, as Mother explained to Bettty-Girl that she had sent Derwood to Piggly Wiggly, just around the corner.

"I just don't understand ..." Betty-Girl tapped her clipboard with those autumn frost nails; she had a schedule to keep. "You're telling me his mother-in-law is up in here layin' a corpse, and he is out shopping for groceries?"

"Yes." Oh, if Mother only had her pink hair brush or wooden spoon.

Eventually, however, Betty-Girl got all of her pictures—including the ones with all the grandchildren, that for some reason included Gio, his mother, and the rest of her fake blonde posse. In every picture I was placed behind Bitsy. And in every picture my face was hidden by her hair. It was high and buoyant, after all.

We were to make the trek now, back across the state line, through Columbus and Starkville (where I would hear no more Ole Miss pronouncements), and finally down the Trace. Nince always preferred the Natchez Trace. We were standing on the steps of the church deciding who would ride in what vehicles for the caravan back. It is a more important aspect of family transportation than one might initially imagine. Car ridership has a pecking order, a social status. One does not want to be stuck in the wrong car.

I desperately wanted to ride with Norma and Rudie. They were with King and Tina. King was the oldest; he was clearly upset that his baby sister was the first to go. He was the spitting image of Dock; he looked just as I remembered Dock looking at Boom-Pa's funeral. It is amazing how such a large and powerful man can look so small when he's lost a part of his heart and soul.

I watched as Mother stood talking to Brother-Man Bill and Betty-Girl. She handed Brother-Man an envelope, and he pulled her into a godly bear hug that was clearly neither enjoyed nor appreciated by one Ms. Debra.

"What's in the envelope?" Livie asked.

"Oh, probably money. Brother-Man Bill has got to get paid,"

Joan, that middle sister, said. Livie and I had to ride back with Joan and Roni. It was not the fun car. We had been demoted.

"What is that Mother's giving to Bitchy-Girl?" I asked as we watched our Mother extricate herself from Brother-Man Bill's hug and offer Betty-Girl a small wrapped gift.

Betty-Girl also hugged our Mother; a less than genuine smile was plastered on her face. Mother wore the same expression as Wilksie had when Wilksie walked into the "Kindy Garden Room." The embrace was fleeting. Mother raced down the steps and got into the car with Derwood, Gene, his wife, and the boys. Now that was truly not the fun car.

"AAAGGGHHH!!!" Betty-Girl shrieked and threw something after Derwood's car as it pulled away from the steps of the church.

"What the hell?" I asked Livie who was laughing hysterically in the backseat.

"Remember when Mother sent Dad to Piggly Wiggly?"

"Oh yeah, when he missed that one picture."

"Yes, she sent him to get a parting gift for Betty-Girl." Livie was smiling so hard her face must have hurt. "I have never seen Mother so happy with Dad. She said he picked the perfect thing."

"What was it?"

"A tube of Preparation H."

THE RIDE TO FRENCH CAMP turned out not to be so bad. While still not what I would consider "the fun car," it wasn't the not fun car either. Joan was filled with gossip. Mostly she dished on Gio and his "choir director friend." They had taken up residence together—roommates, they called themselves. And then there was Conrad. He finally made his last payment to that awful woman with whom he found himself in a charade of a marriage.

"She sued for divorce on the grounds of fraud. And you know what that really means." She nodded at us knowingly.

"Because of the antiques?" I asked.

Livie spluttered out something resembling a sneeze-laugh-cough combo.

Roni, who was driving, looked over at me and smiled.

"What?" Joan asked before dismissing the question and continuing on about how, now that Conrad is free from the awful woman, he has had more time to spend with Wilksie. "He has refurbished her whole house with some rather nice pieces and art too, of course."

Livie didn't care about what Joan had to say anymore and dove into self-preservation mode; she went to sleep. I faced forward in the passenger's seat next to Roni, who held both hands on the steering wheel. Joan pulled a book from her black clutch purse and pretended to read. We were silent for a bit, a good little ways actually, when a lovely piano solo came over the radio. Roni leaned forward, turned it up just a bit, and hummed along. I smiled and told her she played lovely at Nince's service today.

"Is it much different playing the organ versus the piano?" I asked.

"The piano is more straightforward while the organ offers more options. I always recommend learning piano first."

"Why did you play?"

"Oh I always loved music, even as a little girl ..." Roni began.

"No. I mean for my grandmother. Y'all never really got along."

"Mmm. Yes," she replied. And we were silent for a moment before she spoke again. "Randy, I loved your grandmother very much. But, yes—things were complicated."

I listened as she told me about her first husband, who had

died in Korea, leaving her with a young daughter. Veronica played piano at one of the clubs King and Kate would frequent. After one particularly egregious row, Kate left with a saxophonist and King sat at the bar.

"He drank several more highballs while I sipped a glass of wine. Eventually we turned to coffee," she reminisced aloud. "But we talked well past dawn. My mother was so worried. She was keeping Tina and didn't know what could have possibly happened."

Veronica would not even offer a first kiss until his divorce was final. She was certain that would deter him, sending him on his way looking for someone more willing to kiss. He was not deterred. She explained to him that she was unable to have any more children; Christina's difficult birth and other complications left her unable to carry another child.

"I was sure that would have done it. King wanted sons. And Dock wanted King to have sons," she said. "Instead he got down on his knee and proposed."

"So they were pissed that you married their brother," I interjected.

"Yes and no. That was the case for Norma and Wilksie." She smiled. "Dock and Velma had other reasons."

"What?" I asked, and noticed through the rearview mirror that Joan was no longer even pretending to read.

"Dock resented the fact that I would never give King sons. He never forgave me for that," Roni said plainly.

"And Nince?"

"Well, Velma could never forgive me for disappointing her Daddy," she half-sighed and half-laughed. "Ever."

"And here all this time I thought it was because you didn't invite her to that dinner party that one time." Joan couldn't resist.

"If the family did not accept me, would I have lasted this long? I've played organ or piano at nearly every significant family event since India and Brick were married. Yep, I played at your parents' wedding." She said that last bit looking at Joan through the mirror. "I play a role in this family. It may not be a leading role, but I have a role to play. That's why I lasted."

"And of course your love for King," Joan added. "Love is a powerful force."

"Oh it is." Roni said. "But Cassie loved Rudie. Oh very much, she did. There just wasn't a role for her to play."

*   *   *

"GOD WANTS US TO fiND comfort in each other's arms." I think it was Gio, or someone else said it as we gathered by the graveside of Velma Irene Taylor Holloway. It was cold, it was blustery, and it was doing that early-winter-in-Mississippi thing it always does … spit. It is not rain, it is not mist, and it is not "God's tears bathing us in glory." Or whatever else it was that Gio said while continuing to eulogize this generic southern woman he was passing off as my grandmother. It wasn't my grandmother and it wasn't rain. It was spit.

Mother held Derwood's hand. Gene was next to her on her other side, his family beside him. Livie was next to Derwood. Betty-Girl was back in Alabama so I was able to sit with my family this time. And Livie and I sat close, for both warmth and comfort. The service drew to a close, and the family gathered around the casket, hovering over that iron box resting deep inside a hole. The flowers were beautiful, a colorful spray across the silver gray of the casket and the sky. I pulled a handful of the blossoms from the arrangement and brought them to my nose. I said a few words in my mind—perhaps I mumbled them—and I reached into my jacket pocket for the folded piece of paper that held my disallowed words from the heart. I slipped it in the space between the top and bottom lids. Mother caught my eye, and offered a look so filled with emotional complication, pride, and gratitude. I had to step away. Lorraine would have been proud; I was emotional.

⌒   ⌒   ⌒

AND THEN IT WAS THE church. And the supper. A few really older folks managed a "Remember Etty's?" or a "These aren't Dock's." We didn't stay too long. Just long enough for Irene to get there. Her ugly brother, Vernon, was not with her. He was quite ill. But he sent his love, and asked about Debbie and her two beautiful babies.

There was a brief discussion over going to the house, but Wilksie poo-pooed that talk. "The power company was going to take it down. I haven't been in years. I'm sure it's gone," she said.

"There's nothing there but an old trunk," Bitsy said. "At least that was all that was there the last time Wilksie made me go with her. I don't know why she always goes back."

"Oh, I know." Vivian added: "She would make us clean, remember?"

"I know." Bitsy squealed her agreement in a Jayne Mansfield-styled coo. "Abandoned as it was, there was no point, really."

"I'm sure y'all are exaggerating." Wilksie smiled.

"No. The trunk is gone too. It was Etty's," Joan piped in. "You and Conrad went to get it because Conrad thought it might be worth something. And y'all discovered it had been plundered. Oh, Conrad was so upset, remember?"

"Plundered?" Norma asked.

"Made off with," Joan said, then whispered, "Stolen."

⌒   ⌒   ⌒

LIVIE AND I CONVINCED DERWOOD to take us back to the

hotel before we drove to Wilksie's. We wanted to change, and I wanted my own car. Even if it was a rental, I wanted to drive. And Livie wanted to be away from everyone else as well. So she and I took off and headed for the farm. I told her how Wilksie always says that the power company tore it down.

"She's been saying that for like 20 years." I laughed. "And yet it's always standing."

And sure enough, there she was—the old white farmhouse. Dock's mason work didn't look so good anymore. The picnic table was still there. And the barn, you could see a bit of metal roof covered in that lovely English Ivy of the South ... kudzu. At least it wasn't poisonous. The walls had long ago given up the ghost, and it was just a heap of rust and weathered wood and vines. But it was there. We walked to the side porch and crawled through the same kitchen window, and all the floors creaked, not just the ones in the hall. And after about five minutes, Livie was ready to go. She wasn't interested in the stories; there were no forgotten memories for her to find.

We went to Wilksie's. The party was in full swing, and each generation had sort of divided into their own groupings. Two Sisters, King, and Rudie discussed, laughed, cried, and argued over their Velma. Gene and Mother sat with Eddie and Conrad and the next generation of The Three Sisters; they were the only Three Sisters now, and it just wasn't quite the same. And as exciting as Tina, Gio, and his choir director friend were ... Livie and I were done. We bid our farewells and left.

"What are you doing?" Livie spat as we pulled next to the cemetery.

"I need to talk to Boom-Pa," I answered. "And Dock and Etty."

Livie stared at me like I was insane.

"They had to hear what Gio said. And I don't like that. I need to talk to them. To tell them."

"I'm not getting out of the car."

"I won't be long."

"Have you always been this weird?" Livie shouted and I heard the car doors lock behind me.

I walked over to the fence; the gate was locked. I swear I think I may have climbed this fence more times than I ever used its gate. Whoever it is that does those things to clean up after the graveside service must have already done it; the tent and chairs were gone. Everything was smooth and flat once more, save for the bit of unnatural and uneven green spread across the orange mud.

I stood beside Nince first. Her name was there; Wilksie even got the dates engraved already. "She moves mountains, that Wilksie," I said to Nince. "Did you read your note? It's from Livie and me. We made a few changes from when we read it to you before. I hope you like it. I'm sorry for what Betty-Girl did to your funeral. But Nince, you gotta hear what Derwood and Mother did ..."

And I told her. And she and I laughed. I know she did. Livie honked the horn, and I waved at her as I walked over to Dock and Etty. I moved a few more flowers from my grand-mother's grave onto theirs. And we discussed how happy they must be to have their baby girl.

"She was the glue of this whole family, I know," I said to them. "But don't you worry; India is doing her level best to take charge. She'll make sure we're all cared for."

I walked back to Boom-Pa and arranged a few of the flowers for him as well. Finally, he and Nince were laying beside each other once more. I'm sure that brought her peace more than anything. I told him that. And then I sat down in the cold, wet, orange clay—and I told my Boom-Pa all the things Gio didn't.

I didn't notice the rain had picked up until I heard my sis-ter blowing the horn again. The cold, icy drops mixed with the warm dampness already covering my cheeks. And then it stopped. I was under an umbrella and a hand rested on my shoulder.

⁂

"WHOSE WAS IT?" LORRAINE ASKED, blowing her nose and pouring herself another mimosa before stepping back into the tub.

It was a surprise Lorraine had for me when she insisted I come to Oxford after Nince's funeral. You see, she had finally gotten her degree from Ole Miss. Not her Master's; she got that and her PhD in Memphis instead. Nope, it was her MRS. She met her husband in the law library, just like the sorority girls and two of my Three Sister cousins (not Bitsy, clearly). Only Lorraine met her husband by accident. They dated several years before tying the knot and buying a cute, historic bungalow in Memphis. Lorraine and her husband had also recently purchased and renovated an old house in Oxford. The house had been divided long ago into apartments—the same ones Lorraine and I lived in during our years at Ole Miss. It was to be a bed and breakfast; they would make bank during football season. But she insisted that there must be a panel that could slide back in two particular bathrooms, to allow for a thin bit of wall to be exposed. And through that thin bit of wall, those who knew could bathe together in their own separate tubs in their own separate baths in their own separate apartments. She fought with the contractor for weeks over the design. We were testing it out now.

"Would you believe it was Thurgoode?"

"Goodie?" she asked.

"Yep." I laughed. "He scared the shit out of Livie when he walked up to me in the dark. That is why Livie was honking the horn. He said he heard everything I said to my grandfather. He had come down to talk to Dock. He figured Dock might need a talking to after his daughter's funeral."

"So what did y'all do?"

"We went back to his place. His daughter got me a sweat-shirt and shorts to change into; I was pretty soaked." And I explained how Livie and I sat up with Goodie and Melinda, and we talked all night long.

"It's good to be with family at times like these," she said quietly.

I agreed, and I sat back and let myself disappear under the water.

❧   ❧   ❧

Chapter 7
The Ondines of French Camp

Ondine

There is a play I love—*Ondine*. It was written by Jean Giradoux in that glorious theatrical era of the '30s, and is one of those marvelous play within a play, meta-theatrical-type pieces. I was enthralled from the start. I was introduced to the play by the costume design professor at Ole Miss. She had a name, but Lorraine and I always called her Coco Rosselini. But this was before I knew Lorraine, and before I committed to theatre, and Coco Rosselini was just the Bohemian chick who taught Introduction to Theatre. For some reason she took a liking to me and to my dry humor, and she encouraged me to get more involved.

I quickly realized after devouring the play that it was very familiar to me. It oddly brought me back to my childhood and to a magical world I could only see in a vague echo of memory but I could feel all over my very being like being under a warm shower. *Ondine* let my mind swim back to undines and mermen, and I was hooked. I soon discovered it was based on a short novel by Friedrich de la Motte Foqué, a fairy tale really—*Undine*. Of course I read it too. And the recollection of a hardbound version, in a soft blue cloth, on a shelf, in a really cool house with two beautiful statuettes came flooding back.

I did theatre all through high school, and I did community theatre and semi-professional gigs, too. I had done summer stock and had even earned my Actor's Equity card. (Actor's Equity is the professional union for actors and stage managers.) But I never considered it as a career—or as a major, for that matter. I was in my second year of undergrad, and I still hadn't declared a major when I took that intro course with Coco and "History of Film" with Dr. Singlet. Coco Rosselini had an incredible style and ease when it came to teaching all of the various eras and styles and manners of costumes and furnishings throughout history. I eventually took every class I could from her, and I asked her to be on my thesis committee. And Dr. Singlet, the chair of our department; he was a tall, thin, rather paternal sort of man. He presented film, especially early film, with such a focus on history, current events of the time, and a theatrical spin—I loved his classes too. They were like rainy Sunday afternoons on the couch with my mother—and whatever classic film we were watching.

It was the two of them who most influenced my decision to declare a major, and then pursue my MFA. My focus was directing. I was already getting more gigs in the summer as a stage manager than an actor, so I had moved away from that fantasy. And directing allowed me the freedom, the creative freedom to imagine an entire new world and the ability to see it realized. And control it, guide it, create it ... Stage management and directing were what attracted my attention and my talents the most. Acting was just too personal. You have to feel.

Coco Rosselini always said that I missed my calling as a designer to push this directing thing. She knew my tastes and she knew my style, and when I made my pitch to my committee, some years later, for *Ondine* to be my thesis project for my

Masters of Fine Arts in Directing—it came as no surprise to Cocco Rosselini. Dr. Singlet listened intently as I made my pitch; his eyes were closed.

"Have you ever let yourself sink while soaking in a bath, just sink down and allow your shoulders, your neck, your chin, and now your face to slip beneath the surface ... and you open your eyes. The way the showerhead now seems to sway; the picture to the left of you seems to breathe ... "

"I don't take baths." It was Ho-Ho. She taught acting. She wasn't on my committee, but, for some reason, she always inserted herself into our meetings. I think the chair knew I did not like her. (To be fair, she did not like me either.) He just enjoyed watching us interact.

"Or you're swimming in a pool or a lake, a spring. Maybe the warmth of the ocean ... "

"Well, which one is it?" She interrupted for the sixth or seventh time. "I don't understand the symbolism you're trying to achieve here."

"I think the point is ... " my chair finally interrupted her interruptions, "that it could be any of those, based upon an individual's experiences."

"Well, in my experience, it burns if you open your eyes underwater," Ho-Ho countered.

"Was it Holy Water?" I often think of really funny things that may not come across as appropriate or kind, and then I look around the room and realize I said them out loud.

Apparently she understood the symbolism in my comment. The other members of my thesis committee did as well, each chuckling or smiling. Coco Rosselini was actually belly laughing.

"I'm sorry," she said. "I guess no one else found that as comical as I did."

Ho-Ho stopped talking, picked up her things, and glared at Dr. Singlet and me as she stormed out of the office.

Dr. Singlet sighed deeply, took his glasses off, and pinched his nose. I knew he was going to lecture me. "You have got to figure out a way to get along with her," was all he said.

I opened my mouth to speak; he silenced me with a look over his glasses.

"Or I will." His tone was less ominous than his words would indicate—or at least that was what I thought at the time. I would learn otherwise.

～　　　～　　　～

"THAT WAS IT? HE DIDN'T give you a lecture—he just left?" Lorraine was laughing deeply on the inside about my exchange with Ho-Ho. She would laugh on the outside later; she was too busy gathering information now.

"Nope," I said, drinking a glass of not-too-bad-on-a-grad-school-budget champagne from a bottle Rhiannon left for me with flowers, a balloon, and a hot bath filled with bubbles. "No lecture."

"Okay, let's see, what about Squatchy?" That was Lorraine's name for the head of the directing program. It was originally King Henry because of his size and gout and Raymond Burr meets Burl Ives good looks, but Lorraine decided in the end: "He just looked too Squatchy to be anything else."

"He was fine. He doesn't usually see things the way I see them, but he is always interested to see what I come up with." I took a sip of champagne.

"Did he laugh about Ho-Ho?" This was clearly most important to Lorraine.

"Yes, he laughed about Ho-Ho," I said.

"Cheers!"

"Cheers."

"Al probably looked to see what Coco Rosselini did," Lorraine surmised.

She was not incorrect. Al was the technical director. He didn't get a nickname because he was just very Al-like. He was a hyper-masculine kind of man—a very odd thing to be in the theatre. But what he did for the theatre was on the mechanical side so I guess it fit. To be fair to Al, we tried to give him the nickname Al the Mechanic. Then briefly we called him Mike, but we always went back to Al. He just couldn't hold onto a nickname. What he could hold onto was any and all of Coco Rosselini's design choices and everything else she might say or do. We all suspected Al had a thing for Coco Rosselini.

"Ginger Kelly?" Lorraine moved on to the head of the dance program; she was also on my committee. And she was also not named Ginger Kelly.

"Ginger Kelly can always manage a straight face." I laughed. It was true; she had a deadpan style that would make any version of Wednesday proud.

"And of course I already know what Coco Rosselini said," Lorraine added.

"How do you know that? I haven't said."

"Dummy ... do you really think Rhiannon picked out that champagne? I made her put the André back and get balloons and flowers instead." Lorraine mocked insult at my inability to have realized all of that. "Coco Rosselini told her that your play choice was approved. Ondine it is!! And she said that Coco Rosselini also said you'd have more of a story to tell."

We raised a toast to the approval of my thesis project, and we made a toast to Holy Water. And then we agreed to get dressed and go to the City Grocery after our baths.

"Are you gonna fuck that Cedar Oaks boy?" she asked.

"I don't know," I answered honestly. "Are you gonna fuck that bartender?"

"I don't know."

We both sunk down into our respective tubs and watched

the bubbles slowly rise to the surface. The light danced and the walls breathed ... the distortions brought clarity ... and neither of us complained of burning eyes.

Long Live the King

King was the next of Dock and Etty's children to pass. And somehow the thrill and excitement, the pomp and ceremony, the tradition of entering into the Sisterhood of Dowager Widows loses something when it is your brother who makes the widow. And after the sting of the loss of the Dowager of West Alabama just a few years before, well, it didn't do much for the outpouring of sympathy for poor Veronica Brenda Taylor. Not that she didn't get sympathy, oh she absolutely did, but it was their big brother King and not his widow that The Two Sisters and Rudie were most concerned with.

It was either Bitsy or Vivian, I don't remember which, who summed it up best when she turned to Joan and said, "I guess you'll have to play the organ. We can't exactly ask Roni to do it."

"Yes, it is what must be. And that's your role now," the other said with a matching peroxide smile which more than implied, "Bless your heart."

I'm not sure for whom they were sorrier, Roni or Joan. Probably Joan. But of course they were decked out in their finest array of emo-early Victorian mourning attire. They were a sight as they undertook the very important task of finding a suitable family replacement for Veronica. Not that Veronica needed replacing, per se, but they couldn't very well ask her to play the organ for her husband's funeral—could they?

"Well I agree the organist from Roni's church is out of the

question," Joan puzzled over her predicament. *Was she to become the next Roni of the family?* "I don't know what Roni was thinking when she picked her to play at King's funeral." Then she whispered, "She's foreign."

"Well, she is not family, that is for sure," Vivian offered.

Joan was again mouthing the words "She's foreign" with all of her proper diction technique when Norma walked up and flung her arm over my shoulder. She was drinking a martini.

"What are they blathering over?" she asked.

"Who is going to be the next family organist now that Veronica is out of the family?" I answered, sipping my own adult beverage.

"Poor Roni," Norma sighed. "What ever did she do?"

"Well it seems she won't play the organ for their mother's older brother's funeral."

Norma snorted.

Bitsy and Vivian squealed while pulling their sister from the front parlor to the newly renovated Galerie de Glaces, now with less animal print. "Joan has agreed to play organ; the crisis is over!" and "Veronica Taylor; I swear it is true!" I don't know which one said what, but they were both shrill.

Roni was sitting in said newly renovated Galerie de Glaces resting uncomfortably in an elegant jewel-toned leather wingback chair. Uncomfortably, not because the chair was uncomfortable, but because in an identical jewel-toned leather wingback sat the Dowager Countess of Kosciusko. Mrs. India Wilkes Taylor Sable—but you may call her Wilksie—was hosting this morbid affair. Together they were holding court at this "friends and family memorial"—Roni just wanted to be home resting. Her husband's funeral was tomorrow.

Livie joined me and Norma in watching The Boxed Blonde Contingency share their news.

"Hello Liv," Norma said, pointing to the sales pitch going

on at Wilksie and Roni's feet. "They look like they're audition-
ing to be the next Marilyn."

"Monroe?" Livie asked.

"Muenster," Norma and I said, clinking our glasses.

"Where is she going?" Liv asked, as Norma stumbled toward the kitchen.

"To find someone she hasn't told that joke to yet." I smiled.

My shoulder was draped by another arm—Wilksie's. She
took the distraction of her daughters with Roni and Norma's
wandering as an opportunity to swoop in. "Are you two discussing your Mother?"

"We were talking about going back to the hotel and giving
her a call. It's getting late and ... " Livie began.

"Nonsense. You'll call her from here. We'll use Bitsy's old
room for some privacy." She had already had her arm through
mine, her hand firmly grasping my bicep; her other hand held
Livie's, and off we marched to Bitsy's room to call Mother. "I
can tell her what a proud representation of the family y'all have
been."

It is the one thing Mother had asked of me expressly, "Don't
make me talk to Wilksie. I don't have the energy ..."

"Bitsy!" Wilksie called, never shouted. "Come on and talk
to Debra. We're going to ring her from your room!"

" ... or Bitsy," Mother had pleaded when I left.

🐾   🐾   🐾

THE SERVICE AT FRENCH CAMP Baptist Church was what
was expected. It was as packed as that little church had been
since the last patriarch of the community had passed, King's father, Dock. Only not quite, as a few other patriarchs and matriarchs had passed in the years since. We were missing more of
those familiar faces from his baby sister's funeral just a few years

ago. Gio did a fine job with the eulogy. And Wilksie, Rudie, and Norma did their respective duty and sat with Veronica and Christina. There were three of them left, The Three Siblings I guess we could call them.

The next iteration of The Three Sisters sat together. They had firmly grasped that title from the older generation now. And each had their own version of that severe and angled bob that was popular among a certain group of angry women for a time. Livie and I called them the Gashleycrumb Karens and we sat directly behind them. They did their pageant best to listen to Gio as he "fired and brimstoned" his eulogy of a man I did not quite recognize, much as he did with my grandmother. Gio's words were appropriate when he got away from all the preachiness. He painted a lovely picture of a strong Southern Gentleman who embodied family and Jesus and generosity. A true Southern Colonel. A God-fearing man, and a good Christian husband. Each attribute was punctuated by the godliness and "goodliness" of it all; and yes, he said all these would be somewhat true of any Southern patriarch things any Southern family would want said about a beloved family member who had passed; things he said countless times at countless funerals—about countless people. They were not specifically about King, just as they were not really about my grandmother when he spoke those same sentiments then. They were just things.

If Gio's eulogy fell flat, it was nothing in comparison to the debacle that was the organ playing. Betty-Girl had swooped in. Wilksie had called her because she just didn't think Veronica was up to the task of planning her big brother's funeral. And Betty-Girl didn't think Joan was up to the task of playing organ at her uncle's funeral, so she enlisted the help of Gio's choir director friend—only she did this thirty-five minutes before the service was to begin. And, at thirty minutes before the service was to begin, the organ music was to begin. So at twenty-seven

minutes before the service was to begin, Joan and her freshly sculpted hair walked in a huff to the already playing organ.
Gio's friend was not moving from his post; Betty-Girl was clear.
Bitsy and Vivian joined their sister to convince this young man
that he needed to give up his post. Betty-Girl joined the fray,
followed by Gio. King lay in his casket, fifteen feet away, probably wishing his wife had just played the damn thing.

Wilksie stormed in and put an end to it all. She did not
yell and she did not shout—dowagers do not do such things—
but she informed each of them that they were acting no better than a bunch of ... well, she had the decorum to whisper
that last word. But it was clear it had struck each of these fine
Southerners to the quick.

"A bunch of what?" Livie asked me. "I hate it when they
whisper; I can never hear that part."

🌊   🌊   🌊

IT WAS WINDY AT THE graveside; the breeze was strong
enough to make one worry over a coming storm. I think the
best explanations of the weather that day were "It is the angels letting their voices be carried by the winds" or "God has
opened the window to let the fresh air cleanse our sad and tired
souls." Livie and I opted not to take a seat of honor under the
funeral tent and stood together with Goodie near the back. He
was getting on in years, very much so, but it was nice to see him
and his daughter, Melinda. I had not seen them since my grandmother's funeral.

The funeral potatoes in the blue casserole dish were on
point. The others either didn't have enough cheese or they had
too much grease. And one poor soul had used low-fat shredded
cheese, bless their heart. It was also not a good year for chicken,
as the best batch came from the box that someone had brought

from Leonard's 3 Way Quick Stop. We were reaching a point in time when the people of my grandparents' generation, the generation that did all the things, were dying. And it was up to my parents' generation, the generation that expected all the things, to do them. Only they didn't know how as the previous generation never taught them; they just did them. Or they didn't want to learn. And so we are often left with Betty-Girl's choices for entertainment and Leonard's culinary best for chicken.

✍   ✍   ✍

WE CALLED MOTHER FROM LIVIE'S cell. Mother was home resting, Livie was sitting on Nince and Boom-Pa's headstone, and I was talking to Dock and Etty. Mother was especially tickled by Livie's retelling of The Great Organ Debacle. Mother was asking Livie about everyone who was there. Livie would more than occasionally say a name to me, and I would clarify who that was, if they were there, or if they had passed. And she made Livie promise we would put some of the flowers down for Boom-Pa and Nince. I did for Dock and Etty too.

"Mother says 'run,'" Livie said to me, slightly confused.

I laughed, and I took one more set of flowers to put down before we left.

Vernon Dock Taylor—he loved his family.

Fezziwig and Fennig and Phantoms of Fetes Past

I woke up to Wesley's bare ass and the moon staring at me through the first floor bedroom window. My eyes adjusted to the white silvery moonlight. It was a full moon, or nearly so. I was in a substantial four-poster bed, there was a mirrored wardrobe taller than me in the corner, and a writing desk older than my great-grandparents' home along the wall near the window. And Wesley's ass. I was not in my apartment. I was at Cedar Oaks.

"What's going on?" I asked.

"It's Lorraine!" Wesley whisper-shouted.

"Well, what does she want?"

Her head appeared in the window, Wesley squealed and pulled the duvet he dragged across the room tighter. I could no longer see his ass. I, however, no longer had the cover of the duvet. I settled for a hastily grabbed pillow.

"Nope! No gay stuff here!" Lorraine announced. "Seriously though, you need to get dressed; I just got off of the phone with your sister."

"Yeah, um, let me just uh ... " and I dove into my pants and struggled into my socks and desperately tried to get my sweater inside-right.

"Do you think she knows?" Wesley asked quietly, unknotting the mess I had made of my sweater.

"You heard her," I answered ... *Was he joking?* "She definitely doesn't know," I said with an exaggerated eye roll. *I don't think he was joking.*

"Her people know people my people know back home," he said quietly.

I didn't have a reply so I just left through the window. Lorraine smiled at me from the front steps of Cedar Oaks. She didn't say anything to me, thankfully, and we walked to her car and drove home. It was only a five-minute drive. When she stopped the car, she finally spoke.

"You are in for some hell," Lorraine finally said. "I'll explain as I help you pack."

~   ~   ~

MOTHER HAD FALLEN. SHE DECIDED she wanted some-
thing to eat, and rather than ask for help ... she fell down the
stairs. Derwood had been trying to sell the house and get them
something single-story, down-size, ever since Mother was diagnosed. It was the same as her father. It started that way. This
last surgery was to take care of that. It's why she missed That
Sable Boy's funeral. Well, Nince, of course, needed to go down
to Florida and take care of her daughter, since evidently all
Derwood and Livie could manage to do is almost break her neck.
Them and their piss-poor decisions. Only Nince can't drive right
now because she had decided to go horseback riding with Rudie
and broke her leg. Rudie couldn't drive her because he was in
New York with his wife, what's her name—Pennywise. It would
have to be me. I would have to be the one to drive her. Only
there was one more hitch that Lorraine saved 'til the end.

ᰫ   ᰫ   ᰫ

"NOW ISN'T THIS MUCH MORE comfortable?" Wilksie said
from the backseat of her rather gorgeous Jaguar XJR. "And
your grandmother will be much more comfortable than in your
ol' pickup or that old Pontiac she still drives. I told her she at
least needs a Cadillac ... like that one Norma still drives."

I didn't mind driving. I mean, who would? It was a fucking Jaguar!!! Conrad had picked it up for Wilksie as a condo-
lence after Brick had died—or as a celebration for her newly
achieved "dowagerhood." It was sleek and that oh, so British
racing green, with all the retro curves one would come to expect from a pre-Ford owned Jaguar. When Ford bought Jaguar,
they turned these driving machines into glorified Tauruses. We
took the Trace. We were silent as we drove by French Camp.
We did not stop at the home or the cemetery. We did not even
stop at the visitor center.

Nince was waiting for us in the garage. She had probably been there since she got off the phone with Livie. She was seated in one of those woven plastic lawn chairs. How that wide band of fibrous petroleum had not dry rotted over the past 50 years is a true testament to the marvel of American engineering. Her leg rested up on one of her two suitcases. She also had a makeup and toiletry bag. And if I were to tell you Nince was annoyed beyond her senses that her baby sister had to come along to take care of her while she took care of her daughter, then it was clear you were not looking at her. Because, brother, let me tell you, it was written all over her face.

"You help her with the luggage, Randy," Driving Miss Wilksie said from the backseat as we rolled to a stop in front of the open garage where my grandmother sat, looking like a Bernie Sanders meme (had memes been a thing yet) "I'm going to step inside and freshen up."

"Where is she going?" Nince asked as she kissed my cheek. "Mmm. How are you, Randy; thank you."

"She said she was going in to freshen up," I said and picked up the luggage that was not under my grandmother's propped broken leg.

"She's pooping. YOU'RE POOPING! WE ALL KNOW IT!" She shouted over her shoulder into the garage. "Every time we got in the car. It's why Daddy never liked to take her anywhere."

I helped Nince into the backseat of Wilksie's car so she could stretch out her leg. We had a brief, lighthearted argument over the freezer. Me insisting whatever I packed up would melt before we got to Florida versus her suggesting we take a few things just in case I needed them.

"Yes, it would be awfully convenient to gnaw on a partially thawed turkey leg should I get hungry on the drive." I laughed.

"We didn't send you to Ole Miss to get smart," she rebutted.

Wilksie stepped back into the garage from the house. She

walked past me as I was putting the things back in the freezer Nince had just pulled out. She looked flustered.

"Did you have a nice poop?" Nince asked.

"Velma," Wilksie whispered. "Velma, there is something amiss with your facilities."

"And I guess there's nothing wrong with yours," Nince said, turning to get out of the car. "Is it clogged again?"

I closed the freezer and turned in time to see Wilksie give an uncomfortable nod in my direction. She mouthed something I couldn't see or hear. Now I understood how Livie always felt.

"I'm sure the boy has seen a clogged toilet before," Nince answered and then said again, after another set of missed mouthed words from Wilksie. "Fine India, I'll have Billie do it."

We stopped at Billie's. She was just across the street and down the hill; her driveway was just before the bridge. She lived in a tiny wooden shack. I'm not convinced there was indoor plumbing. Billie was an older woman, a few years older than either of the two ladies in the classic British touring sedan outside of her house. I took her by the arm and helped her to the car. Wilksie rolled down the window and gave a little cough.

"She wants you to give us a little privacy, Randy." Nince rolled her eyes.

"You gon' have some kinda drive," Billie said to me as I helped her back to the porch of her house. "You take care of your Granny, now. Hear me?" And she kissed my cheek.

"Now, you are certain you have left the door open for her?" Wilksie asked as we drove on 82 toward Montgomery, then Eufala, then Tifton.

"I always do," Nince answered. "She knows the side door to the garage is always open, in case she needs to go in for something. And I never lock the door to the house from the garage. She can get in any time I need her to."

"She doesn't have a key?" I regretted asking.

Wilksie laughed. "Why on earth would she have a key?"

"So she can get in anytime she needs without leaving the door unlocked so ANYONE can get in if they want," I reasoned.

"Randy, you just can't go around giving keys to those people," Wilksie said. "They can't have free access to our homes, too."

I dropped it. My Ole Miss learning was not helping me understand. Or actually, it was. I understood perfectly. What my Ole Miss learning was not providing me with was the tools to help them understand what it was they were saying. We stopped in Georgetown and ate at a little hotel restaurant that overlooked the Walter F. George Reservoir. It is not important that we stopped there, but neither are the many distractions and excuses we fill our time with while avoiding the inevitable. We sipped coffee, I picked at my remaining french fries, and Wilksie had excused herself to freshen up.

"Wilksie knows all of the places to stop for lunch." Nince smiled. "The ones with the nicest facilities."

"Shall we?" Wilksie asked as she reappeared. Her lipstick looked fresh, her eyes were bright, and she wore her lovely smile.

"Do we need to call Billie?" Nince asked.

"I'm glad Mama died before she could see how vulgar you've become."

⌒　　　⌒　　　⌒

I ONLY STAYED A WEEK this time. I had to head back to Ole Miss as soon as Mother was home from the hospital. I had obligations, I had class, and I had a chair of the department who needed me back for something urgent. So I had to get back.

I suppose it was a brief respite for Derwood and Livie. Derwood, of course, lived and breathed everything related to the care of his wife. Livie was fortunate to both live and work close by. She always made herself available. But she had a life to live, a career ... a life. I always admired her ability to handle it all. Career and family.

Nince and Wilksie stayed longer, bringing Derwood and Livie's respite to an end. I would drive Wilksie's car back; it only made sense. And she and Nince would fly back to Montgomery, where Rudie could pick them up. He would be back from New York, and that gave them a few weeks to really help with Debra.

I made the trip to Kosciusko in one long marathon drive. I blared music, I sang loudly, and I had a quick indiscretion with an LSU frat boy in a jeep; he shared I-10 with me. We first winked and nodded at the gas station just past I-75. We spoke briefly at a Mickey-D's in Tallahassee—and then christened a stall at a rest area just beyond Pensacola. I veered north in Mobile; he headed west.

⌒   ⌒   ⌒

HO-HO WAS AT HER fiNEST when I returned, and I was livid as I drank a beer with Lorraine in the bath. She was obviously mimosa-ed up, and we were thoroughly abusing the woman who was probably never as awful as we made her out to be.

"And you couldn't just say no?" Lorraine asked, stepping back into the tub after refilling her champagne. She opted to cut the oj for calories.

"I did," I said, "and Dr. Singlet reminded me of my assistantship, and that part of my contract meant stage-managing two shows. And they wanted me for *A Christmas Carol*, directed by the fourth sister from Macbeth."

"And she was okay with it? She hates you as much as you hate her." Lorraine was not pleased.

"She requested me."

"Oh, she is such a conniving, cunty thing ..." Lorraine growled. "I'm taking you to Grocery. We're going out."

I slunk down in my tub and exhaled a lot of bubbles. I didn't want to run into Wesley. And I didn't want to see the rest of the Oxford Queers. I wanted something easier, something quieter than Bible-thumping queens. Also, there was a good chance Ho-Ho would be there too. And I certainly didn't need that noise.

"Or the Hoka?" Lorraine was saying as I came back up for breath. "We could go to the Hoka instead."

Now that idea I liked. The Hoka had a more down home, cozy, wear your Birkenstocks kind of vibe—and if you have a spliff, no one will mind as long as you puff, puff, pass. A great venue for old classic movies, indie films, theater, and live music. I had seen a film noir festival and several great bands there. And I was fortunate enough to have done my own work there too. I directed a few low-budget plays for a local community group, and I also stage-managed a higher budget world premier of a play by an impressive local author. The building itself was a little sketch, but that also suited the Hoka.

Not like the Cotton Gin, which was an old cotton gin that had been renovated—and was quite the high-end hot spot for alum. The Yoknapatawpha Arts Council hosted a reception there for the world premier of that play performed at the Hoka. Squatchy, the head of the directing program, directed the show, and he needed my Equity credentials as a stage manager. The show was cast with several professional actors from the Chicago area and one graduate actress who was a favorite of Squatchy's. Everything ran smoothly until after the Sunday matinee.

Sunday was the closing day of the Arts Council's Written Word Festival. They had arranged with the director and me for an author's reception following the final matinee. The Cotton Gin was just around the corner from the Hoka; it would be a perfect venue to host the author and festival attendees. The Cotton Gin put out its finest array of Southern cuisine, barbeque, and a big ol' boilin' pot of crawfish. There was an open bar, and the beer and booze—they were a flowin'. Every notable VIP from the artistic, writing, and University communities was there. And eventually so were the cops. It was Sunday, and Oxford and the rest of Lafayette County were dry on Sundays. No alcohol could be sold, at all, whatsoever. At least that was the argument the producers, the director, and I used as we were being handcuffed and led from the place—no alcohol was being sold; it was a private party.

Oh, it was a chaotic scene. The police all came running in through the front door. The kitchen and waitstaff all fled through the back door. The patrons, or guests, rather—again, nothing was sold; it was a private party—ran in all directions. I always found it funny and not at all believable when I watched chaotic scenes in movies, people running about from something; there'd be terrified extras running from the left ... and then they'd be running from the right. So, in my mind, some of them are not running from the danger, but toward it. It makes no sense. But then chaos rarely makes sense. And in the dimly lit, smoke-filled rooms of the Cotton Gin, the folks were indeed running about in all directions.

It was Ho-Ho and Dr. Singlet who bailed us out, or at least picked us up. There we sat in the holding cell: Squatchy, Deandra (the Equity actress from Chicago), Chris (the Equity actor from Chicago), Katie (the grad actress who was not Equity, but getting a really good shot) and of course myself. Dr. Singlet wore a tired expression, but found the situation rather comical. He and Squatchy had a very good rapport. Ho-Ho looked like a cat with a mouthful of canaries. And the officer releasing us looked as though he had gotten an earful from his superior who had clearly had an earful from the mayor of Oxford, the chancellor of the university—and even the governor—calling to complain over the handling of this situation. The City

Police eventually released an apology to us, to the university, the Equity actors, the Actors' Equity Association, and to the Yoknapatawpha Arts Council.

It was Ho-Ho who drove me home. The others all piled into Dr. Singlet's car. I sat uncomfortably for the long, three-minute ride to my house. I'm not sure Ho-Ho was any happier about it. It was also Ho-Ho who explained to me about the Arts Council, the mayor, the chancellor, and the governor.

"What I don't understand is why you were there," she said in her staccato, nasal pitch. "Squatchy (she didn't say Squatchy) can't pass up free liquor, and he'll pay this week with his gout—we all will. But you should know better."

"It was a private party," I argued.

"It was in a public place," she insisted.

"It was like renting a venue for a wedding or a bat mitzvah," I offered.

She launched into a mini-tirade about me bringing up Jews just because she is Jewish. That no one at that venue was there for a wedding or a bat mitzvah, and who did I think I was that I was so special to come to Oxford and flaunt their traditions and ways? I should know better. My people were from Mississippi, after all.

I listened to her monologue, unpacking all of the snipes and snide remarks, the quips about who she thought I was, and how she told Dr. Singlet all along I should not have been accepted into the program. It was a lot. And it was difficult to hear such harshness delivered by a short, round woman whose hair was equally as short and round with that stop-start voice of Porky Pig—so I did that thing I do where I dissect and describe all the unflattering pettiness I can manage. I got out of the car and thanked her before offering one more little quip of information about me and my family she clearly had not researched. It left her stunned-face and open-jaw sitting in her car as I turned and walked toward the two faces looking out my bedroom window at us.

It was Rhiannon and Lorraine. "What did you say to her at the end? We couldn't hear what you said when you poked your head through the window," they implored as I climbed through my window and joined them laying on my bed.

I told her what my Great-Grandfather Fennig liked to tell folks, much to my Great-Grandmother Fennig's dismay: "You can't have a Fennig without having a little Jew in ya first!" And then he would laugh and laugh. He was a tiny little man, 5'1", and Jewish. He was on the Vaudeville circuit, while, on the other side of my family, Dock was trying to play ball for the Yankees.

Oh, word got around fast, and it did not take the Trace or I-55 to reach the Dowager Countess of Kosciusko; a simple phone call sufficed. And Wilksie had no sooner hung up the receiver than her white-gloved finger was spinning the rotary on the phone as swiftly as she could. Wilksie thought the touch tone phones were vulgar. And the Dowager of West Alabama was notified of her grandchild's indiscretion.

And then the phone rang. Rhiannon answered. Her eyes went big, and she handed me the phone. "RAIN-de!" the voice on the other end said with a note of anger but a volume of concern. "You are not so grown that I can't have you pick out a switch! What is this I hear from Wilksie that you have been sent to prison?"

❧   ❧   ❧

OF ALL THE PLAYS I worked on in undergraduate and graduate school, of all the plays I did professionally up until this point, Nince had never attended one. And then there was *A Christmas Carol*, as directed by Ho-Ho. Well Nince came to that. And she brought Rudie, Norma, and Wilksie with her. It seems Nince was worried about me. After the debacle of my rolled up pants at That Sable Boy's funeral, summers in that den of iniquity, New York City, and then this going to prison thing, she was not certain Ole Miss was living up to its former standards.

And then there was Mother. My mother had been ill, and she had another surgical procedure. Due to my class obligations, teaching obligations, and stage managing this play, I was also lacking in tending to my familial duties. So the Four Siblings descended upon Oxford that early December—Ole Miss, my apartment, and the City Grocery.

Ho-Ho may have been a talented actor, and she may have had a way with working with actors (the ones she liked) in a way that elicited some very strong performances. She made some good, if interesting casting choices, and she did well with giving creative control to her choreographer, music director, and designers. Ten minutes into our first production meeting, I realized this was not because she was an incredible collaborator who trusted her colleagues. Nope. She just ignored the things she didn't like or didn't think she had to do. So all those decisions fell to her stage manager. Me. Being in the union, I understood the rules surrounding my role and responsibilities quite well. Being a grad student with other responsibilities and obligations, I was not under Equity rules when stage-managing for the department. It created great conflict between Ho-Ho and me as we butted professional heads. She did not see me as a professional. I did not find her behavior to be professional. Countless times, we were in front of the chair, Dr. Singlet, hashing out our woes.

"He is always throwing his credentials around like they mean something. He is just a student, and he forgets that," Ho-Ho sputtered during one such confrontation. She had a cloth beach bag of cold and flu medicines, nasal sprays, and Ho-Hoes (not Oreos but Ho-Hoes), hence her name.

"I was asked, because I was a professional, to perform this task for this lady who also claims to be a professional yet refuses to follow the rules," I replied with no expression at all on my face. "And now, we are in the midst of tech week, and she has decided she is staying home."

"I don't feel good. I am sick and my diabetes is reacting to my cold medicines."

"And not the Ho-Hoes?" My mouth did that thing again where it says what I am thinking before I can truly think about it.

And of course Ho-Ho once again stormed out of a meeting after my rude and disrespectful remarks—she always did. I was scolded by the chair briefly for my lack of respect. I assured him that, indeed, I had very little respect—especially after her behavior this week. I would do better to mask it, but it was not likely to change.

"Just get through this show, Randy, and then you can concentrate on your thesis," he said. "And I'll tell her she is not going to be on your committee; she has been lobbying, but it is clear that would be unfair to you."

In addition to the demands of tech week, I had to help Nince and Wilksie come to terms on where everyone would stay while in Oxford. Norma and Rudie figured they could all stay at my apartment. Nince would have been fine with that, too, but she was concerned about the judgment coming from her younger, more particular sister. Wilksie wanted a suite in the five star hotel that Oxford did not have. Lorraine came up with the solution.

"I've got it, Randy!" she said excitedly as she turned off her bathwater and stepped in. I was thinking about it the whole time I was in Ho-Ho's class, and I think I finally came up with a solution."

"Are you going to tell me the solution or just tell me you have one?" I asked, my head somewhat floating, somewhat resting against the back of the long tub.

"Well, that depends on the level of your bitchitude!"

"Sorry." I sighed. And then my bitch level went up again, "What the fuck was she in class for? She has not been to rehearsal all week!"

It was true—she hadn't been to a single rehearsal all week. And it was tech week, which is when all the technical elements are combined with the performance elements, and they are rehearsed. The lights, sound effects, set changes, things that "fly" in and out, entrances and exits and timing in black-outs, costumes, and costume changes ... all come together during this week. It is the stage manager's job to coordinate these things, call the technical cues, run the rehearsal, and learn, themselves, the timing of things and how to ensure the show opens with all the elements coming together. The director's job is to approve all the levels of all the various elements, the visual impact, and that they do, indeed, tie into their vision or concept of the production and with everything they had discussed with their designers. It is very difficult for them to do that from home, with flu meds and Ho-Hoes on their lap. So she didn't. She stayed home and left the task to me, her stage manager. She had not been to rehearsal since that fateful meeting with Dr. Singlet.

"Okay. She was NOT in class," Lorraine said, realizing the source of some of my frustration. "And you need to get laid or something. Shoot."

I took a sip of my beer during her pause, and closed my eyes to listen.

"Dr. Singlet stopped by class. He watched us work our monologues with one another. Abby said that was what Ho-Ho wanted." Abby was Ho-Ho's prized student. "He was most interested in our feedback and less, the monologues."

"Yeah. That sounds right." I sighed.

"Anyway, he pulled me aside to ask how you were."

"Oh?" I sat up, a little more interested. "What did you say?"

"That you were pissed, but it was not beyond your skill set."

"Mmm," I said and slid back down.

Lorraine continued. "I was honest. And he agreed. He said he figured it was probably easier without her there, but you were just too idealistic and stubborn to realize it. He meant it as a compliment."

"Well then, I shall take it as one." I sat up again, the warm water falling from my shoulders and back. I splashed water in my face and took a sip of my beer. "And so what is your plan for the solution to my other problem?"

"Easy. It came to me while Abby was doing that over-done 'Mr. Parnell' one she always auditions with. I hate that monologue." Lorraine was excited. "And I thought, Cedar Oaks! Wilksie would love to stay at Cedar Oaks!"

So with that, a trip to The City Grocery was needed. I had to meet Lorraine there because of our first full dress rehearsal. Lorraine was lucky enough not to be cast. And Rhiannon, she was also fortunate enough to be spared working on this holiday tradition. She was there too; she was part of Lorraine's master plan. And so was Wesley. Yes, imagine my surprise when I walked in and Wesley and Rhiannon were sipping on some frilly holiday cocktail while fiercely discussing whatever it was Rhiannon was sketching. Lorraine spied me and shot a glance to her married bartender; he immediately poured me a beer.

"Okay Randy, sit down; we're gonna go over the plan." Lorraine waved her hand at me from over her head as she shouted across the room.

I sat down next to Lorraine. Rhiannon whipped around her sketchbook, giving me a view of what it was she and Wesley were huddled over so intently. It was a spectacular rendering of mid-19th-century dress, with all the layers, frills, crinolines, puffy elbow sleeves, low slung shoulders, ribbons, and bows. In the rather flattering rendering of this dress was one Ms. Wesley himself.

"RAIN-de!" Why did he have to say my name like my grandmother? "I'm going to get my dress!"

Lorraine's plan was quite simple. She knew Nince and Norma would want to stay with me. And she knew Rudie would need to be where all the action was. So Rhiannon was going to stay with her new boyfriend. She had finally dumped the free-loading boyfriend and moved on to a fellow designer, though nobody knew about it except for me—and now Lorraine and Wesley. Nince and Norma would take Rhiannon's room. Rudie would take my room, and I was going to sleep on the couch. And that left Wilksie.

"I just knew Wilksie would love to stay at Cedar Oaks," Lorraine explained. "So I walked right over here and waited for Wesley and asked what he needed to make it happen. It didn't take us long to arrive at this. And when Rhiannon agreed to make the dress ..."

"Oh you are gonna owe me ..." Rhiannon smiled at me and raised her glass.

⌐   ⌐   ⌐

IT WAS FRIDAY, A LITTLE after lunch when they rolled into town. Rudie drove, Norma was by his side, and Nince and Wilksie sat in the back of Norma's large '80s Cadillac. She loved the size and the color, that pearlescent white, and swore she would drive it 'til one of them was dead—or at least have someone drive it for her, like in Rudie's case. I helped unload luggage from the car. Rudie took his back to my room. Rhiannon showed Nince and Norma where to go. And Wilksie, of course, had to powder her nose.

"I am telling you that I heard what I heard," Wilksie was saying to Nince and Norma as they walked back out onto the front porch.

I was putting Wilksie's luggage for the weekend back into the spacious trunk of Norma's even more spacious car. Rhiannon was clearly trying not to laugh; she was in the doorway watching the three ladies walk down the steps. And Lorraine had come from around the side where her apartment was. She wore a rather curious expression.

"Wilksie is hearing voices in the bathroom," Norma said to me with her Ethel Merman simplicity. "And your aunt needs a drink!"

"I do not need a drink," Wilksie said. "And I do not need to calm down."

"I am also his aunt," Norma added.

"His grandmother could use one too." Nince laughed.

Wilksie was not laughing. "Randy. Ooh, be careful with that one; it has my delicates," she said, pointing at the small, squarish, hard-sided piece of luggage I held in my hand. "And it is true, I tell you. I heard a woman's voice, just as clear as if she were right beside me. And she said, 'Are your people here yet? Do you have time for a quick bath?' I swear I have heard that voice somewhere before ..."

We didn't get much further into that discussion before I needed to take Wilksie to Cedar Oaks and get her settled. Rudie stayed behind with Rhiannon to watch golf and sip a bourbon beverage. Rhiannon was from Kentucky and her Daddy kept us in good bourbon. (Oh the Derby Party we had that one year, shew!) But Norma and Nince wanted to see the house too. So they came along for the ride to Cedar Oaks.

Wesley was waiting for us in the entrance hall. The front door, which I had never used, was open and a grand arrangement of flowers sat atop a round, lion-footed table—probably from the early 1800s. We followed Wesley up the grand staircase to the room he had prepared for Wilksie. It was beautiful. Another arrangement of flowers filled the room with the sweet aroma of soft white and yellow roses with baby's breath. The rest of the house was decked out in its Christmas finery, and Wesley was eager to show Wilksie around. We were joined by Miss L'Anita. She was the primary caretaker and Secretary of the Women's Auxiliary. Wesley had convinced her that it was an opportunity like no other to allow the Dowager Countess of Kosciusko to stay at Cedar Oaks. While they gave the grand tour, and Wilksie lapped up every complimentary word, Nince rolled her eyes and huffed at least twenty dozen times. Norma shot me side eye glances and comical looks every time Wesley sauntered by.

The original plan was to have an early dinner at City Grocery—Nince, her siblings, and myself. A family dinner before the show. Lorraine invited herself, reminding me it was her plan.

"Besides, someone has to go with them to Fulton Chapel since you have to be there for your call time."

Lorraine was correct; they would need an escort to the main stage theatre on campus. Meanwhile, Rudie had invited Rhiannon because they were both kind of tipsy and wanted another drink. And Wilksie invited L'Anita and Wesley because "they were both so accommodating and gracious."

I suggested we change the plans a little, since we had gone from four to nine of us for dinner, and get catfish from Cedars. Alas, Rudie's and mine were the only votes for this option. We agreed to meet at City Grocery for a four o'clock supper so I could leave in time for my call. The food was delicious; I had the shrimp and grits. And the conversation was hilarious. Wilksie wasn't sure what a stage manager was and kept trying to figure out my role in the play. She peppered Lorraine with questions, trying to determine why they didn't just call the stage manager a personal secretary. Rudie grilled Wesley on the Rebel football team, trying to determine why they were having such a shitty season when they had two big guys like Wesley and myself on the team. Wesley must have felt as though he were in testosterone purgatory. Norma, Rhiannon, and L'Anita chatted Memphis and Louisville; apparently, L'Anita was going to come to our Derby Party this year. Norma said she would come too ...

"But only if I can leave Wilksie in Kosciusko!" she snorted.

Nince ate soup. She picked at her salad. And she watched, she listened, and she took everything in. I would look up from my grits, or look over after sharing a laugh with Lorraine and Wilksie, maybe an enthusiastic chuckle from Rudie—and there was Nince, watching me. Her face wore little expression, but her eyes seemed to smile. Maybe even approve.

"Well, good afternoon, Randy, Rhiannon, Lorraine ..." It was Dr. Singlet. "Enjoying dinner before the show tonight?"

I made the introductions and then made my excuses. I had a show to get to, and I had to change. Dr. Singlet took my seat, another round of drinks was ordered, and I left The Four Siblings at City Grocery with Lorraine and Rhiannon, Wesley and L'Anita, and Dr. Singlet. I was a little unsure as to what they would talk about, but I was fairly certain it would be a lot.

The headsets were abuzz with chatter, and not because of the unrehearsed changes to the light, fog, and orchestra cues during a rather pivotal Scrooge and Ghost of Christmas Yet to Come moment. No, instead the technicians were concerned with winning a little wager over who would spy The Three Sisters and their brother first. Well, it was a wager nobody won, as it was quite obvious when these ladies and their brother walked through the door. Everybody saw them.

Norma's was ermine, Nince's was mink, and Wilksie's was fox—floor length, and a beautiful gray, white, and almost blue in the fur. Their hair was flawless, high and buoyant, of course—could it be anything else?—and all three wore varying shades of deep brunette. Fingers and wrists and necks bejeweled—Norma had clearly emptied every one of her Ziploc bags. It could have only been a grander scene if Wilksie had worn the tiara she brought. Nince would not let her, no matter how much Norma, Rudie, and Rhiannon had begged. The Three Sisters took their seats. They were flanked by Dr. Singlet and Ho-Ho. Ho-Ho had made a miraculous recovery this afternoon and was ready for opening night. Rudie ended up in the light booth with me. Rhiannon thought he would enjoy the show better from there. She was right.

Chapter 8
A Well of Souls

A Star Is Born:
Another Show, Another Time

N ince's house was filled with excitement that morning as we got ready to head over to Wilksie's. We were leaving early, trying to get on the road while it was still dark. Boom-Pa and I were loading the car. Livie was getting dressed in the bedroom. Mother was trying to fix her hair in the bathroom. Nince was putting things away in the kitchen while also trying to hurry the others along.

"Debbie, honey!" Nince called. "It's fine. You look lovely."

"Thank you, Mother."

"And a simple scarf or hat, you won't even notice that little thing with your hair." Nince smiled at her daughter. "Livie, honey, we need to get going!"

Livie was ready. There were no tears this time over a dress and stockings; Livie wore a pair of shorts and sneakers. It was summer, it was hot, and we hoped Boom-Pa would turn the a/c on in the car. We knew he wouldn't do the roller coaster with Nince in the car.

Mother had closed the door to the bathroom after her

discussion with Nince; the sink was running, and you could hear the fan come on. I walked in from the garage to get anything else that we needed for the car.

Nince handed me a large, silver-wrapped box to be taken to Boom-Pa for loading. "Be very careful, Randy," she said to me. She seemed so excited. "It is a very important gift."

I carried the box to Boom-Pa and repeated Nince's statement about the importance of the gift. Boom-Pa rearranged a few things, a few times, until everything was the way he wanted it. Then we carefully placed the box in the trunk on top of everything else, so it would not be crushed.

"I'm gonna smoke this cigarette; then we're leaving." Boom-Pa walked out of the garage and into the driveway. "Tell them women to hurry up; if they ain't in the car when I pull out, then they ain't in the car." He lit his cigarette and walked to the side of the house, proudly looking over his land, appreciating the beautiful summer blooms. He loved his land—he loved his home.

I ran inside to warn the women. Livie was in the kitchen; she had a glass of water. Mother and Nince were in Nince's bathroom. Nince was scolding Mother.

"Just hold still, Debra," she said sharply. "You know this cream will help with the puffiness around your eyes." I imagined a pink, white-bristled brush or a wooden spoon.

"Boom-Pa says hurry, 'cause when he leaves he leaves," I said to everybody.

"You tell Daniel he better not leave!" Nince yelled from the bathroom. "Not even as one of his jokes!"

"Ow!" Mother winced.

"Well, hold still!" Nince scolded.

Boom-Pa drove, of course, and Derwood was not on this trip. Livie, Mother, and I were in the back. We were not bribed with cokes and candy, and we were not drugged. We were a bit older—Livie, in high school, and I was in middle school, so we were threatened instead. Well, I was, but Livie always complained of getting car sick, so she chose the Dramamine option and was therefore drugged by consent, I guess. It was an important occasion, the reason for this particular trip to Mississippi—two important occasions, actually.

The birth of Laura had occurred some months prior; this was to be her first introduction to the entire family. She was Eddie's baby daughter and named for his mother. And Rudie was beside himself with pride and joy and all the beaming that comes with being a grandfather for the first time.

We were also celebrating another landmark occasion, Dock and Ettienne's anniversary—their 75th! Wilksie was hosting the family for a large dinner party. And Nince had thought up the perfect gift for her mother ... and her father too, it would turn out.

The magnolia tree Wilksie had planted several years before was standing a bit taller. Its waxy green leaves provided shade; its fist-sized white blossoms offered a floral redolence that was almost overpowering—like a fine lady with too much perfume. Boom-Pa parked on the street and had his cigarette lit before he was out of the car. He popped the trunk lid, but before he could grab the carefully wrapped package, Nince already had it in her protective arms. Mother was reapplying her lipstick and adjusting the little scarf she wore. Liv was trying to wake from her drug-induced coma and wiping the drool from her face. I was out of the car and being pulled into a huge hug by Wilksie.

"Debra!" Bitsy called. "Debbie! Come on inside, girl! I can't wait to catch up!" (*Own:* you have to say it the way she does; *on* is pronounced *own*.)

Bitsy was on the front lawn, flanked by her sisters, Joan and Vivian. Her arm was outstretched and her wrist held just so, the sparkling from her finger was nearly blinding in the Mississippi morning sun. The aging confederation of ingenues I'll call my cousins appeared to be running in place, screaming, as Debra joined the excitement and the four of them disappeared into the house.

"Which one is this?" Nince asked.

"Your grandmother and her jokes," Wilksie answered, glaring at Nince as she led me into the house.

That familiar yet ever changing fireplace was now a sleek and brilliant white, as were all the furniture pieces. Two rounded, egg meets golf ball-like chairs served as the focal point around the fireplace. Sort of like an '80s homage to the wingback chair. It wasn't all white, as there were pops of color, like a yellow phone, pink and teal throw pillows, and a few "objects d'art." Above the fireplace, in a rather colorful, gilded, matted frame concoction, was one of Wilksie's own paintings: a still life of oddly shaped fruit in a weird little bowl.

Bald Don Johnson, or Conrad as his mother named him, was animatedly explaining to Mother his vision for this room he had just redesigned for Wilksie. "I mean, honestly Debra, everything was so dated and just ... we went straight from museum to mausoleum. We did not pass GO. We did not collect $200. So I just had to do something."

Mother stood wide-eyed and attentive, laughing appropriately, and desperately looking for an out. Bitsy held her by the arm, out of affection or incarceration; Mother did not seem sure which. Joan brought a tray of cocktails for them all. Suddenly Vivian let out a squeal that was then shared by all four of the Sable children as Eddie walked in carrying baby Laura. Rudie was right behind him, beaming proudly at his son and his granddaughter. And bringing up the rear of the baby train was Amazing Grace. Grace, as she had not quite yet earned the Amazing prefix, was a sweet bundle of Alabama country girl. Kind and soft spoken, but she could skin a hog and take out a deer with her own shotgun. She would earn the Amazing prefix in the coming years as Eddie fought with his demons.

Laura was passed around like the flu; everyone had their turn with her. But it was Rudie who was there to take her every time she fussed; it was Rudie who helped Grace with every need his grandchild had; it was Rudie who gave his entire heart to this little girl—the namesake of his beloved wife. Not that Grace or Eddie didn't participate in the raising of their daughter; they did ... when Rudie would let them.

Livie and I took our turns with Laura. We sat on the sleek, reflective white surface of the hearth while Rudie gently placed her in my lap. Grace was beside Livie, and Rudie hovered, in case we were looking like we would break her or something.

"Now hold her head, hold her head, you gotta support their neck, you know?" Rudie cautioned in his low-key panic kind of way. He said this to everybody he handed her to.

"Rudie, you better get away with your nonsense before I tell Boom to go long!" Norma snapped at Rudie, pulling Laura back over her shoulder.

Boom-Pa set his drink down on the piano and raised his arms. "I'm open, Norma!"

Grace laughed; Rudie did not. And Laura let everyone know she was hungry.

"Oh, why give me that precious baby, I think she must be hungry or something." Wilksie strode over to Norma, arms outstretched. "Follow me back to Bitsy's room, Grace; you can have some privacy there."

Rudie chased after Wilksie, who was now clutching Laura to her chest, looking over her shoulder at her wide-eyed brother. "Now hold her head, hold her head, you gotta support their neck, you know?"

"Rudie Taylor, I will have you know I raised four healthy children! You better get away." Wilksie said all of this with a smile.

"Now you know it was Mama who raised your brood," Rudie shot back.

Norma snorted. Nince grabbed my hand and squeezed it. Mother grasped her neck.

"Rudolph Mornay Taylor, just because you are my brother does not mean I won't get my gun and shoot you in your knee-cap." She did not say any of this with a smile.

The Show Must Go On

Opening night of *A Christmas Carol* had closed. I was in the midst of doing my final checks for the next evening's show and giving notes to a few of my technicians about some minor changes when I heard it. The gossip, the chatter, the talk. There was a cast party, of course—but I wasn't up to bringing Rudie and The Three Sisters to a party filled with mostly under-age undergrads who couldn't hold their liquor. So I suggested we meet back at City Grocery. Lorraine and Rhiannon were happy to skip the party as well, so they served as escorts for my family until I could arrive. But there was this chatter, this buzz of gossip that came all the way from the Square in Oxford. "Randy's relatives were on the balcony with the Oxford Queers."

Well, of course they were—and none other than Ms. Wesley herself was holding court. All the LGBT—we didn't quite have the alphabet we do now—of Ole Miss were gathered around to see Wesley, the Dowager Countess of Kosciusko, and her siblings. It was as though they were the ruling family of the Kingdom of Alassippi on a state visit. Wilksie really should have worn her tiara, but her floor-length Russian fox with the silver gray hood had to suffice.

A beer was thrust into my hand by Lorraine's married bartender. "Lorraine ordered you a shot too. She said you would need it!" he called after me.

I was already walking toward the balcony. And, yes indeed, there the fur-clad sisters sat. Wilksie and Lorraine were drinking champagne. Nince had a glass of scotch. Norma had two martinis. Rudie was not to be outdone by Norma, only he had Old Fashioneds instead—plural. Wesley was drinking something with an umbrella. Rhiannon appeared with the shot of tequila from the bartender and one for herself. We clinked glasses and slammed them before walking outside.

"Randy!" My name was called by all as I stepped out onto the balcony. Filled with queers and relations as it was, RAINde rang like a jarring cacophony of moments and memories juxtaposed into a flipbook of still images. With every flip a different picture, a different memory, a different moment that moved into another, but not the next moment—everything was out of order. Nothing was where it belonged. The *whats* of the memories were clear—just not the *whens*. I needed another shot.

It was quite the party, or maybe the Wesley and Wilksie show. But the two of them shared stories and embellishments, recalling life in Kosciusko and Winona and getting a few digs in at Starkville. The grandeur of the neuvo-antebellum was on full display and the Oxford Queers were here for it.

"You forgot to mention your oldest went to State!" Nince mentioned in a throwaway comment.

"And you also forgot to mention why!" Norma added.

Maybe not everyone was here for it.

Rudie occasionally threw everyone for a loop by asking Wesley about football and the Ole Miss team. "They say it's the sanctions," Rudie said to Rhiannon. "But I swear, that boy don't know a thing about football."

Rhiannon laughed as she, Rudie, and I slammed another tequila. Norma and Rudie argued over whether Wesley was a lineman, maybe a tight end.

"He is not a tight end. I assure you, Rudie," Norma snorted.

"Well, he is just too big to be any good at being a wide receiver."

"Oh, I believe he manages." Rhiannon laughed.

Soon enough "last call" was announced. And everybody knew what that meant: slam your drinks and go. But Rudie and Norma showed up with a tray full of drinks and decided they were going to teach us youngins how to really drink. Lorraine's bartender, the restaurant manager, and a young lady who might have been a server who I also think I had as a student in one of my acting classes stood anxiously by. It was 11:58 and they needed to be closed in two minutes.

I leaned over to Nince, who was warily, but skillfully, drinking her second scotch from Rudie's tray. "This is how I went to prison, you know," I said.

Now, why or how we did not get arrested, I do not know. Two police officers showed up, and the manager was a wreck. The owner was called, and the waitstaff had snuck out the back. We were no longer on the balcony; we had been ushered downstairs by management and the cops. The Oxford Queers had also managed to escape, save Wesley, who sat nervously afraid he would be kicked out of Cedar Oaks for this transgression.

"They have an image to keep, and if their caretaker is arrested ..." Wesley needed smelling salts, he was so distressed.

I sat at a table with Nince and Rudie and Rhiannon. Lorraine was talking to the bartender, who had to call his wife and explain why he was late. Rudie sat staring at Wesley, a confused expression on his face as he tried to figure out this large, broad-shouldered, effeminate fellow. Norma continued to sip the drink that she held discreetly under the table where she sat. Wilksie was engaged in a rather lopsided conversation with the police officers, the manager, and the owner.

The officers recited the law, that Oxford and the surrounding Lafayette County were dry on Sundays and at midnight on all the other days. So at the stroke of twelve, bars were to be closed and empty—no exceptions. The business could lose its license, and those involved would face a fine and even a few nights in the pokey.

Wilksie complimented them on their knowledge of the law and how handsome they each looked in their uniforms and how awful proud their mamas were of them. She learned where they were from, where they attended school, and the names of their teachers. She discussed her memberships in clubs where some of these fine ladies must also have some affiliation.

The manager and the owner took turns explaining their plight to the officers, and Wilksie as well. Wilksie overrode everything the officers tried to say in return, primarily their irritating need to keep mentioning the law.

"The law, the law, is that all you boys talk about?" Wilksie scolded and then mentioned every prominent family from Yazoo City to Biloxi.

It was her third time launching into the speech about the Daughters of the American Revolution weeping for the mamas of these Southern Gentleman who would be ashamed to learn that they raised boys who were so disabused of the notion of chivalry, and honor, and duty that the tide turned in our favor. Wesley sat enraptured, eating up every word of this Master Class on how to wield one's feminine power without so much as a drop of perspiration.

We were allowed to leave. The Three Sisters stood on the Square. The landmark white courthouse built in 1872 served as a dramatic backdrop to their furs, their perfectly styled hair—even their eyes seemed to shimmer like the jewels they wore. It is a striking picture of these three ladies whom I love—powerful, forever emblazoned in my mind. I have so many of those pictures in my mind. I wonder if they would lose their power, their importance, their sentiment, were they one of thousands of pics I have on my phone now. But we didn't have phones that stored precious pictures and even the mundane in those days. We couldn't capture every last moment of significance and then make them somehow less significant. We hold them in our memories, our minds, and our hearts. We lay them on dashboards, like the song says. The streetlights reveal a clearer picture in reverse.

Wilksie and Wesley were given a ride to Cedar Oaks by one of the officers. The rest of us walked back to the apartment. I heard Rudie whisper to Rhiannon.

"Don't tell Randy," he said, "but I think someone put too many cherries and umbrellas in that Wesley boy's drink, you know what I mean?"

That Same Fete from Before

We had moved the party outside to the bricked courtyard between Wilksie's studio and her home. It was decorated as tastefully as could be allowed with all the 75th Anniversary finery that could be found at a Party City. Wilksie had vetoed several of the options offered by Bitsy, Joan, and Vivian, but they got their decorations in just the same. There was even a tall, tiered cake, complete with a wedding topper for the bride and groom. The family was ushered around the cake table for a picture; I was stuck behind Bitsy and her hair. I am always stuck behind Bitsy and her hair. Livie fared no better; she was stuck behind Vivian's.

Boom-Pa was about to take his turn with the camera when Joan let out a terrific cry. Everyone stopped to look, first at Joan because of her rather vexatious outburst, and then to the happy couple being led through the gate by Gio and some man who must have been one of Bitsy's husbands. He wasn't the undertaker, and he wasn't the attorney, not the first one ... he might have been the grocer?

Ettienne wore a smile that was bigger than her entire being. Her whole family was there, it seemed—her children, their children, and in some cases, her children's children's children. Her hands went to her mouth and held her chin as she smiled. She looked about the bricked patio, scanning the decorations and especially her family. Oh, she was surrounded by her family. She could not imagine anything finer.

Dock held Gio's hand. He was a bit frail for being such a tall, large man. Not large like he was heavy or fat, goodness no; he was as lean and thin as they come. But he had these broad shoulders and hands the size of an iron skillet. He looked about the courtyard at what must have been a score of faces— blurred, vague, even unfamiliar. Dock smiled and nodded and held Gio's familiar hand tighter. His eyes did not share in the enthusiasm of his smile until they did when they met the gaze of his Nince. He let go of Gio's hand and reached for her.

Nince handed me the gift-wrapped box. "Hold this carefully."

The two embraced in a long hug; there were tears and there was laughter too. The family shared in the smiles and the laughs and the love, and everyone soon settled in their groups, their cliques, their people within their people. They segregated by generation, or by a common last name—this branch of the family tree here and that branch over there. They all paused and took notice when Eddie came out of the back room with a freshly awakened, fed, and changed Laura. He placed her in his grandmother's lap, and Rudie resisted the urge to tell her to hold her head—mostly because Nince was standing on his foot and Norma was threatening to pinch him. Each generation came together and surrounded Etty as she held her great-granddaughter.

"Randy? What is in that box you been holding for your Nince?" It was Dock. I was so honored he remembered my name, I forgot to speak. "Did ya hear me?"

"Yes, sir. I think it is a gift for Grandmother Etty," I stammered.

"Well, bring it on over so my bride can open her gift," he said with clarity.

Etty passed Laura off to Dock with the help of Eddie. That baby nearly disappeared in his enormous hands. Oh, Eddie was a proud Papa for sure. Rudie hovered, of course. And Nince and I placed the wrapped gift box, nearly the size of Etty herself, across her lap. Etty giggled like a school girl as she peeled back the silver-white paper from the box.

"Such fine paper," Etty whispered, tracing the scrolls and swirls with her ancient hands. Hands really betray age, don't they? "Save me some of this paper, won't you India?"

Nince was the only one who knew what was in the box. She hadn't told Boom; she hadn't told Debra. She did not confide in me, and she certainly did not confide in Dock. "Daddy keeps a secret as well as Norma and Rudie."

Etty struggled to remove the lid from the box. Nince helped her lift it off and passed the lid on to me. Mother had moved in behind me; she took my arm as she leaned against me for support. She was tired, I knew, but she was also where she wanted to be. With her family. She squeezed my arm tight and rested her head on my shoulder as Etty let out a cry.

"Oh Velma. Oh my!" Etty gasped, pulling the sleeve of something dark, something heavy, something furry to her face. "It is fine. It is fine indeed."

And with that, the tiny frail woman celebrating 75 years with the same man jumped to her feet. I use jump loosely, but she moved rather swiftly for such an old gal. Dock even commented on it to her great amusement. Eddie took Laura from

Dock, and Dock stood to help his wife put on her new, very own, knee length, mink fur coat. Ettienne's hands covered her smile and giggles as her handsome groom bowed as low as he could, extended his hand, and asked her for this dance.

"Dock, you silly fool, there is no music." Etty blushed.

"Ettienne Mornay Taylor, from the moment I met you, I can count on one hand the number of times the music has stopped. And even then, when I couldn't hear it here ..." He pointed to his head before bringing her hand to his heart. "... I always heard it here."

It was a beautiful picture, Dock and his bride. With one arm around her waist and the other holding her hand next to his heart, her head rested on his chest, his eyes closed tight. And the two danced to the music in Dock's heart, mind, and soul. I would love to be able to say Etty and Dock danced the night away under the stars there, in Wilksie's courtyard, but they did not. They were old, and they tired easily. And we were offered another, perhaps even lovelier picture for that flip-book of memories. Dock asleep on a settee, his arm draped around a fur-clad Ettienne, who was also asleep—her head still resting on his heart. And across their laps was their sleeping great-grandchild, Laura Evelyn Taylor.

◿   ◿   ◿

Chapter 9
Eddies and Estuaries

Laura Had a Terrible Summer Too

It is most certainly a sad thing when a child is tasked with bury-ing their parents, and yet that is something that happens every day. Eventually, naturally, we will outlive our parents. And we will be tasked with that burial or cremation or some other fu-neral rite. It will be left up to the children. So, there must be, there must be some acceptable age when it seems natural that a child would face the task of laying their parents to rest. Perhaps it is somewhere in their 60s or 70s, or, should their parents live longer, in their 80s or 90s. And why not? Dock and Etty lived that long.

On that same token, a parent should never have to bury their child. And I do mean never. It is not right. It is not natural—and there is just no age that can erase the hurt, the pain, the un-natural wrong of being predeceased by one's own child. Yet that too is a tragedy that occurs every day. Add to that an unpop-ular war, an unforgiving public, and a life of mental, emotion-al, and physical scars that we expect our soldiers to live with. Oh, we help them cope along the way. There are plenty of reme-dies both prescription and not, pills and liquids and smoke—we offer these as the only remedies to deep pain and trauma. And then we shame the folks who rely on what we have pushed to help them battle their demons—and eventually they succumb.

Eddie had demons. Laura buried her father. And Rudie buried his son.

↞   ↞   ↞

IT WAS MOTHER WHO CALLED to tell me Eddie had passed. "Laura found him, bless her. And she called 911 and she even administered Narcan—but he never regained consciousness." She was crying.

"Oh God, I'm so sorry." I didn't know what else to say.

Derwood put Mother and Livie on a plane. He was unable to go because of issues with his own mother. Livie offered to fly with Mother to DC, but she didn't think she could stay long—work, life, family, commitments. She wouldn't even stay for the funeral; she had to get right back. Amy was pregnant. Amy is Livie's wife. They each opted to carry a child for their family; Amy was first. And after their daughter was born—they named her Vilma—Amy learned that she actually enjoyed being pregnant. Livie saw what happened to her wife's body and decided she wanted no parts of that, so Amy was now carrying their second child too.

We all have them, don't we? Commitments. I had them too, but I was on an extended holiday having closed a show I had toured with for the past 13 months. I had also closed a relationship I had toured with for longer than 13 months. I use the word relationship loosely—as relationships are just not my thing. Oh, and I was terrible to him. Of course. I don't know why. Probably because I always am.

I met Mother and Livie at Ronald Reagan; it is an easy in and out airport, and the Metro is right there. Livie complained about how far we had to walk to everything as she pulled Mother's suitcase along with her own. Mother complained about the wheelchair Derwood insisted she take as she has never been steady on her feet since that fall down the stairs, what, 15 years prior?

It is amazing how time passes linearly, but our remembrances twist and shape themselves into a timeline all their own. Madeleine L'Engle and tesseracts come to mind, from one of my childhood favorites, *A Wrinkle In Time.* I think time reveals its wrinkles upon reflection, much like a mirror reveals those on our face … on our hands.

"I have my Mother's hands," Mother said while gripping and ungripping the armrests of her chair. I can look at mine and think the same thing now. They are nearly the size of Dock's, but they look so much like Nince's.

We were on the Metro, barreling through an underground tube toward Woodley Park. It paid tremendously to be the favorite nephew of my grandmother's well-connected sister. I had an extended, rent-controlled lease on an apartment with a stunning view of Rock Creek, covered parking, and walking distance to the Metro all courtesy of Norma's former in-laws. They were not in politics anymore; they just owned things. And I was right next to the zoo!

Livie took the train back to Reagan International while Mother and I took my car and drove down Connecticut Avenue, through Chevy Chase, and decided to stay off the Beltway. Instead we kept on Connecticut until it was no longer Connecticut. It was Georgia Avenue now. And we were approaching a little place called Sunshine. Sunshine, Maryland.

"Well this is a lovely little area," I said as we drove past modest homes on large lots with rolling hills and mature trees.

"Does it look familiar?" she asked, looking out of the window. She was thin this time. Thinner than the last time I saw her certainly. And once again she managed to come through chemo with her hair intact. She was so like her father. And Nince would have been proud of her weight. "What's funny?"

"What?"

"I asked if any of this looked familiar to you; you laughed, and I said, 'What's funny?'"

"Oh, yes. Sorry. I was thinking about Nince and Boom-Pa for some reason. Um. No. Should it?" I answered.

"Well, it is a bit different. Things do change, don't they?" She answered in her usual way of answering without answering.

"Wait, have I been here before?" I looked at the scenery with a bit more interest than my former modest appreciation of the lovely Maryland countryside.

"Well, of course." She rolled her eyes. "We're looking for a white church."

"All the churches are white." It was true, with red doors; very cute. "What do you mean of course? When was the last time I was here?"

"This one will have a lot of cars in front of it. Now don't be funny. What have I told you about being funny?"

"Not to be funny."

"Especially at funerals," we both said. I laughed; she glared but smiled.

And there it was. The little white church with a tall steeple and red door. And there were quite a few cars in front of it, just like she said. I added mine to the mix.

"And when was the last time I was here?" I asked again.

"Well, the first time was when you were six. We stayed at Rudie and Laura's farm; it's just around the bend there." She pointed off in a direction that had neither road nor meaning.

"And the last time?"

"Well, it was only the one time." She closed the car door. "Honestly Randy, you make things so difficult."

"Debbie!" A bundle of sheer black lace and gauze and Ultimate Lightest Platinum came bounding toward us.

Her mother was more subtle; she glided. "Why Debra," Wilksie said as she took Mother's hands in her own, "I just know Velma is looking down on you just as proud as she can be, and thinking how lovely you look. You've lost weight."

"I have," Mother acknowledged, then laughed. "... without even trying."

"Your mother is just so lucky." Bitsy grabbed me by the arm and started marching me toward the family, but not before she shared her jealousy over my lucky mother's effortless weight loss. "I just starve myself half to death or throw it up to look like her."

"Velma might have found this side effect an attractive bonus; she sure did hers." Wilksie held Mother's hand as they walked. "But Debra, honey, I think you look rather thin. We're going to have to do something about that."

"I'm working on it," Mother answered.

"Yes. Well, I'm just a little leery of the kind of food they might serve up here. I've never been to a Yankee funeral." Wilksie touched her hair with her free hand, as if to make sure the high, Aqua-Netted mound had not managed to actually move.

THE YANKEE SERVICE WAS FINE. It was not Baptist. The chicken was not Etty's, and there were no biscuits to compare to Dock's. Not that there were a whole lot of people there to know the difference. There were also no orange ruts in the cemetery. It did alternate between rain and drizzle at the graveside; the angels were weeping over our loss of such a young soul. And then there was a rainbow as the rain slacked off and cleared.

The general consensus being it was Laura, Eddie's mother. It was her smile welcoming her baby boy into Heaven. At least there was still that bit of comfort, assigning Divine commentary upon the random meteorological events.

We ate at a local restaurant, a diner. And we met a lot of family from Eddie's mother's side. They all remarked how Eddie's daughter, Laura, looked so much like his mother. She had height from both sides of the family. Wilksie and Rudie took after the Mornays when it came to height, but the Taylors were all tall people: King, Norma, and Nince are proof of that. Laura had the steel blue eyes of the Taylors, but the softness of her grandmother's. She also had the elder Laura's smooth complexion, warm smile, naturally blonde hair, and her kind, gentle heart.

Laura stayed by Rudie's side. When she had to handle some sort of business matter relating to the burial of her father, Norma took over with Rudie. It had been a rather difficult summer for Laura. Much like the Stolen Summer of Velma Irene Holloway, Laura starred in her own version of that sad movie. Her father's mental illness and addiction had taken their final toll. And helplessly watching the inevitable decline of his only son, Rudie took a turn of his own. His eyes lost their light; like a switch, it was gone.

"He looked like that when Laura died," Norma whispered to me. "It was years before it came back on."

"I don't believe it will this time," Mother said; she held my hand tight. "Not after losing a child."

I thought he looked more like Dock than I ever believed before. Really it was King who took after Dock; Rudie favored the Mornay side. But I remembered Dock having that lost look too, only Etty and Nince reminded him of where he was. I guess we all have those people in our lives, or that person, who reminds us of home, makes us feel safe, helps us know who we are. Rudie had also relied on Nince, and she was gone now too. Once upon a time, it was his wife, Laura. And Eddie, his darling little Eddie. They were all gone. Norma and Laura were there, of course, and Rudie cherished them. But Rudie was a caretaker, Goddammit, he was never supposed to be a burden.

"You look angry," Mother said to me, picking at the breading of the Maryland Fried Chicken on her plate. She wasn't eating it. Just sort of poking, dismantling it with her fork.

"I am," I answered honestly. "I don't know why. I'm trying to pinpoint it. I just feel ..."

"I know." Mother smiled a "not happy" smile, but a smile. "I'm going to try to figure out what this congealed sweet stuff they call cornbread is. Why don't you go rescue Laura?"

She was right. Laura needed to be rescued. She was in an awkward exchange with Bitsy and Wilksie. And Laura's grandmother's family members were all there to observe.

"How is your mother holding up with all of this?" Wilksie asked Laura. "I know they split up years ago, but I couldn't help wondering if a mother would attend the funeral of her child's father, even in estrangement."

"You could ask your daughter," Norma replied.

I stifled a laugh as Wilksie was stunned into a momentary silence.

Laura was less able to stifle hers; she excused herself in a disguised coughing fit. I grabbed the glass of water that had been sitting in front of her and followed.

"Are you alright?" I handed Laura her water. We were standing by a huge fish tank that separated the dining area from the bar.

"I am. Norma told me that Wilksie and Bitsy have been obsessed with whether my mom should be here. Wilksie finally worked up the nerve to ask."

"I'm sorry. My God, you've got so much dropped in your lap

right now—I can't imagine." I felt so awkward. A fish swam by; it was greenish-blue.

"Yeah, but it's been a minute too. It's not like any of this is new. Dad's been sick his whole life—well, my whole life anyway. And Grandpa, he started downhill after Velma passed." Laura responded with what I can only describe as calm. "I believe this is going to be very hard for him. Norma has been a godsend. He trusts her. And Mama tries ..."

"We always called her Amazing Grace because of all she dealt with." I smiled what I hoped was an understanding smile. "At least Mother always did."

"That's sweet. Yeah, Mama took a lot of crap before she finally packed me up and left."

We stared in silence for a moment, both looking through the large tank into the dining room. The bubbles from the aerator rose to the surface, the fish followed their normal routes around the dancing plastic greenery and through the unnaturally colored plastic coral. My eyes followed that bluish-green fish as it picked at a fork. Someone had dropped a fork into the tank.

Wilksie broke the silence with a laugh, and Laura spoke again. "Oh, and Wilksie tries, bless her heart, but she can't go anywhere without ... Lord, I was about to sound so mean."

"No, I get it. It is one thing having a relationship with your grandparent's siblings through your grandparents. It's a different thing when you begin to develop one on your own. It is nice though. I cherish the one I have with your grandfather."

"Oh, he thinks so much of you. He goes on and on about you playin' football for Ole Miss," she said. I think she actually believed him.

"Yes, he used to talk about it, all the years I went. Whenever I came to visit Nince, he came over and we would drink, laugh, and he would ask me about Rebel football."

She laughed, Laura did, truly laughed as we discussed the

times her Grandpa, Nince, and I would sit on her back porch
and drink margaritas, argue, and enjoy the feeling of family. Or
the time all of them came to Oxford and we nearly got arrested.
We laughed and we hugged. It was wonderful to see her relax,
to see her eyes soften, and to watch that ever-reliant warmth and
comfort of family seep in.

Hungover in Oxford

I woke up in the bathtub. I was still in my clothes from last
night, mostly. My shoes and socks were off. The light was also
off, but a candle was burning, so there was a bit of light, casting
shadows to dance about. My head was pounding. And then I
heard water in the pipes ... the tub was filling. But I wasn't wet.

"Good morning, sleepyhead!" It was Lorraine.

"How did you know I was here?" I sort of managed to say
... or something to that effect as Lorraine had an answer ready.

"Silly, I put you there last night." Lorraine laughed. "Norma
and I did. Your Nince reminded us you don't like to sleep in
socks."

"Where was she?" I asked.

"She was laying on the floor counting the things she would
tell your Mother to clean, reminding us about your socks, and
telling Rudie to turn down that dang TV." She explained that
my grandmother didn't do this in any particular order, that
Rudie was not watching TV—he was passed out in my room,
and that it turns out Wilksie can hold her liquor better than any
of them.

"Why do you say that?" I asked, my head pounding. "And
how is your head not hurting? Oh God, and now I hear the
phone."

"Silly, I popped a cork first thing and made a mimosa." She answered like it was the dumbest question in the world. "And Wilksie has already rung once. That's her calling now, I imagine. Apparently, we're having coffee and pastries at the Faulkner House in 45 minutes."

"GOD DAMMIT WHY IS OUR SISTER SO WELL CONNECTED?!"

"Oh yay, she finally got through to Norma." Lorraine laughed. "She was annoyed that nobody would answer, so she called me."

"How did she have your number?" I asked.

"She knows a lady who knows a lady who knows my mama. It's a garden club thing," Lorraine answered simply, as though this were anywhere remotely next to normal. "Honestly, some days you act like you've never been south before."

Breakfast was delightful. The Ladies Auxiliary of Southern Something-or-other put out a delicious spread of pastries, biscuits, assorted jellies, and an omelet station. This was all done under tents. The tables were set with real china and silver, the chairs covered in white linen on this fine, decidedly mild and bright Mississippi December day. It was as though they had ordered the weather, these garden club ladies.

We were greeted by several representatives of the Ladies Auxiliary. They all wore big hats. They also joined us for breakfast. Other guests included the provost and the dean, the vice-chancellor, an undelighted Dr. Singlet and Ho-Ho, and a few other folks the ladies of the Auxiliary deemed necessary. Wilksie and Lorraine chatted with the ladies, drank their tea, wore their large hats, and had a marvelous time. Nince also wore a hat. Wilksie apparently came prepared. But Nince did not wear the same wide smile of her younger sister and Lorraine. She smiled appropriately, don't get me wrong; Nince always did exactly what was required.

Norma was different. "I will punch you like I did when you were little."

"Oh, you are so dramatic." Wilksie stepped back from trying to place a large flowered hat on her eldest sister's head. "It is a tradition of these ladies to wear these hats, so we shall wear them."

Norma's fists were raised.

"It will keep the sun out of your bloodshot and hungover eyes." Wilksie smiled.

"I have sunglasses."

And she did. The kind Jackie O would have coveted. Her Wilksie assigned hat sat on the chair beside her. Rudie was beside her too; he also wore sunglasses. His feet were propped on the same fine linen-covered chair as Norma's borrowed flowered hat. He may or may not have been sleeping. He was. My sunglasses were also intact, on my face, and shielding my eyes from the unnecessarily bright morning sun. Winter in Mississippi is generally kind of cold, damp; it is always spitting a fine cold mist—and it is generally gray. I do not know what magic Wilksie and her Auxiliary of Southern Belles possessed on that day.

Dr. Singlet and Ho-Ho were also a bit worse for the wear. Clearly they had been to the cast party, at least Ho-Ho had. They donned their own eyewear and sipped on their own tea or coffee or what have you. Norma, Rudie, Rhiannon, and I were drinking what have you—with a little assistance from the flask Norma carried. And Wilksie, well, let me tell you, she was on fire.

"So tell me," she said to Ho-Ho, "what part did you have to play in the production we saw last night?"

"I directed," Ho-Ho stuttered. She was confused because they sat together at the show the night before. "We were introduced last night at Fulton Chapel. Just before the show."

"So we were." Wilksie smiled. "Velma, is she the one you

told me about? Velma was telling me all about my nephew and his part in the production. All the technical elements that had to come together. And to think you had to miss all that, bless your heart."

"Yes. I was quite ill." Ho-Ho choked. "Randy really came through—the consummate professional. Our department is blessed to have him."

"You'll have to include that in all your letters of support," Wilksie said, and then she directed her attention toward the vice-chancellor. Oh, Wilksie was gonna get me another scholarship or get me expelled before the day was through.

Back to Laura; Back To Rudie

"Yeah, Grandpa still talks about when you would come to visit Velma; she would call, and he would come right over." Laura and I were sitting with Mother now.

Most of Eddie's mother's side of the family had gone by now. We were in the "special room" of the meat and three that was a local Sunshine favorite. They didn't call it a meat and three, and neither did the family from Laura's mother's side. I guess that's more of a southern thing: one meat and three sides. Two if you ain't that hungry. And, upon confirmation of the guest's hunger level, the waiter or waitress always followed up with the question, "Cornbread or a roll?" Debra would tell you to get the roll, as she never quite came to terms with what they called cornbread.

"I would be more inclined to eat it if it came with strawberries and whipped cream."

It was a lovely wood-paneled and linoleum floor kind of establishment. And there was that fish tank that separated the bar area from the dining area. Rudie sat at a corner booth with Norma. He looked tired and worn and ready to go. I knew Laura would need to leave soon, but I also knew she was enjoying this peaceful time with family.

"Oh yeah, well, we had some good times for sure." I smiled.

"You taught Laura to swim on one of those trips. Do you remember?" Mother interjected.

"No ma'am," Laura answered. "It was before that. I was in middle school and early high school when Randy was at Ole Miss. But he did teach me to swim, yes, ma'am."

"Why did I think it was when you were at Ole Miss?" she asked.

"Probably because you weren't there, but you heard about it from Nince or Rudie. And usually when I was there and you were not, it was when I was at Ole Miss. Before that, I lived with y'all."

"Yes. And we drove up every summer," Mother answered, certain she was not wrong.

"Except the summer you were first diagnosed," I reminded her.

"Oh, that's right. Well. I knew he taught you to swim." She changed the direction of the conversation back to its origins—back to when she was right.

"I do remember that." Laura smiled. "I could swim some, like doggie paddle, but you taught me to float on my back and not to be afraid to open my eyes under water."

"I think I do remember now. We had gone to Lake Martin, right?"

"Yes. And I remember you saying to me that when you open your eyes underwater, you can see things in a whole new way. It's a whole new world where everything dances," Laura said. "Oh, the way you described it made it sound way less scary and way more exciting."

"Wow, I think that's how I sold my thesis project. I think that's the same year I discovered *Ondine*. I had to be in high school. No, I was in undergrad when I discovered *Ondine*. So I guess it was when I came back to visit."

"Wrong again." Laura smiled. "The reunion."

"That's right!" Mother almost shouted. She could forgive herself for getting the facts mixed up; she always got the facts mixed up—but she could also relish in the fact that her know-it-all son was getting the facts mixed up too. And she did.

That opened the door for more conversation—and soon Norma and Rudie were part of the discussion. Norma's snorts brought a concerned Wilksie and a curious Bitsy to the party. And soon our little corner booth, the one Laura and I chose to get away from the sadness for just a moment, was filled with family. Filled with that immutable bond of love and shared experiences, and, of course, what good is a funeral without a little raucous laughter?

I was in the midst of retelling the story of me trying to get a picture of Nince with her sisters. You see, Nince was busy patrolling the room, sniffing glasses as she was concerned there was too much alcohol at this family reunion. There were about three years where Nince decided alcohol was a thing NO ONE should touch. It was only Nince who felt this way, as her siblings were certainly not a part of her tea-totaling bandwagon. And they were not shy about snapping back at their glass-sniffing sister.

"Norma, what's in that glass you gave my grandson?" Nince wore a glare like some folks wear mascara.

Norma didn't get the chance to answer before Rudie had his arm around me and was raising his own glass to Nince. "Liquor? He doesn't even know her!"

"Alright, alright." I was laughing, and Nince's stern face cracked just a little. Rudie always made her laugh, despite herself. "Y'all all sit down so I can get a picture ... The Three Sisters."

"We can't all sit down on that loveseat," Nince announced. "It will collapse under the strain of my two sisters."

Norma's face screamed "Oh no you better didn't!" as she handed Rudie her cocktail and flounced down on the loveseat. She was joined by Wilksie, whose smile to Nince also belied commentary of a sisterly nature. Rudie laughed, and not quietly, and Nince looked at me and then the loveseat. With a giant eye roll and a huge huff, she made her way toward the loveseat. She had just placed her arm around Wilksie and was about to sit down on the arm when the front legs just gave out. The front of the loveseat hit the tile floor with a loud thud. Both Wilksie and Norma bounced—and we all worried Rudie would never catch his breath again as he collapsed in a fit of laughter.

"And what did she do after that?" Rudie asked me. He knew the answer.

"That was when Nince took my glass out of my hand and swallowed the contents like a shot." I laughed. "And her look dared me to tell anyone."

"She took that shot like she did at City Grocery," Norma piped in. "Remember that, India?"

Wilksie smiled her toothsome smile, giving her take on the behavior of her less-than-civilized siblings and their tour of Oxford. "Mama would have been so embarrassed."

"Oh, and remember what Money-Penny wore to the reunion?" Mother dipped her toe back into the conversation.

"I do," Cassie said. That's right. Of course Cassie came to the funeral of her former stepson. She really was a lovely person.

The conversation naturally dissolved at that point. Each of us, in turn, made our excuses or found our reason to leave. Mother and I had a bit of a drive to get back to DC; Norma opted to ride back with us. Her home was in Chevy Chase, just outside of DC. And Norma ribbed Mother about Cassie the entire way home.

"Oh the look on your face, Debbie ..." Norma laughed. "Thank God I have on a thick pad!"

Chapter 10
Dashboard Photographs

I Don't Like Mirrors; I Don't Like Reflections

We are beneath the surface, all of us, looking up—up beyond the break and into another world. A realm of rigid structures and men, neither thing willingly bends. From our vantage, however, they do ... they do bend and dance and breathe distortions. We are the audience and we are the Ondines in this cautionary tale, viewing the action from the depths of a stream or a spring, a pond or a lake—perhaps some gentle river winding its way home.

The lights cast shadows and movements as the beams and shafts are also filtered—through colored gels and gobos and scrims. We see lights dance above the surface as a lightning effect flashes and the cushioned, muted sound of thunder is heard as if from beneath the waves. The filter of the water brings a new clarity, an altered perspective, and we are introduced to another. She is not in our realm, but she is of our realm. She is like us; only she is nothing like us at all. A figure, we cannot see her too clearly, as she is above the surface, beyond the waters. Another flash of dancing silver, a ripple on the surface, and her visage comes into view.

"Ondine!" We hear her name called from off stage left. And then stage right, "Ondine!"

"Randy?!?" Light from the side door flooded the little theatre we called a black box, but it wasn't.

It was painted black, but it was a small performance space for about 150. The stage was somewhat of a modified proscenium, like a framed picture or perhaps a polaroid. So while we did not get to experiment with a thrust or arena-styled presentation, there were still boundaries to push. And I was trying to push them all with my thesis production of *Ondine*. We were in the midst of a tech rehearsal. The lighting designer, sound designer, and I were trying to get the right looks and levels and timing of our cues. Rhiannon was having a costume parade in the various light levels, and I was trying to give my thoughts and approvals of her designs as well. All the elements were coming together.

"Randy!" It was Ermaline. She was the bullet-bra, beehive-wearing department secretary. "There's a call for you. It's your mama."

It is true. She looked like she stepped out of a 1953 *McCall's* catalog. And she was probably the sweetest person, genuinely so, who has ever lived on this planet. She was one of those women of an indeterminate age. You know those ladies; they could be anywhere from their mid-20s to their early 50s. You just don't know—and you sure as shit are not about to ask. She led me toward the department office and then back into Dr. Singlet's office.

"You can use his office for a little privacy 'n stuff." She always ended whatever it was she was saying with "'n stuff."

"Mother?" I sat back in Dr. Singlet's chair and nearly fell over; it reclined rather easily.

"I forgot to warn you," Ermaline said. "I put in an order for a new chair 'n stuff." And she closed the door.

"Randy," Mother said from the other end of the line. "I told her not to interrupt you if you were busy."

"No, no. It's fine," I said. "Is everything okay? Are you okay?"

"I'm fine. I'm a little tired is all. But I wanted to tell you I was so proud of you." Her voice was choking. "I wanted to be there, but ..."

"Um, Mother," I stepped in; she did not like losing composure. "I know."

It was an aggressive surgery they performed, in an attempt to take a rather aggressive little mass that managed to make its way to her lung of all places. How something that started in her colon, presumably, found its way there—I just don't get the science of any of it. Or the fairness. The woman never smoked a day in her life, and they are telling us she has lung cancer now. But with this surgery and some radiation, they think they are onto something. And that is the reason my mother was not able to attend my thesis project. Nobody was. And now she was calling to apologize to me.

"Nince is here. She so wants to be there too," she continued, "and your father."

"No they don't." I answered her matter-of-factly; it really was rather simple. "They both want to be with you, the one recovering from major surgery. It is where they are supposed to be. And I want them to be there too. I'm fine." I wanted to be there too. I did. But I also didn't. And I wasn't fine.

Had I known going into the surgery how serious it all was, I would have been there. I would absolutely have put all this on hold. But in Mother and Nince's great wisdom, they opted to withhold the information from me, so I wouldn't "do something foolish and risk not graduating." To be fair, I had been spoken to in the past for relying on some fellow grads to teach my classes while I was back and forth to wherever it was my mother was having her variety of experimental treatments: Johns Hopkins in Baltimore, Shands in Gainesville, even some place called King's Daughters. This time they were in Orlando. Closer to home. Their home.

She put me on speaker phone so I was forced to talk with everyone who was there. I did so curtly. I still hadn't gotten over their decision not to tell me. Mother and Nince—I understood them, so I wasn't surprised. But I was livid with Derwood, and felt particularly betrayed by Livie. We spoke for maybe ten minutes? Maybe 15? I answered the questions about how rehearsal was going. And I promised Nince I would relay her well wishes to Lorraine and Rhiannon. And I promised I would be on the first plane out of Memphis once this show closed. It would be Spring Break; I wouldn't need to miss any more classes.

"And you are where you need to be too, Randy. Don't you worry over me. I love you. Now break a leg or whatever you say to the stage director." She never just said director. "My son was the stage director!" she would say, even when I wasn't.

I hung up the phone. I sat back and fell to the floor. The chair flipped right over, my legs flew into the air, and I landed with a rather loud crash. A few books and pictures fell from the shelf that the chair and I struck on our way to the ground. And I laughed. I laughed hard. I laughed so hard until the tears just streamed down my face—and I didn't even notice the moment my laughter turned to sobs.

"Oh, bless his heart," Eramline said to Dr. Singlet. They were both in the doorway moments after the crash. "He just hung up from his mama 'n stuff."

Dr. Singlet didn't say a word. He helped me up, he hugged me, and he held me as I wept. When I was through, and I had caught my breath, blown my nose, and I was about to launch into an embarrassed apology ... "Now, shouldn't you be in rehearsal? You're Equity, I think you've gone beyond your break."

I smiled. I thanked him. And I thanked Ermaline on the way out. She blessed my heart 'n stuff.

The rest of rehearsal went well, if somewhat awkward. Rhiannon's costume designs, the set, all enhanced by the lighting ... they gave credence to my concept that we were watching all the scenes of this play from beneath the surface of the waters, rivers, lakes, and streams. The lines and definitions and boundaries all blurred, distorted by the dancing shadows and light when they move and breathe and reflect. Everything bends beneath the surface, including us. We were the "old ones" who knew how this story would end. And we were her sisters—the other Ondines—helpless to save her yet destined, perhaps, not to learn from this cautionary tale. We were all watching this struggle, this battle of coming to terms with one painful truth ... we are not to others what they are to us. Even in love.

LORRAINE AND I WERE BATHING, going over the ins and outs of the rehearsal we'd just had. Lorraine was my Ondine, and she was doing a spectacular job of conveying the imperfections of perfection. One scene was troubling her, and we were in the midst of a deep conversation.

There is a beautiful and heart wrenching moment as Ondine describes to her love all the treasures she has stolen from him: a boot, an old picture frame, or maybe just a fork. She has placed these things in a careless yet deliberate manner all over the oceans and streams and rivers, the world in which she truly belongs. Ondine knows her love is to die, and she is doomed to forget who he was the very moment he takes his last breath, the moment her sisters call her name for a third time. So she hides these objects of his about her world of rivers and oceans, knowing she will one day find them again and wonder what these beautiful and unfamiliar things are. She will cherish these unfamiliar treasures she finds and hold them, collect them, love them ... and in doing so she will always be true.

The phone rang; it pulled me from the depths of discussion as Rhiannon shouted through the door it was for me. I think both Lorraine and I held my breath as I went to answer the phone. I knew it was Mother again ... or worse, it wasn't Mother.

"Was it your mother?" Lorraine asked breathlessly when I returned.

I slipped back into the water, letting the warmth embrace me.

"Randy?" She asked again. "Who was it?"

"It was my boyfriend."

"Wesley?"

"Wesley is not my boyfriend."

I heard Lorraine sit up in her tub. I imagined the bubbles I know she always used sliding off her shoulders. I wanted to distract or evade or follow my mother's sage advice and "Run!" But the gate was locked and the fence was too high, and the pull of the water had me in an eddy-like trap, a whirlpool from which I could not escape.

⟁   ⟁   ⟁

WE MET AT ONE OF those summer stock gigs. Upstate New York, somewhere in the Catskills, at a barn turned performance venue with a rather impressive summer schedule. *Kiss Me Kate* and *Taming of the Shrew* were done in repertory style for four weeks, followed by four weeks of another pair of shows, *Ring Round the Moon* and *A Streetcar Named Desire*. Aaron was an intern, an apprentice actor earning points for his Equity card. I stage-managed. And when the diva Equity lead found a mouse in his room in the cabin he shared with Aaron and two other apprentices, the solution I found was to give him my small apartment above the theatre box office. I took his room in the cabin.

Aaron had essentially chorus roles in *Kate* and *Shrew*. And he played the boy who lights Blanche's cigarette in *Streetcar*. After the mainstage shows, the interns would perform a cabaret act—a late night showcase of musical theatre favorites. I hate musical theatre, none of them are my favorites—though they often pay the bills. But I had a growing fondness for the strikingly handsome Aaron. Slim, athletic, with eyes the color of blue you only see in the compacted ice of a glacier. And they cut through you, bore into your very heart and soul ... at least they did me. And a ship called Titanic, as I recall.

It was Aaron I told first about *Ondine*. There was a stream not too far from our cabin. It wound its way from its source, through and down the mountains. Spilling and tumbling and flowing its way into larger streams, then rivers, then finally the bay or the ocean. I had scored the remaining third of a bottle of tequila and a six-pack from behind the bar. I bought it; I didn't steal it. It was late, or maybe just incredibly early; the cabaret had ended whatever time it was. I drove Aaron back to the cabin, parked my truck, and he started inside. I walked down to the stream.

The moon was bright on the water, almost full. And the light danced in the ripples and tumbles of the cool stream before me. A footpath to the left carried me up to a granite ledge that hung over the deep pool below. The stream fell onto the end of the granite before spilling over, continuing its wandering journey. The sound, while not a deafening roar, still offered an echo as it crashed against the hard stone. I set the tequila bottle in a shallow indentation of the stone, filled with cool water from the falls. It was the perfect spot to chill any beverage. I set the six-pack on a drier bit of rock; no need to soak the cardboard case. Or my socks and shoes; I took those off and set them by the beer. I cracked open one of the Molsons, took a large swallow, and I somehow lost the sound of the footsteps behind me in the echo of the water.

"Do you feel like sharing a beer?" I found the footsteps; they belonged to Aaron.

Though startled, I didn't react. I simply said, "Sure." I slid over as if to offer space on this offshoot of granite that held ample room.

"You had my mind racing after telling me a little bit about that play." He was awkward in his approach, as though it wasn't really the play he wanted to talk about. When he sat down, he sat closer than he perhaps needed to.

"I do love it," I said. "It is a powerful piece." I stretched my legs out and let the fall of the water massage my toes. "I've read it a dozen times already."

"What attracted you?" His eyes felt so icy warm; it was like he stared right into me. His shoes were off too, and when he sat down, his feet met mine under the falls.

My mind muttered, "Your eyes." And I'm not sure my mouth didn't as well. He blushed. I stammered on, "Um, I mean ... it's such an emotional piece, but the way the story is told, the Old One speaks directly to the audience as though the audience is a part of it all, complicit. And the richness of it, the interruptions, the discrepancies, and contradictions ... it allows someone like me to connect."

"And who is someone like you?" he asked. His fucking eyes. Why did he always have to look me in the eyes?

"Um. Someone who avoids emotion." I laughed. "Wanna take a shot?"

I stood and walked over to the indentation filled with cool water and an emotion-avoiding bottle of tequila. I took a swig and then pointed the bottle in his direction. He walked over to me; his eyes held mine as he took the bottle from me and tipped it back. I set the bottle back down. The spray of the water felt cool as it splashed back from the rock. I turned to look at him. He was about to speak when I reached forward. My hands found the sides of his face; he had just one dimple on his left cheek. And this slight imperfection with that one tooth. God, he was beautiful. I pulled him into me as I stepped backward into the cascading water. Our mouths opened at the sudden chill of snow melt and spring water pouring over us—and then met in their own warm embrace. Let me tell you ... that moment, that kiss—it was the single sexiest moment of my entire fucking life.

The rest of it was pretty hot too. We made out, me made love, we made hot fucking sex ... at one point the action fell apart as we slid from the ledge and fell a hilarious four feet down into the pool of water below. We were inseparable for the rest of the summer. And tear-filled as we parted. I went back to Ole Miss. His hometown was Toronto. I found it very funny that I had a secret boyfriend I essentially met at summer camp who no one knew, not in any of my realms. And he lived in Canada. And I liked that.

⁂   ⁂   ⁂

"AND Y'ALL HAVE BEEN TOGETHER how long?" My tub was starting to go cold; I think Lorraine's anger kept her bath rather heated.

"Oh, let's see ... this was the summer before my junior year in undergrad?" I tried to recall.

"That's five years," Lorraine said.

"Really? That long?" I was trying to do the math. "Huh."

"Huh? That is what you have to say? Huh?"

"Do you hate me?"

"Yes," she said matter-of-factly.

"I do too."

"I know you do. And that hurts my heart because I also love you. A thing you seem to have a real hard time ever doing."

⚜   ⚜   ⚜

AARON FLEW INTO MEMPHIS AND he rented a car. He knew I had so much going on, rehearsals were late into the night, and this show was ... well, it was *Ondine*. He was crafty, Aaron, and he made his way to Bryant Hall, and up the steps, and into the theatre just as we went to places for final dress. He saw me in the back and waved; I motioned him over. Our knees touched as he sat, and we exchanged a quick kiss as the lights went dark.

The Ondines called, the lightning flashed, and we watched as the two worlds met in a confluence of desires and dreams and intentions. And the Old One guided us in and out of the estuaries, the creeks, the lakes, and the eddies and whirlpools of our story. Two lovers, neither could be true to themselves when in the other's realm. As Ondine told Hans of all she had taken, had hidden, and how she would always be true ... Aaron's hand held mine, I could see, I could almost feel his tears as they streamed down his face and fell on the hard granite of my soul.

We stayed at his hotel, no Cedar Oaks for Aaron. And though we shared a bed that night, after an obligatory round of not our best sex, I don't know that either of us slept as we held each other 'till dawn.

Aaron had asked to see where Faulkner lived. So he and I drove to the cemetery. I brought a towel from the hotel and spread it out next to his monument. We sat in the light breeze, the sun dappled through the new leaves, and we didn't really talk.

"Nobody knows who I am, do they?" Aaron broke the silence.

"What?" I stared hard at Faulkner's name etched in marble. "I mean, Lorraine does. She'd like to meet you."

"And you won't even look up at me while I'm trying to talk

to you." Instinctively I reacted as if to a dare; our eyes met briefly before mine darted away again. "See?"

His fucking eyes.

"We can still make it by his actual house if we hurry," I
said. "I have to get to my call time."

"I figured it out last night, during the play. I watched your
whole entire being run away from every emotion you gave us
on that stage. Every moment, every feeling, every image was a
snapshot of what you have been ..." And then he laughed a heavy
sigh. "No, I'm wrong about that. You're not running away; you
are stealing them. That's what it is. Randy, you steal every painful thing in your life and hide it away, only to find it again like
Ondine in your play. And when you find it again, you hold on
to that pain like some newly discovered treasure or like it is the
only thing you ever loved."

"Great material; maybe I can use it in my thesis."

"You probably should. It would be the truest thing you ever did."

That one stung. I looked up at him. Into those eyes whose
glacier blue burned right through me. I felt so cold ... I felt ... "I
don't love you," I finally said.

Aaron stood up. "Yeah ya do," he said. "You wanna know
how I know?"

I didn't answer. I stood to face him though. I wasn't going
to be talked down to. His eyes were less cold.

"Because you brought me to a cemetery to break up with
me." His hands held my face as he planted one last, long kiss
on my trembling lips. He walked back to his rented SUV and
looked back one last time. "Everything important to you, everything that means anything to you ... it happens in a fucking cemetery in Mississippi. A fucking cemetery, Randy!"

I looked over at Faulkner; he had heard the whole exchange.
Not really. He was dead. But my mind was doing that thing
where I cover up feeling ... anything. And so all it ever does is

make some fucking lame joke. There were no orange ruts and there was no one to comment on the weather.

I walked back to my apartment. It started to rain, a light spring shower, but it served the function of hiding the tears on my face. I took a bath. I took the coldest bath I could stand to submerge myself in. I wanted to be numb. And every time I began to feel something, I sank to the bottom until it went away. Or until it didn't. And when it didn't ... I believe it was Aaron I told I didn't do well with emotion.

I met Lorraine outside, and we walked together to the theatre. She was my Ondine, and we walked hand in hand as I gave more notes and thoughts and discussions on the performance. Lorraine listened and nodded as we walked. She was quiet. She said nothing; she absorbed it all.

At the bottom of the steps to Bryant Hall she stopped me. She took both my hands and looked me deep in the eyes. I stared back; I hoped my eyes weren't bloodshot. I would just blame it on the Holy Water from the bath.

"RAIN-de." My God, why am I hearing her say my name like they do? "When I first came here to Ole Miss, I wasn't sure I wanted to stay. I didn't think I would fit in. But the actors, they talked about you as a director. An "actor's director" they called you. You have a way of tapping, helping us tap into places so deep within ourselves, to portray such truth to our emotion—because what we feel is so real. But my God, Randy, no direction you have ever given taught me as much about feeling as the last 35 minutes when I just couldn't bear to let you be alone. I felt like such a thief sitting there on the side of my tub like that. Listening to you tear your whole self apart to get at your heart and ..."

I hugged her—and held myself together as we embraced. I was still raw; I wasn't sure I would make it through my opening night. Nothing more was said; we just hugged. But I think it was enough acknowledgement for Lorraine that I wasn't mad. And I was grateful she maybe didn't still hate me.

We parted ways at the top of the stairs. Lorraine went backstage to the dressing area and the rest of the ensemble. I poked my head in the tech booth and checked on my stage manager. Everything was good to go. We were at half-hour to curtain when I went to the back to say my final finals to the cast and crew. Lorraine was almost luminescent in her shimmering translucent gown, the long white-blonde tresses she wore over her little brunette pixie transformed her into the Ondine I had always envisioned. She was everything I described to Aaron that day under the falls. In another time. In another world.

"Randy!" Ermaline poked her head backstage. "Randy you've got some flowers 'n stuff in the grad-office. Just pull the door to when you leave, and it will lock behind you 'n stuff. Oh my, the roses are just breathtaking. I've never seen that color before."

Livie, I thought. She knew I loved roses. Or Mother. Mother probably asked Livie to send flowers. And I was right. There was a beautiful arrangement of mixed flowers, an absolutely gorgeous spring bouquet with a card. "Break a leg!" it said. "I love you, Mother." Livie sent a bottle of tequila and a note bemoaning how difficult it was to get in this hellscape of a nearly dry county. And then there was the large vase overflowing with roses. Ermaline was right, they were absolutely breathtaking 'n stuff. They were white, these roses, such a pure, pure, pale white, they were almost blue. There was no card. But the vase rested on a package wrapped in a similar fashion to the ribbon tied round. I hastily opened it. It was two books. A hardbound copy of *Ondine* in French and a clothbound copy of *Undine* in German. They were purchased at a used bookstore in Toronto.

☙   ☙   ☙

AS IS OFTEN THE CASE, each performance grew stronger, and each actor found more and more of what they were searching for. And, in doing so, they gave more and more to the audience. I was lucky to have an amazing ensemble who trusted me. And I told them all again and again in a teary-eyed and semi-drunken rambling at the cast party.

"Randy! Randy! SHHH! RANDY!" Lorraine thought she was whispering. She put her finger on my lips, and partially in my nose as she shushed me. "I told you when I first met you. Everyone says you are an actor's director. And you are."

Even Ho-Ho, who again inserted herself on my thesis committee's discussion after the production had closed, was complimentary. She went so far as to offer to guest lecture one of my acting classes so I could stay an extra week in Florida. Dr. Singlet agreed that would be fine. Now I had time to drive and not fly. I felt like there was more freedom that way. And I started to pack my baggage. All of it. I packed all the praise, all the success, and the coming down from the high of having worked so hard ... and everything that didn't work ... I packed all of that away. I did not have time to deal with those things, plays and praise, and disappearing into a world I am able to create and craft and design ... I had to get back to Orlando. Get back to Mother. Back to family, and sickness, and real life. I had to disappear into that world where there was no room for Aarons ... there was barely room for me.

Mississippi Yearning

They were waiting for me, The Blonde Contingency, and, of course, high and buoyant were their heads of hair. It is hard to mention them without saying that tired old joke. They sat in order of hair color, not age: Joan, being the mousiest, was on the inside of the booth; Vivian in the middle; my most platinum cousin was on the end.

"Randy!" (Or RAIN-de!) Joan shouted across the restaurant. Attempting to stand from her inside position in the booth and get my attention, she knocked over a glass of water.

The hostess greeted me as well, and I pointed toward the apologizing and embarrassed woman and her two annoyed sisters. "I'm with them. I think we need some extra napkins."

We were at Perkins, on 436, also known as South Semoran Boulevard. They needed my opinion on something that was somewhat of a delicate matter—my cousin Gio, Bitsy's boy. My mind reeled at all the possibilities of this conversation, Livie and I having joked about it much of the night before, if not much of our lives. I was staying with Livie during this extended Spring Break, because Nince and Norma were staying with my folks. I had gotten over my anger, but not all of my hurt, over my family's decision to keep me in the dark on this one. I understood, but did not agree with their sentiment of keeping the seriousness of it from me until after my thesis project was done. And it was done. All of it. My thesis and the surgery. And Aaron. And two out of three were successful, it seemed. Didn't Meatloaf sing something to that effect? I put that other matter away, maybe next to a fork, maybe a boot, maybe a forgotten book on a shelf with a rose petal crushed inside. But that was not why I was at Perkins with Bitsy, Joan, and Vivian.

Gio was about to open a large new church. It was one of those mega-churches and was being built just outside of Orlando in a little community called Sanford. Sanford is a lakeside town that boomed when the St. Johns River was a primary means of transportation. I-4 runs right through it, and several high dollar neighborhoods are on its outskirts. Gio and his new wife were building a home in one of those communities, Heathrow. His choir director and best friend was also newly married. Oh, and it is quite the story, especially when delivered by three aggressively smiling southern belles with an agenda.

In turn, they each delivered their lines and told me how this choir director friend and Gio dated a set of twins—two sweet little girls who were a part of the congregation and staff at their previous church. This was when they lived just outside of Atlanta. They had a double wedding. It was so precious: the brides matched; the grooms matched. They all shared the same bridesmaids and groomsmen. And now they were about to be neighbors too. That's right, Brooks, that was his name, Brooks. He and his little bride were building a house next door to Gio and his little bride. It was all rather sweet and clearly "clandestined"—at least that is the word one of my cousins used while explaining all this to me.

"They married two young ladies?" I clarified.

Joan looked at me, confused. "Well, what else would they marry ... dogs?"

"They are not what one would call traditionally attractive, no, bless them ..." Vivian tried to lighten the mood. "But I would not call them dogs."

"Oh you're bad." Joan laughed. "They are very sweet, if a little boxy and plain."

"We are not here to talk about Gio's marriage." Bitsy took control of the conversation. "We are actually very concerned for Debra. She is not well, is she?"

"No," I agreed. "She is not well. She has cancer. All over. She is not doing well at all, but she is fighting. Recovering from an aggressive surgery actually."

"Mmm." All three offered the same reply, followed by their own version of "so sad" or "bless her heart."

It was clear they had rehearsed this little play or pantomime (if only there were music), and each had prepared a little monologue. Vivian's was about her concern for Nince, Norma, and Wilksie and the amount of time and attention they were giving my mother. They had, of course, all come down for the grand opening of whatever the name of Gio's megachurch would be. And it seemed that Debra's recovery from that surgery, well, it was stealing some of Gio's thunder.

Joan was next. Her concern was for Norma and Velma's health. Should they really, at their age, be around my mother who was so clearly ill? What if they got sick too? She was also concerned about Derwood. He didn't need his in-laws helping him; he needed to hire a proper nurse. She was about to insinuate something about Livie's laziness in this matter, but I think Joan had a brief moment of being able to read the room when our eyes locked at the mention of my sister.

"Livie has a career and a home, and she manages to see our folks at least three nights a week," I said plainly. "I am grateful she is so close."

Realizing Joan's script was not working, it was time for Act 3. Bitsy took center stage.

"What my sisters and I are trying to say ..." Her smile was not unlike Wilksie's, though more aggressive; she did not possess Wilksie's capacity for nuance—nobody does. "We find it imperative that Debra come to the opening services this Sunday ... Randy!"

"I'm sorry." The poor soul wearing a giant squirrel costume, whose job it was to wander in and out of the aisles between tables and interact with guests, provided an easy distraction as I tuned out the ridiculousness these insipid women were spouting. "What?"

"We think your mother should attend the opening of Gio's church. It's this Sunday," Bitsy repeated.

I stared at the three Cheshire Cats staring back at me, and then I looked back at the human-sized squirrel. "I mean ... I'll ask her. I guess it'll really depend upon how she's feeling."

"We feel if your mother doesn't go, then Velma and Norma won't go either. And that would be sad and silly, now wouldn't it?"

"Mmm," I offered as my reply before putting on my own aggressive smile. "Sad and silly doesn't even begin to describe it. But I don't believe, even if my mother isn't feeling well, that it would be cause for Nince or Norma to miss the grand opening."

In unison, The Three Sable Sisters breathed a sigh of relief and sat back. We ate our breakfast. We were finishing our coffee, and the waitress brought us our check. One of the three informed our waitress that they were in the presence of a true southern gentleman; the other two nodded in my direction. I reached out my hand for the check.

"So what time is the ribbon cutting?" I asked.

"Oh, Randy," Vivian giggled. "You make it sound like a car wash."

"Similar concept." I laughed, placing some cash on the table for a tip as I stood.

Vivian did too—laughed, not tipped. Joan looked confused, but smiled. "Oh you are a wicked little Dickens." Bitsy grinned and hugged me.

"Aren't I though?" I kissed them each on the cheek and we left.

We hugged and said our goodbyes in the parking lot too. They drove away in Joan's new Saab, an anniversary gift from her husband. I got into my used Toyota pickup. I apparently left my lights on, and I needed to find a kind stranger to offer me a jump. I needed a lot of things. And the stranger turned out to be pretty cute—and helpful.

What I Found Down By the Pond

"RAIN-de!" It was Nince.

It was the morning after Dock and Etty's big party. Livie

and Mother stayed at Wilksie's. I opted to go to French Camp with Nince and Norma. I knew I would have to sleep on that lumpy old couch, and I knew it was a little creepy, but I also knew it was a lot more fun. At least for me.

"RAIN-de!" Nince whisper shouted again. "Come help me with breakfast."

I opened my eyes and saw Nince, her head anyway, poking in from the kitchen doorway. She saw I was awake, was satisfied I would not go back to sleep, and disappeared back into the kitchen. I sat up, stretched and yawned, and got my socks on. I walked into the kitchen to see Nince; she was trying to roll out biscuits. I knew her thoughts on biscuits right away; canned ones are easier, but there were no canned biscuits here. Not at her Mama and Daddy's. She had a mess of flour, well, everywhere—her hands, her hair, and all over the table.

"Oh, Nince," I said as I noticed her frazzled distress. "Can you work on the bacon or something?"

"Canned biscuits are just so much easier and cleaner," she mumbled as I took her place rolling out the dough while she fumbled about looking for bacon and the grits.

I placed the biscuits in the skillet she had already greased— she had that part down. Nince poured me a cup of coffee. It was awful. Weak, like tea, but she was such a wreck this morning I didn't want to complain. I heard the toilet flush, and then steps in the hall. It was Dock. I wiped my hands and we all greeted each other. Nince set a hot cup of coffee in front of her father.

"You didn't get much juice outta this bean." Dock smacked his lips and tasted his tongue, as though more flavor would be found.

"Randy did the biscuits!" Nince exclaimed. I'm not sure if she was throwing me under the bus or attempting to praise my efforts. "And I've got bacon going. I'll do the grits and Randy can do the eggs."

"Sounds good." Dock smiled, and then winced as he sipped his coffee.

"What's that happenin' in my kitchen?" It was Etty. She was calling from her room.

"Well," Dock shouted back from his chair. "It looks like Nince got Randy up to make the biscuits she was wrasslin' with. She never could make biscuits."

"Oh, bless her!" Etty called.

Norma stumbled in at this point. I guess the inter-room chatter woke her. She didn't speak; she just poured coffee and sat down.

"Norma just got up. She's a ball of sunshine," Dock kept Etty informed.

Norma tasted her coffee then spit it back into her cup. She got up and poured it out in the sink, along with the remains of the pot on the stove. And she loudly, or as loudly as one can, scooped coffee grounds back into the filter of the stovetop percolator, glaring at my grandmother the whole time.

"Do you need help getting up, Mama?" Nince called back.

"Oh, no thank you, dear," Etty giggled. "I'm just wondering how we gonna eat all this food ..."

"It's not that much, just breakfast; there's five of us this morning. Daniel's sleeping in, he told me," Nince said as she was glaring back at her sister who was making an unnecessary spectacle out of making coffee.

"Boom tied one on last night." Dock laughed while Norma touched her hand to her temple.

"But Gio will be by, and he brings so much over from that man's store," Etty said; she was in the doorway now.

"I'll get your coffee once it's decent, Mama." Norma finally spoke, though she still stared daggers at her sister. Norma did not enjoy mornings.

"What man?" Nince asked.

"Oh, Elizabeth's latest. I can never remember their names. He owns the Piggly Wigglys." Etty took her seat at the table beside her husband.

"Don't you look fine." Dock smiled and kissed his bride's cheek.

Etty giggled and pulled her new fur coat tight around her. "I slept in it. It is so cozy."

We were just cleaning up from our first breakfast when a small caravan arrived. Gio and Bitsy led the way; their backseat was loaded with boxes from the Pig's Bakery and Deli. The rest of The Blonde Contingency followed. Liv and Mother's more natural blonde allowed them to be unwilling members of this club. They rode with Joan and Vivian. Wilksie brought up the rear. She was in the backseat of her Lincoln. She had decided to purchase it after her latest unfortunate incident had caused the Mississippi State Highway Patrol to order a governor placed upon Wilksie's car. Well, she wasn't going to suffer the indignity of chains on her own vehicle, so she purchased a more sensible car and hired a "boy" to drive her.

We ate our second breakfast. Etty was pleased as punch her family was at her table. They were smiling and laughing, and she was eating a cheese danish and wearing a fine mink coat. Norma and Nince cleaned up; Mother helped too, though Wilksie tried to keep her at the table to discuss ... you know ...

"Women's things." Wilksie smiled. "Now why don't you go find Gio; he took some of the pastries down to the ..."

I knew who she meant. Thurgoode and his family, and the other folks who lived in the row of houses down the clay road. She did use the word folks, but yeah, there was that other word too. Livie was about to get up to go with me when Wilksie put an arm around her.

"Yes, a fine chat for just us girls." She smiled her toothsome smile.

Livie mouthed the words "Help me!" and she began to blink

her eyes. I'm not up on my Morse code ... but her message was clear. I paused long enough to think of something to say in an effort to rescue my sister. But I didn't get the chance.

"Now you run along now, RAIN-de." Again Wilksie flashed her trademark punctuation. "And Daddy, you go on and get dressed; you don't want to hear us hens cackling anyway."

✍   ✍   ✍

I LEFT THE KITCHEN AND made my way down the porch steps toward the picnic table. I sat down under the shade of the pecan tree. The breeze was so fresh and clean. I could hear Wilksie and Norma, though I could not make out what they were saying. And I couldn't tell if it was arguing or laughter, but since Livie hadn't figured out how to escape yet, I decided to go wandering on my own. Maybe I would go find Gio. I walked toward the cars; it seemed like a good idea to find that man who drove for Wilksie. Maybe he knew if Gio had gotten back yet. In my world that demanded quick turnarounds; it seemed like Gio had plenty of time to walk down to Thurgoode's and those other houses and back. I didn't even really want to find him. He was older than me—and weird. He made me feel, well, like he knew things about me that I didn't understand.

The man Wilksie hired wasn't there. At least he wasn't sitting in or standing by Wilksie's Lincoln. I looked down the highway toward the cemetery. Would the guy have walked to town? I wasn't going to. I decided to walk toward the barn, Goody's, and the pond. The clay was slick. It had rained this week, quite a bit actually. And everything seemed so vibrant and even more colorful with the orange dust washed away. I avoided the puddles in the ruts; some were quite large, but Mother would kill me if I ruined these new sneakers.

I pondered briefly over Mother—like why did she insist

on Livie and me looking like little magazine models or fresh out of the New Mickey Mouse Club in a backwoods, nowhere, Mississippi town where everything was covered in a sepia film or kudzu. It made no sense to me. And there was zero chance my white shoes were not gonna get soiled. There was zero chance Livie was going to put on the dress Mother insisted she pack, not unless she got Nince involved. Oh God, I hope that's not why they kicked me out of the house—to gang up on Livie! I started to go back when I saw something white blowing, maybe waving from a tree branch near the pond, just up the way. I decided to walk a few yards further. Was it a flag? No. It was a shirt. And folded on the branch next to it were some more clothes. And on the ground were a few more mismatched items: clothing, shoes, and hats.

Along the tree line, just up from the bank of the pond, I saw some figures standing. The shadows and light played so it was hard to make out faces on their dark skin, but Wilksie's driver and another man, plus two younger teens were standing in a half circle. I didn't recognize them. It wasn't Thurgoode; I could tell that much. And I could see the back of Gio's head as he knelt before them. One of the younger teens had their hands on his bare shoulder. I stopped in my tracks, and then quietly tried to secure a more secluded spot so I could see just what was going on a little bit better. I crouched low. I rested my hand on a broken bit of blackberry bush, the dried brown stem of thorns attaching itself violently to my hand.

"Dammit!" I muttered, pulling the thorny stick from my palm.

I looked back up to see one of the men and the teens making their way from the trees to the water. Then Gio did too. I could see now that they were all naked. The other man was pulling the white shirt from the branch where it hung; he buttoned the shirt as he walked back toward the road. It was Wilksie's driver. He carried the jacket of his suit over his arm as he made his way back down the orange clay road—back toward my great-grand-parents', back toward Wilksie's Lincoln. I pretended to pick blackberries as he passed by my not-so-secluded location. I ate a few. They were still closer to red, not black, and rather bitter.

"Wanna go swimmin'?" he asked, blowing me a kiss as he passed me by.

I blushed a crimson deeper than those unripe blackberries and managed to mutter something stupid. He just laughed and then whistled a little tune as he walked on down the road. I watched him walk a little ways; he never looked back. I took a deep sigh of relief; my heart was pounding. I turned my attention back to the nudity in the pond. Gio and his friends splashed about in the muddy water, floated, roughhoused, and a few other things I could not quite make out from my vantage point—especially when they all went behind that tree again. I soon had to adjust myself, and not because of the thorny briars, and then looked up in embarrassment as my eyes met Gio's from across the way. He said something to his friends, and they all stood in their glory, watching me now. I tried to crouch lower, to disappear, but the stab of pain and the trickle of blood from my knee let me know the jig was up. I stood, I turned, and I ran. I ran like that small town boy from Bronski Beat ... I ran so fast I couldn't hear Gio and his friends laughing.

⌒   ⌒   ⌒

"DID YOU FIND GIO?" MOTHER asked as I came breathlessly through the front door.

She was sitting in the front room, the living room we would call it—parlor was Wilksie's word. A book was resting face down on the green, yellow, and orange chevron-patterned afghan that covered her lap. She must have dozed off.

"Randy?" she asked again.

"Um, he was down by the pond, I think. I didn't walk that far." I blushed.

"Come here; you look flushed," she said, and her hands were all over my forehead looking for signs of fever.

"I'm fine." I wiggled from her clutches. "Where's Livie?"

"I can't believe you didn't see her. She's out back with Dock," she said.

"I was out front."

"Well, you should run find her. Apparently, there are puppies." She smiled.

"Puppies?" I asked, walking toward the kitchen to see if I could see out of the side window.

"You better run see." She smiled a tired smile.

I did. I bounded out of the kitchen door to see Dock and Nince at the picnic table. A yellow-meated watermelon was cut up on the table. Nince was eating a slice. Norma and Livie were in the grass. Norma had a puppy in her lap and was laughing as Livie had about four of them.

"Randy!" Livie shouted joyfully. "Puppies!"

We played with the puppies and ate watermelon that afternoon. Gio caught an earful from Wilksie for being gone so long. Etty threatened to make him get a switch if he was down at that pond.

"You ain't too grown for one, now, you hear? Just 'cause you can drive a car." She giggled, mostly poking fun at how annoyed Wilksie was. "And India will whoop you good with it."

It was time for everyone to get going now. The folks staying in Kosciusko had to get home to change for dinner. The folks in French Camp had to start getting ready so they could meet the folks in Kosciusko at the restaurant owned by one of Bitsy's friends. And Boom was heading back home; he had a medical appointment at the base in Montgomery.

We were having an anniversary dinner for Dock and Ettienne.

Yes, another one. While the garden party at Wilksie's was per-fection (save for the tacky decorations as provided by Bitsy, Joan, and Vivian), it was just not enough for the "Paterfamilias and Grand Dame of the Taylor Clan"—at least according to those same three Marthaless Stewarts who were now sitting across the table but way further down from me. We were eating at the fin-est steak and pasta joint in town. Think Ponderosa meets Olive Garden with a heavy Tudor, Ye Merry Olde England flair. So classy. But then Bitsy's friends were always classy.

I sat next to Livie. Nince was on my other side, and Norma was directly across from me. We were at a large table in a sec-tioned-off party room. Faux wooden beams and trimmings en-cased us like a Henry VIII hug. It was *so* authentic. And at a head table sat our guests of honor, Dock and Ettienne. Etty wore her fur and a huge smile. Dock wore his best suit and a look of bewilderment. And both of them stared at the enormous side of beef that was placed before them. The bone on the rib-eye was thicker than Etty's forearm, which Dock used to pick up the steak and take a bite, much to the amusement of his bride and chagrin of his youngest daughter.

"Daddy, you behave now," Wilksie could be heard saying throughout the evening.

Gio was at the other end of the long table with The Blonde Contingency plus Conrad. He shot me knowing looks from down the table every time I looked his way, so I did what I could NOT to look his way. Livie asked me what was wrong.

"I'll tell you later," was all I could say. I hadn't told her yet because we could never find the time to be alone.

Livie shot an annoyed look and then stared down the table to see what the trouble was.

"I haven't figured it out either, Livie," Norma chuckled, sipping her drink. "But something has got him from that end of the table."

Livie, Norma, and I all stared down the table. Mother

looked at us periodically, confused, but she was being pulled into conversation by Rudie, Eddie, Bitsy, and King. Yes! King and Roni made it to the dinner; we were not sure if they would. Tina was home on bedrest with a difficult pregnancy. But she insisted she was fine and sent her love and congratulations to the happy couple, and of course to the family as well.

We were having our various coffees and desserts and after dinner drinks. Some had several after dinner drinks as well as during and before dinner drinks. An altercation was brewing. Norma was watching with a raised eyebrow as her younger brother and his son were having tense words. Eddie had been one of those with before, during, and after drinks. I needed to pee.

"Livie," I whispered to my sister. "Livie, walk with me to the bathroom."

"Ugh. Fine." Livie rolled her eyes. Not at me but at the thought of going to the bathroom. "Do you think Mother would notice if I took these hose off? What a pain in the ass they are."

"She may not, but Nince will." It had been the discussion the ladies had sent me away for earlier in the day: Livie being a responsible woman and dressing appropriately for her family.

While we wandered through wooden-beamed rooms, she told me, again, about the horrors of being berated by The Three Sisters, her mother, her great-grandmother, and, worst of all ... that Bitsy. Granted, we were a bit jaded in our opinion—we were most certainly Team Mother. But I assure you Bitsy did her level best to earn the ire of the Fennig siblings. Her son too. As I was now finally able to let Livie know about what happened to me while she was having her little life lesson ... I was having one of my own.

"What?!" Her jaw dropped. I mean we knew, but we didn't, you know?

"Let me pee and I'll tell you the rest." I ducked inside the men's room.

I was washing my hands when in walked Gio. He looked at me, offered a wide grin, and walked over to the urinal. He spread his legs wide and didn't stand close enough to the urinal in my opinion. He unzipped and began his business. I could see his reflection; he was looking over his shoulder at me in the mirror. I blushed hard; I don't know why—and I rushed out of the door without saying a word. I could still feel the heat on my neck and face as I came out of the men's room. I frantically looked around for Livie. She must have gone into the restroom. Damn. Unless she went back to the table. She wouldn't do that. I peered around the corner and looked toward the back room to see if I could find her. I could not. But that did not really mean anything; she could be anywhere in this maze of Tudor timbers and sconces, tables and patrons. The restroom door opened and I turned anxiously to tell my sister what just happened ...

"Well hey, Randy." It was Gio. "I was hoping for a chance to talk to you."

My face went hot again as I watched him sidle over to the cigarette machine, put in some change, pull the little knob, and retrieve his Marlboro Light 100s—the same brand I would try to smoke in a few years because my first boyfriend also smoked them. It didn't work, neither the cigarettes nor the boyfriend. I was not built to be a smoker. And it was the boyfriend who was an asshole that time.

"I was thinking it would be fun if I drove my little cousin back to Dock and Etty's tonight. I don't mind." He smiled and winked and slammed the bottom of his cigarette pack against the hard part of his palm several times.

"Uh," I managed.

"Only if I can go!" Livie interjected. "But I think Mother would have a fit; she's tired and we have to head back early tomorrow."

"That's too bad." Gio winked. "I was hoping we could go for another swim."

"But I ..."

"Oh, and Randy," He stared directly into my eyes, deep and brown and threatening his were; wide and blue and frightened were mine. He peeled off the light plastic wrap and slid a cigarette into the corner of his mouth ... "I wouldn't tell anyone about this. It would be a real shame." He watched me as he left, went out the front door, and into the night.

"You didn't tell me you went swimming with him," Livie whispered in shock.

"I didn't, Livie!" I defended myself. "I swear!"

We walked back to the table. I was trying to figure out if Livie believed me. Eddie and Rudie were arguing. Rudie had told the waiter not to bring Eddie anything else with alcohol in it. The row got louder so King, Norma, and Nince sort of escorted or herded them out to the parking lot. Bitsy asked if Gio had found me. Wilksie was trying to get the rest of her family out the door before another scene could occur. And Mother had a coughing spell that required her to sit down on the bench by the front door. She leaned her head against the cigarette machine and closed her eyes.

✍   ✍   ✍

Chapter 11
Ripples

Last Call and Lamentations

Spring Break was over, and the Perkins' incident with the Miss Clairols left me wanting to get back to Ole Miss, back to Oxford, and back to not being with family. I could have said "back to being away from these people," but that has a harsher connotation, doesn't it? And I do remember lecturing my grandmother on the use of "these people" or "those people" in polite conversation. Yet the former might make one think I missed them. I did not. And I felt terribly guilty for it.

"While I appreciate you listening to me go through my audition monologues, I'd much rather talk to you," Lorraine said. I could hear the water move in her bath as she reached across to the toilet for her pitcher of mimosas. "You are very quiet."

"I'm sorry." I sighed and slowly let myself sink to the depth my tub would allow. My eyes remained open. I found comfort in the distortions, the bent light, the shimmering of everything. My eyes stung, burned a little ... and the bubbles rose to the surface as I laughed. "It's Holy Water!"

"You know—some days you make it very difficult for yourself," she said. "And for me."

"What?"

"I was talking to you and you went underwater and missed what I said," she said louder. "And it was very important information."

"I'm sorry. What did I miss?"

"Well, you'll just have to ask Rhiannon about it now."

"She's not here, I think she's in the costume shop." I was getting annoyed. I was tired, and it had been a pretty shitty Spring Break.

"Nope. She should be at City Grocery waiting for us," Lorraine said gleefully. "... and that's where I'm going too. So hurry up, Mister, or I'll call Wilksie and tell her how you are gonna make a lady walk to the bar by herself."

"You're the worst!" I said. "The worst friend ever!"

"I know. That's why you love me." She giggled.

"I know." I did too, and I sunk back into the bathwater and watched the walls breathe.

$$\approx \quad \approx \quad \approx$$

WE WALKED UPSTAIRS AND INTO the bar area. Sitting at the bar was Lorraine's married bartender's wife. Lorraine made a beeline for the balcony while I nosily ordered our drinks. I say *nosily* because I really had to get a look at this dude's wife. And I did. I got a good look at her. She was sipping what I was hoping was Sprite through a straw—and she was clearly showing off a pregnant belly. She wore bright red lipstick and was rather heavy-handed with the masonry she must have used for foundation. I'll give her credit, no prenatal acne could force its way through all that spackle, blush, and powder. She was well-denimed and fringed, looking somewhat like a knocked-up wrangler cheerleader. I do not believe she was old enough to be sitting at the bar. And her hair was ... it was just like ... well, beneath all the macaw eye shadow, denim, and pregnancy—she looked just like Lorraine.

I carried our drinks out to the balcony along with a couple of shots for Rhiannon and me. Lorraine nearly tipped the tray her bartender friend had handed me as she grabbed for her glass and mini-bottle of champagne.

"Thank God she doesn't look a thing like me! I worried over that." She poured the bubbly into her glass. "And she's fat!"

Rhiannon and I locked eyes, tipped our shot glasses, and drank. Lorraine raised her glass too, sipped, and stared at the back of the pregnant wife of the married bartender she was fucking. She had a troubled, perhaps puzzled look on her face. Furrowed brow, silently muttering something—at least her mouth looked like it was forming words. Rhiannon was just as bubbly as Lorraine's beverage. And she was talking to Wesley, who was equally as animated and excited.

"Did they tell you?" Wesley asked. "Did they tell you about the dress?"

"No," I said, and looked at Lorraine and Rhiannon for a clue.

"Well, Rhiannon found some stunning fabrics ..." Wesley began.

"Were they the portiérs from your room or the parlor?" I asked.

Lorraine spit out her drink, Rhiannon chuckled, and Wesley was confused.

"Why would she make my dress out of curtains?" Wesley asked. "No, she found, what did you call them?"

"Bolts," Rhiannon said.

"Yes, that's right, bolts. Bolts of fabric," Wesley repeated. "She found two bolts of fabric that were just perfect!"

"I actually bought three," Rhiannon said, "... but the third one is for trim, so I won't use much of it."

"Three bolts; that's a lot of fabric," I said, imagining how much I was going to owe Rhiannon.

"Are you kidding? These dresses use a lot of fabric to lay

properly over the hoop. And Wesley is not exactly southern belle proportions ..." Rhiannon began.

"Girl, I'm right here ..." Wesley cautioned while sucking in his waist.

"I am using like 40 yards of fabric ... but they are partial bolts and remnants, so I got them at a really good price." Rhiannon smiled. "You know I can be thrifty."

"Is it done?" I asked.

"Oh, Lord no," Rhiannon said, "but I have the fabric cut and draped. I hope to do some fittings at the end of the week. It really depends on Jason's show. His opens in two weeks. I'm designing that one, remember?"

"Ooh, that's right. He wrote this one, yes?" I asked. Jason was a third year grad-student, also with a specialty in directing.

"He did," Lorraine added to the conversation, though she was still very much looking at the back of the pregnant lady at the bar. "It's pretty good, too."

"Last call!" shouted the married bartender.

Rhiannon and Wesley downed their drinks. They decided to pull a late night in the costume shop. Lorraine and I stared at each other over the last of our own beverages. We drank them in silence; then we both stared at the married bartender.

"I don't think I can do it anymore," Lorraine stated simply. "Fuck him, I mean. I just don't think I can after seeing her all pregnant like that."

"Looks like neither of us are getting laid tonight," I replied, watching Wesley and Rhiannon sashay down the stairs ... well, one of them was sashaying.

"No. And it's a shame too. He was pretty darn good."

"And he has that ass!" I said. I had often admired Lorraine's bartender's bubbly derriere.

"Oh it is nice." Lorraine smiled a wicked smile. "He has that baseball player butt."

We both continued to admire it as he put things away behind the bar. His pregnant, fringe-wearing, Lorraine doppelganger was finishing whatever it was she was drinking. We took our last sips and headed downstairs, still talking about his ass.

"And don't you dare to touch it," she giggled.

"What do you mean?" I asked, "How can you not grab it while he is pounding away?"

"You make it sound so ... athletic." She frowned.

"It's the only sport I like." I laughed.

"Yeah, well, grabbing is fine." She giggled. "But I sort of slipped a finger in one time ..."

The long and the short of it was he clenched his butt and exploded ... then Lorraine had to calm him down because he was afraid he was gay. It took hours of talking through the bathroom door to calm him down. And while we laughed about it the whole way home, it was kind of sad in retrospect.

"Poor dumb guy," I said.

"I know." Lorraine agreed. "And I never touched his little bung hole again."

"And that is the real tragedy," I declared.

"Are you okay?" Lorraine managed to ask without bringing down the mood.

"No." I laughed. I didn't want to bring down the mood either. I threw my arms wide and screamed at the heavens. "I AM NOT OKAY!"

Lorraine shushed me but laughed along with me.

"I'm never okay. But I'm fine," I said more quietly. "I'm always just fine."

We locked arms and began our march home. Lorraine talked about the bartender some more ... a few more stories of tribute as we shared our lamentations over his ass.

"Thank you." It sort of fell out of my mouth.

"Of course."

Laura and Rudie

W e were back at my place, Mother and I, after Eddie's funeral. A few weeks later maybe? Mother was doing well. Her last surgery and round of treatments seemed to be working. She was gaining strength and she had purpose. But Norma. Now it was Norma who was having her own battle with that dreaded c-word. It was her ovaries. A diagnosis she did not want to believe, so she ignored it and told no one—for too long.

"I never even used them for anything. I thought they were dried up and shriveled and dead," Norma explained to me in the living room of her Chevy Chase home. "I couldn't even have children."

"Bless your heart. They couldn't give life, but they can taketh away," Wilksie said sagely.

"What kind of morbid dumb shit is that?" Norma shot back.

And that is precisely why Mother had to move from my Woodley Park apartment to Norma's home. And why Wilksie had to go—back to Mississippi, back to Kosciusko, and back to her own world. And as fate or luck would have it—or just the way life works out sometimes, I was called back too.

"Hello?" I answered the phone. It was a Tuesday. I don't know why I remember that; I just do.

"RAIN-de!" It was not Nince, but holy cow did she sound like her. Not just the accent, but the tone. "Rudie wants you to come home."

"What?"

"It's Grandpa. He's fine ... he's safe. I mean we found him and all, but he went missing again. And he wants you to come for a visit."

"Oh God, Laura, I'm so sorry."

Rudie had moved beyond the just slipping stage. "Slipping" was the time he picked Mother and me up from the airport. It was a few months after Nince had passed. We flew in to do some things at the house. Mostly it was the removal of furniture, as the house was under contract. Rudie picked us up in Montgomery. There is this one particular intersection, where roughly six lanes of traffic meet eight lanes of traffic ...

"STOP!" I screamed as we were approaching a very red light at that very intersection at a very high rate of speed.

He did. And then I explained to him the meaning of lights.

"That's right. That's right. I remember now," he said, and then continued to drive us to his home on Booger Holler.

It was his habit to get into his truck and drive. Some days it was to the store and back. Or the meat and three he liked to go to. Some days it was to Eddie's. Only Eddie didn't live there anymore. He had passed away. And the new tenants, while kind, were growing weary of the visits. Other days it was to Nince's ... Velma's, only Velma didn't live there anymore either. Some couple from Birmingham bought it as a weekend home. Laura would find him sitting on the back deck talking. Sometimes to Billie, the little lady from across the way, and sometimes to no one.

"Well, this time was a little scarier," Laura explained. "He crossed the state line and drove all the way to French Camp. They found him at the cemetery. I didn't know who to call, so I called Wilksie."

"Oh God." I let out one of those laughs you laugh when someone tells you something that is more terrible than it is funny. "At least she has an in with the cops."

"Yeah." Laura sighed. "But not so much with my Grandpa. He didn't want to talk to her."

"I could see that. She can be very Wilksie about a thing."

I sympathized. "Is there anything else I can do? I mean, I'll fly down, of course."

"Umm. Yeah. Would you? I hate to ask," she said, "... and it's a lot."

～　　　～　　　～

RUDIE DIDN'T WANT TO TALK to Wilksie. He wanted to talk to Velma. But of course Velma was gone. So he asked for me. Wilksie tried to reason with him, but between his dementia and her reasoning skills, they were not on the same page. They were not even in the same book. In fact, he wouldn't stay with her, not at her house anyway. They stayed at that family funeral lodging spot we always use. And Wilksie was unhappy about having to spend the night at that motel somewhere between Ackerman and Weir. But someone had to watch over him or the cops wouldn't release him—and Laura couldn't be there until the next day. Rudie would have preferred to stay at "Mama and Daddy's," but Wilksie told him the power company bought it and tore it down.

Laura made it there the next day. Tuesday. And she called me. I made my own arrangements; I was able to score a flight to Memphis. Lorraine and her husband picked me up at the airport. I spent the night at their house, as I arrived so late that Tuesday. But I arrived at our Bates Family Motel on Wednesday. I was lucky enough to arrive before the stale coffee and plastic pastries had been put away. Rudie had also saved me a cheese danish.

We were drinking coffee and eating our danish and having a fairly banal conversation about weather. He didn't seem particularly excited or worked up over the fact I was there. He greeted me as though we shared breakfast every morning. He was concerned about the heat. It was going to be a hot summer.

"And I was sorry to hear about your mother."

"My mother?" I asked.

"Yes," he said, sitting back to take a sip of terrible coffee. "That's why I wanted to talk to Velma. But nobody will let me."

"I don't understand, Rudie." I watched his eyes. They were both distant yet present.

"I lost my Eddie. And it hurts. But now Velma has lost Debra. And I need to talk to her."

"You were there the other night. I don't know why you didn't tell her then," Wilksie reasoned. "Besides, Debra is not dead."

I looked up at Laura. It was clear she didn't get it either.

"Take me to the cemetery," Rudie said simply. "I want to go to the cemetery."

So we did. Laura, Rudie, and I piled into my rental. Wilksie got into the backseat of her Mercedes. Her driver closed the door.

"Does Wilksie have a governor on her car again or a suspended license?" I asked Laura.

"Neither." Laura laughed. "She told me she just didn't like to drive anymore."

At first glance the cemetery hadn't changed much. The gate was open, and it was daylight—those were the biggest changes from the last time I was here. Rudie was quiet. He walked over to Nince's grave and sat down. Laura walked with him. I waited for Wilksie. Partially because I am a gentleman, but mostly because I wanted to rib her about the driver.

"Randolph Scott, you better hush now." She smiled that Wilksie smile.

Rudie waved me over. I squinted in the sun toward his direction. Laura was also squinting. I thought she was squinting. It turns out she was just holding her forehead in frustration, understanding, and a bit of amusement. Because you gotta laugh to keep from crying some days—a stupid saying that is so often true.

Next to the headstone that held my Nince and Boom-Pa's names was another, polished and shiny, with that new car smell. Benjamin David Fennig and Debra Holloway Fennig. There were no dates. And it didn't say Derwood.

"Oh, your grandmother asked me to do that," Wilksie said simply.

I pointed to Nince's grave.

"Before she died," Wilksie said. "She liked the one I ordered for her and Daniel. And I just hadn't done it. But after Eddie's service, sorry Laura, it sort of put me in a mind to do it."

"That's morbid." I wasn't sure if I should laugh or be angry. I looked at Laura; she was trembling as she attempted to subdue her laughter. Her hand never left her mouth.

"I'm not the one who bought my children cemetery plots for an anniversary present. That was your grandmother," she said defensively, using the red nail of her finger like a sword. "And I did not purchase this one; I merely facilitated it."

I was speechless. For a moment. And then it occurred to me to call my mother. And it occurred to me to wonder if I had cell reception in the middle of this absolute nowhere of orange clay ruts and white marble surrounded by chain-link.

"Hello?" It appears I did.

"Mother?" I said. "I need you to talk to Rudie. He thinks you're dead."

"WHAT?!? What gave him that idea?" she asked. "Norma! Rudie thinks I'm dead!"

"WHAT?!?" I could hear Norma too. "What the hell did my sister do?"

I explained. I think the most remarkable aspect to my Mother's reaction was how nonplussed she was. It was as though I had explained that dolphins come to the surface to breathe. She relayed it to Norma. Her reaction had all the plusses my Mother's did not. And then I gave Rudie my phone.

Rudie sat on Velma's grave and talked to my mother. I'd like to say they talked for hours. How poetic and lovely would that be? *As the sun set, their words followed* ... But it wasn't like that. These beautiful little moments we want to celebrate in our minds, they are just that—moments. And moments do not last. And also, the cell reception was not stellar. And once Rudie had adjusted to the fact that Mother was not dead, they talked again about Eddie. And then the call ended. It was maybe five minutes, ten tops.

Laura put her arms through mine and laid her head on my shoulder while Rudie talked with Debbie. "Thank you."

We held each other for that five, maybe ten minutes tops ... but those minutes were familiar and safe. I felt safe. I felt connected ... to family. I hope she did. We talked about doing a drive by of the old place, but Wilksie made it sound like a bad idea.

"Oh, the power company finally tore it down after all these years, I'm certain, not to mention that it could trigger poor Rudie."

We reluctantly saw her point on that last argument. So we didn't make the drive. Laura and Rudie left that afternoon. It was just a few hours back to her place. I drove to Oxford.

The notice was short. Lorraine could not come down. And worse than that, the bed and breakfast, my old apartment—it was rented for the week. So I had to settle for a regular old hotel. I walked the campus and tried to visit my old haunts. Most of them were something else now. Cedar Oaks still looked lovely, if a bit more touristy. City Grocery was going strong. And Proud Larry's. Square Books too. In fact the entire square was thriving, vibrant, and alive. I was not. I was not vibrant and alive. I was not okay. I wasn't even fine. I had fallen into a world in which I did not belong.

No. I hadn't fallen. I hadn't fallen at all. This world in which I did not belong was falling down all around me. Drowning me.

I walked to the cemetery. I'm not sure why. Faulkner is

buried there. I tried to remember where. I had this strong, crazy urge to talk to him. Why? I don't know. I'm not what one would consider a Faulkner aficionado. But I did. And there he was. So I knelt on the ground beside him. It didn't seem right to sit on the large marble slab. I told him all about the brunch we had at his house that one time. And how remarkably mild it was that December day, gah, so many years ago. And then I told him about a boy I knew, Aaron. I don't know why he came up. We had only dated briefly in undergrad and grad school. Really it was just summers and the too few times I let myself escape into the safety of his world. I was awful once again—I was always awful. And I broke up with him right here in this cemetery, right here at this grave. The truly sad part ... I could have loved him. I truly could have. Maybe I even did. And then I realized I had told ol' Bill here, laying under that cold slab of marble, all of this before. And it didn't do me any good then and it wasn't doing any good now. So I tried to tell him about what just happened, back in French Camp. Back at that cemetery. But then I got emotional. And poor Lorraine wasn't there to see it ...

∿ ∿ ∿

RUDOLPH MORNAY TAYLOR PASSED AWAY in his sleep three weeks later. He was laid to rest beside his beloved first wife, Laura, and his beautiful boy, Edward. It was a simple, quiet, somber affair. Laura, his granddaughter, came alone though her mother, Amazing Grace, did send the loveliest flowers. I drove with Norma and Mother; Livie was able to attend too. Wilksie was there with Conrad. The Blonde Contingency was unable to attend. They also sent flowers. And of course the same representatives of Laura's (Rudie's first wife) family were there. We all agreed it was a broken heart that took him.

"Just like Daddy," Norma whispered.

I draped my arm around her shoulder and pulled her close. She let her tears fall and held me tight. Mother gasped gently, as she never misses a thing, and grasped Livie's hand. Laura stood to my left. She held my other hand.

Cassie came to the graveside service. She looked both beautiful and a wreck. It was clear Rudie's passing had hit her hard.

"So many regrets," she said as her painfully thin arms reached for Laura.

"Oh don't be silly." Laura reached for her too, trying to comfort her. It always amazes me how the ones who should be able to truly mourn are often the ones who are tasked with consoling everybody else in their grief. And Laura was a master of it by now. Or maybe it was shock. But she was so composed and strong. "He always loved you; you know he did. Y'all were good friends right on through."

"I know dear." Cassie smiled. "But we all have them. It's unavoidable. And so will you. We all do. One day."

"Thank God her cheerful ass didn't join us for dinner," Norma said as we drove to the same meat and three we ate at after Eddie's service. It's a family favorite. "Their side of the family." Norma's toothsome grin was a welcome sight.

And after dinner we all parted ways. We swore we wouldn't let it go so long or be another funeral that brings us all together. And we meant it. People always do. I think people generally mean the things they say at funerals, more so than they do at other times. Perhaps grief, or the presence of grief, brings out the honesty even when we are being dishonest.

Laura's connection with her father's mother's side of the family, while not severed, was dissolved. Rudie was the last real bond. They have spoken on occasion, in the years since, and have exchanged greeting cards. But despite the promises, I don't believe they have gotten together.

Norma's Turn

We didn't either. Not really. I mean, we did in the sense that Norma and I lived in the same-ish town. I was in the District, she was in the Beltway. And eventually Mother moved in with Norma as Norma's cancerous ovaries did their worst.

Derwood held down the fort in Florida. His retirement and Mother's continued remission allowed him the freedom to spend more time on projects at home. He also had his own mother to contend with, and a sister. And Livie lived not too far away, so he was not lonely. She was married now, of course, to Amy. They were discussing the possibility of having more kids. Livie was still determined not to carry them.

Wilksie, of course, flew up to be with her sister. And she, of course, flew back when either one of them became intolerable. You know how it is ... the fights, or disagreements, or differences that come when discussing whether a glass is half full or half empty. Or if it really fucking matters when you are dying.

"It's like I told That Sable Boy; you can't just sit there acting like you're dying all the time. You gotta live," she argued.

"He *was* dying," Norma said, "... and so am I."

"Well, not today." Wilksie would smile. "And if you are not going to die today, you might as well live."

This went on for eighteen months or so. Mother would fly home to be with Derwood on occasion, but the bulk of the time she stayed with Norma. Wilksie flew back and forth from Jackson. On Norma's good days, I would meet them all for lunch or dinner at a nearby favorite of Norma's. It was not a meat and three. Sometimes if it was just an okay day, we would meet at her home. Other days I would meet Mother. Other days I would meet Wilksie. A few times I was able to meet them both.

Mother was sipping a glass of wine; it was nearly empty before she spoke. Wilksie had scotch. Actually she had two. She remained silent for a very long time. I sat and listened to the silence. I had a beer. And I knew it was coming. I also knew they needed a minute sometimes, just to not be in it all. You know?

"It's going to be tonight," she said, and took another sip of wine. "Or tomorrow morning, early."

After a long moment of silence, Wilksie agreed, "Yes."

And then it was as if they were free. They each ordered another drink. Wilksie ordered a beer and a shot of tequila for me and then regaled Mother with tales from the time she, Norma, Nince, and Rudie came to Oxford. Oh they were hilarious, embellished—and yet not at all the same as the last time she told them. But they were told with that unique brand of Wilksie sincerity and truth.

"And that effeminate boy, the big one. The one who longed for you. What was his name?" she asked.

I laughed. "You mean Wesley! Yes!"

"What was it you promised him that allowed me to stay the night at Cedar Oaks?" She batted her eyes as though she were waving a fan to hide the naughtiness of her insinuation.

"Not what you think." I laughed. "But my roommate made him an amazing gown, so he could pose on the balcony like he was an antebellum Evita. I had to pay for it."

"And you never?" She ordered another.

"Wilksie." I smiled and raised my shot glass. "A gentleman does not kiss and tell."

⁂

I GOT THE CALL AT four. A last shot of morphine allowed her

the final rest she needed. I made coffee. I took a shower. And then I called Livie.

"Are you okay?" she asked.

"Fine," I lied. "I mean, I'm always fine, right?"

"I know." Livie did know. "You were always closer to everyone. I did like Norma though; she was a lot of fun. So sad. How's Mother?"

"Tired." And I told her she was probably relieved too. A lot like after Nince had died. It was like she had already grieved.

"Should Dad and I come up for this one?" she asked.

"I think that would be nice. Yeah," I said. And I meant it. Norma would have appreciated it. And I think Mother would too. She could use her husband. And her kids.

We talked a little more, but I was clearly distant. Livie finally interrupted one of my ramblings. "Hey, look. I know you have things to do, and I should probably call Dad, and then I should check on Mother. Ugh. You are better at these things than me."

"Yeah. I have to call Laura and then a list of other folks Mother and Wilksie asked me to call."

"Bitsy?" she asked.

"Yup."

"I love you, Randy."

"I love you, Livie."

⟆   ⟆   ⟆

NORMA BUCKED THE BURIAL TREND. She was cremated.

"As was her artiste husband," Wilksie stated the obvious.

Norma's ashes were placed in a lovely urn. Wilksie had selected it from a collection Rudie brought back from his time in Asia—as a hotelier, not a sailor. And Conrad gave them his seal of an antique dealer approval. The urn was placed inside a vault beside the urn containing the ashes of Norma's artiste husband. And that is how Norma, the headstrong girl from French Camp, Mississippi, came to be buried in Arlington National Cemetery.

Wilksie was astonished. "I was astonished." She even said so. "All these years Norma told me that artiste husband of hers was buried at Arlington National Cemetery. And I never believed her ... until I made the arrangements for her to be interred, and, sure enough, here we are."

She wore that same look of guilty relief Mother wore. They were both tired. We had decided to gather at another one of Norma's favorite spots on the National Harbor for dinner. It was quite the family affair. Livie, Laura, and I sat at one end of the table. We each had our beverage of choice to slowly sip while we watched the show. Mother and Gene were at the other end of the table with the Bleached, Flaxen, and Tow-colored Girls, plus Conrad and Gio. Gio was without his wife AND his choir director/brother-in-law/best friend. They were fun to watch, all of them. Animated, and laughing, and seemingly free of the tensions and baggage that weighed them down before. Maybe it is time— or age—that changes things. Or perhaps dynamics shift when the parents are no longer around, not because they are out ... but they have passed and are not coming back.

Wilksie stayed out of it. She carried her scotch. Her hair was flawless, and she watched everything from a decided distance—a barrier of proxemic choice. She wandered over to my father and Gene's wife, Bev. It was a second marriage for both. They had a daughter named Alice; she was thirteen. Gene's boys were not able to come. Livie and I watched and commented as our father did his uncomfortable best to make small talk with Bev, Alice, and now Wilksie.

"Here comes his, 'I have to take a shit' face," Livie observed. "Should I rescue him?"

"Nope. Your mother just raised her empty glass toward him." Laura was not without her own observations.

"He's saved!" I laughed. "I'll go join him at the bar; do y'all need anything?"

They showed me their empty glasses.

I met Dad at the bar. He was worried Mother was overdoing it. She was. But she was surrounded by family for the first time in a long time. The circumstances were what they were, it is true—Norma's funeral and all. But this was family, and haven't we already established that there is a family reunion-like pull to a funeral? Not everybody shows up, but everybody is invited. You can't say that about a wedding. Wilkise joined us at the bar. Derwood raised Mother's wine glass and excused himself. I ordered another round.

"And, of course, whatever this lovely young lady would like," I said as Wilksie took the stool formerly occupied by my father.

"Why Randolph Scott, you were always a gentleman." She smiled.

I couldn't help notice, though, that Wilksie's smile had lost something. Something in its tone. Its authority.

"RAIN-de." She reached out and took my hand in hers, and stared into the mirrored backsplash of the bar. "I'm alone. It has occurred to me that I am alone. Mama and Daddy are gone. King. Rudie, and Velma. And now Norma has left us. I don't have my family, Randy; I'm all that's left."

The bartender broke the tension of the moment as he gently slammed a tray of drinks in front of me. I was beginning to suspect he was growing tired of the lingering nature of this party.

"Oh, sorry," he said. I wasn't convinced.

"Yes. Well ..." Wilksie's voice cracked, and so did her armor, "I just know that I'm next. I mean by default it only makes sense. But I find myself entirely selfish for even letting it cross my mind, and yet it is all I can think of. Everyone else is gone.

I am next."

"Nope. We're not gonna do it, India Wilkes Taylor. Not today." I said, and then ordered a round of tequila shots for the tray. The bartender begrudgingly complied. "A wise woman once said, and you'll forgive me if I paraphrase ... 'Well, you're not gonna die today, so you might as well live.'"

"Your mother raised you right." She smiled; it was almost back.

"You all did." I smiled too, and I managed to carry the tray in one arm and escort Wilksie with the other.

Livie's eye roll did not go unnoticed, at least by me. I laughed. So did Laura. And Wilksie joined us for a shot of tequila.

"Did I ever tell y'all about the time we—all of us, my siblings and I—we all descended upon RAIN-de for a weekend while he was attending Ole Miss ..." It only got loftier from there.

◆   ◆   ◆

THE PROMISES MADE AT THE end of the evening were easier to believe. We were all on the same side of the family after all. We were from French Camp. We were the Taylors. But we weren't. Livie and I were Fennigs. Gene was a Holloway; Mother too, until she married. And Wilksie, who had just pointed out that she was the last of them, even she was no longer a Taylor. She was a Sable. Her children and their children were never Taylors. We were generations removed, all of us. And yet again, despite the promises, we knew we would all meet, all of us, one day, on that familiar bit of orange clay in French Camp, Mississippi.

◆   ◆   ◆

Chapter 12
What the Water Knows

Debra's Last Wish

"No," Mother insisted. "I am not crazy, and I know what I want."

"But Nince's ... Mother, it was awful." Livie tried to intervene, tried to speak some common sense.

But Mother was not common. She was quite uncommon actually—and she had her uncommon sense. And she had her reasons too. We were sitting in her room, a homemade hospital room Derwood had constructed to make her life easier. We had finally, after years, over a decade really—we finally had come to some agreement on Mother's treatments. It seems the medical ones, the experimental ones, while they were good at attacking and killing some of the cancer, they were also good at attacking and killing some of Debra. The havoc they wreaked on her body ... they left her drained and sick. But the other treatments—the homeopathic ones, the physical therapy, the emotional therapy, the well-being of the mind, body, and spirit ... they really did little to fight the actual disease. They allowed the body, mind, and spirit to feel more at peace as the end arrived. And, at the end of the day ... at the end of your life, isn't peace better?

Today's row was over the funeral. Yes, Mother was rather involved with her own funeral. She did not want to leave anything to chance or to her grieving children, or her husband who she knew would no longer be in a position to make decisions. Yesterday's row was also over the funeral. It seemed Mother had some peculiar choices. And they were bitter pills to swallow.

Like her request for two services. Just two services. One would be at Gio's church, in Sanford. She felt as though it would honor family, and at the same time it would be large enough for Derwood's family not to feel overwhelmed by her side of the family. But she did not want Gio to give the eulogy. That was for Livie and me to write together, and I was to deliver it.

"And be funny," she said. "But not too funny ... you know I don't like that."

Wilksie brought up the fact that it was Gio's church. "Wouldn't it seem odd that he did not speak at his own church? After all, he delivered a lovely memorial at his grandfather's funeral. Oh and Velma's. He did such a lovely job for your mother."

"I was there." Mother smiled. "And I want my son to deliver it. Gio can introduce him."

"I will confer with Gio." Wilksie smiled.

That was yesterday. This was today.

"And I want Betty-Girl. Why can't we at least get her on the phone? She organized so many funerals for this family. I want Betty-Girl."

All three of us looked at her like she was crazy. Even Wilksie, whom one might think would be on board with this tradition, was aghast. "But Betty-Girl. Oh Debra, I don't know if she is still in the business."

"She is," Mother said. "And I know for a fact, she will do everything I say, the way I want it. And she will make sure it happens. Just the way I want."

"But she hates us," Livie said.

"Oh, that is an ugly word," Wilksie scolded.

"She's an ugly woman." I couldn't help myself.

Wilksie flashed a smile.

"And she is also a highly anxious, OCD mess. And paranoid too. And a real bitch. So she will do everything exactly the way I lay it out, to a T. To a fault even. And I want Betty-Girl."

The three of us—Livie, Wilksie, and I—were about to launch into yet another round of why it was a bad idea ...

"Okay," Derwood answered. And that was the end of that.

Even for Wilksie. She put on another smile and said, "I'll give her a call and make the arrangements."

◈　　◈　　◈

IT IS TRUE THAT NOT all promises are kept. Especially to family. Especially under duress. (Funerals and dying mothers fall under both the family and duress categories.) But sometimes promises are kept. And thankfully that was the case with Laura.

"I think it's her. I mean it could be." I typed this into Messenger ...

This was preceded by a picture and a message, all waiting for me when I sat down at my computer to check the news, read the gossip, and start the morning. And as I scrolled through, I could see a few more pictures had been sent. Another of that same lady, this time standing next to Rudie—my great uncle, Nince's brother, and Laura's grandfather. They were so young.

"Good night, she is up early!" I thought as I took my very first sips of the strong, dark nectar that would awaken my senses and allow me to function. "How is she up so early? They are an hour behind."

I stared at the picture—an old, grainy, black and white photo of a woman dressed plainly yet sharply. She was posing with her purse while outside a structure that looked like it belonged on the set of the *The Long Long Trailer*. But the woman looked more like a cross between Ethel Merman and Rosalind Russell, and less like Lucille Ball. So I guess, to be more accurate, it looked like Auntie Mame walked over to the Collinis to pose for a picture in front of their trailer. I know that Lucille Ball also played *Mame,* but she was terrible in my opinion, and we should all just forget it. But this picture of a young Norma was striking, well put together, attractive even—but not pretty. Pretty is so delicate and sweet. Norma was not delicate or sweet.

I took a sip of coffee and started typing. "I'm pretty sure that's Norma."

The three little dots appeared. Laura was typing away; I took another sip of coffee and scrolled through social media while awaiting her response.

"Good Morning! I was going through some boxes of Grandpa's and found these. I thought that might be Norma, but I wasn't sure. For Norma to be such a loving and gentle woman, from my experiences, that picture sheds a different light. She looked like she had zero time for funny business. My mom says I have Norma's eyebrows; I think I have her RBF as well. LOL"

"Ha!" I typed. "I can see a bit of the Taylor side in you for sure. My mother thinks you look like your grandmother."

"I get that a lot too," Laura agreed. "Do you know who the others are?"

"I think it's King, and your grandfather is on the mule. But maybe it's their father and one of them?" I made my best guess. "I know King and Dock looked a lot alike; your grandfather was smaller than they were, I don't know. I'll show them to Mother when I head over later."

"Oh, please do. And call me."

I DID. AND WE SPENT several wonderful late mornings chatting on the phone, FaceTiming, and going over pictures she found in various boxes and albums her grandfather held onto. Mother had a story for each one. And she shared every one that she could. Livie was less interested in the family dynamics, but she enjoyed seeing Mother so engaged. And she brought Amy and the kids over as often as she could. Mother would read to them whatever book they brought and did her best to interest them in the pictures. And Wilksie? She had her spin on the stories Mother would tell, but she would rarely contradict.

"Oh, that's not how Mama would have told it" was the closest she would get.

And Derwood appreciated her presence more than any of us thought. Where he and Nince did not exactly see eye to eye, Wilksie always demurred with a smile that gently suggested he rethink—and he would, sometimes arriving at a new conclusion and sometimes not. Nince wouldn't have taken his conclusions into consideration. But that was Nince. Wilksie's method of control was more subtle, allowing the natural tendencies of those she was up against to be her allies. She was patient, Wilksie was. And that was a character trait she alone possessed among her siblings—patience. Livie, Derwood, and I didn't have it either.

I was sitting in the bed with Mother; we were FaceTiming with Laura. She had discovered another trove of pictures, this time in a box of her father's.

"Mama had it in her attic since the divorce, and she forgot all about it, she says. And I found these two pictures of Daddy," Laura shared.

"Oh my goodness, would you look at that! It's Eddie and Gene. This was at your Nince and Boom-Pa's house before they retired to Alabama. I don't think you really remember it; you were young. It had a pool."

"Because you couldn't tell by the picture," I quipped. I mean, it was a picture of Gene and Eddie in bathing suits ... by a pool.

"Don't be smart."

Laura giggled through the exchange, then showed us the next picture. "And then there is this hottie!"

And there, lounging on a towel on the diving board was my 15- or 16-year-old mother in a two piece bathing suit. Eddie and Rudie were bobbing in the water beneath her. They both wore mischievous grins.

"Alright, Debra!" I laughed.

"Yes. And right after that, your father and my brother decided to splash me with that cold pool water."

"Is that the summer you met Dad?" I asked.

"Mmm." Mother closed her eyes and thought for a moment. "Eddie stayed with us the summer before my junior year. So yes. I met your father at school, at the end of the summer."

"It's crazy to look at that picture and think that in ... what? Two, three years later you would be a mother," I said. "I mean, the whole picture is like a metaphor for how your life can change in an instant. One minute you are peacefully laying in the sun, not a care in the world. The next you've been splashed by cold water and you are pissed off at your bratty brother and cousin. And then, boom! You're a mother ..."

"Yes! With two bratty children of my own. If that is in any way, shape, or form a part of your eulogy for me, you can call Gio right now."

Our laughter was interrupted by Livie slamming open the door. "She's here!"

And we heard the last of Derwood's cry, " ... the fuck is she here for?"

Wilksie answered the door with "Why Betty-Girl! What a surprise to see you all the way out here! We had no idea you would actually come ... here."

And moments later, in walked Betty-Girl. All raw-faced and beady-eyed, and clipboarded, as I remembered her. She was followed by a red-faced, speechless Derwood and Wilksie, whose shocked smile was so wide, I thought her eyes would surely pop.

"Oh, my poor Debra!" Betty-Girl exclaimed. "As soon as you called, I knew I had to rush to your side."

"You called her?" Livie asked. I'm not sure she was aware her face looked as disgusted as her tone.

"Laura," Mother said as though we were all at a Sunday tea. "You must know Betty-Girl; Mother and Rudie used to attend her husband's church."

"Brother-Man. Yes. Yes." Laura's smile faded to her aforementioned RBF.

"Do you know Brother-Man?" Betty-Girl called to the back of Mother's iPad..

"Everybody knows Brother-Man," Laura acknowledged.

"I love you, Laura. I'll talk to you soon," Mother said.

"I love you too, Debbie! And you RAIN-de." Then she disconnected.

"She says your name just like Mother used to."

"I know," I said and I kissed my Mother's forehead.

"Okay, everyone leave me alone with Betty-Girl. We are gonna have a little chat," Mother said.

And we did. We did just as we were asked. And we never learned the full extent of their chat. Laura got a clue, but that was later.

Also, I did remember the pool. At least I think I do. Didn't I learn to swim in that pool? I think it must have been Livie who taught me. But there was someone else. Only I can't really see them. It's like I'm underwater, looking up, and they are there, on the deck of the pool, arms waving. I can see the movement ... everything breathes, the light dances, the colors collide ... and then it all scatters as whoever it is jumps in.

IT WAS TWO WEEKS MORE. If you know, you know—I think that's the phrase that's become popular. And appropriate. Dying is so pretty in movies. It is not in life. I'd like to tell you otherwise, but I can't. But I will tell it as simply as I can.

Mother had a restful afternoon. I spent it with her. Livie did too. Amy and the kids peeked in when they stopped to pick Livie up. Derwood and Wilksie were going to sit with her for the evening. Livie would be back for the early morning. And Wilksie would be asleep in the chair, and Derwood would be on the very edge of the bed beside Mother. Liv would wake them, send them to bed, and take over. I would be back at lunchtime, and generally wake her up. It was our routine.

"Yeah?" I answered the phone.

"Yeah," Livie said.

It was 3:32 in the morning. I think it was Wednesday.

GIO'S CHURCH WAS LARGE, INDEED. Massive even. But then so was Mother's service. Livie and I had no idea so many folks would come out to celebrate our mother's life. Derwood was less surprised. He came from a rather large family—all of them were there. And they had so many friends. Livie and I were so grateful for their love and support, especially for our father. Oh, he was broken. But he was not discarded, as some broken things are. Nor was he ever really repaired. And why should he be? Our mother was a part of his life since he was in high school ... and for all the good and bad of it. And they had a good run of it too. Not as long as Dock and Etty, but Mother didn't make it 'til old age. Derwood had a longer go of it. But he was never quite the same.

When two souls pledge to make that lifelong journey together, and that pledge is forged deeper with every step, every turn, and every climb on that journey ... when does the journey end? Does it end when one of them stumbles and falls? Not if the other is there to help, to rest, or to carry. Does it end when they come to a crossroads and do not agree on the path? Sometimes pathways diverge and meet again a little further on. Does it end when one of them can no longer journey? My father would tell you no. Not as long as you can still share the journey, describe the journey, take a few steps along the path, and rush back to share what you have seen, what you have learned, what you have known. And that is what Derwood did. Though broken, and though he was missing a large part of who he even thought he was, he journeyed on because our mother told him he had to.

"These are dying last wishes, dying promises, so you have to honor them," Betty-Girl had instructed as she went through the checklists on her clipboard. Mother had nodded her head in agreement. Betty-Girl and my mother went through every item with us. Betty-Girl read and explained; Mother clarified when needed.

And yes indeed, Item Number One: "My Husband." It included a laundry list of things he should do; people he should call; folks he was to talk to. His suit was picked out for the service at Gio's church, and he had another suit for the graveside service in French Camp. It was a little lighter, because it could rain or be cold and you would need to layer—or because it would be blazing hot and you would need something light. Mother had clearly been to a weather roulette funeral in Mississippi.

Her final instructions to our father, her husband ... "Live as long as you can. Our grandbabies will know me through you. And I will know them through you as well, so tell me about them every chance you get."

She told Livie that she was never to force her children to wear stockings. Not really. But she did advise Livie to let them be who they are. "I fought that with you and Randy, but y'all were both so rotten, you turned out the way you were gonna turn out anyway." She laughed. "But when I met Amy, I knew you were where you belonged."

And it is true, Livie's wife is the home my sister needed ... They have two kids—a girl and a boy. They are beautiful, my pride and joy. I spoil them rotten. Livie and Amy yell at me, but Dolph and Vilma think I am the coolest uncle ever ... 'cause I am.

Item Number Three on the clipboard was "What to do with Randy." Oh she had some words for me, Mother did.

"Ask Livie before you decide to tell the story about that time Livie threw her shoes away at the airport. I don't want her embarrassed," she said, "and I think the coke bottle story would be a cute one for the eulogy. And make appropriate eye contact; look at everyone. And keep your hand out of your pocket. You always did that whenever you got on stage; it's why you could never be an actor. "

"If you are not writing these things down, don't worry Randy; I have them," Betty-Girl assured me as she tapped her clipboard with her same autumn frost nails.

"I know them all by heart," I said to Betty-Girl, resisting the urge to reach out and peel that little bit of skin from her eyebrow.

∽   ∽   ∽

GENE'S BOYS WERE PALLBEARERS, AS were some cousins on Derwood's side who were particularly fond of Mother. But the caveat added to Betty-Girl's clipboard was that "only family members are pallbearers, and they must sit with their families."

"I love that idea, Debra," Betty-Girl said, taking her notes. "We should have done that at Velma's."

Wilksie sat up front with Derwood and his mother. Livie and Amy and the kids were also up front, and they saved a spot for me. Gio sat to the side, near the organ, which was played by Roni. Oh, Roni was so honored to be asked, but was afraid she was too old. Betty-Girl suggested Tina help her. And it was a good suggestion (Alright, Betty-Girl!), so that is what happened. The Blonde Contingency was seated right behind us. It was on Betty-Girl's clipboard that Bitsy should always be right behind me in the photographs.

"But won't that block her face? Randy is so tall," Betty-Girl questioned.

"Yes," Mother smiled. "But you'll know it's her because of the hair."

Betty-Girl wrote it all down.

🐾　　　🐾　　　🐾

LAURA AND HER FAMILY SAT on one side of the church, while Lorraine and her husband sat on the other. I was so surprised, and touched, to see Lorraine. Betty-Girl did all her homework. Per Mother's instructions, Betty-Girl had them placed on opposite sides because she knew I would look at them when I spoke. And if they were on opposite sides it looked like I was looking at everybody when I went back and forth between them. And with Livie up front, I had the entire congregation covered. Mother was so clever. She should have been a director.

The service was lovely; absolutely it was. Gio's church was very welcoming, and Mother was right—we needed the space. While she was not in the garden club or a member of the DAR, not that Wilksie didn't try, she was a woman who reached others in her own way. So it was not surprising to see kids Livie and I went to high school with, and other friends who grew up with us. When you only look at a person through your own lens, you miss so many facets of who that individual was. Mother had a lot of facets. More, sometimes, than I ever gave her credit for.

I told the coke bottle story. And I was funny.

⌒   ⌒   ⌒

LIVIE HAD THE WINDOW SEAT on this flight to Montgomery. I didn't complain this time. The aisle seat had more legroom, or at least it had the aisle. We didn't speak much; in fact, I think Livie slept most of the way. The flight attendant was flirty. Maybe it was his job or maybe he was just friendly. But the only times Livie opened her eyes were to roll them every time he offered me another beverage, cookie, or blanket. She made sure I noticed too; she would tap me on the shoulder each time.

"Stop it, Livie."

She giggled and went back to sleep.

We stayed at the Bates Motel, between Ackerman and Weir. I explained to Livie that Boom-Pa was born in one of these towns. She nodded with vague interest. She was never one for history. Derwood stayed with Wilksie. And Wilksie insisted his mother stay too. Grandma took Bitsy's room. I was thankful when Wilksie asked him to drive her home. Amy and the kids were part of that caravan. The Blonde Contingency took rooms at the family funeral lodging spot. We shared plastic pastries and crappy coffee just like last time. Livie pointed out that the only difference was Bitsy didn't hit on me. Vivian laughed out loud; Joan looked confused; Bitsy just smiled. I noticed again how alike, yet different it was from Wilksie's. I don't know if it was experience or intent that betrayed the difference.

What began as a cool drizzle gave way to a damp mist, and finally the bright sun illuminated a blue and cloudless sky. Oh you can imagine the commentary on the divine nature of that weather pattern. It was shared by most every grouping of mourners who stood around the familiar green tent and as-troturf. The preacher from the French Camp church led us in prayer. And he said a few words that could have been said about anyone. And then I was tasked with thanking those who attend-ed and letting them know there would be a light supper in the fellowship hall back at the church. And would everyone allow the family just a few minutes by the graveside ...?

Betty-Girl sort of took the wind out of the somber sails at that moment as she shouted, "Letters out!"

And while the mood was unintentionally lightened—Livie, Laura, and I all laughed out loud for a moment—we had a lovely moment just the same. Derwood did not laugh, but you could see the smile and appreciation in his damp eyes. One of the items on Betty-Girl's checklist was to ask each family member to write a letter.

"Your mama was so moved when you placed that letter of yours into Velma's casket. She never forgot that sweet moment and how very much it may have helped you. So she asked that you write her a little letter, just a little note, if you want to. And then slip it to her, you know, at the very end," she said to me.

And I remember how very pretty Betty-Girl was at that mo-ment, looking at her through the tears that were forming. Water has a way ... doesn't it?

✑   ✑   ✑

THERE WERE NO COMPARISONS TO Etty's chicken or Dock's biscuits. Nobody even made biscuits. The chicken may or may not have come from a gas station. There were other items: Salads and brownies were a top choice for the church ladies to bring. And at least one really good coconut cake.

Thin white arms reached up to me from a wheelchair and pulled me into an awkward hug. I held her, bent over as I was while she cried and spoke words I couldn't really understand.

"Who is that?" Livie asked me without making any actual sound, but I could read the words while I hugged the old woman who must have been one hundred and forty-two.

"I'm pretty sure that was Irene," I told her.

"And who is Irene?" Livie asked.

"Gah! Why is it you still don't know anybody?" I rolled my eyes.

"I know her," she said, pointing at Amy.

Poor Amy, she was holding her own with the Fair-Haired Sorority and the twin sister wives belonging to Gio and his friend. Dolph and Vilma were doing what kids do, and running about on a sugar high from all of the brownies, cookies, congealed salads, and cake. There were a few other children there. We may or may not have been related. A lot goes on in that triangle of Ackerman, Weir, and French Camp. And a lot doesn't.

"I do declare, Livie, you are letting your children run around with reptilians." I did my best Wilksie and pointed toward Dolph and Vilma.

Livie spit out her drink and then punched my arm. "Okay, now do Norma."

"Why are Popeye's nephews playing with your kids?" I said, with a toothsome grin. I ran my tongue over the front of my teeth and made a little sucking sound.

"God, I miss Norma!" Livie laughed.

"What are y'all getting into over here?" Laura joined the party. "I thought I heard Norma for a minute."

"Now do Nince." Livie was nearly in tears.

I got real serious for a minute, and my voice dropped to a whisper. "Look at 'em," I said. "Just look at 'em. They have always been such ugly children."

Wilksie interrupted our laughter. "I can tell from across the room that y'all are admiring Vernon's great-grandchildren."

"Oh no, was it that obvious?" I asked.

"No." Wilksie smiled. "I just know my siblings, and y'all three had that same conspiratorial look about you."

♠   ♠   ♠

THE PARTY MOVED TO WILKSIE'S. And despite the number of people there, it felt empty without Norma and Rudie, King and Boom-Pa ... Nince. The cocktails did not flow, like at previous fetes, and the generation between Nince and me ... they were so different. Or maybe they weren't, and it just takes that generation removed to know. Dolph was plastered to Gene's side as Gene told some story about Mother from when they were younger. And Vilma took a real liking to Joan, much to the annoyance of Bitsy and Vivian. But I felt removed from the conversations, despite the fact that they were stories about our mother. Livie too—she felt it. Eddie was brought up nearly as often as Mother, so it was comforting, I suppose, to see that Laura also noticed the disconnect. And I realized then, what I watched with such enthusiasm, delight, and eager wide eyes, everything that was said and done by the Original Three Sisters, King and Rudie ... and Boom too—we were of no consequence to Dolph and Vilma. They longed for the adventure, the mystery, the danger, the excitement of Debra's generation. We were boring. And Wilksie was old. And the others were gone.

♠   ♠   ♠

I WOKE UP EARLY; IT was well before dawn. But I couldn't sleep. Something was calling me. Pulling me. I knocked on Livie's door, and Amy answered.

"It's like 3," she said. "What?"

"ᒐ stealing your kids."

"...?"

"I'm stealing your kids. And it's 5 ... if I had known you would let me have them at 3, I would have knocked sooner." I smiled.

She did too. "Kids! Your crazy uncle has some wild hair across his ass ... go brush your teeth, and be sure to mind what Randy tells you. I'm going back to bed."

Livie snored through the whole exchange.

But they found us soon enough. It was after sunrise. I saw Livie and Amy pull up to the chain-link fence. And they saw us—Dolph and Vilma and me. A blanket spread out on the ground. Dolph and Vilma were selecting flowers they could pull from Mother's grave and were happily making the others just as pretty. Nince's and Boom-Pa's were especially well decorated. And so were Dock's and Ettienne's. And I was so grateful that Betty-Girl had ordered the dates to be engraved in another month's time.

"Why did you come here so early?" Livie asked. We sat in the morning sun. Livie absently played with a bit of the disturbed orange clay, tracing lines with a stem from a carnation Dolph had given her.

"They needed a proper introduction," I said. "How are they ever going to know Mother if we don't tell them about Nince and Boom-Pa? And there is no Nince without her brothers and sisters. And Dock and Etty ..."

"You're weird," Livie said.

"I love you too."

She rested her head on my shoulder, and we watched as her kids took Amy from graveside to graveside and shared the stories they had learned. The sky was nearly as orange as the earth.

"He was too!"

"Nu uh!"

"Randy! Randy!" the kids yelled as they ran my way. "Who was Uncle Money again?"

"I'll tell you as we walk back to Dock and Etty's." I laughed.

"We can't do that. Wilksie said the power company tore it down." Livie looked confused.

"She always says that. It's her thing."

We did walk back. Well, Amy drove. The house was indeed a wreck, but visible through the overgrowth of scrub pine, young pecan trees, and weeds. Kudzu had not taken the house, but it had the barn. And remarkably, that ridiculously old and weathered picnic table still sat under that pecan tree. Someone had cleared the poison ivy from before. I doubted it was the power company. I also doubted Wilksie had anything to do with it.

Livie was inspecting the table before she would let Dolph or Vilma sit; Amy joined us, carrying a bag from the car.

"... this what you needed me to bring?" she asked, confused.

"Yep," I said, as I removed the watermelon from the bag. "Hey guys, ready to have your mind blown?"

Dolph, Vilma, and Amy oohed and ahhed when I sliced open the dark green melon only to reveal its sweet yellow meat. "Your Great-Great-Grandfather Dock used to grow these ..."

Oxford One Last Time

Livie and Amy went on back to Kosciusko. It was a long drive back to Florida with Derwood, his mother, and two kids. And the sooner they said their goodbyes to Wilksie and picked up Derwood, the sooner they could be on their way. I took my rental car and drove north. I went via Winona instead of the Trace. It had been a while but the route was just as familiar. And by the time I was in Batesville, it was like going home.

Once again Lorraine and her husband spoiled me. And

my old apartment was available for the rest of the weekend. Lorraine came down as well. And of course she took the apartment next door.

"I talk about this all the time to friends," Lorraine said. "About how we would take baths together in college. I get the strangest looks."

"I swear we need to make this an annual tradition." I laughed and sipped the cocktail I had poured.

"I'm so sorry I couldn't make the graveside."

"Oh my goodness," I said. "Don't be; it was so kind of you to come all the way to Florida. Livie loved meeting you."

Yes," she said, and took a sip of her champagne. "It was like learning a whole new side to you, meeting her. And that story. Oh—all I can think of is your poor mother and that coke bottle sticking out of her foot. And y'all just left her there as she called and called for help."

I laughed. "We thought she wanted us to put laundry away or something."

"Rotten!" Lorraine laughed too.

"Besides ... I was like four and Livie was seven. What good would we have been? We were just kids ..."

"You wanna go to City Grocery later?" she asked.

"I do."

I slipped back down into the warm water and let it envelop me, surround me ... hold me. I opened my eyes and let the distortions of the surface bring clarity. The bend in the light illuminated the shadows of my mind. And I allowed the water to carry me through all the old rivers and streams of my memories. Here is a fork, here is a shoe, here is a watery reflection in a handheld mirror I placed there long ago ...

"Hey!" Lorraine brought me back to the surface. "I forgot to tell you something. Oh and it's good. Remember that dress your roommate made for ... oh, what was his name?"

"Oh my God! Wesley!"

"Yes, Wesley! Oh, whatever happened to Wesley?" she asked.

"He became a pharmacist and got married."

"Oh, good," she said. "Not to a woman, I hope."

"No. Not to a woman."

"Good."

"So the dress?"

"The dress ... Oh, the dress! Yes! One of the ladies who does the caretaking for Cedar Oaks now—she found it in a closet and has put it on display. It's on an old dress form. And it is a wonderful example of the finery and craftsmanship of the day, as this lovely dress was made for a plus-sized or more regular-sized woman, but had all the finishings and finery worn by a true antebellum lady. And it's survived all these years."

"Rhiannon made that dress," I said.

"I know. I was there." Lorraine laughed. "But these experts think it's the real deal!"

☙   ☙   ☙

WE TOOK PICTURES AT SUNSET. And it was a hilarious evening of drinks and music and laughter. Wesley and Lorraine re-enacted a scene from *Gone with the Wind,* sort of, as Wesley was never gonna have a waist like Scarlett's. And Rhiannon kept the mint juleps flowing, made a few adjustments, and tied a few bows. I was dressed as a southern gentleman; Rhiannon had pulled a few things from the costume shop.

The Oxford Queers came by. They all *oohed* and *ahhed* and serenaded, while Miss Wesley posed and promenaded the best she could on the balcony. Cedar Oaks had never seen a finer lady grace its balcony. Rhiannon was the photographer; I am sure this ended up in her portfolio somewhere. And finally we were interrupted by the familiar sound of truck engines gunning, and pinstripe and khakied boys shouting "Faggots!"

A shotgun blast in the air nearby and the sound of police sirens sent everyone home. Wesley and I stayed in the second floor ballroom and finished the mint juleps. And once the sirens, shot guns, and shouting had ended ... we did gay stuff all over the place, until finally—bent over the balcony with her hoop hiked up nearly over her head, I was buck ass naked and in my groove behind him—Wesley sing-shouted, "Look away! Look away!" and we collapsed breathless in a heap of petticoats and skirts and bows. I do hope nobody was looking.

I woke up because the sun was shining into the room and hitting me directly in the eyes. Wesley was awake, his head was on my chest, and he was staring out the window. His light brown eyes were rather pretty in the light.

"I don't want to do this anymore," he said.

"Do what?" I asked. But I think I knew.

"This—" Wesley said. "This whatever it is we're doing."

"Fucking?"

Wesley took a deep breath. I think reducing it to those terms, while true, was hurtful. "Yes."

"Wesley. Look ..." I began. "I like you, I do. But I ..."

Wesley started laughing. And once he started, he couldn't stop. And I couldn't help it, but I found myself laughing as well.

"I don't know what's funny," I finally said.

"You are," he said. "And you are sweet. But good God, Randy, you are not husband material."

He was right. We lay there for the rest of the morning. I think we had a quickie and then I left. I saw him the following Wednesday at the Grocery. And we hugged at graduation. I sent flowers and a nice bottle of tequila to him and his husband for their wedding. I was invited, but I didn't go.

The Most Sensible One

It was six years after Mother died and a few months beyond that when I was summoned. The Dowager Countess of Kosciusko wanted an audience. I readily agreed and took the opportunity to see Laura as well. She was eager to hear about my time with Wilksie.

"But what about Gio?" she asked. Her jaw was on the floor.

"She told me she wanted me to do it."

"I mean, I get it … but why?" Laura asked again.

◢   ◢   ◢

"RAIN-DE," WILKSIE HAD SAID TO me. The emphasis was both in her smile and on the rain. "I've put a lot of thought into this. And you are going to deliver my eulogy."

"You're not …"

"No," she said. "Not today … I still have some living I need to do."

I argued a number of good arguments as to why it should be Gio and not me. He was her grandchild. He did such a lovely job at his grandfather's and so many others. He was a preacher, for Christ's sake; this was his wheelhouse. Or what about Conrad, or one of her daughters?

"He doesn't know me." She smiled. "None of them really do."

"What do you mean, he doesn't know you?" I asked. "Wilksie, he has known you his whole life."

"He will talk about the DAR. He will talk about the garden club and the artists' guild. And he will celebrate every institution, organization, and philanthropy with which I have been involved. And more than likely, he will tell the story of how my husband, and everyone else, came to call me Wilksie."

"You always tell that story."

"Of course I do," she said. "It's my story."

"But that's your name," I said.

"No, Randy. That is not my name. That is who I chose to be—and then who I became to others. I made choices in my life to do as I pleased and to be who I wanted. And to let everything else go by the wayside. And it was all fine because I was Wilksie. But I did not come into this world as Wilksie, Randy, and I want everyone to know who I am."

"Okay," I said. "Before I accept, can I ask you something?"

"Randy, honey, you are here. I think you've already accepted." She smiled and waited for my question.

"Why is it ... every time anyone mentions the old homestead, or whatever you want to call it ... why is it you always answer that the power company tore it down? You knew they hadn't."

Her smile faded, but it did not disappear. "Because they all left, Randy. And I was the only one who stayed. Oh, life was hard at Mama and Daddy's and not at all like the stories we all shared. King, Norma, and Rudie ...and Velma, especially Velma ... they all left a terrible life to find something better. And they did. And they didn't. Each one of them. They exchanged one terrible life for another, maybe a better life, and then they made something of that."

"Look at the life you built!" I looked around her everchanging museum of antique furnishings.

"Yes, look at it. And I stayed behind. And I took the terrible life I was given, and I made it better. I chose every aspect of my life, and I changed it when and how it suited me."

"Wilksie ..." I began.

"Call me India."

"India ..." I looked into her determined eyes.

They stared right back. "May I ask you a question?"

"Of course."

"Why did you take that old trunk?" Her eyes flashed and she had that trademark inquisitive smile.

"I, uh ..." I stammered as the wave of memory rushed in, and I struggled in the surf for an adequate why.

"One night, Norma and I had quite the row. Do you remember?" She asked this out of the clear blue as well.

"Y'all always fought." I still wasn't sure where she was going. "It was how y'all talked to each other."

"But the love was there, always."

"And that was clear, Wilksie ... India."

"Thank you, Randy." She paused and took a sip of the tea she was drinking. Sweet tea. "It was when she was sick. And there was that night I just had to come stay at your apartment in Woodley Park. Do you remember?"

"I do."

"Well, I was so beside myself that evening, I could not go to sleep." She continued, "I perused your bookshelf, and I found this darling, blue, hardbound book. It was an older book and clearly worn. I took that as a sign it must be a good read."

I wracked my brain to think of what book she may have pulled from my shelves to read. I didn't have book-books; I had academic books: books on acting and design, theory and criticism, and tons of plays and scripts.

"Oden or Onden ..."

"*Ondine.*"

"That's it. It was in French."

"You read French?"

"Of course. You can put that in my eulogy." She winked. "It was beautiful. Oh, Randy, I was so moved. The play, oh, I can only imagine now what you might have done with it. I know your Mama was so ill when you were in school. I regret we didn't send anyone to represent the family. Oh, you can laugh at that ..."

I did.

"But you did it so respectfully all these years—representing the family. I don't know why we didn't think to be there for you. And I'm sorry for that, Randy." She took my hand.

This, I was not prepared for. The eulogy was enough of a surprise—but when you really think about it ... maybe not. It is a very Wilksie thing to do, making waves. She was making them with her funeral choices, that's for sure. And, like a celestial body commanding the tides, she was reaching for the forbidden shores of emotions I had long since left behind. I did not come here to feel things.

"Who was Aaron?"

I was even less prepared for that. "Someone I have not thought about in a very long time."

"Mmm." She smiled. "I don't believe that is true. Come with me, Randy."

I followed her through the once-again-remodeled Galerie de Glaces. It was more what it should be, a connecting corridor with lots of windows showcasing the beauty of her courtyard. The courtyard was filled with blooming hydrangeas of rich purple-blue and roses of every variety ... pinks and reds, yellows and oranges, and the softest of whites.

"I have been cultivating roses ever since Mama planted her first bush. Mama was so patient with me as she taught me to prune and cut and graft." She held my hand as we admired her roses. "But I could never get a rose to have that pale blue of that rose you pressed between the pages of that play. I could develop a rose with deep purples or the palest of lavenders ... but never the iciness of what I believe that flower must have held before it dried. I can tell by your eyes, Randy, they must have been breathtaking."

"'N stuff" popped in my mind. That's what Ermaline called them, breathtaking n' stuff. I don't know why I remembered that.

"The closest I ever got was painting," India continued as she unlocked her garden studio—or shed, as Norma had called it.

We stepped through the doors and were surrounded by stretched canvases, paintings in and out of frames, brushes and paints ... all of what you might expect in an artist's studio. And on a large wooden easel that used to belong to Norma's artiste husband, a still life she was working on loomed large. A large vase of roses sat upon a blue bound book, *Ondine* in a fine gold script. The book lay on my great-grandmother's trunk. The water in the vase gave distortion to the long stems and leaves and all that could be seen through the vase. The greens of the stems and leaves gave way to shades of white and the palest of blues. And I let myself get lost in my thoughts, lost in my memories, and lost in his eyes.

"Blue roses are not found in nature. The closest anyone has really gotten, outside of dyes and sprays, is a rose called *Applause*. I found that appropriate, but it wasn't quite right. I'd still like some in my garden, and at my services too."

"It is beautiful," I managed.

"Do you know the meaning of a blue rose?" she asked. Her arm found its way into mine and she held me. "It means unattainable. And I immediately thought of you."

"Of me? Why?"

"Because you are unattainable. You always have been." She took me by the hand and brought me closer to her work in progress. "And you've never seen your worth. Like that old trunk of Mama's that begged you to take it home. Oh, it called to you, Randy, and you could not resist. You were drawn to that trunk, not because of what you found inside of it. There was nothing, I presume?"

"No ma'am. It was empty when we found it."

"No ... it wasn't empty. It was filled with memories. It was filled with the memories of all it once held. I can't even begin to imagine what all has been kept in there. Pictures, and linens; I believe Mama used it as a hope chest for awhile. And then there was the time Norma took it to Memphis. Of course it also traveled with you." Her eyebrows raised and her smile widened.

I blushed.

"Oh, RAIN-de. There is so much more in that empty ol' trunk if you just let yourself see what is there. That Sable Boy saw it in me, and he helped me see it in myself. I believe a young man named Aaron saw it in you." She lifted a hand and wiped something wet that was forming in the corner of my eye. "So did your mother ... and your Nince. And everybody knows Rudie and Norma thought the world of you. We all did. I wish I knew how to get you to see it yourself. Find and see what is good, RAIN-de, and stop seeking what hurts you."

I stared at the painting for a long time. And Wilksie stood with her arm in mine. The silence felt nice. It felt right. And it was pretty good. The painting. Not really. But it *was* better than the fruit and bowls that were a part of that slideshow of memories playing in the silence.

"I want you to have this one, RAIN-de, when I am done."

⚭   ⚭   ⚭

I LEft INDIA'S AND STARTED the drive down the Trace toward Laura's. I'd pass through Starkville and State on the way, and I'd hear Nince's voice, of course. But first I stopped at the cemetery. I sat in the orange clay ruts; I threw little crumbling balls of orange and dust at nothing in particular—I just liked the way they sort of dissolved in the air. She would most likely get her way, India would. And I would deliver her eulogy. At least that was the general consensus of all of us in the graveyard.

✎   ✎   ✎

"YOU REALIZE YOU HAVE YOUR mother to thank for this," Laura said to me. We were drinking a beer on her back deck. She looked at the same water Nince and Boom-Pa once did.

What do you mean?" I did not follow.

"Well, when I made that long haul drive back home from your mother's service at Gio's? You remember Betty-Girl rode with me."

"Oh yes I do, now that you say it."

"Well, Betty-Girl told me that your mother began planning her funeral the day of Velma's service," Laura said. "Debra apparently had some very specific words for Betty-Girl. She didn't say what they were—just that they were "very specific and her intent was clear."

"What was her intent?" I asked.

"I asked that too," Laura said. "I didn't understand her answer, though."

"Oh she just smiled a peculiar smile and told me some story about a mermaid hiding all these little things so she could set it all right or something. I don't remember exactly what she said, but just that I was gonna honor it all ... every word." Betty-Girl nodded earnestly as she told Laura what she knew.

✎   ✎   ✎

IT WAS A RAINY DAY in Mississippi when the Dowager Countess of Kosciusko left this earthly realm; the Angels bathed us in their tears. The entire state of Mississippi would mourn. The Governor issued a proclamation from his mansion. Ole Miss, State, and even that college in Hattiesburg sent delegates to the funeral. And of course The Three Sisters were there. Front and center. They all wore furs, and they all wore blonde. The names of the colors had changed, but the shade remained the same. Gio delivered a beautiful welcome and opening prayer. And then he asked me to step to the front.

I did. Laura squeezed my hand as I walked past. Lorraine was there with her family as well. Gio took my hands in his when I reached the front; his sad, tired eyes looked into mine.

"Thank you," he whispered. And he hugged me tight. The gratitude was real.

I could see Livie trying to see around Bitsy's hair. It was all I could do not to laugh.

"We are here to celebrate the life of a woman I think many of y'all would be surprised to find you don't know. I have known her my whole life, and yet, I just met her for the first time not too long ago. India Wilkes Taylor Sable. An interesting name, with a wonderful story that our dear Wilksie loved to tell ..." I began. "She told it to me for the first time when I was just a boy. But I was too young, and I didn't really listen. I spent too many years not listening. 'My Mama named me India,' she told me, 'because she was the most sensible one in the whole dern book ...' "

⟡   ⟡   ⟡

Fin

(The End)

Closing Credits

People Who Helped Make This Happen

I certainly did not take this journey alone. There are so many who helped me along the way:

Stephanie Fowler, I think you would hold my hand through any journey; I appreciate every facet of who you are, more than you'll ever realize. **Patty Gregorio,** oh the things you put up with! And the things we have shared ... **Susan Wimbrow**—your insight, your love, and your experience added so much flavor to this venture.

There are a few folks who might argue they did very little, but that is a silly argument as each contribution was invaluable. **Ella Kinney Burnett, Mike Burnett,** and **Laura Otts Ramsey,** y'all took me down culinary memory lane, and conjured other memories too. **Lorraine Cotten,** you were another well of information and memory. And then there is **Amber Green;** it is like you only know how to lift people up. **April Schlaat Mason**—you have superpowers of contacts, memory, and a knowledge of all things Oxford. **Husayn David Frazier**—I never send anything out that you haven't read first. It's like you know me. And **Samuel Andrew Heller**—the same applies to you. I love you! And of course **Michael Parker**—how can I not thank my husband?

I must also thank **Barbara Lockhart.** My respect and admiration for you knows no bounds; your insight and guidance are like gifts raining down from the heavens.

Mary Lib Morgan of Perfectly Penned - my editor, oh, the patience you possess. I think you would agree, it is always an education!

Derek B. Lingle - you are a treasure.

Joseph Traylor - thank you for your kindness and your talents.

Kelly Russo - your work on this project, in many ways, helped shape my work on this project. What you are able to glean and then share through your art ... you are amazing.

Carol Heller - I mean, your stories were the source of inspiration—the spring to the river. *And* your love.

And I must acknowledge those whom Tom Brokaw called The Greatest Generation, my grandparents' generation. Offspring of a generation back home from war, they lived through the Great Depression and the Cold War, with World War II and a moon landing in between. I can't help but admire their greatness and their weakness. They have both. We all do.

And **Eva Middlelbrooks**—you were in my heart, my mind, and my instant messenger or texts every step of the way.

🍃   🍃   🍃

Books by Andrew Heller

Samuel Smythe and the Mystery of the Missing Papers

Samuel Smythe and the Mystery of the Snake Bird

Samuel Smythe and the Mystery of the Urbane

A Bunch of Ellipses: Two Plays

Mama ChaCha's School for Girls
(Or What Every Queer Boy Should Know.)

The Ondines of French Camp

About the Author

Andrew Heller received his MFA in Directing from the University of Mississippi and his BA in Theatre from the University of Central Florida. A Florida native, he now resides on Maryland's Eastern Shore with his husband. He has worked as a director, an Equity stage manager, and an educator from pre-k through college. Andrew has done extensive work in theatre both for and by young people and has written several children's theatre adaptations including *Alice in Wonderland* and *Dragons!*

After a twenty year career in education and theatre, Andrew now writes, plays in his yard, and helps others share their stories through his work at Salt Water Media. He loves junk stores and Halloween. Andrew is the proud dog dad of Oswald and Rupert and the human dad to his amazing son Sam.